BLACK MAGICK BOOK ONE

DARK & FLAME

USA TODAY BESTSELLING AUTHOR

M.L. PHILPITT

Author' Note

Dark Flame is the first book of Black Magick, a paranormal romance series of interconnected standalones that are recommended to be read in order. This will be the first series in a new fictional world.

This is a <u>HEAVILY</u> revised edit of Cure Bound, my debut (removed from sale Dec 2024). It has undergone major edits that alter the plot, characters, world, and lore. If you have read Cure Bound in the past, I *promise* this book is vastly different. New plot, new ending, new story. The only similarities remain in the main character's names and the general underlying plot of Harlow's blood is the cure to vampirism, and Alec taking her.

This book has content some people may find triggering. You can read the content warning list on the last page.

This book uses Canadian spelling. This means words will have U's in them, "re", or double LL's. (colour vs color, centre vs center, signalling vs signaling, etc.) These are not typos.

Playlist

"Calling From Above - Edit" by Bassnectar
"The Wolf in Your Darkest Room" by Matthew Mayfield
"Like A Villain" by Bad Omens
"Eyes on Fire" by Blue Foundation
"How Villains Are Made" by Madalen Duke
"Rain" by Sleep Token
"Make Hate to Me" by Citizen Soldier
"Paralyzed" by NF
"Pleasure" by Crosses
"RUNRUNRUN" by Dutch Melrose
"Flesh" by Simon Curtis
"Bloody Mary" by Lady Gaga
"When Darkness Comes" by Jeris Johnson
"Haunted" by Isabel LaRosa
"Dead of Night" by Ruelle
"Morally Grey" by April Jai & Nation Haven
"You Put a Spell on Me" by Austin Giorgio
"Everybody Wants to Rule the World" - Lorde
"Take Me Back To Eden" by Sleep Token
"older" by Isabel LaRosa

"eyes don't lie" by Isabel LaRosa
"The Death of Peace of Mind" by Bad Omens

A NOTE ABOUT WICCA

This book is heavily inspired by Wicca/Paganism, but is not an exact depiction. The elements play a crucial role in the entire series, and at one point, the main character draws protection runes. Although described within the novel, feel free to use the following images as visuals to assist.

PROTECTION RUNES

ALGIZ RUNE

PROTECTION AND
WARDING OFF HARM

THURISAZ RUNE

DEFENSE AGAINST
HARMFUL ENERGIES

**PLEASE NOTE, THERE ARE MORE PROTECTION WARDS.
THESE ARE THE ONLY TWO MENTIONED IN THE BOOK**

THE ELEMENTS

FIRST INTERMISSION

Freya

Hello. Bonjour. Ciao. Hola. Olá. (Insert your chosen language here.)

I know, I know. Intermission already, yet the story hasn't even kicked off. Thing is, I've been watching all this play out since for fucking *ever*, but now you're here and I'm so damn happy to have someone to share the drama with.

It's been a *long*—like endlessly long—few centuries, and now, we're about to experience two idiots falling in love despite being enemies.

Well...eight idiots, actually, but they're not all enemies to one another. Four couples, starting with a witch and a vampire. I'll admit, when Hecate—that's the Goddess of magick and witchcraft, by the way—first prophesied their stories to me, I wasn't particularly excited about the drama that'd be unfolding, but damn if they won't all undoubtedly win me over. Call me an old softie for the slow bonding until they realize how right they are for one another.

But before that happens, there are three main pieces of information you need to know. The boring, pre-story shit that sets the scene, so to speak.

Stick around, because here we go...

First, I'm going to take you back a little bit, to when I was given the prophecies and essentially who I am and what my entire role is.

Bear with me, because I'll be showing you this scene from an outsider's perspective rather than a direct recounting. Sorry about the random perspective shift, but humour me. When you've been around since the dawn of time, you get bored and find amusement in the little shit.

Anyway, sorry again. Here we go...for real this time.

Freya, First Witch and earthbound representative of the Goddess, stands above the small pond of water that reflects the vivid moon above and the twinkling stars scattered around it. She breathes in deeply while waiting, tipping her face to the sky to enjoy the few moments of peace.

The night is calm, while the world is not. The chaos feels never-ending.

The pond ripples, and the moon shifts into a new shape. A shape without a design. A woman without a body. A soul without a manifestation.

Daughter, the being greets, her melodic voice chiming through Freya's mind. It's a familiar and tranquil sound, reminding Freya of the very breeze that blows around her.

"Hecate."

I tire of my witches dying from their ongoing wars with other beings, especially now.

"What is now?"

That detail does not matter yet. The bigger concern is how my witches must be on the same side as the others. I have seen the solution, though the witches involved will not be born for some time.

"You're giving me a prophecy?" Freya puts the Goddess's strange dialect into a more simplistic explanation.

A promise. There will be four who bring a truce to the fighting. See here.

The pond swirls again, and Hecate's spiritual figure is replaced with a series of images quickly flashing over the surface.

A witch standing in the arms of a vampire, without fear, as he grazes his fangs up and down her neck. Around them: a kingdom of vampires bowing.

A witch standing beside a wolf, her hand buried in its fur. The wolf shifts into a man and pulls her into his arms. Around them: a pack bonded.

A witch standing with a mortal, her head on his shoulder. He's holding a sword, a city from the future as their background. Around them: a world protected.

A witch standing hand in hand with a warlock, their joint elemental magick swirling together to create a myriad of white and green. Around them: covens united.

The image swirls again, returning Hecate's undefined form to the surface.

"Vampires?" Freya questions, thinking of the human male who became the first vampire after making a deal with a demon—one of the original fallen angels. The new vampire spent centuries spreading his disease to innocent humans, ruining their souls and ensuring they'd end up in one place only: with his master in Hell.

It must happen to end the war. The vampire I am showing you will be a king amongst their kind. With a witch by his side, others will follow suit and obey, understanding witches should not be targeted. In turn, the covens will learn that vampires, while creatures of Darkness, can be led to the Light.

"But when this vampire taints the witch–a Sinclair, if her red hair is indicative-he'll spread Darkness into her, ruining one of your daughters."

Perhaps that is what is needed. Balance, after all, is the only way the world truly functions. The Goddess's manifestation fades away again, the outline of the moon becoming clear once more while her final words ring through Freya's mind. *You will see this come to pass, Freya. Help if you must, but do not intervene in a manner that will change the outcomes. It is the only way.*

Freya settles beside the bank, the images of the couples imbedding into her mind, where they'll remain for the centuries they'll take to come true. Until then, the bloodshed continues while she can do nothing but let fate run its course.

Fate, of course, is a fickle bitch. Despite the Goddess's visions, fate has her own plans for the couples...and she isn't kind.

From the journal of Clarice Sinclair...

June 1521

I have recently concluded casting a protection barrier around the coven's territory while asking myself, when will the Goddess save us? When will She protect her daughters?

We have been at war for much too long—and we are losing. Too many of our coven have been lost to us in recent months. We are a fraction of what we used to be.

Today marks the day we have lost yet another, this one particularly close to me. My dear sister, Elizabeth, was attacked by a vampire. Drained of her blood, all to feed the undead soul originally bred from demons. I do not understand why Hecate is allowing demons, and thus the Devil, to win.

After her body finished burning on the pyre, Hazel, the High Priestess of the coven, announced she has been working on a new curse with some of the elders. A spell I am in disbelief over her performing. She has nearly forsaken Hecate by using black magick—a dangerous feat, but one I now pray will benefit the cause.

Before Elizabeth's body burned, Hazel collected a few drops of her blood, explaining the use of a deceased witch's blood would ensure the curse's potency. With it, she cast the hex onto our bloodline for all those coming after me. Elizabeth was the eldest Sinclair daughter, the first-born; therefore, it will only affect the eldest daughter of each generation of Sinclair women. This means Annabelle—Elizabeth's daughter, my niece, and a mere baby—has now been placed in danger by our High Priestess.

I do not agree with Hazel's choice. She has not helped witches but sentenced future Sinclair women to death.

A cure to vampirism now runs in Annabelle's blood. In the blood of every first-born Sinclair witch.

The High Priestess claims it will assist in extinguishing vampires from Earth. That if the Goddess does not wish to save us from the demons' children, we must come up with our own solutions.

I will protect Annabelle in ways unlike any before. She's a baby and will now be hunted by the vampires who wish for humanity again. Hazel seeks to end vampirism, but the demonic bloodsuckers will not be satisfied with a couple sips to change back. No. They'll likely drain my niece for dead. And if not her, then every first-born Sinclair witch the future produces.

The High Priestess did not end the war between witches and vampires.

She's deepened it.

Clarice

A Few Months Ago...

May 15th

"We've just gotten reports of breaking news. What you see here behind me is the house of Emily and John Sinclair, who tragically died in a house fire. At approximately midnight, neighbours phoned 9-1-1 about smoke nearby. When police and firefighters arrived on scene, two bodies were found burned beyond recognition, but are presumed to be the homeowners, Emily and John Sinclair. Their adult daughter is alive and unharmed—as is the house, save for minimal interior damage, strangely enough. It has left authorities questioning how a fire large enough to trap a family inside did not seem to have lasting effects on the structure. Foul play is suspected, but no leads have been released yet. Tim, back to you."

Me again. Makes no sense, right? It will soon, I promise.

For now, we must wait a few more weeks.

Oh, don't bitch. I've waited centuries, witnessing entirely too much bloodshed. Needless to say, I'll do *anything* to help the first couple get together.

Get your popcorn ready. It'll be a show.

Oh, remember that thought I had after the Goddess's visit? *Fate, of course, is a fickle bitch.* Remember that point, won't you? It sets the stage for what's to come.

And oh, it's *good*...

ONE

Alec

Present

From the roof across the street from her house, I observe her.

The witch belonging to one of the world's strongest covens. The witch belonging to a family that's been taunting vampires forever.

Yet *this* is what's left of the great Sinclair bloodline?

While it abhors me to admit this about an enemy of my kind, the Sinclairs have always been renowned throughout the magickal community, and both desired and feared by vampires. Her family is the very source behind so much of my own pain.

Harlow Sinclair doesn't deserve such a recognition.

For three nights, I've watched her avoid the windows unless she's triple-checking they're latched before heading to bed. She doesn't leave the barrier surrounding her property. She paces her house, chewing on fingernails I doubt have anything left to them, giving me long-awaited glimpses through the cracks in the window coverings.

I'm not the only vampire who's been hanging around, waiting for her to leave the safety of her magickal bubble. Luckily for her,

I've discarded the others who dare believe they have the rights to *my* prey. Unfortunately for her, though, I'm an immortal with all the time in the world. At some point, she'll need to leave, and I'll be here when she does. Unless it's when the sun is up.

The interest I hold in her isn't the same as all the other vampires who have come around. No, my needs go much deeper. After so many centuries of getting revenge upon the family who once stole mine from me, killing them has become too easy, simplistic, and, if I must admit it to myself, boring.

There's a better path forward, and while one might refer to it as fate, I believe that concept to be stupid and something only witches are entertained by. The history behind my fight with the Sinclairs is the very reason behind my newest plan.

When I killed Elizabeth Sinclair centuries ago, their coven leader cursed the Sinclair bloodline to get rid of my kind. Instead of the plan succeeding how the witch hoped it would, she created endless targets for any vampire who craves humanity—there's quite a few. Immortality can grow tiresome for those who haven't received the forever they imagined. Since Elizabeth's death, I've been wiping out every Sinclair witch and warlock born, cure or otherwise. I only spare one from each generation so they can continue the bloodline and keep my revenge alive...because I can. Because when you live forever, one must find their own form of entertainment.

While it's been a thrill, it's grown tiresome. It's too simple and doesn't bring long-lasting satisfaction to the grief festering inside me. So now, the only remaining Sinclair will pay for her ancestors' actions through other means. One that'll profit off the very attribute me murdering Elizabeth created.

A way that extends her pain until she's nothing but a corpse.

I won't only kill her; I'll use her until she's begging for death.

Sinclair moves into view again, climbing into her bed in nothing but an oversized shirt, giving me a brief view of bare legs. It's amazing how little modesty humans have compared to centuries ago. If only this girl knew about the vampires outside her window, she'd cover up a bit more.

Especially that pretty little neck of hers.

When the witch falls forwards and plants her face into her pillows, the sound of sobs comes from within the brick house and barrier. She's crying again, for fuck's sake. I release a long, pained groan, disbelieving I'm about to subject myself to *this*. To her. Her whining is too much. She may be a witch, but she's as emotional as a human. Can't handle the death of her parents for shit.

As tragic as that was. Her mother, Emily Sinclair, was the only witch from her generation, having no siblings; therefore, I had no choice but to keep her alive. Dying in a fire is such a wasteful death. When hearing the news, I felt something for the little Sinclair woman. Something the mortal side once would have understood, but the creature I've been for a long time hasn't felt: sympathy. Perhaps because it's the one Sinclair death I didn't have a hand in, a true accident leaving her alone in the deadly and dangerous world filled with predators lurking in the shadows.

A predator like me.

The witch burrows into her bed and pulls the covers over her head. The night vision accompanying my vampirism cuts right through the darkness, allowing me to catch her subtle shifts in bed while her cries are loud enough to alert any being in the area.

Another night of not leaving her house. I sigh, the long-winded noise disrupted by the shuffling within the shadows beside the building. Curious, I pace to the edge of the roof, spotting the other vampire getting as close to her as the barrier allows him to. Trying to get near *my* prey.

My hiss is low, a warning that causes his eyes to dart up. He doesn't take my warning as it's meant and returns to inching his way around the building, searching for an in to the impenetrable barrier built by magick. I've long tried what he's about to attempt, and it's useless.

With another sigh, this one of annoyance, I step off from the roof, the ground rushing quickly towards me. My shoes make a nearly silent *thud* with my landing, and I cross the street towards the Sinclair house.

"Did you not understand my warning, or do you not know better? Go the fuck away."

The vampire turns, pupils red around the edges with his increasing thirst. "We can all have a sip. Do you not smell her? I can all but taste the humanity coursing through her veins."

Of course, I fucking smell her. Her blood is a fine perfume, like the sweetest wine after a lifetime of sobriety, like meat to a starving carnivore, like everything right and wrong in the world. Most humans' blood carries similar notes of iron and whatever they've consumed that day. No one, not even previous generations of Sinclairs, have ever smelled as pleasant as this one. The High Priestess who created the cure made their blood appeal to every vampire to draw them to their deaths, but I've been around many Sinclairs and it's never been like this. Not so...appealing. She smells like my own personal meal, all for me and me alone, which is an alarming thought.

"She's not yours," I state firmly.

The vampire scoffs, turning to face me. "And who the fuck are —*oh.*"

"Yes. *Oh.* Leave or die. Those are your options."

For a moment, it seems like he's about to obey me, but the idiot continues tempting death by shaking his head and gesturing towards the house. "Not until I get what I've come for. You should know better than any of us how long immortality is. Aren't you tired?"

He's hoping I dread vampirism as much as him and appealing to that possibility. While I can appreciate others' desires, mortality holds no temptation for me, and it hasn't since the day I died and woke up immortal. Humanity is nothing but emotions and pain, a pointless end to a pointless existence.

"I warned you," I mutter. Killing my own dwindles our numbers, which isn't preferable, but when they don't fall in line, there's no other option.

I turn towards him, and in a flash, my hand is buried in his chest, having torn through flesh and bone until his dead heart rests in my palm. I yank my arm back, ripping the organ from its home, and a spray of black blood spurts onto my clothing. The vampire's eyes widen as he comprehends the final seconds of his undead life before falling to my feet, truly dead. Fisting the heart to ensure nothing of his defiance remains, I drop the squished, bloodless tissue on top of his body.

"That's for believing you'll get near what's mine."

If only he obeyed, then he would have learned of the opportunity all my subjects will soon be given: the chance to regain mortality...for a price.

Backing away from the body that'll disintegrate with the sunrise, I return to the roof across from her window and resume my watch.

It's hours later before my nose picks up the trace of another being right as my senses comprehend her beside me.

A woman appears from seemingly thin air, her arms clenching her purple cloak shut. Her hair, an almost white-blonde, blows in the breeze, lifting from her face. She peers at the house with pastel-purple eyes—a feature all witches have—that narrow on Sinclair's bedroom window. "Hm. That won't do, now will it?"

Her scent of mud and leaves and nature drifts my way. It's the distinct perfume most affiliated with a witch. One who's probably come to defend her own. Too bad for her, her mission will result in her death.

My fangs lengthen, body poised to attack, but my single step towards her is blocked by an invisible wall mere seconds after she waves her hand. I push into it, but the force is strong enough to keep me out, and my growl is a warning for her to fuck off if she won't let me kill her.

"Give up," she says in a bored but musical tone. "You won't get through my barrier, so stop injuring yourself trying."

I straighten, tensing against this strange witch and the uncertainty of her presence. "Who are you?"

"Will you attack me if I lower my shield?"

I shake my head, meaning it because she doesn't seem like a threat and, without a doubt, she'd only replace her spell if I make another move to harm her. She lowers her hand, allowing the night air to once again pass between us.

"Good," she murmurs with a small, satisfied nod when I don't budge. "My name is Freya, and I'm here to help. That's all you need to know."

"You're a witch." Leading into the question of why a witch would help a vampire found lurking outside another witch's home.

"And you're a vampire." She, this *Freya*, rolls her eyes. "You'd think a king of the vampires would be smarter, but what do I know? I'm only a millennium old and tired of waiting for this particular phase within the timeline, so if we can get shit moving along, that'd be great."

A millennium... "You're the First Witch," I deduce, taken aback by the ancient lore in physical form poised in front of me. Not that I've been interested in tracing witches' lore throughout the centuries, but one hears things. I'd never gotten a name, nor confirmation she—Freya—was even around. The First Witch, a physical representation of the deity witches bow to, sounds like a tale they'd tell their children.

Never would I have guessed this tiny woman would be it, though, given how powerful the stories claim she is. She looks young, maybe early twenties in relation to human years, and barely reaches my shoulder. Her hair brushes her waist, making her almost childlike in appearance, despite being around since the beginning of Earth—long before me or any other vampire around. Regardless, she's clearly adapted to the modern world in her tight jeans, Converse shoes, and some ruffled kind of top while retaining the traditional witch's garb by covering herself in a cloak.

"Very good." She dips her head to my deduction.

But if the First Witch has come, it's likely to protect the only remaining Sinclair. "You're here to stop me."

"No, like I've said, I'm here to help." She lifts her hand towards the Sinclair house, and a ripple of red passes over the once-invisible dome. As the sparks of magick fall, so does the barrier that's prevented me from entering.

Immediately, the little Sinclair's scent intensifies, every note jamming a stake into my body. It's stronger, infinitely so, than what I've gotten so far, shooting the desperation of hunger down my throat—the need to capture her, drain her dry, and seek satisfaction from this thirst.

Fuck, she's sweet.

I force my gaze away from the sleeping witch, who's seconds away from being in my grasp, to question, "Why would you help? Do you have any idea what I'm about to do?"

"Yes, and good luck, Alec. She'll make you wish you had some." Freya turns, her cloak swirling around her ankles dramatically.

Despite being able to finally get my mark and knowing, realistically, I shouldn't waste any more time, I reach for the retreating witch, not yet finished with this conversation. She's created more questions than has given answers, and, by the cloak, I tug her back to my side.

"Wait. I never told you my name."

"I'm aware." Freya smiles sweetly and bats her lashes theatrically. "I also know all. Remember who I work for? You're really not that smart, are you?" She circles her finger towards the sky. "I know who you are, what you've done to Harlow's entire family, and what you plan to do to her starting today. But don't worry, 'cause I can't interfere. Not allowed. Orders from the boss lady."

I stare at her. She stares back. Never have I been so wordless until now.

"You're a very strange being," I finally manage.

"Right back at ya, Your Majesty. Blessed Be."

"Fuck off with the witchy bullshit." She doesn't seem fazed by my insult, her expression unwavering. But if she insists on staying, then she can give me more than whatever unhelpful drivel she's spouted so far. "What did you mean by that last part? That she'll make me wish I had luck."

Freya's mouth stretches into a large, knowing smile seconds before she disappears in a blink, the faint whiff of nature lingering where she last was, leaving my hand gripping nothing but air.

Fucking witches. I shake my head and turn back to the house across the street. Without the barrier spell up, more of my kind is bound to descend soon, so I hop from the roof to the ground, landing near my recent kill.

You're mine, Sinclair.

TWO

Harlow

"*M*ommy, help me! It's dark...so dark. Help!"

As quickly as the thought passes through my nightmares, it shifts to something more recent. Something more painful. The recurring memories that plague me so often since two months ago.

"*Mom! Dad!*" *But the fire blazes on. It's too much. Too—*

No!

I rip myself from that memory, clawing at the blankets constricting my legs like a snake swallowing its prey. They're too much, too tight, too unforgiving, and panic rises, my heart hammering until it's painful enough to rip me from sleep and away from the cavern of hell I find myself continuously tripping down: the memories of *that* night and the earlier childhood screams for my mother.

Fucking claustrophobia, a fear plaguing me since I was a kid. Makes sleeping impossible when the blankets continuously tighten around my body, resulting in a sensation of being enclosed somewhere inescapable.

My eyes open, mind repeating the four little words that try to convince my mental state it's all okay.

I didn't mean to.

I didn't mean to.

I didn't mean to.

It's a stupid attempt and something the internet suggested. That therapist's website was so full of bullshit. Nothing changes what happened weeks ago, and nothing ever will.

Nothing chases away the shadows that have consumed me. Literally, not the metaphorical ones. The literal shadows that bend, shielding my bedroom into near obscurity. The slithery voice—nothing decipherable—snakes through my mind, like a barely there caress that taunts me with both heartbreak and desire. With endless power while being powerless.

They won't go away. They've been a part of me since the accident. Every day, they're *here*, trailing me throughout the house. No matter how much sunlight I allow in, the shadows bend, shutting it all out while keeping me captive. I have no control over them, no way to make them go away. They're suffocating, making the walls feel that much closer, playing on my claustrophobia.

I'm positive it's punishment from Hecate. She's chosen the one thing that makes the world feel smaller, the one thing that could affect me so much. It's the most logical explanation as to why shadows are tormenting a witch without magick. Why they won't go away—because they're here on *Her* orders. Which is contradictory, considering shadows represent Darkness, while the Goddess is everything Light, good, and natural.

This is Her cruel reprimand for accidentally killing two of her children, a witch and warlock: my parents. Murder is one of the wickedest things a witch could do to another. Mom and Dad taught me that early on, which is so ironic, it's nearly laughable.

If laughing is even possible for me anymore.

Not only are the shadows punishment, but they hold an allure I find concerning. For a few moments every day, when they're at their strongest, the slithery sensation feels like a hug rather than a threat. They make me feel just a bit better. At peace, though not a comfortable, calm serenity. More like I'm on edge, faced with a threat I'll need to react to. But there's a strength in that too. They tease me with the desire to leave this house and prove to every immortal around why I'm no longer the same witch I was and why they shouldn't fuck with me.

I don't listen to that random urge because, for one, I'm still partially convinced the shadows are solely in my imagination and I'm making all this up, which suggests I'm nuts. And two, I'm nuts.

I mean, a slithery sensation, physical shadows that taunt me, a voice in my head. What else could it be other than my parents' deaths have made me clinically insane?

Oh, yes, the voice—the singular reason keeping me semi-sane while distracting me from my self-hatred, grief, and the fact my life changed in a single night. A few minutes of time, really. Funny how a little stretch of it can have such lasting effects. No buildup, no warning. It just happened, and I was too far gone to stop it.

Amidst it all, the thing keeping me grounded is *his* voice. A voice that only ever murmurs my name, in an almost disapproving tone. Mind you, it's probably evidence of my newfound insanity.

Newfound? While the shadows are new, I'm half-convinced I was already on the train to nowhere since my twenty-fourth birthday five months ago, because that was the first time I heard the voice. Even then, it was only my name, spoken in a manner that felt like my mind was being stroked while simultaneously drifting through the rest of my body, making me come alive.

I never admitted any of it to Mom and Dad because even witches shouldn't be hearing voices. I'd never heard of it happening, not that my knowledge of my own kind really extends past whatever my parents taught me and what's inside my grandmother's grimoires. Most witches grow up within a coven, with a High Priestess to guide them on the Goddess's path, but not me. I lost that opportunity a few centuries ago, when my ancestors cursed me to be the way I am.

The *way I am* is the entire reason I was put into this mess. It may have been my ancestors' actions, but Hecate never once thought to get rid of it? Help save us? How many Sinclairs have died because of it? Ridiculous our own creator abandoned my bloodline.

The fucking vampire cure. The cure to *goddamn vampirism* is the entire reason vampires continue to target me. Why I've grown up inside a house coated in protection spells and never allowed out past sunset when the vampires emerge.

It's the cure's fault my parents are dead.

But it's also mine, and no enchantment can change that. I should know, because the days following the accident, when this house and its items were mysteriously alright and unburned, I poured over Gram's grimoires for something that'd change the past, reverse time or something. A spell to bring them back.

Pointless, because if there was a way, it'd require powers to do it.

As usual, waking up is due to nightmares, and then nudged along by the stream of self-hatred and misery. At this point, it's useless to attempt falling asleep again. Getting through the night is a miracle in itself, so with a groan, I push myself up and start another day of pretending to be fine. Pretend to no one but me, myself, and I. Oh, and my shadowy friends, of course. This whole house is tainted with memories of Mom and Dad, and I hate it survived the burning with very few marks to show. Probably another one of Hecate's punishments: to force me to live within the physical manifestation of everything I once had and everything I've lost.

I switch on the bedside lamp, letting the room fill with a soft light. It teases the edges of the shadows, attempting to push them away. My phone lights up with my tap, the time reading 2 a.m. and nowhere near a decent time to get up.

"Oh, for fuck's sake." Two in the morning means I only slept three hours, but it isn't all that surprising. I haven't slept a full night since their deaths, and at this point, I may never sleep again. Perhaps I'll die of exhaustion and all my problems will be solved.

I slide from bed and yank on pyjama pants I'm not entirely sure have been washed recently before heading out of my room, passing the shut door of the one once belonging to my parents, and into the bathroom. On the way, I regard the bundle of rosemary and sage on the hallway window's sill. It's extra protection that doesn't require magick to activate, though I'm certain the barrier that somehow found itself around the property is keeping the monsters away.

Each night, I'm tempted to toss the herbs away and leave the house and its protection. To let the vampires who are undoubtedly stalking this place come after me. If I'm lucky, one of them will drain me dry and end this miserable existence where I have to pretend to be a grieving daughter rather than a murderer.

But every time I go near that front door, that finicky thing called self-preservation keeps me inside and safe.

Self-preservation...and that smooth voice. Between him and the shadows, I truly am convinced Hecate is playing a cruel game. Seeing how tight she can pull before I snap.

Won't be much longer now.

Mom would kill me if she knew I was having such thoughts about the Goddess, but it's difficult to think anything positive about Her. All things considered, She abandoned me when my parents did, leaving me alone with my miserable thoughts, a random male voice, and bleak shadows.

I finish in the bathroom and pass the same window, pausing to look at the flowerbeds in the backyard Mom once religiously tended to. They're dying now, uncared for and unloved, and it's with a sharp stab in my heart I realize, yet again, I've failed. I should be caring for them. Keeping the one thing I have of Mom still alive. She'd like that.

Tomorrow, I decide. *Or rather, later today. When the sun's up,*

I'll head outside, get fresh air, and see if I can revive Mom's precious plants.

With a bit of renewed energy joining with my misery, I turn into my bedroom's doorway.

Only to stop when it's *not* the way I left it.

For one, the shadows are completely gone, and for the first time since that night, they're not forcing impossible weight on me.

Maybe it's my hallway plans that did it.

The second thing isn't giving me a chance to consider my missing shadows for any longer. Because the guy perched on the edge of my bed certainly wasn't here before.

The room goes still. He doesn't move, and I *can't* move. Can't do anything but study the stranger—albeit, a handsome one— who's invaded my home unannounced and got by me.

There's only one kind of person who could manage that.

A vampire.

All those self-preservation instincts kick into overdrive, mind whirling with every possibility of what to do, given my current limitations. I'm already at the door and have a head start if I run, but he'd probably catch me before I made it to the stairs.

How did he get in? My gaze darts to the window. The barrier is held up by magick; he couldn't have possibly slipped through. It's built specifically to keep creatures like him away.

Unless it's no longer up...which is entirely possible. My hands curl in on themselves. *Fucking useless tools.*

Maybe he's one more thing to add to the ever-growing pile of ways to torment me.

In an abrupt movement that seems to ruffle no part of the surrounding air whatsoever, he gets to his feet. Silent, steady, and stealthy, letting me take in exactly how he towers over me. Easily a foot taller than me, not that height really matters considering the strength their kind has.

Hair so black, it shines like the nighttime sky against the dull backdrop of my bedside lamp. It curls around his ears and masks the tops of his eyes—also deep and dark as a void of nothingness. He's like a nightmare come to life. His skin is pale, a common attribute of vampires, but unlike others who look like walking corpses, this one makes it work. There's a sexiness to him, enthralling in that lethal way so many of them are. It's simply one way they lure in their prey. Every flawless inch of him is a hunter.

I slide my foot behind me, managing to gain a fraction more of distance between him and me.

His head ticks to the side instantly, his immortal hearing catching the subtle movement. His lips curl until the tips of his fangs peek out. I jolt at the sight of his weapons, my stomach coiling in warning.

"Don't be stupid. If you run, I'll be forced to chase, and I promise you will not like it when I catch you."

His voice is strangely soft, silky almost. A purr reverberating throughout my body, warming my insides in a way I can't decide is pleasurable or not. Likely a protective instinct and nothing more... even if it feels like my body's trying to tell me something else. Something bigger. Something begging me to *hear* him and realize what I already know.

My heart pounds in my chest, hands forming fists. I can't fight my way past him; one pinch of a finger and his strength would drop me instantly. And my magick...well, yeah. Words are all I got. I'm left with talking him down.

"H-how did you get in here?" One hand wraps around one of my wrists, fingers brushing along old scars I know to be there. It's an anxious twitch I've never been able to get rid of.

He doesn't reply, leaving me to my own conclusions: the barrier failed, exactly like so much in my life has.

"Wh-what do you want?"

I know what he wants. It's the same as all the others who stalk my house.

"You."

Of course it's me. It's always me. Ever since my ancestor cursed me to live like this.

"Get out," I demand, my voice strangely calm and steady. The questions of how and why matter less than getting him to leave. Even though I'm about to lose a fruitless fight without being able to defend.

He takes a step, and I do too, crossing my bedroom's threshold. The stairs are only a couple feet away. If I run, I can get downstairs and maybe out of the house before he catches up. Maybe. A slim possibility at best. And if I managed it, where would I go? He'll catch me no matter what. Hiding with neighbours will only result in their deaths. Running to the police would get me locked up in a psychiatric ward. And that's *only* if I manage to escape that far.

I lift my hands for the first part of my lie, ready to fake my way to safety. "You're a brave vampire to be entering a witch's home. Leave, or you'll burn."

"Yes, yes," he drawls. "You Sinclairs have always had a penance for fire. Destructive little things, aren't you?"

His comment hits the part of my heart closest to where grief is stored, but I try not to reveal the little power he could so easily gain with a few choice words.

"You seem to know a lot about my family."

All witches are born with one kind of elemental magick, which can command, control, and create the natural world related to the element: earth, air, water, or fire. My powers are bred in fire, exactly like every Sinclair before me. It's the comfortable heat I've grown up with—and now miss almost as much as Mom and Dad.

He chuckles, the sound almost depraved and teasing. "Probably more than you."

"Which tells me you've had dealings with us in the past. So you'll know I'm not the witch to piss off."

"Then do it."

He wasn't supposed to call my bluff.

I wait for the familiar tingle of heat in my palms, the feeling of freedom rushing through me. Of control and power and strength.

The feeling I called upon to save my parents when vampires attacked our home.

The same heat that formed balls of fire to kill the pointy-teeth assholes.

The magick I haven't felt since then.

Come on, come on. Body, if there's a time to work, now would be it. Hecate, if you could give me a thirty-second break from my punishment, I will pay you a tribute every single day for the remainder of my pathetic life.

The vampire takes another step, a dark brow arching in a daring manner. This is all a game to him, and with that look, he's goading me to fight back. Oh, how I'd play his game...if only my magick worked.

Witches aren't taught magick necessarily. Enchantments and control, yes, but we're born with the power and it's unlocked with puberty. I've had my magick since I was thirteen and managed to control it by seventeen, when I gained a much better handle on my ever-fluctuating teenage emotions—*thanks, hormones*—considering a witch's magick is so closely tied to our emotional being.

I call upon fright and self-perseveration to save me, like I did the night of my parents' deaths. For my magick to function again. I think about every lesson on control Mom and Dad taught me in lieu of us having a High Priestess and push it away. Control isn't what I need right now.

Come on, come on, come on!

The vampire laughs, his melodic voice cutting through my determination. "Oh, this is good. You don't have your magick, do you?"

I refuse to answer, to admit any weakness to my new enemy, to address what truly happened the night my parents died.

"Harlow, run!" Dad's voice comes from down the hallway, and there's only one thing that would suggest the sharp fear in his tone.

I bolt towards the kitchen since the back door is the closest to me and the farthest away from the crash that just came through the front of the house, and hopefully the direction the vampires won't expect me to go.

My hand's on the door handle when the loudest scream chills me to my bone, masking the natural heat from my magick.

Mom.

She's by the stairs, throwing shield after shield up against one of the intruders, but it's the one who came up behind her, its teeth jamming into her shoulder, that distracts her.

Beyond her, Dad is fighting against two more—and losing.

I can't run. They'll die.

Mom screams again, and I whirl around, calling every flame buried within me. Every ounce of my fear and anger burns through me.

I only aim for the one feeding from Mom, to burn him to death and kill him in one of a few ways vampires are able to be killed: burning, decapitation, and ripping their heart out. Instead, my magick comes out in a massive wave that knocks me to the ground.

And the world burns in a mirage of red, orange, yellow...and black.

I tried to save Mom but instead killed both my parents and the attacking vampires.

When I woke up, I no longer had access to my magick, shadows bathed my surroundings in an inescapable blackness, and a barrier was erected around the house. I figured it was the last act of my power. The emotion that went along with saving them did the one thing I never knew was possible: drained me entirely. The barrier was my magick's final protection.

The stranger grins, his fangs seeming larger. He takes another step forwards, but I jerk my hands in his direction again.

"N-no, that's not it. Stay away from me or I'll—"

"You'll what?" he asks mockingly. "Push me to death?"

In a flash I miss entirely, a movement quicker than a blink, he's standing in front of me, his body closer than I've ever been to a vampire. His head hangs over mine, his fangs dangerously close.

Apparently that self-preservation that's been keeping me alive the last little while is broken, because when my head screams at me to run, I remain, captivated by his gaze. His voice. By *him*. By the way, as inexplicable as it is, he feels safe and familiar.

This must be one of his powers. A thrall or something that compels me to want to be near him so he can strike.

Then he opens his mouth, and every ounce of that comfortable reaction wanes.

"Harlow Sinclair. Oh, how much fun we're about to have."

It's not what he said. Not that he knows my first name.

It's *how* he spoke it.

It's the exact same as the voice in my head.

Fuck this.

I turn and run.

THREE

Alec

She so wisely and stupidly tries to escape, though it's taken her longer to attempt than I assumed it would.

I let her go, cocking my head to listen as she rushes down the stairs, her heartbeat thrumming. The rate it's going is enthralling. So few things make someone's heart beat that quickly—fear and lust being two of the most common.

Both make my fangs extend far past the gums, the urge to satisfy those parts of me elevating my own excitement as I wait a moment, granting the little Sinclair a brief head start.

The *magickless* Sinclair. That was certainly a surprise. As far as all my reports go, she has powers. Or *had*, at the very least.

The front door of the house opens and shuts before I move, slowly following her scent through the house.

Her fucking *scent*. Being at the distance I've been for days, I wasn't graced with nearly the same amount of it until entering her home earlier, but *fuck*. She smells like pure sin, the ultimate temptation luring me to death. That's what humanity would be for me: death.

Thankfully, I was wise enough to feed last night, capturing a human in the next town over, so it'll keep me going for a few days.

At the very least, until Sinclair is behind bars and the temptation passes.

I maintain my pace to be no faster than a human's brisk walk, allowing her to get farther, knowing with every step she takes, catching her will be that much more thrilling.

At our core, vampires are hunters. Chasing prey, letting their fear tinge the taste of their blood...the only thing sweeter is the vein between a woman's legs. The hunt is half the fun, and Miss Sinclair is appealing to the monster inside.

Outside, my hearing picks up her feet smacking against the cement on my right, so I head in the opposite direction. My night vision has her about a block away, entirely too close and easy to catch, so I slow to allow her to believe she's winning for a short while and take a detour.

Sinclairs have always been a prideful bunch. There's never been one who hasn't fought me, and it's fun to witness the second they realize they've lost. The light of determination that fades in their eyes right before the light of their life is snuffed.

My steps pick up.

I rub my tongue along the pointed edges of my fangs despite the fact I will not be feeding from the being who'd rob me of my abilities. They're out because my body is responding to the hunt, the chase, and the ultimate high of soon being the victor.

Eventually, I chase her, the human neighbourhood becoming a blur of muted colours and scents until catching up, even going a few feet past her before stopping.

She slams into me, her gasp as delicious as her fear, but she quickly spins on her heel and bolts down the connected road, as though she has any chance of escape. Even with her few minutes' head start, I still caught up, so what she's attempting now won't get her far enough. At this point, running will tire her out, so I'll let her do this all night if it so pleases her.

Something shifts inside me. A *need* urging me to satisfy it—whatever *it* is or why it's come.

There's something about this Sinclair that's different from the others, though I can't place why I feel it at all. She hasn't done anything to warrant the thought.

Whatever it is, it's something beautiful.

Something...*sinister*. Something that makes me think Sinclair has more going on than she'd ever let slip.

I shake my head of the unwanted thoughts and notice she's now a block away, so I run, stopping in front of her again, this time my hands latching onto her upper arms as I walk her backwards, forcing her to the nearest streetlight pole.

She gasps, her vibrant purple eyes wild as she scans the surrounding street for a saviour. No one's coming for her, and any human she hopes to convince would be sorely mistaken. Or she will be when their heart ends up crushed at her feet.

No one's taking my magickless, pathetic, money-making witch from me.

While she's scanning for help, I'm studying her. Her hair, the signature mark of her bloodline, is a shade between red and orange, so representative of the flames she controls. Or, used to control. It falls in long waves around her shoulders, mussed from running. I've always despised the colour on her ancestors, but on this one, it captivates me. Her cheeks are rosy, puffed with her heaving breaths, calling my attention to the spattering of freckles decorating her face. A quick count has me determining exactly how many. Her eyes, a few different shades of purple—not remotely concealing her witch identity—are mixed into a colour so lovely, even I can't help but notice the story they tell.

A story of pain and loss I find myself curious about. There are too many questions circling around this Sinclair. Why she doesn't have her powers; why she and her parents don't live with the Highridge Coven, the very coven *her* ancestors began; and why she's all alone in this human town are a few of them.

In truth, her being powerless makes my job easier. She'll have less fight without them, making her practically human. A witch's strength is their power, and without it, they're nothing special. But the questions still remain.

While she's scanning for help, trying to pull herself from my hold in a few pathetic attempts, I finish my study of her. She's barely tall enough to reach my shoulder, and the skin beneath my grip is broken out in goosebumps, a stupid affliction from the cool night-time fall air. They coat every part of her skin bared to me. She's dressed in pyjama pants with little images scattered on them, and the same shirt I watched her wear to bed. It's shapeless but taut enough over her chest to reveal nipples erect from the cool air. I tear my gaze away, ignoring how the sight sent an aching signal to my fangs, and catalogue the rest of her. There are marks around her wrists—white lines that are only visible in the dark with help of my enhanced vision.

More questions arise over them, but ducking my head, I distract both myself and her by dragging my nose up the column of her neck, her skin soft as silk and so easily crushed beneath my palm if I wished it to be.

"Oh, little witch, you have no fucking idea what you've unleashed by running."

A goddamn addiction.

Feeding from her may not be possible, and I'd never sully myself by fucking her, but I'd happily chase her around my property for as long as she's able to run. The thrill of the chase will be enough; her fear will feed my bloodlust. If I won't be killing this Sinclair, nor allowing her to continue her life as normal to create the next genera-tion, then her punishment needs to be long-lasting and satisfying— for me. Hunting her until she dies sounds like an exhilarating idea.

"Little witch," I muse into her skin, more for myself. The

moniker came from nowhere; I've certainly never humanized her ancestors this way. "Little witch...no, that isn't right. You might be short, but you're certainly not little. You have too much willpower to bow, don't you? I sense you're about to make my life very fucking hellish."

She jerks in my grip, whimpering, her pulse skyrocketing. Knowing it'll amplify her panic further, my tongue darts over her pulse. *Fuck, she tastes better than imagined.* And this is only her skin. Her blood would surely destroy me.

"Just do it already and leave me alone." Her throat bobs with her swallow.

I pull back slightly, but she quickly avoids eye contact, staring towards the nearest house. "What are you talking about?"

"My blood. The cure. It's why you're here, isn't it? What you want. What all you assholes want. Bite me and get it over with."

I open my mouth, ready to reveal all the ways her life's about to change, when something scrapes the ground nearby, earning my immediate attention. I straighten from Sinclair, partly disturbed by the fact her addictive scent distracted me enough I didn't hear the intruder's approach. Probably some stupid human out for a night-time stroll.

I turn when my senses begin prickling, the urge to keep the witch behind me protected, growing inexplicably strong, especially when spotting who's approaching.

Three vampires whose attention is locked on the woman at my back.

"Leave."

"Your Majesty." The middle one steps forwards, claiming leader-ship over the others. He dips his head respectfully, but that respect is quickly extinguished by the flash of red overtaking his black pupils. "You have the Sinclair witch. I didn't realize you wanted to give up your throne."

"Why I have the Sinclair girl is none of your business," I reply dismissively. "Run along before you piss me off." I've already killed one of my kind tonight and have no qualms about taking out three more if they don't obey.

"We want a taste," the middle one pleads, while the vampire to his right hisses. "We all have our reasons for craving mortality, and there's a cure not two feet from you. Only fair you share."

"In time," I declare, knowing Sinclair's listening intently. Can't give away all my secrets yet.

I see the attack before it comes. When two of them launch themselves at me, I'm forced to spring into action. Fighting with Sinclair was the only battle on my nightly plans, but they're making me choose otherwise.

They both reach for me, obviously trying to distract me so the third can go for Sinclair. Which is exactly what he does, darting around me, so I quickly pivot directions, heading his way. The other two attack at the same time, and I lose track of whose hits come from where, charging forward. My hands grasp one's head and I yank, ripping it off his body and ending his life.

I turn for the other two when my ears pick up the sound of quickly retreating steps. She's running, which isn't much of a bother. For one, she'll be quick to catch again, and two, it's one less thing to focus on while I deal with this infuriating irritation.

Whoever these vampires are, they're obviously much younger than me, and therefore slower and weaker. One manages to get his arm around my neck, but with a twist of my feet, I'm out of his hold, gripping him by the shoulders instead and jamming my fangs into his neck. Not to feed, but to latch onto his skin, and with a quick jerk, I yank.

His skin ripping creates a shrill sound, followed by the thump of his undead body becoming, well, actually dead as his head is torn from his neck. Blood drips from my mouth. I spit out as much as I can, the taste sour and sickening, before standing to my full height and descending on the final vampire.

"You." I bore down on him, my steps silent through the pool of blood seeping from the two bodies on either side of me. "You will remain alive, and you will spread the word. You want mortality? I'll grant it to you, to all vampires...for a fee."

He hisses, his eyes darting around for an escape. "You don't own the cure, Dormer."

"I do now," I affirm slowly, words paced. "And *you* will not touch what is mine. Spread that to everyone you know, and attach this warning to it. If anyone goes for her, they'll be dealing with me, and I promise to make the rest of their immortal life *extremely* long and painful. Look for my missive. Keep pissing me off, and you'll be banned from mortality and I'll instead take your life."

With a disgruntled huff, he slinks away before taking off in a blur down the road, leaving me bloodied, with the Sinclair witch getting farther away, and two dead vampires by my feet. I should clear them away so the mortals don't attempt to examine the bodies and learn something is different about them, but in reality, the dumb beings will simply confuse themselves with theories that'll result in scientific study that goes nowhere for the next few decades but keeps them entertained. If they were going to figure out vampires—as well as witches, shifters, and all the other otherworldly and celestial creatures out there—are walking amongst them, they would have done so a century ago.

Leaving the dead vampires behind, I run in the direction Sinclair's syrupy scent is taking off to. I catch up when she's three blocks away, running the opposite way from her house. She's trying to escape where she believes she won't be looked for, so I suppose the witch has a bit of a brain.

I stop in front of her, her responding screech echoing through the street. She halts, panting, her gaze taking me in, paying particular attention to the blood dripping from my fangs.

"You cause a lot of trouble. We need to go before more descend."

I lunge, wrapping a hand over her mouth, fingers pinching her nose. I count to five so I don't accidentally suffocate her, given that time can pass in a blink if I'm not careful.

She fights for a moment, struggling in her powerless way, before her body drops limp, her head against my chest. It's then I really take her in, the deep colour of her hair sticking to my shirt and brushing against my arm, probably the silkiest thing I've felt in centuries. Her scent invades my nose, making something inside me move—which is impossible because everything inside me, most noticeably my black heart, is dead. Not the scent of her blood, but *her*.

Pushing it all aside, I reach down to lift her, noting how ridiculously light she is. I could break her with the gentlest touch. This witch needs her powers because if her life ever comes down to a fight, she'd lose.

I suppose, luckily for her, she'll never need to fight again, with magick or elsewise. Unluckily for her, I'll be the one she'll wish she could fight.

Keeping her close to my chest, I turn and start the journey to her new life.

Towards her captivity.

FOUR

Harlow

The pain in my head dulls, slowly drawing me from sleep. Discomfort thumps front and centre in my forehead, and I groan, opening my eyes to pure darkness. My heart begins pounding a bit faster. I shift, confirming I'm not tied down, and I immediately breathe easier having control of my limbs. At least I have that going for me.

Unilluminated places end up having a sense of entrapment, and my claustrophobia is a bitch about it. With that fear out of the way, my mind's able to focus on the rest, the immediate problem.

Like what happened and where I am.

I shift my hips, the ground hard beneath me. Certainly not my bed, warm and comfortable. I move my arms again, this time paying attention to my senses rather than not being tied down. Dirt, I think, and rocks. I lift my hands to my face, waiting for my eyes to begin making out shapes. After a minute of this, I give up since nothing seems to be changing. It's not that concerning, considering it's only a bit obscurer than my shadow friends, and those I've gotten used to.

All at once, memories flash through my mind. The vampire in my room. The one who spoke my name in the *exact* way I've been hearing for all these months.

Impossible. I've imagined the entire thing. The voice in my head...yeah, don't have an answer for that one, but it can't possibly be the same. If that's the case, then vampires must have powers that my parents never mentioned. Unless they didn't know either, in which case, who knows what else vampires have been hiding, or what other abilities my captor will likely use against me.

More plausible: My terrified, traumatized brain injected my kidnapper's voice into being the replacement for my mental one. They're two different things, but circumstance forced my mind to blend the two realities.

Yeah, that's what I'm going with.

Returning to the last thing I remember: that vampire chased me, caught me—because why wouldn't he have?—and then other vampires showed up. He fought them off but I didn't bother sticking around to see the ending of that. Whoever won didn't change the outcome they all wanted me for. He must have won, considering he caught up to me, this time caked in blood, like he just walked off a horror-movie set.

I don't recall anything after that.

If only I had my magick still, then none of this would be an issue. Instead, I sit up and wait for my eyes to adjust to the impossibly dark room, for shapes to begin forming.

Minutes pass, and still nothing. I remain where I am, rocks digging into my thighs, rather than stand. My luck, the asshole stuck me on the edge of a cliff and with one wrong move, I'll topple to my death.

Although death may end up being the better option than whatever he's planning.

Over the years, many vampires have come for me—for the cure, anyway—but my parents always had so many charms on me, my blood was made to smell like a mortal's, allowing me the chance to live a semi-normal life. It helps vampires can't come out in the daytime either, so as long as I'm inside by sunset, I'm good. They've attacked the house, but none have managed to get through the barriers.

Until this one. The nameless vampire who beat me.

I scoff. What's it matter, anyway? No matter the bloodsucker's name, they're all the same: rich, ancient, and cocky as fuck. He's one of many whom I'll burn to death the moment my powers return.

At this point, I'm still working on the how. If my magick wanted to cooperate, I'd like to think it would have last night when my life was literally in danger. Although, I suppose I'm still in danger. Maybe. I don't really know what's about to happen, but I do know having light would be nice so I can plan my escape accordingly.

Goddess, give me the fucking strength to defeat this vampire.

As though my prayer to Her is answered, a dull light flickers in the distance, casting a glow that barely reveals my surroundings. The dirt-covered and rock-decorated ground, the windowless stone wall at my back, and the thick metal poles across from me that lock me into a not very large space.

At all. Not large at all. Small, in fact. *Too* small. Mentally, I try to count the estimated size of this place, coming up with six-by-six feet or something close to that, and only about four feet above my head if I was standing.

Prison?

A cell that feels entirely too tiny. The concerns of where I am and why are gone for the immediate future, the panic slowly setting in given how close the walls are to one another...and how I'm stuck right in the middle.

Claustrophobia's always been such an inconvenience, and freaking out about my cell's size shouldn't matter as much as the fact that I'm *inside* one. But it's where my brain goes.

Getting to my feet, I wipe the dirt off my pyjama pants and walk to the bars. Thankfully, I still have my flip-flops on from my two seconds of logic before escaping my house. Taking the extra moment to slip them on meant running faster than in bare feet.

I wrap my hands around the frosty bars and shove my face through the metal as far as they'll allow me to, studying my surroundings while breathing in the stale air. Stale, but it's free too, so I'll take it. Better than the cell's air.

It's the same damn air, but rationalizing the different compartments of this horrible place will help me feel less scared about the four walls around me. Sticking my face between the bars makes me feel less trapped. Like the walls aren't *so* close.

For once, I'd rather have the shadows around.

Wherever I am, it's a jail of some sort. A matching cell is across from me, with two more on either side, both sides of the short hallway. At the end is a door, and I long for it to open, for that vampire to return only so we can get this over with.

I should be more frightened, I realize, but somewhere over the years of my parents' protection, I suppose I rationalized this possibility. That at some point, a vampire wouldn't be satisfied with merely a sip.

I twist around, taking in the cell with better detail, my back against the metal. It's cold, and my oversized shirt rides up, the chill pressing to my skin, but I accept it. Accept the fact I'm not so numb yet that I've tuned every sensation out. I slide towards the ground, bringing my knees up to my chest, and rest my head on them, unsure what's to come.

I'd gotten good over the past couple months at pretending. Pretending I'm not dying inside while compartmentalizing my problems. Losing Mom and Dad, and the guilt and grief that have been plaguing me since that fateful day, has been momentarily shoved into a pretty little box and put into a much safer place than I currently am. Once I'm free—and I vow I *will* get free, even if I'm unsure how at this point—then I'll return to hating myself within the confines of my home with my friendly shadows hanging around.

I wonder when they're coming back for me. Or has the Goddess given me a reprieve from that torture method considering my new problem?

Even so, once I get out of here, home is no longer safe without the barrier. If I escape, then I'll be attacked by the next surge of bloodsuckers waiting. With a considerable look around, I realize this cage is the safest place for me. At least until I get my magick back. Or find a coven willing to take me in.

Not the one I was born into—they kicked me and my parents out when I was a kid, so I doubt they'd take me back—but another one.

Ironic that being imprisoned by a murderous vampire is the safer option. At least he keeps out the multiple others and, from what I've seen, he'll protect me from them.

Like a dog protecting his bone from other canines. At this point, I'll take whatever protection I can get.

From down the hallway, a loud crack sounds out. By the time I manage to get to my feet again, using the cell bars as leverage, a quick sliding of metal against metal clangs and a blur of black ends up towering over me, backing me into the cell bars.

Him.

He sneers, looking down at me over his nose. Strands block parts of his eyes, but not enough I'm unable to see the black pupils of the soulless creature.

"Sinclair." It's that voice again; the same one I've been hearing for months. It reaffirms the revelation I'm still pretending doesn't exist.

"Asshole, bloodsucking kidnapper," I greet in return, failing to come up with possible explanations why his voice has been in my head.

"Enjoying your new accommodations?"

"Fuck off." My heart quickens with his nearness, which he probably hears. He's too close, but not in an alarming manner like the size of the cell. There's a strange feeling coursing through me as I tip my head and meet his dead gaze straight on. "Better yet, burn."

He smirks, looking entirely boyish, and a mere fraction of what his actual age likely is. I hate, hate, *hate* to admit this, but my captor is actually hot. I noticed it when finding him on my bed, and I notice it now.

In a psychopathic way, of course.

"Good thing you don't have your magick. For me, anyway." His lips purse, momentarily hiding the sharp tips of his fangs. "How did that come to pass?"

I remain silent, my jaw locking and holding in the answer.

Clearly, he doesn't care all that much about my secrets because he continues to say, "You are somewhat of a disappointment. My history with the Sinclairs dates back a long time, and none have been quite as...lacking...as you are."

"Then send me home. Wait for the next one of us to come around."

He chuckles, the deep reverberation bouncing throughout the room, a threat on its own. "That won't be happening."

There's only one way to end this. I might be magickless, but I'm not powerless, and my power is the very reason vampires seek me out: my blood.

I tip my head back into the bars and squeeze my eyes shut as I do the very act I've always dreaded ever happening and bare my neck to the bloodsucking demon who doesn't deserve my permission.

"If you're going to do it, stop playing around and just fucking do it."

"Do what?"

"Bite me, obviously," I reply with a bit of a huff. "That's why I'm here, aren't I? You want the cure because you're tired of being a vampire. Poor little soulless creature, forced to endure forever..." The kidnapping is a bit much when he could have bitten me in my bedroom and gotten this over with. "What a fucking cliché."

He makes a humming noise that reverberates through my body and straight to my core. My eyes clench again, only this time for a reason other than fear.

A moment later, he takes my offer and lowers his head towards my neck. I hold my breath when his hair tickles my cheek. I never believed I'd ever invite a vampire to bite me, but the sooner he's human, the sooner he'll release me. And if he doesn't let me go, at least I have a fighting chance.

Lips cold as ice but silky as water cruise my neck in the space below my ear before dipping into the curve of my shoulder. My heart races both in fear and anticipation. A vampire's never bit me —for good reason—though I've been curious what it'd feel like from time to time.

Hooking a finger in my shirt's collar, he slides it as far as the material allows, clearing a space for his mouth. His lips part, and sharp pricks slide over my skin. His chilling lips freeze me pressed against the poles, waiting for him to jam them into my skin.

Up and down, he teases me. Taunts me. My hands clench the bars, tapering the storm of emotions brewing—frustration, disgust, anger...desire.

Then he pauses, and I grip the poles even tighter in anticipation of the bite. My thighs press together. Any second, he'll—

His chuckle, dark, dangerous, but also musical, blows against my skin. "Oh, Hellion..." He pauses, his tone trailing off towards the end before he lightly huffs. "Hellion. Yes, that's much more fitting for you."

A freaking *nickname*? This asshole's taunting me for the cure, chasing me around my neighbourhood, and now he's *naming* me.

"Thought you're not supposed to name your food. Makes you grow attached."

He smirks, his lips brushing against my clavicle. "You are very far from being my meal. Your first mistake was assuming I'd like to end my immortal life. I'm at the top of the fucking food chain, so why would I give that up?"

"What?" My eyes fly open and I rip away from him, shoving into the bars hard enough my hips will likely bruise. A bruise is better than anything he has in store for me, because if he doesn't want my blood, why am I here?

The vampire cages me in with his arms. He ducks until he's eye level, his fangs catching my attention. They're so intriguing, mystical, and entirely attention-stealing, despite his next words deserving all my focus because they suggest my downfall.

"I won't be drinking your cursed blood because I'll be *selling* it."

FIVE

Alec

"There are numerous of my kind who've been trying to get to you, but unfortunately for them, I've succeeded, which makes you mine. Which also makes you my property to do with as I see fit."

In the past few hours, I've been excited to return and break down what her future will hold. To watch her pay for crimes she's technically never committed, but rather will be held responsible for what her ancestors did. It should be no different than the rest of her life. Witches are notorious for following family and coven tradition.

"No," she breathes. Her pupils constrict, and she somehow manages to lean farther away. If I didn't have faith in the bars, I'd be worried they'd break against the force. But considering these are the very cells that once held criminals much more dangerous than a mere magickless witch, they'll do.

I let her work through her new reality. My limited experience with humans—which is essentially what the powerless Sinclair is— tells me they require processing time. And considering she's about to spend the rest of her life in this small box, I'll grant her the few moments.

I lower my arms and back away a couple paces, the space more for me than her because being around her is...unsettling. It's the simplest term to describe the tension in my body.

Sinclair's attention darts to the cell's door, which I left open. No matter what she tries, any pathetic escape plan she comes up with will fail.

"Don't do it."

Please do it. Make this fun.

"Then let me go. If you don't want to be human, you have no need for me."

"Did you not hear me moments ago, or is your hearing that bad? You are too valuable for me to release. You truly have no idea how many vampires seek to end their immortality."

"I have an idea." She glances towards the open cell again, her jaw working back and forth. Surely she realizes she won't beat me, but her fragile hope will likely tempt her into trying regardless. "Why? What have I ever done to you?"

"You're paying a debt owed."

She grunts, shifting her feet. "What else can I offer you?"

"Nothing."

"You realize selling my blood will be useless at some point? Eventually, you'll run out of vampires wanting to be human."

"You have no idea how vast of a network we are. For every one of us that dies or will eventually become human thanks to you, three more are made. I'm not worried about running out of immortals."

My ears pick up her rough swallow. "I will not be your blood whore."

"Yet. You will after tomorrow."

Her face flashes white, all that lovely blood draining from it. "Tomorrow?"

I remain silent, not quite willing to disclose everything.

My silence apparently becomes the final straw for her because in a blink, she twists on her heel, her flat shoes smacking against the stone as she hooks her hand on the bars and pushes herself through.

She'll be unable to escape the dungeons, so I remain where I am and wait. Her uncoordinated steps approach the door, her hands grasping the handle as she yanks, probably using all her meager strength, pointless hope continuing to drive her. It's charming.

After another moment of her heaving on the locked door, I tread from the cell to take in the scene. The scrap of a witch is pulling on a door that'll never open for her, her flat shoes that are nothing more than thin pieces of foam—flip-flops, I think mortals call them, which is an absurd name—dragging over the stone floor. She grunts, yells, and smacks her palms against the door in an endless cycle that only irritates my ears.

She stops at my weary sigh, twisting back to face me.

"If you're done now..." With my speed, I move in front of her, spinning her around as I grasp her very fragile throat and begin walking her backwards to her cell.

She claws at my hand, shouting all sorts of unsavoury things, some in an entirely different language, which I guess to be spell incantations. Based on the lack of magick swirling from her, she hasn't gained any of it back between her home and now, rendering her once again completely at my whim.

She spits at me, the ball of saliva landing on my cheek. I don't bother to wipe it away, instead showing her how her pitiful attempts at challenging me are cute at best.

"Fuck you, bloodsucker."

"I'm good, thanks. I don't fuck witches."

Her mouth parts in what I assume would be the start of a witty comeback, but we've reached her cell. I toss her in and lock the door, slipping the key into my pocket. Something discomforting moves in the base of my stomach, but I ignore it. Certainly can't be pity. Pretty sure that emotion isn't something I, as a vampire, am capable of having.

"Stay. I'll return later."

"Like I could go anywhere," she snaps. "What's tomorrow?"

"Tomorrow is when you become useful. If you'll excuse me, it's nearly dawn." I need to return to my quarters to rest and regenerate, because I suspect every moment with this Sinclair will be a trying one. Exhausting in ways I haven't felt since being mortal. Hellish, a tribute to her new name.

She scoffs. "Right. Sunlight burns you guys. Like fire, so remember that for when my magick returns. Rest up—or don't. I don't care either way."

"You should, because I'm the only thing here that'll keep you alive." With that, I turn on my heel and stalk from the dungeon, her cries and shouts music to my ears. The thick metal blocks much of the sound, and if I were human, she'd be inaudible to my weak ears.

I ascend the circular stone steps back to the main part of the castle, quickly going through each of the hallways until reaching the main set of stairs that'll take me up to my wing. It's minutes away from daybreak, and though the windows have long been redone with sunproof enforced glass, I prefer being certain.

Entering my quarters, I head straight for my cell phone—a modern piece of human technology I'm still appalled by all these years later—and open one of a few conversations, this one with my oldest friend, practically a brother to me.

ME

I have her.

CEDRIC

Still think you should kill her and end the Sinclairs altogether. It'd be easier. Quicker.

ME

Consider the retribution in Cora's name. Besides, at this point, it's fun. Start sending out the missive to those we've already chosen.

CEDRIC

As you command.

I toss the device away, knowing by the time the sun sets later today, the message will be in the hands of some hundreds of vampires, all hungry and eager to get a look at the youngest Sinclair. After all, before selling a product, my customers need to view her.

After preparing to rest, I drop into the centre of my bed—a habit from my human life. Vampires may not require sleep the way we used to, but we do need occasional rest every week or so to regenerate. Where that rest happens could be anywhere as long as it's sunless, but I've kept to the habit of sleeping in a bed.

My final thoughts before sleep consumes me are for two separate women. One being the redhead in my dungeon, probably inventing every escape plan possible. The other, long gone but still ever so present.

For you, Cora. Sister. All for you.

<h1 style="text-align:center">SIX</h1>

Harlow

I'm sorry, Mom and Dad. I failed. I suck. I killed you and now I'm about to die in a vampire's lair as some blood bag–slash–cure.

Goddess, how my life has changed in twenty-four hours.

After the vampire, whose name I still don't know and at this point almost don't care to, leaves, I sit with my back to the door, bringing my legs up beneath me and slipping off the flip-flops to tug the edge of my pyjama pants down over my toes. After hours of being here, the chill is starting to penetrate my body. I rub my arms and legs, willing friction combined with my clothing to be enough before lowering my head. If he's going to be gone for the day, no amount of yanking on the bars will help, so I may as well preserve my energy to fight later.

Hecate, give me strength. What do I do? How do I get out of this? Please give me a sign.

My silent prayer is useless. She can't hear me. I doubt She's even paying attention. Without my magick, I'm nothing more than a human. It's been a fact plaguing me for weeks, but regardless, I've tried not to allow it to bother me. Lighting candles and practicing incantations that did nothing were activities that allowed me to feel closer to Her. Enough that I still felt like one of Her daughters.

But now...now I'm further away than ever. By allowing me to be taken by the witches' enemies, it's like She's forsaken me. Again.

"Goddess, don't leave me behind. Please. I'm so lost without my fire. Like I'm partially dead already. I can't handle losing you as well."

Silence. Or so I think. This cell isn't equipped with windows, which means the sky isn't available to me. Just another form of the distance between me and the deity.

Minutes pass with more silence until my prayer is answered. Answered in a way that proves she is indeed punishing me.

The slither along my neck causes me to shiver as the cell grows so black, I can't see a thing. The accompanying chill is different from the dungeon's air, similar to being abandoned in the Arctic, and is unmistakably the very thing harassing me for months.

"Stop. Just stop. Go away. Leave me alone."

Maybe if I begin screaming, the vampire will return. And then what? Beg him to get me out of here? Admit shadows are stalking me? He'll think it's a lie to get free, and then he might leave me here longer out of annoyance.

My mind has to stay sharp and not focus on too much, so with a defeated sigh, I unfold my body and shift away from the door, turning to face it instead. I scrape as much of the nearby dirt in front of the door, giving me more to trace through. My powers may be gone, but activating runes is something else entirely. The blood in my veins designating me a witch might be enough to trigger them, and if not, then at least drawing them is a distraction.

I start with the Algiz rune, designed for protection and warding off harm; a straight line down with a V, like two arms, coming from either of the upper sides of my line. Beside it, I draw Thurisaz, another straight line with a V coming out from the right side. Another protection rune.

I spend the rest of the day tracing the runes while ignoring the weight of the shadows, the proximity of the walls closing in, my body going numb with the cold, and my hunger increasing until my stomach twists uncomfortably.

The walls are closing in.
They're too close.
It's too dark.
It's suffocating.
The walls are coming closer.
So close.
Too close.

...

Time means nothing down here. A day may have passed or a mere hour. Either way, it's been too long and I need that vampire to return. Fighting against him is a distraction from how small this cell has gotten.

I've tried to stand, to walk, to remind myself there's *space*, but the anxiety has rendered me useless, and the longer I remain inept on the ground, the worse it's getting.

This day needs to come to an end. Everything must *stop*. The cell needs to be larger...

For the millionth time, I trace my runes, but they're not really doing anything to calm me. So I try to recall some of the advice Mom and Dad have given me over the years, for once welcoming the memories. Since their deaths, I've been trying so hard not to think about them, but now I need their teachings more than ever.

When we first learned of my claustrophobia, Mom always told me when spaces felt too small to recount something calming. I discovered reciting incantations helps, and though I no longer have the ability to conjure them, the empty words are still comforting.

For the first time in hours, I use my voice, my lips dry and parched.

"Without the flames, make me warm." If I had my magick, that would heat my body.

"Fire, Water, Air, and Earth, I summon you." To call upon all elements, most used by High Priestesses.

"Fire, be gone." To extinguish the flames.

On and on, I recite as many spells as I know. Ones for healing, for the elements, even for cleaning my bedroom. Anything and everything while I trace the runes. The walls eventually back up. Even the shadows seem to lighten; something that would have been nice to know weeks ago...

Once the walls allow me to breathe again, I lift my head, gazing around at the prison that hasn't changed in the hours passing. At least I hope it's been hours—multiple. I'd like to say my grumbling stomach would be screaming more than it already is if days had passed.

I need to get out of here and not allow whatever that sicko vampire plans. Without my powers, I'm left with whatever my body can do—which isn't much against an immortal. I'll never be able to take him on physically, and even if I get a chance to bolt, he'll catch me, exactly as he's done every other time.

It leaves me with few options: making deals, which I doubt he'd take if his entire thing is to profit from the cure in my blood.

The cure...*of course.*

It's impossible to fight a vampire, but less so a human, especially one who wouldn't be adjusted to the clumsy and slower speed.

Before I fully rationalize the likelihood of this working, I'm crawling all over the cell's floor, searching for a tool. I pass over smaller ones I won't be able to properly grip until finding a flatter, longer one. One already in a semi-useful shape.

With it, I drag myself to the cell's bars and begin sawing the rock, sharpening my weapon.

The muscles in my upper arms are burning with more effort than they've ever been forced into, but the rock is much sharper, filed to the point it'll hopefully be good enough for my needs.

When the door down the hall clangs, I tuck my new weapon into my palm and return to my old position, head lowered and knees up, feigning misery rather than near victory. An anxious energy makes it difficult to appear beaten, nerves and excitement mingling knowing this can be over for good if my plan is successful.

At the last second, I wonder if he has cameras in here. It's a place to store prisoners; one would think he'd want to watch them, but the fact we're inside a *dungeon* of all things tells me the vampire's not exactly living modern. So hopefully he has no way of seeing what I've done.

In that familiar whooshing sound of his speed, the cell door opens and he appears, no less irritatingly sexy than he was last time. He's wearing black slacks and a black button-down, both immaculate and no doubt expensive. His hair is damp, as though freshly showered. A spare drop of water drips from a strand when he tips his head towards my runes and merely smirks before stepping over them, his shiny shoes dragging through the design.

Well, that answers that. If the runes worked, he shouldn't have been able to enter. They're designed to keep danger out, and he's the definition of danger.

As he enters the cell, the darkness lifts, the room becoming larger when the shadows evaporate. Just like my bedroom. Whatever's been sent to torment me seems threatened by the vampire, and right now, I'm not entirely sure which I'd prefer.

The devil you know and all that.

"Cute. You really thought those would work?"

I lift my head, facing him directly while pretending my stomach isn't in knots. "I hoped." I curl my hand tighter around the rock, ensuring no part peeks out.

"And if they did, what should they have done?"

"Kept you away."

"You think I wouldn't have found another way to get to you?" He flicks the metal bars closest to him. "These cells were erected centuries ago to keep humans within them. Long before I knew about the existence of vampires or became one myself. I could bend them open if I so desired."

Centuries. So he's old as fuck. "How old are you?"

His nose lifts up, as though insulted by the question. "Doesn't matter, nor is it something you need to know."

"What about your name?"

"Also does not matter to you."

"I should know the name of my captor."

The vampire moves closer, his steps silent over the dirt. He bends slightly, hanging over me, parting his lips just enough the tips of his fangs peek out. Their fangs come out when they're fighting or feeding, according to all the documents my parents had me read.

"Around here, people have to earn the things they want. So what will you give me in exchange?"

Like I'd give anything to him. My freedom's enough. "Never mind. I don't want it that much. I'll be sure to write *the vampire who kidnapped me* on your tombstone when I kill you."

His lips twitch before he straightens. "You're much more entertaining than your ancestors."

"I'll be sure to add 'entertainer' to my résumé."

Along with vampire slayer by the time I finish here.

SEVEN

Alec

There's no plausible reason for me to be down here, considering the party isn't until tomorrow night, but something urged me to visit. That difference about her I can't place. It's strong. Intriguing. Inebriating, even. Addictive for sure. Something I want to break first.

Her willpower, perhaps.

Whatever it is, it led me down here.

"If you want it on your résumé, you'll need a reference, no?" I grin, playing into her sarcasm.

"What would you know about that? Aren't you from before the time of résumé writing?"

"I didn't sleep my lifetime away."

"Whatever." She huffs, crossing her arms tight over her chest and making her shirt pull tight over nipples, which suggest how cold she is. The sight makes my mouth parch—which is physically impossible for my kind. "Why are you here?"

"Humour me, Sinclair." I settle on the ground across from her and bring up my knees to rest my hands on. I can't recall the last time I've sat in a cell with a prisoner. Never? Socializing defeats the purpose, and it's wiser to keep distance.

Yet there's something *off* with Harlow Sinclair, and I will discover what. After all, how can one build a profitable marketing plan if they don't know their product inside and out?

She can't see me as well as I can her, but based on the way her brows rise, she's surprised by my seat choice.

"You'll dirty that fancy clothing of yours."

"You care?"

"Nope. Just making a statement."

I hum. "Getting the sense you talk a lot. Use all those words to make yourself useful and tell me about yourself."

Her face scrunches before she laughs, the sound lyrical and pleasant; a light chime reminding me of a certain harp that was played in the ballroom during my mortal years. Certainly something more pleasant than this dungeon has ever heard. They're not screams, for one.

"You're funny for a vampire. When I made the résumé joke, I wasn't looking for an interview, so how 'bout I don't and we say I did."

Her attempt at humour gnaws at my annoyance when all I want is to learn the intriguing witch's secrets. "I'm serious."

Her lips purse before she insists, "Not without something in return."

"That's not how captivity works."

Her chin lifts. "It's how bargaining does. We both want something."

I'll entertain this...for now, simply because I'm curious. "What is it you want?" I ask, knowing her answer could be one of a few things.

"Food and water. I'm hungry. If you're planning on keeping me alive to sell my blood, I need to, you know, stay alive."

No better than a human, but I suppose comparable to myself. While my body doesn't feel hunger pains the same way, I would grow weak and get thirsty if without blood for too long. A weakened, starving witch would be easier to manage, but her point about staying alive is enough to have me agreeing.

"Very well then. Tell me about yourself."

"You don't know everything already? Getting the sense this was premeditated and you didn't happen upon me at random."

My mind wanders upstairs to the files I have on the Sinclair family, though they're not very detailed—their coven shielded them well. "You're right, but there are facts about you I'm unaware of."

"Why would you want to?" Her lips pick up with her confused sneer, her nose scrunching.

My question exactly. "Humour me. You grew up around humans. Must have been difficult at school to hide your powers." From what I know, witches and warlocks spend years mastering their control, and usually around one another so they don't accidentally alert mortals to otherworldly beings.

She's quiet for a moment, and her bottom teeth scrape over her lip, making the skin red with the flush of blood. I roll my own together when a ghost sensation of teeth along mine causes me to experience my first shiver in centuries.

"Wasn't a concern. I was homeschooled."

"Hm." I suppose it's safer that way. Without a coven for protection, her family was sitting ducks—a stupid phrase Cedric recently taught me. "Why don't you live in Banff?"

The day word got out the remaining Sinclair, Emily, her husband, John, and their daughter moved across the country, it struck me as odd. But witches have done stranger things, so after a brief check-in to confirm their new location, I left well enough alone until the day I planned on coming for Harlow.

"Random. What's in Banff?"

I scrutinize her expression, the genuine confusion, for a lie or joke. She's unaware of what's in Banff and her family's history with the mountains? "The Highridge Coven. *Your* coven. The coven every Sinclair has been a part of."

"Oh." Her voice is small, hurt. "Them. I didn't know their location. They kicked us out when I was a child."

"How old were you?" It's a test question because I know the answer. She was eight.

"Not sure."

"Liar."

Red flushes her cheeks. "I'm not lying."

As an immortal, I've experienced countless lies over my years, but after a quick study of the witch, she truly isn't. Her heart isn't quicker than earlier. She remains still and without a nervous twitch. Her breathing is paced. She looks genuinely confounded. Interesting...

Before I realize what I'm doing, I'm across the cell, crouching in front of her and studying her like mortals stare at poor animals caged up in zoos.

She presses back into the bars, her hands scrambling on the dirt. "Wh-what are you doing?"

Ignoring her, I study her eyes. The strips of different purple shades like a clematis flower prove to me she wasn't lying. They're too clear, honest. Innocent.

Innocent is a dangerous thing to be. It makes me hungry, hard, and eager to hunt.

Before my thoughts get away from me, I return to my spot across the cell. "You're telling the truth."

She rolls her eyes, snorting derisively. "Told you. Anyway, next question if you have more."

I have many. Humans usually retain memories from around eight-years-old, so why doesn't she remember what was a big life event? Getting kicked out of a coven is major for witches, who trust their own above anyone.

"Homeschooled," I muse, instead choosing a more direct topic. "Quiet life. You have a job?"

Another eye roll, this time making me twitch. "I'm twenty-four.

Obviously."

"Wasn't sure, considering you still live at home." This is solely a taunt because without a coven, no doubt her parents wanted to keep her nice and close and safe. Away from the vampires who'd descend, seeking the cure.

"Not all of us have castles, or whatever this place is."

"What gave it away?"

She taps the bars at her back. "The row of cells for one. The fact this place screams torture chamber."

"That's down the hall," I admit, thinking of the room so often used for prisoners during medieval times. It was a different world back then, and before vampirism, torture methods had to be more creative. My nose can still pick up the metallic scent of death that never quite left. "You've gone off track. Your job?"

"Yeah, I work, and yes I still live at home. Economy sucks, not that you'd know. I'm a secretary for an accounting firm."

Certain jobs have existed as they are for centuries, but others are more recent, in the last two to three hundred years. A secretary being one of them.

"As in, you answer phone calls from rich mortals?" I verify we're both speaking of the same thing.

"Ironic statement coming from a rich asshole."

"The great, ancient bloodline of the Sinclairs has been reduced to working for another person. A *mortal* at that." Stating the fact makes me chuckle as I picture centuries prior, dating back to Elizabeth Sinclair. How prideful the coven was. How they ruled above humans, not the other way around.

"It pays the bills. Besides, we were blending in, and it's a pretty basic job."

"Are they missing you?" I realize too late she may misconstrue it as interest when it's...well, I'm not sure why the inquiry into her life.

She shakes her head. "I quit when my parents died."

Yes, the mysterious fire that engulfed their house and took two witches whose power was fire while leaving the third alive and their house still standing. There are many things that don't quite add up, but the questions die on my tongue when I catch the tear beading by the corner of her eye.

Her sniffle is nearly inaudible, if not for my enhanced hearing. She wipes her face before her hands rest in her lap, one wrapping around the other wrist, thumb stroking the scars on her skin. Those are a question for another day.

I understand the *concept* of grief from losing a loved one, but the actual experience of it is different for vampires. After losing Cora, I thought of only destruction. I want to probe the subject, even if it results in her breaking down, but don't. *Can't.*

A Sinclair has never cried in front of me. All the years of murdering them, not one has shed a tear. Screamed, yelled, fought, yes, but none looked so...mortal as this one. It's all the more reason to continue talking, but instead, I find myself across the cell again.

She stiffens, but I'm too occupied studying her to care about her feelings over my proximity. Coupled with that addictive scent I swear is lingering upstairs because it's haunting me through my halls, there's something not quite right about her.

"Don't touch me," she bites out, even though I haven't lifted a hand towards her. Her deterrence only makes it more tempting. Miss Sinclair shouldn't have made such invitations.

"Explain why I'd want to."

Her heartbeat, which was already beating quickly, kicks off into marathon speeds. It's a tune I could very well rest to, knowing it's driven by panic.

"Your heartbeat is extremely fast," I murmur, despite her not answering my latest demand.

She turns her face away. "Fear does that."

"So does intrigue. Lust. Pleasure. Joy. Excitement. Adrenaline. Numerous emotions could be the explanation, each one as probable as the last."

Her teeth grind against one another, the sound a bothersome disruptor to her heartbeat. "Go fuck yourself."

"You have such a mouth on you, Sinclair. It's alluring." Grinning, I stand and head for the cell's entrance. "Thanks for the talk. See you tomorrow."

"Wait." She scrambles to her knees, one foot resting on the ground. "I answered your questions. You promised me food and water."

Pesky little thing. Without replying, I exit the cell and lock it behind me before speeding from the dungeon, a mere blur throughout the castle as I go retrieve a few items from my stores, stocked the other day before retrieving her, knowing she'd need sustenance beyond air.

With the same speed, I return to the dungeon to drop the apple and water bottle in between the bars. She gasps, having not seen me enter, and I'm gone before she could attempt to spot me.

"Until tomorrow, Hellion. Until tomorrow."

EIGHT

Harlow

'm still processing the vampire's visit long after he goes—long after I've finished the apple and drank a few sips from the water bottle, opting to conserve it since I don't know the next time I'll receive any.

I remain in the same position on the ground, creating warmth from my body. The rock I filed down into a weapon remains close so I don't accidentally misplace it in the dark. I didn't count on the vampire to visit so we could only *talk*. The two times he got near enough, I debated going forward with my plan, but considering I was on the ground beneath him, he still held the upper hand. There will be a better time, and it's probably when he lets me out of the cell.

With his absence, the pressure from the small space returns, but this time, driven by determination and the strength of the single fruit, I pace the cell, trying to keep myself mentally grounded.

It also works to exhaust my body. I soon retake my place, makeshift weapon in hand, and curl up. Ignoring the walls and the shadows that creep into their places, I shut my eyes, managing to doze a little.

Sleep only lasts so long before I'm awake again. Without windows, I can't tell if it's day or night, but I take the time to continue working at my weapon, wanting it to be as sharp as possible if this is to work.

At some point, the door from down the hallway opens again, so I return to my earlier position, seeming every bit the pathetic witch he revels in me as. Legs drawn up with arms around them, the hallway lights flick on, basking the room in a dullness that removes some of the suffocation.

My cell opens, and he steps over the useless runes he ruined at this last visit. He crosses the cell, snapping his fingers. "Up. My guests will be arriving in an hour, and your appearance leaves something to be desired."

That'll be a no. I remain seated.

He steps towards the entrance, flicking his fingers for me to follow. "Come."

Still a no.

Two steps from the cell and without turning around, he rumbles, "You'd do well not to test me, Sinclair. You won't like what happens."

I speak for the first time since he's entered. "You won't kill me. It'd go against your entire 'sell the witch' plan."

He whirls, black eyes glinting in the dull light. "Death isn't the most painful thing I can do to you. In fact, death would be a reprieve. Get up, unless you'd like me to demonstrate some of those ways."

Grumbling beneath my breath, I do, because if I have *any* chance of getting free, step one is leaving the dungeon. There's no other option other than listening to him, at least for now, even though obeying him is the last thing I want. He doesn't need more power over me than he already has.

Clenching my weapon, I position it so the sharp point is against the thin skin of my palm and follow him towards the door I tried to escape from yesterday. It groans beneath the weight, but his strength makes it seem like he's opening a thin closet door.

He steps to the side, gesturing. "Go first. I don't trust you not to fall and die or something ridiculous, assuming it'll be your ticket to freedom."

I skirt by him, pressing close to the doorframe to avoid brushing his arm. "And trust you to catch me if I do?"

"You said so yourself that I need you alive. So yes, catching you is precisely what I'd do. Noting that, don't be stupid and test my benevolence. Just walk quickly."

I study the skinny stone steps twirling in a circle, the top unable to be seen from here. The distance between each step seems rather high, and after lifting my leg to the first one, I already know this will suck.

"Why the fuck are these steps so far from one another? Who the hell were they built for?" I mutter beneath my breath, managing my second one, my burning calf telling me I'm not fit enough for this.

Surprisingly, he responds—because of course his vampiric hearing allowed him to hear my grumble. "Humans have shrunken over the centuries. The men once meant to use these stairs were quite large, at least by today's standards."

Not that I want to act interested in *anything* this vampire says, but that was oddly intriguing. It once again makes me wonder how old he is and all the things he's seen.

"Why's that?"

"Humans no longer live off the land. Everything they consume is manufactured. Coupled with natural evolution. The biggest thing to fear nowadays is corporate greed and retinas burning from social media, so humans' bodies are no longer built for surviving in the wilderness."

Did the vampire just make a joke?

I glance over my shoulder and nearly trip on the next step at the sight of his lowered face, half masked by his hair, revealing a barely there smirk. He looks entirely roguish, and *that* is the only nice thing I'll ever allow myself to think about the asshole.

Halfway up the stairs, right when my legs are burning from the workout, he sighs. and I have a fairly good idea why.

"Not all of us are equipped with immortal energy, asshole."

"You could at least attempt to walk faster."

"Do you *want* me to fall and break my neck?"

We're close to the top of the steps, and this might be my best chance. If the change can happen on a staircase, surely that'll make it easier to get rid of him. He'll be weak and easy to kick down.

I reposition the pointy rock into my palm, squeezing tight to dig in and—*Fuck, this hurts like a bitch.*

What the vampire has in store for me will hurt more, which becomes my motivation to keep going. No matter what, though, my skin refuses to break. Maybe I didn't make it sharp enough…maybe my body's natural protective instincts are taking over and not allowing me to push it in as much as it needs to.

I stagger on the next step, which gives me an idea, and since we're only two from the top, it's now or never. For the next one, I purposely trip myself by not lifting my leg as high while simultaneously tightening my grip on the rock. When I land, knee on one step, palms catching me on another, there's an instant sting, the rock successfully making a slice.

The vampire sighs again and mutters something about witches being no better than humans. Except humans are completely powerless, while I'm not.

I lift my bloodied hand, slowly unpeeling the fingers to check the injury; a small slice about half an inch long. Just enough for blood to seep from it.

I straighten and turn towards the vampire, readying myself for what I hope will be my final interaction with him. He catches the scent of my blood almost immediately, black eyes dart to my injured hand, his nostrils flaring with his intake of breath—of my scent.

Before he realizes what I'm doing, I push my sliced palm against his mouth, ensuring enough of the blood stains his lips, knowing it's likely enough when the tip of his fang grazes my hand. It's sharp like a knife, and I'm momentarily stricken by that alarming fact.

But that's all the thought I give before twisting back around and taking off up the final two steps. Although I've never witnessed the transition from vampire to human, I have a vague enough idea how it works. A few drops, and within a moment or two, the transition will start. I've always been mildly curious in a masochistic way, and even though this is probably my only chance to witness it, I don't stick around.

NINE

Alec

That fucking witch. She isn't that stupid?

I touch my lips, wiping away drops of her blood, seeing them stain the tips of my fingers.

She is. She fucking *is*.

I spit whatever blood I can out, praying my body ingested very little. But still, it doesn't change the fact I've officially tasted the witch; the one whose blood smells like temptation brought to life.

She tastes fucking *divine*, like I first assumed. My hunger amps up, my vision turning red with bloodlust. I may have drank only hours before stalking her house, but Sinclair has me feeling like I haven't eaten in a month. Like I've been starving myself and she's the answer. The *need* to drink and to never stop.

Hunt.

Chase.

Feed.

Fuck.

It all switches on, which confirms one thing: her little plan failed. I'm not mortal. Since only my tongue got a small taste, I assume my system didn't absorb enough to trigger the change. Even so, that minor lick was enough for my every sense to attune to her.

In the half a second of lucidity before I'm completely taken over, I think, admittingly with a bit of admiration, that she's the only Sinclair to try to ever change me to get free. Her plan was clever, and disconcerting for me that I hadn't suspected she'd do something like this.

Hunt.

Instantly, I'm at the top of the stairs, staring down the long, stone hallway lined with tapestries and stained-glass windows. She's almost at the end, near the foyer, where her chance of escape is. Her breaths come out in rapid succession, her heartbeat so impossibly loud. She's more scared now than when she was running through her neighbourhood, probably because she *knows*. She knows what she's done, the monster she's enticed.

Chase.

Without having been changed, I'll beat her to the door.

But now, I'm fucking *pissed*. While I have no desire to alter my plans, the primal side of me is demanding to end it altogether—to end her life. She thought she could win, and I'll prove to her every way she will not.

Hunt.

I take a regular step before pushing myself down the hall, my speed making me a blur until passing her and stopping at the front door, only feet from where she's running to.

She gasps, nearly slamming into me, but I snap a grip around her neck and squeeze, spinning us both to shove her against the doors. Fear radiates from her, the scent almost as pleasing as that blood of hers. I could very well drown in both. She scratches at my hands while her legs kick; both motions are useless.

"Hellion, you've made a big fucking mistake."

Snarling, I press close to her. She's soft, softer than any woman I've been with since my human life. Vampire women are different... colder, vicious. Miss Sinclair is probably all hearts and flowers. Good and Light, masking the very grimness reflecting in her expression—the truth behind her.

"Wha…?" She trails off, scanning me, pausing on my fangs, erect in their rage and hunger. "It didn't work," she whispers, going limp with defeat. "It should have."

I pinch on the spot that'll cut off her airways, careful not to make it fatal. "Seems you've overestimated yourself."

"Why didn't it work?" She claws at my hands.

I don't answer, my mind and body not exactly equipped to handle a conversation meant to depict the rationality of how the curse within her blood functions.

"Your life might be dependent on the fact it didn't, so be thankful. Now, give me one reason I shouldn't end your life like you tried with mine."

I squeeze tighter, earning a gasp but no plea. Shame. I want to hear her beg for her life. Beg *me* for something only I can give her. Show me a bit more of that fighting spirit that drove her to this ridiculous plan.

Her ancestors all died too quickly. A few meager attempts with magick to beat me, but in the end, I still got them. This one is the only one putting up a halfway decent fight, and another side of me enjoys it. The primal side is demanding I let her go so she can continue fighting, making a game out of her freedom, all while I play with my prey.

Hunt.

Chase.

Feed.

Yes, that's what I'll do. Why strangle her to death when I can set her free on my land and hunt? Maybe I'll take days to track her, purposely letting her live every second in terror that at any moment, any turn, any tree, I could be right there. The unknown will kill her well before I do.

The chase, the hunt…it'll do.

She scratches at my hand, her nails doing nothing to my hardened skin. "You can't kill me. You need me."

"*Need?*" I roll the word around in my mouth, its flavour sour and unwanted. "Believe me, I need nothing from the Sinclairs. You were a passing opportunity and nothing more. Don't believe your life has more value to it."

"Fine." Her eyes flutter shut with her concession, and for that I nearly let her go. My grip loosens, confused she's giving up. After all that, she's decided not to fight?

The part of me that wants to dominate and prove she's prey to my predator is upset. The game hasn't gone on nearly long enough, leaving my cravings unsatisfied.

"Kill me then," she continues, her voice both soft and hard at the same time. "Death will be better than this miserable existence."

Hunt.

Chase.

Kill.

...Protect.

The red covering my eyes fades ever so slightly into a dark pink. A bit of lucidity returns, and my hand loosens more.

Protect.

Why is that singular feeling almost as strong as my need to kill her?

Through my confusion, I repeat her last words in my head. They weren't a plea to be saved, but an agreement to die.

"Why would you want to die?" I prick the tip of my tongue against one of my fangs, using the sting to stop me from acting on one of the few feelings coursing through me. "You give up too easily."

"Because life isn't worth living anymore."

I release her entirely, laughing as she falls to her feet, clutching her throat. "And that, Miss Sinclair, was your second mistake today. You want to die, so you've given me every reason to make your pain live on."

With my next deep breath, my fangs retract into my gums and

my eyes return to their normal black, vision in full colour once more.

She glares at me, watching my transformation. "Why don't you ever call me by my first name?"

"Given names are a sign of respect, and Sinclairs have never deserved mine." I spin on my heel and snap my fingers. "Now, follow. We must get you ready."

Her steps don't trail behind me right away, not that I expect them to. She won't attempt escaping again, even as she's right in front of the main doors. Her plan failed, and I anticipate her conceding for good, given the limited outcomes of any attempt she has in her.

"Then what should I call you? What's your last name?"

So she learns. Once on the bottom step, I peek over my shoulder, studying her standing there clutching her oversized shirt, her ridiculous pyjama pants dirty from her time in the dungeon. Are those pineapples all over the pink pants? I've never seen a witch seem so... human. It's unnerving.

"Earn it, and maybe I'll tell you." I take another step, and this time, so does she.

"How?"

"First, by following. Second, by obeying every command I give you tonight."

"What's happening tonight?"

"You'll see." I end the conversation by walking up the stairs. She'll follow, or she'll continue making unwise decisions.

After a moment, her quiet paces trail behind me, those damn flat shoes making annoying slapping noises against the stone. They're almost eye roll-worthy and soon will be gone. Burned so I don't have to be subjected to them anymore.

I lead her all the way to the guest wing, every paced human step I'm forced to take exasperating. It's unnatural to move so slowly, but finally we make it to the spare room I had prepared for her to use.

I push open the door to the bedroom and cross to the ensuite bathroom, hovering until Sinclair appears in the doorway. Lips part as she takes in the room that's much cozier than the cell. For one, it has a bed.

"What are—"

I snap my fingers, ending the stupid questions. The *whys* and *whats* are unimportant. Her little stunt downstairs has already put us behind. Within the hour, hundreds of vampires will descend to get a look at what I'm selling, and she should be shackled in place and ready before then.

"Into the bathroom. Shower. There's soap for you to use. Don't wash your hair because we don't have time for you to dry it, and looking like a drowned animal won't do. There's a brush in there, and a dress. Once you're ready, meet me out here. You have fifteen minutes beginning now. Do not make me come looking for you."

Her brows lift as she slowly treads into the bedroom, staring at the large bed with longing. "You're letting me shower?"

"Yes. You stink like a cell. You forget, vampires have heightened senses and no guest of mine deserves to be subjected to you. Get clean."

Her eyes narrow into little violet flames that match the vibrancy of her hair so perfectly. "Gee, sorry, if I knew kidnapping was on the calendar, I would have showered and primped for you."

"Yes, well, next time be smart and think ahead," I reply, playing into her sarcasm. She forgets, I've had centuries at perfecting an attitude, and once lived with a woman who was much more irksome than her. "You're down to fourteen minutes."

I drop into one of the two armchairs positioned beside the unlit fireplace. In recent years, after a lot of convincing, I had a modern heating system installed in the castle, rendering the ancient fireplaces useless. The temperature makes no difference, hot or cold, but I was reminded that if I wish to keep this Sinclair alive, the place needs to have some human, livable conditions.

Propping my chin on a hand, I regard her from across the room. She hides her anxiety and hatred well as she stares back unblinkingly at me.

"Give me one good reason why I should listen."

"You want my last name, don't you?"

"Not that bad."

"Your life."

"Again, I gave you permission to end that downstairs."

Yes, and that permission made me uncomfortable. "You're getting clean one way or the other. *How* you get into the shower is dependent on you in the next thirty seconds. Either you march your ass into the bathroom or *I* wash you."

Sinclair scurries across the room like a little mouse and, with a final glare, enters the bathroom and slams the door shut.

"If you drown yourself, I'll change you into a vampire myself as punishment," I call out just loud enough she'll be able to hear me between the thin wood.

Now *there's* an idea, especially if she keeps pissing me off. End the Sinclair line by turning her into one of us. Her ancestor will roll over in her grave—or wherever her coven placed her body. The cure would be no more, but the Sinclair bloodline will live on forever, suspended in time.

Maybe in the future when she's outlived her worth.

Shutting my eyes, I focus on the sounds coming from behind the door. The shower switching on, her steps moving through the room, clothes hitting the tiled floor. The water loses its sharp pelts to softer ones as she steps beneath the spray, and her sigh is loud enough, it's like she's standing right beside me.

I watch the time tick away on my cell and after about seven minutes, the shower turns off. Another one, and her towel drops to the floor. My staff were instructed to hang the dress on the back of the door, so if I can guess, she's retrieving it now.

Exactly at the fifteen-minute mark, the door opens again and the little Sinclair emerges, dressed in the gown I chose before retrieving her from the dungeon.

She looks up, that vibrant red hair dry as I've instructed, falling in a wavy curtain around her face. Her gaze no longer holds hatred, but curiosity.

What's even more curious is the thought passing through my head. The one I'll never dare admit, even to myself.

Exquisite.

TEN

Harlow

The shower is purely otherworldly, a gift from the Goddess herself. At least, I'm pretending it is rather than a forced chore from the asshole vampire on the other side of the bathroom door.

A shower because I *stink.*

Yeah, well, no shit. Live in a cell and you would too.

I could very happily stay in here forever, but I'm getting the sense he'll stick to his word and will come for me. So, too soon for my liking, I leave the hot water and dry off with a towel hanging on the nearby rack before heading for the garment bag on the back of the door.

I debated checking it out before my shower, curious to see what kind of horrendous outfit's been chosen for me. No doubt something extremely revealing so all his "customers"—vampiric assholes, to use another nickname—will be able to see parts of me I'd rather they didn't. All of me. *Too* much of me for what's comfortable.

Comfortable. That's a ridiculous notion in general, because none of this is comfortable. Rather, it's the exact opposite. Like knives beneath my fingernails uncomfortable.

Hecate, help me get through this, I pray, crossing the space to the garment bag. At this point, who knows if She's able to still hear me. I unzip the bag, expecting...not this.

My grip on my towel slips, and it falls to the floor, leaving me naked and gaping at the dress.

It's floor-length, modest. Oddly modest. I reach up and pull it from the hanger, fingering the chiffon material and bodice decorated with the tiniest beads. It's extremely extravagant, much more than anything I've ever worn, and not very modern. Which makes sense, given my captor is a vampire, but it also has me wondering whom he stole this from.

The time is ticking away, so I step into the dress, slipping my arms through the off-shoulder sleeves and pulling up the small zipper on the side.

How it fits so perfectly is a damn mystery. Unless he had this made for me... Nah, that's too ridiculous to even consider.

Glancing towards the mirror, I'm taken aback by the reflection, but don't remain for long, instead heading for the door, preparing for yet another round with the vampire.

He looks up as I return, and if I didn't know better, I'd believe his eyes flashed red before returning to their flat black. He gazes at me for what feels like forever, his expression unreadable, chin on his hand. I fist the sides of the dress, ready for the torture to begin so I can return to my cell and plot escape plan number two.

"Who'd you kill for the dress?"

If I wasn't paying so much attention, I would have missed his flinch. That's interesting.

"Does it matter?" He lifts his head from his hand, his rumble oddly gentle for his words.

I shrug, because at the moment, other people's lives aren't my focus. "Guess not. Also, why this one? It's modest." The heart-shaped neckline doesn't dip too low, the skirt tickling my feet.

"They're buying your blood, not your body."

Thank fuck for that confirmation. Still, my questions keep pouring out of me, like a fountain I just can't put a cover on. "Yeah, but everything I've been taught about vampires claims you guys are extremely sexual. Like, when you eat. Wouldn't you want to appeal to that side of the others for a sale?" Heat warms my cheeks. I rambled and didn't mean to admit that or place the idea in his head.

Between Mom, Dad, and Gram's old books, I've read up on our enemies: vampires, as well as the shifters. Vampires are notorious for linking sex and feeding together.

Suddenly, he's right in front of me, looming in that way he seems to enjoy. He backs me into the wall with a smile too malicious, all fang. In the safety of my stupid thoughts, I admit he's sexy like this. One arm lifts, bracketing my right side, and although I'm still free to run, his influence certainly doesn't make it possible.

"Tell me...what exactly do you know about my kind?"

Gulping, I tear my gaze away from his enticing eyes, staring at the patch of skin where his collar meets his neck. "That you like to have sex while feeding."

He makes a humming noise, his smile growing even more devilish. "That we do. For vampires, so much of our lives are felt in numbness, passing us by. So we seek delight in indulgences and risks. Blood satisfies our food requirements, and fucking satisfies *us*. Maslow's hierarchy of needs—I assume your human education taught you that? For vampires, both are high on our hierarchy, so combined..." He flicks a tongue against his fang, but I feel it as though he were between my legs, flicking something else. "Combined, there's nothing greater. Nothing more fulfilling." He pauses, his head tipping to the side. "Has a vampire ever bitten you?"

I shake my head, unsure if words are able to be formed. It's messed up I'm having *any* reaction to this vampire whose name I don't know and who's kidnapped me.

"Probably for the best." He pushes away, dropping his arm and granting me the much-needed space to breathe. "As for your question, the vampires who pay will not be drinking straight from you, so there is no need to show off your body more than what is necessary. The purpose of all this is because not every vampire believes there are any Sinclairs still alive, and we must prove you are."

At least that's something.

He moves towards the door, gesturing for me to follow. "We have to get you situated before my guests arrive."

"No shoes?" My feet are bare, and the castle's stone hallways won't provide much comfort. My flip-flops are in the bathroom, and I skipped putting them on, assuming he'd have something to match the dress. My mistake, obviously.

"No."

Biting down on my retort because it won't change his mind, I follow him out of the bedroom, leaving it after a longing look and wondering how I might be able to work it into a deal. The bed, the room's temperature, and the bathroom are all infinitely better than the dankness of the cell downstairs.

He leads me through the hallways and to the staircase we came up earlier. The more of this place I take in, the more I realize this is an *actual* castle—stone walls, tapestries, random statues and knight costumes.

Makes me wonder again exactly how old this guy is, or whom he stole the castle from.

Downstairs, he walks me down the hallway away from the front doors. Another look, this time for any cameras positioned towards them or staff lingering that'd stop me, but the area appears empty.

"If this place is as old as it looks, how did you get modern plumbing?"

"I've updated it."

He takes another turn before stopping abruptly at an arched doorway. I come up beside him, taking in the room with a low, appreciative gasp. As large as two theatres with high, painted ceilings, I'm awed by the beauty of the mural depicting a sky within a lightning storm. In the centre of the ceiling, a very intricate glass chandelier hangs, almost obnoxious with its size. Teardrop glass hangs rather low, like it could be reachable if attempted. The ceiling-high windows across the room are draped in dark curtains that cover any indication of the outdoors and where we are. On the opposite wall, a series of paintings hang, ones the size of my entire apartment. They depict various landscapes: mountains, vineyards, fields, and oceans. The room is vast and wide open, a huge ballroom, empty except a dais at the opposite end with a throne erected on it.

An actual throne. I cast a look towards the vampire. Again, who *is* this guy?

The vampire crooks a finger, and reluctantly, I cross the room behind him. My feet make slapping sounds on the ground, the chill from the hallways having numbed my feet to the point this floor feels warmer.

We reach the dais, and the throne looks so much larger up close. It has a dark cushion, lined with a black filigree, the back arching high in a series of twisty vines. It's pretty.

The vampire steps up beside it and reaches for something behind the seat, dragging forward a set of cuffs attached to a chain, the other end connected to the throne. He comes towards me, his intent obvious.

"No."

"This isn't a debate. Give me your wrists, or I'll get them myself. I won't be gentle, so make the correct choice."

Gritting my teeth, I lift up my arms for him to clasp the metal around. He opens the cuffs and lowers them beneath my wrists, but stops suddenly, his gaze intent on the white scars.

He snatches my right arm, lifting it for closer inspection. "I noticed them in your room. Where did these come from?"

"Not sure." I've had them for as long as I can remember. I assumed they were some witchy birthmark or something, but Mom and Dad denied that, and said they didn't fully know either. That they appeared one day. Not the first unusual thing to happen to a witch and won't be the last.

"Lying won't help your case, Sinclair." His finger drags over the largest one on my underside. His pad is smooth, and nearly as distracting as his touch. "Did you do this to yourself?"

"No." I yank against his impossible hold. "I'm serious. I've always had them."

He looks up, black storms clashing with my face. "The bit I recall from my human life, people aren't born with scars like these. Who did this to you?"

"I don't know! I don't care, and neither should you."

My words seem to register because, after a long pause, he drops my arms. "You're right, I don't care." He clasps the cuffs around my wrists before gesturing to the dais. "Sit."

I do, my body feeling as though it's no longer present. Careful not to trip over the dress as I walk up the platform, I situate myself on the top step, only a foot or so from the base of the throne. The vampire steps by me, but I'm no longer paying him attention.

Too busy studying the cuffs on my arms.

And the way the scars match up almost perfectly to the edge of the metal.

ELEVEN

Alec

Sinclair takes her seat on the dais, looking exactly what she's supposed to be portraying: a broken captive, saddened by her new life.

Her head's low, and she's staring at the cuffs with a strange intensity. If she had her magick, I'd be convinced she was working to get them off. And maybe, I'd think that was the case—that she was hoping it'd return now and help her get free—until she strokes over one of the scars that interestingly line up with the cuff's edge.

Like she's been cuffed before.

Arguably, there'd be numerous suitable reasons for her to have been in handcuffs in the past, but none of them should have been so lasting that scars formed. The scars are...concerning. Not sure why, but they are. She's been hurt before, and either she's doing a damn good job at lying to protect the bastard or she truly doesn't remember.

Knowing what I do about humans, trauma is one of the worst forms of ongoing pain a person can survive through. Being cuffed long enough to leave lasting scars would surely result in a kind of trauma one doesn't simply forget.

Something else is going on, and I vow to figure it out. Why... because I must know all about my little captive. For her own safety, of course, which in turn is for my benefit. If someone out there wishes to harm her, they'll have a bitch of a time getting to her. I've found her, claimed her, and she'll be protected from anyone else.

Lost in thought, I miss the moment the others begin showing up. Most walk straight to me, bowing deeply as they use the appropriate greetings, but their eyes remain on the witch. She stiffens under the attention and subtly shifts closer to me, making me smirk. Despite her hatred of me, I'm the safest killer in the room. At least, to her.

A short while later, the ballroom is full of vampires in their finest, eager for the first party in a century I've put on. After so long of hosting them, they've grown tiresome and boring, but tonight, it's serving another purpose.

After all, no investor will provide money without seeing the goods. I don't even need to show the witch off; she's doing it all on her own by simply being here.

The Sinclairs have always hidden themselves away so well, and time for vampires is fleeting. For some of them, the last time they thought to seek out the cure may have been during a previous generation. When they failed, they disappeared for what felt like a couple years, but decades passed, and they began their quest all over to find the current living Sinclair. Vampires are, unfortunately, so easily deterred.

Most of them. Not me.

Age. Personality during our human lives. So much can decide how we act as an immortal.

I snap my fingers at Sinclair. She twists with a glare, and I snap again, this time pointing by my feet. "Here."

She doesn't move at first, her lips pursing. She seems to be in debate with herself and, after a quick glance toward the crowd, most of who are raptly watching, she scoots herself backwards. It becomes a complicated laughing matter, the dress bunching beneath her and getting tangled.

Finally, she makes it beside me, muttering, "Dick."

I reach down to pet her hair, aware of the hundreds of interested eyes drilling into us. They can all smell her blood and the cure it holds, and by tonight, I anticipate the number of eager vampires who are ready to end their immortal lives to be high.

Interestingly, she doesn't flinch, playing the part I need her to well. I lean close to murmur, "Continue being good, and I may be satisfied enough to hand over my name. The audience is very captivated by you."

I am too. In part.

She reaches for my hand again. "I don't care about your name anymore. I want to go home."

Oh, she couldn't have said a more perfect thing. Raising my voice ever so slightly so it's heard by the entire room, I tell her, "This is your new home. You're never leaving, so get that silly notion out of your head."

Her eyes blaze an interesting mix of irritation, fury, and something even more depraved. I stroke over her hair again, dragging my fingers through the silk. Her hair is softer than anything I've felt in a long damn time, and it's only the audience preventing me from getting lost in the sensation.

More and more stop their own conversations to observe. Towards the end of the night, I'll offer one lucky customer the chance to be the first: to change right after the party. They can bid on the chance.

In truth, I need to confirm that earlier was simply because I didn't ingest enough. Can't build a business on a broken product.

A familiar figure breaks away from a nearby group and strides forwards, his attention bouncing between the witch and me. He passes her and comes close before dipping into a low, mocking bow.

"Your Majesty."

Like every time someone's approached tonight, Sinclair glances at me, the throne, and then the walls around us. She's presumably finally pieced together who I am. A part, anyway. A role.

Cedric straightens from his bow before all proper etiquette—the little he holds on to—disappears, and he slouches, shoving his hands in his pockets. Up close, it's obvious the little care he puts into his appearance. The rumpled suit, his unbrushed hair, the drops of blood in the corner of his mouth he's never bothered wiping off after his latest feeding.

Speaking low and hurried so our conversation won't be heard by Sinclair or the others, he asks, "So this is her? Took you long enough."

Her eyes narrow on us, our conversation a mere hiss to her ears.

I bob my head in a single nod at the man who's been my longest friend, dating all the way back to our human lives. Cedric and I changed shortly after one another, and we've been putting up with each other ever since.

He grins before crouching in front of her. She leans away, pressing herself into the throne's side, her cuffed hands coming up to hide herself; a useless endeavour, because Cedric reaches and grasps her chin, angling her head towards him.

I watch them.

I don't like it.

"You certainly are a pretty one, aren't you?" He strokes her cheek, and every nerve in my body tightens in response.

After all, she's *my* prey. My conquest.

Cedric has as much reason to despise the Sinclairs as I do. Difference is, he took a different approach to healing himself. He's numbed himself with alcohol, blood, and fucking to the point I barely recognize him anymore while I've chased revenge.

"Fuck off." She tries to jerk away, her attempt causing the cuffs to clang against one another.

Cedric chuckles, gripping tighter. "With a mouth on her too. Keep it up, sweetheart. Our friend here doesn't like when your kind fights back. He may accidentally kill you, and we can't have that, can we?"

My eyes drill into where his thumb sweeps over her pulse, which is beating faster than normal. Even faster than when she found me in her room. An interesting fact I tuck away for later.

Clenching my hands around the throne, I muster everything into my words, unwilling to beat my long-time friend over someone as minor as her. "Get your hands off her." The threat, the desire to kill, slips into my tone, not acknowledging our friendship and only recognizing him as a threat.

Both glance towards me with varying expressions of confusion. Sinclair with a bit of fear, but Cedric smirks before slowly—too slow for my liking—releasing her face and returning to my side.

Before he says anything, I utter my words quietly. "I need her alive and unharmed."

"Mhm." He claps my shoulder. "Your pupils are red. You seem a bit...threatened."

Fuck.

I snap my fingers, and a human servant comes rushing forward with a glass of blood. I down it in one go and give her the glass back. It helps a little.

Cedric watches, amused. "Good luck, and nice to meet you, Harlow Sinclair." He shoots a final wink at her and then glances my way, laughing when the same sensation starts making me tight again.

Once we're alone, she twists to me. "What the hell is your problem all of a sudden?"

I gesture for another glass of blood, chugging this one just as quickly. I'm debating signalling one of the humans over again, this time demanding a vein, but the concept of feeding straight from any of their bodies doesn't interest me at the moment. So I take a third glass, this time sipping it to prolong the healing. Like a glass of bourbon mortals would consume slowly after a long day at their pitiful jobs.

"What's your name?" She moves on to her next question. "You told me if I played the part, I'd get your name."

"My last name," I correct, lifting a finger off the glass. "Night isn't over yet."

"Asshole vampire it is then. Your choice."

I hide my smirk behind my glass and catch Cedric's attention from across the room. He's leaning against a wall, his own glass of blood drained, while he talks to two businessmen from across the world. He glances over their shoulders at me. While our conversation hasn't been loud, many of the older ones here, Cedric included, can overhear.

"Dormer. That's my last name."

She blinks, her snark momentarily slipping away. I'm learning, with this Sinclair, surprise is key to dismantling her.

"You're a king?"

"The castle didn't tip you off?"

"Assumed you stole it."

She's not far off. "I once conquered it."

She snorts, scanning the tapestries, all of which are original and date back centuries. Some even before my mortal birth. "Isn't that stealing?"

"It's different. Conquering is a sign of strength."

"When did you do that?"

She's probing for my age in that indirect way of hers. "A while ago."

"Were you a king in your human life too?" Her voice picks up, like she's genuinely interested in my backstory. No doubt it's a ploy, and she thinks that by playing nice, she'll earn her freedom. Or she's searching for a weakness. Either way, it won't work.

"Yes." It's a slight lie. Technically, I was a prince at the time.

"King Dormer," she mocks. Her jabs irritate and fascinate me all at the same time. "How'd you become king of the vampires then?"

I tear my eyes away from the interested crowd to the witch sitting ever so pretty by my side, like the perfect little captive. Her cuffed hands are a striking difference from the dress, her hair unruly around her face, the splattering of freckles looking brighter beneath her rage and determined eyes are focused entirely on me.

I could get used to this. Fuck the cell she'll later return to.

"You're awfully interested."

One bare shoulder shrugs, which only shifts hair forwards. "If you don't tell me, I'll need an inscription for your headstone. *Here lies the asshole vampire who once stole a king's castle, named himself as the new ruler, and then took over the vampires too.* Do they know you're a fake king?" She nods to the crowd.

A few gasp, others chuckle. I let her speak freely, because it's only providing a show that'll encourage the bidding later.

"They know enough."

She huffs, shaking her head. It blows her enticing scent towards me, and between my hunger, her taunts, our audience, and my vastly declining mood, those forbidden and strange feelings from earlier return. Before they consume me, I need to regain control of her and of myself.

I snap my fingers, earning her glare once more. "Stand."

Defiance exudes from every pore, but a quick glance to our audience shuts her down. It's wise since she has no idea how unsafe she is inside a room full of vampires who desire draining her dry.

I point to the space beside my throne, and she shuffles there, the clanging of her cuffs the only noise in the suddenly silent room. Hundreds of eyes are on us with a mixture of interest and hunger. Few begin showing those very signs of hunger, which only adds to my next taunt.

I reach for one of her wrists, bringing it up to my face, her pulse deliciously rapid. Given both her arms are clasped together with a little chain separating the cuffs, they move together.

Just the sweet, addictive smell of her has my fangs lengthening, and I drag them along her pulse point, keeping my attention on the audience. Sinclair gasps but wisely doesn't try to yank away. I trace a vein, inhaling deeply before lifting my head, pretending to ignore the subtle scent of her desire that flares so suddenly...and enigmatically.

"So you see, my friends, how mortality is but a bite away. I know many of you are here out of curiosity, to see the youngest and remaining Sinclair witch for yourself, while many others are here for the chance to end your immortal life."

A few nods of agreement. A shuffling amongst a community who lives within stillness.

"Of course, I have claimed the Sinclair witch as my property, which makes the cure mine as well. If you wish to be human, you may, for a fee. Gaze upon the witch tonight and be in contact tomorrow."

More hissing, more murmurs—more interest.

Sinclair shifts beneath the weight of their gazes. Before I comprehend my ridiculous actions, my thumb strokes over one of her many scars to ease her, the curiosity behind their origin still lingering. It's bothersome not to have all the facts about her.

"But"—I pause, letting the single word bounce around the room—"this is a party, which means a celebration is in order for my successful capture of the witch. I have no desire to be human; therefore, I will not be claiming the first drink, so one of you may take it. For a price, after the party, one of you may remain behind and be human before morning hits. This can be your final night as an immortal." I pause again, letting the buzz of conversation carry before providing more enticement. "When the sun rises, you may stay up with it. Her blood will be the final blood you'll ever have to drink. So many possibilities."

"Straight from the vein?" one calls from the left side of the room.

Initially, I did debate the extra fee associated with drinking the cure directly from the vein, but knowing my kind, so many are careless, and it'd be a risk they wouldn't stop when commanded and they'd try to drain her dry. Fighting a vampire mid-feed is a nuisance I don't need nor want.

I glance towards Sinclair, spotting true terror in her expression. For the first time since meeting her, the mask has fallen. She said that no vampire has drunk from her before, and that memory brings a surge of something twisting inside me. Something protective.

No one will, if I have anything to do with it.

"No. I don't wish my asset to be drained dry by accident. You all understand."

Some sneer, some laugh. Sinclair audibly sighs in relief, and my thumb does another sweep of her scars, this time slipping beneath the cuffs. Her pulse jumps.

I bring her wrist back to my mouth, pressing my lips to the vein that exudes temptation. She shivers before trying to yank away, obviously not enjoying her body's response to my touch. It's not her fault, though, and it means nothing of what she's probably guessing it does. Exactly how she described vampires and sex going together, the influence of a feed, even when accompanied by fear like Miss Sinclair's feeling, dulls that fear into something else. Something that makes them compliant for us.

Lust.

And Harlow Sinclair is dripping with it.

TWELVE

"So...how many of you want to be mortal come sunrise?"

Dormer, my captor and a literal *king*, clenches my wrist again, his finger tracing my scars. The touch is almost tender, which is completely ridiculous, and I wonder if he realizes he's doing it.

A vampire steps forward to call out a number. He's one of many, which still, my brain hasn't processed. My parents hid me from vampires my entire life, and here I am, a buffet for his guests. Even more shocking is the fact I'm not getting attacked by any one of those numbers, thanks to my captor, who's doubling as my body-guard. And my pimp, based on the actions unfolding around me.

"A thousand!"

Dollars?

Dormer makes a displeased noise. "That's all mortality is worth to you? Come now. I know you've spent the last three hundred years gambling your way to wealth."

Three hundred. Okay, so my captor's older than that. Old enough to have been around when kings and queens were a thing. Although, in some countries, they still are, so that's not much to go off of.

He casts me a quick smirk, like he knew exactly where my thoughts went.

"Ten thousand!" another one shouts.

Again...dollars?

A few sips of my blood is worth *ten thousand dollars*?

And why'd I never think to do this years ago?

My captor hums, the vibration going up my arm, making me shiver. I shouldn't enjoy the feeling of his touch as much as I do, but when his fangs dragged over my pulse, my thighs pressed together to hide the truth of what I'll never admit to either of us.

It's science, that's all. He already said the feed is pleasurable for these assholes. Surely I, "the prey," get affected by whatever powers they're working with? Gram's books didn't cover that part, so it's only a theory.

"Twenty thousand!"

"Thirty!"

"Fifty!"

Dormer brings my wrist back to his nose, inhaling. It's erotic in a way it shouldn't be. "Miss Sinclair has never turned a vampire mortal. Her blood, for what it's worth, is virginal."

"Eighty!"

Hate to admit it, but he's good...

"One hundred!" a voice yells, louder than the rest. A vampire pushes from the back of the crowd to the front, hands in fists and eyes tinged red and a bit manic, almost terrifying as they pin me to the spot. "One hundred thousand dollars to end this fucking life *now*."

My kidnapper straightens in his seat and releases my wrist. He leans forward, scanning the rest of the crowd. "Would anyone like to beat that?"

The vampire who made the insane bid glares at the room, as though daring anyone to shout a higher number. No one does, and after a moment, my captor nods towards the buyer.

The buyer. The bids. My goodness, is this Stockholm syndrome? Even my thoughts are lining up with the vampire's.

"After the party, you will be human. Between now and then, get the money transferred to me. Payment first."

The vampire who won bows before retreating into the crowd, presumably to go follow those orders.

"Is he about to lug in a whole chest of gold coins?"

Dormer glances my way, amusement dancing in his expression. "We've adjusted to modern times and keep bank accounts."

"Did he really just pay one hundred thousand dollars for my blood?"

He reaches for my wrist again, too quick for me to react, and flicks where my skin meets the cuff. There's no reason for him to be touching me since the bidding is over, yet he does. "Some of us have been vampires for a long time. After so long, most of us have grown our wealth. Unlike humans, we have the benefit of time and a lack of need. Wealth is agreeable, of course, but we don't use it to buy food, houses, or vehicles like humans do. We don't engage in normal society, so jobs and education aren't open to us. When you don't *need* something, it's easy to allow time to work in your favour."

That actually makes sense.

"You underestimate exactly how desired your blood is," he adds.

Except I know that all too well. I've survived the attacks on my house, and the ones who were successful in getting through.

And how my parents' lives ended as a result.

Pushing the past aside to get through the present, I point out, "Except by you."

He's about to respond when a loud shrill comes from the crowd. The entire room falls silent, turning towards the interruption. A vampire storms his way to the front, a finger jabbed in our direction, his braided hair tossed over one shoulder.

"*You.*" His snarl focuses on Dormer. "You call yourself our king, but then take control of the one thing in existence that can save us from this cursed life by putting a goddamn price tag on it. You are no fucking ruler of ours."

Dormer smiles at the one who's interrupted, but it's a smile full of maliciousness. A smile promising death if the vampire continues. A slow tilt of his lips before he murmurs, "The witch has been available for any of us to kidnap. I'm simply the one with the means to do it."

I step back a few paces, feeling the sudden urge to get away. A quick peek at the crowd tells me my motions haven't gone unnoticed.

"Fuck the money!" the vampire shouts. "And fuck you! Hand her over and let us *all* drain the witch dry."

I don't notice if there's a signal or anything, but suddenly, the vampire is a blur towards me. Instinct has me quickly skittering back, cursing the cuffs that keep me stuck to a short vicinity. Before I've fully taken a step, my captor is out of his seat, a shadow coming between me and the attacking vampire. For once, a shadow I welcome.

Everything happens quickly then. Anarchy breaks out and I, the magickless witch who's chained to a chair, am absolutely *fucked*. There's *running from the vampire who appeared in my bedroom* brave, and then there's stupidity. This would be stupidity.

Two more break away from the crowd, streaking towards me. My captor throws the first attacker clear across the room, his body thudding against a painting of an ocean. He lands on the ground, the crowd around him dispersing in a loud hush. I doubt that killed him, but my attention is on the next one coming my way.

Dormer zips from one end of the room to the other, cutting off the oncoming attack with a vicious snarl I'll hear in my nightmares for years to come—if I live that long. Blood splays right before the vampire falls to the ground, dead, his head rolling away from his body.

Oh, Goddess, get me the fuck out of here.

Dormer's a blur towards the other, cutting off that attack and repeating his own. Another head, another body, and plenty more blood spilling onto the once-white granite floor.

He whirls to face me, a monster in human form. Blood-coated fangs elongated, with more blood coating his chin and even the tips of his hair. He seems so much…bigger. His body takes up more space as he seethes. His eyes, a vibrant red, pin me from across the room, as though daring me to react.

He looks dangerous, yet my stomach clenches in a way that whispers something else. That familiar slither of the shadows glides over my neck but doesn't linger, as they frequently seem to not when around Dormer. This time, it's more like a nudge in the direction he—my monster, captor, and protector—stands.

A motion comes from behind him as the first vampire he tossed out of the way gets unsteadily to his feet before sprinting towards Dormer. I open my mouth to warn him because, as messed up as everything is, my captor is my best bet in a room full of war-hungry bloodsuckers. At least to him, I'm valuable and not a meal.

As fast as a sound leaves my throat, Dormer whirls, catching the vampire by his neck in an unyielding grip. He lifts him off the ground, the man's feet dangling a few inches above.

When Dormer speaks, it's a deep growl masked by fangs and gore, and with a ferociousness I could never have made up. "You thought you could usurp me? That was your first mistake. Your second was thinking you could touch her."

"My liege—" His words cut off when my captor's hand punches inside his chest. I think I shriek, all bravado disappearing when Dormer twists his hand and yanks from his chest a black organ—a heart.

The vampire slumps forward, his pale skin flushing even whiter before the body is dumped unceremoniously on the ground. Keeping the heart in his grip, he turns to the audience.

"Take what happened here as a fucking warning. The Sinclair

witch is *my* captive. *Mine* to do with how I see fit. If I choose, I could lock her away from all of you, ensuring her family line ends—and thus the cure. See it as mercy I'm granting you the ability to regain your dreaded human lives." He holds the heart up before rotating his wrist and dropping it beside the deceased body. "If anyone dares to question me again, this will be the outcome of your stupidity. If any of you even fucking *look* at her, you will die. Leave, now, all of you."

Like magick, every vampire in the room disappears in a massive blur, obeying his command before they end up on the wrong side of his mood. Only two remain: the one I've guessed to be his friend, given he's the only one who approached all night, and the one who won the bid on my blood.

That one drops to his knees, his head lowering. "My liege, I hope our deal still stands—"

"I don't break agreements with those who show respect," Dormer interrupts with an irritated flick of his hand that gives me an idea of what he would have been like as a human ruler. "Stand. You'll receive what you paid for shortly."

Right. With everything, I'd almost forgotten about the bid. *Almost*, but after being nearly attacked by three vampires, pouring a bit of blood into this guy's mouth—or however Dormer is planning on doing this—seems so insignificant.

He turns my way, pinning me with that gaze of his that makes me want to bolt while also remaining unmoving. Eyes that are no duller than moments ago, blood now drying, crusting on his face.

He's like a nightmare and a dream come to life. A physical embodiment of fear, yet as he approaches, I'm overcome with a sense of safety wrapping me in its arms. For better or worse, he saved me. Only to protect what he believes is his investment, but still. For now, I'm breathing because he didn't allow them near me.

I'm frozen in place as he stops short, his hand darting for my arms. His fingers are stained with blood, but thankfully it isn't the hand that ripped out a heart. That one is coated in gore up to the wrist, and the scent tickles my nose.

As though reading my thoughts, he wipes that hand on his pants before unclasping the cuffs with a jerk of the metal. "You better hope on your life this works."

The cuffs drop to my feet, my wrists immediately lighter, but the vision that slams into me pushes me right back down.

"Come on, time to go." Cuffs land by my feet, my arms feeling lighter than they have since I was put in here.

Dormer yanks me towards the other vampire, snapping me from my thoughts. A memory? Whatever it was...I glance towards the scars on my wrists. *Impossible.* Maybe it was a premonition of what's to come, even though I've never had those before. It would explain hearing his voice, if so.

At this point, I'll lump all the weirdness together and tie it in a giant bow marked with a big question mark. Topped with my shadowy tormentors, of course.

He snaps his fingers and, seemingly out of nowhere, a guy appears with a goblet—a human, based on his blue eyes and scared demeanor—handing it off before he skitters out of the ballroom. I watch him go, wondering how many people Dormer has captive here.

He gestures towards me, slipping a knife from his pocket, telling me all this was pre-planned. Unless he walks around with weapons on him for fun. "You'll bleed into the cup, and that is all that will be required."

His friend wanders closer as Dormer places the blade by the meaty part of my hand, and I shuffle my feet until I have him in a better view, just in case he's someone I need to worry about attacking me once the bleeding starts.

The slice that'll be the start of so much more—the lineups outside the castle about to ensue—is only stopped by the other vampire interrupting. "Wait. How do you know how much to bleed from her?"

"A few sips is all it'll take," Dormer answers.

"Are you certain?"

"According to the history of my family, yes," I chime in, irritated. The bloodsucker is about to be handed immortality at *my* expense, and he's complaining?

The look he gives is like I'm a bug on the bottom of his shoe—worthless of his attention. "You have every reason to lie."

"Yeah, but I'm not."

"Both of you, shut it." Dormer's command is only enforced by the quick slice on the same palm I cut with the rock. It re-opens the wound, enticing a curse out of me that all three vampires ignore. Assholes probably haven't felt pain since they were human.

"That fucking hurts," I hiss, but it gets worse when Dormer presses his thumb beside the cut, forcing blood to well faster. It slides to the edge of my hand before dripping into the goblet, the small amount forming a pool of everything I've spent years avoiding.

I jerk my hand away, my movement clearly unexpected to him because he doesn't stop me, and the next drop doesn't join the others in the cup. My pitiful resistance only lasts so long when Dormer appears behind me, his arms coming around my waist to regain control. He pushes even harder into the cut, and I twist to glare, hoping those heightened senses of his pick up on the level of hatred I have for him.

Just in case he can't, I mutter, "I fucking hate you."

"I'm aware."

He abruptly pulls back, satisfied with the inch of blood in the cup. He releases his hold, his body disappearing from behind me before reaching into his pocket and pulling out a silk handkerchief, handing it to me.

His nostrils are flared, his voice a grating command. "Clean yourself."

Taking the handkerchief, I wrap it around the cut, fisting my hand to soak up as much of the blood as possible before the others get triggered.

Dormer passes the goblet to the other vampire, who eagerly snatches it. Dormer's friend comes up on my other side, his attention on the show about to take place.

In truth, I *am* curious to see the outcome of what my ancestors did as well. Out of all possible chances at witnessing the transformation, this is probably the best and safest one.

The vampire lifts the cup to his mouth and tips it back, his throat working in large gulps as he swallows it—*me*—down. Dormer crosses his arms and observes all his hard work with a look of satisfaction.

After all...one hundred thousand dollars made this possible. One vampire, and a few drops.

I'm never getting out of here. There's nothing I can offer him that'll replace this business opportunity—money that's unfathomable to me. It's a realization as heavy as the shadows Hecate keeps sending after me.

The cup lowers, and the vampire wipes blood from the corner of his mouth, swiping it against his fang for what'll be the final time. "Your blood tastes like honey." He glances towards Dormer. "You will be making a fortune off her. How long does it take to work?"

"Few minutes."

"And if it doesn't? I'll need more."

Dormer snarls, inching himself closer to me. "You've gotten plenty."

The other vampire opens his mouth, presumably to argue, but then he gasps. His black eyes wildly dart around the room, as though seeking answers to a question he isn't asking, before a full-body shudder drops him to the ground, a pained cry filling the room.

His shrill scream is loud enough my ears would likely bleed if he went on for a while. He manages to get on his hands and knees, and his back bows, his head lowering to the ground.

"Fuck," Dormer's friend whispers, his tone amazed.

This is the cure at work. This is why my ancestors did this. To eradicate vampires, one bloodsucker at a time. Maybe there will be an upside to captivity...

The screams fade into pants, and the man's head darts up, his gaze landing on me. Only this time, he no longer has fangs but straight, human teeth that grin in a non-malicious manner. Brown eyes instead of black, and his skin darkens with the newly changed blood coursing through him.

"It worked," he whispers, a sense of wonder filling his tone.

THIRTEEN

Alec

*I*t *worked.* All my planning is paying off. All my years of hunting Sinclairs only to end the line in a way most satisfactory to me.

For you, Cora. All for you.

Beside Sinclair, Cedric watches on with an equal measure of shock and wonder.

The newly changed vampire manoeuvres himself to his feet, swaying with his shitty balance after hundreds of years of perfect poise. He's upright, but with a harsh cry, abruptly falls to his hands and knees again, adopting a position identical to the one he was in moments ago.

Blood pours from his mouth in a wave, and I yank Sinclair away from the mess. He gurgles, his brown eyes screaming with a silent plea: *Help me!*

Another choke, a sob, and he slumps to the floor, his mouth open as blood slowly pours out.

Sinclair makes a noise while Cedric curses, stepping towards the buyer. He crouches and checks the pulse he had for the few short minutes, feeling for what we can both hear has stopped beating.

"He's dead," I state before Cedric can announce it.

He jerks his head in a nod. "What happened?"

Exactly what I'd like to know.

Satisfaction from seconds ago dwindles as my gaze narrows on the witch. "*You.* You did something to your blood." I'm by her side instantly, grabbing her arms and hauling her to my chest so she can get a front-row view of my fangs before they jam into her neck to drain her until she's dead. May as well get some use out of her. "What the fuck did you do?"

Fear radiates from her in a sour scent, and she tries to fight, her little attempts nothing short of pathetic. Her eyes are blown out, her skin a bit paler than normal, making the freckles pop. "I, I swear, I have no idea. It didn't work on you either, so maybe I'm broken?"

"On you?" Cedric approaches, getting annoyingly close to Sinclair. Too close, and I feel that rumble in my chest that demands he back the fuck up.

Before I kill my oldest and best friend, I demand, "Leave, Ced. Forget what you saw here. I'll be in touch."

"Alec—"

Sinclair practically lights up with excitement at hearing my first name.

Damn him.

"Cedric. *Go.*"

He sees my face, nods, and is out the door instantly, leaving me and the witch who has a whole lot to answer for.

"I'll repeat. What. The fuck. Did you *do?*"

"Nothing!" She yanks on my unyielding hold until her skin turns red. The sleeves of the dress she has no right to be wearing slip farther down her arms, and it takes every bit of restraint not to rip it from her body, to protect the material. "It worked; he turned human. We all saw it!"

"He didn't *stay* human."

"That's not my problem." Her face tips up defiantly, but beneath that very defiance, fear is crumbling her walls. A few more seconds and I'll make it into nothing more than rubble. "It's over, *Alec*. Let me go home."

She's making demands when I'm barely clinging to my sanity. Watching fucking *years* of effort and centuries of revenge become meaningless. I have her lovely throat in my grip before realizing what I'm doing, walking into her until she steps back, my grasp the only thing preventing her from tripping.

"Test me, witch, *I dare you*." My hold tightens. "If you're truly useless, your life is now meaningless."

She isn't, not yet. It's the mantra I repeat to myself so I don't accidentally kill her, because until I know for certain, she might still have her uses. Amidst the fog coating my vision, I consider what she said. That the cure worked to transition him, though mortality didn't remain.

So before I tear her throat out or call back every single one of those very eager and hungry vampires to hand her over to them for the slaughter, I pick her up and run her straight down to the dungeon, opening the door nearest the exterior one and dropping her into the smallest cell. She stole my sanity, so I'll steal the bit of space the other one gave her.

Don't hurt her.

And, of course, that pesky voice that won't leave me alone. The instinct that says to hunt, chase, and feed from her is the same one demanding I leave her be.

I'll listen to neither and leave her to rot until I figure this out.

She scrambles to her hands and knees, eyes darting around the dark cell as recognition sets in. I shut the door as she reaches for it, hands clenching around the poles. She presses her face into them, and then dares use my name in her plea. As though she has *any* right to beg me for shit after what she's done.

"Alec, please, you can't leave me in here!"

I laugh, one full of darkness that channels my every ounce of hatred towards her into it. "Oh, believe me, witch, I certainly can."

She smacks the post, realizing begging isn't doing shit for her. "What did I do to deserve this? Tell me!"

Miss Sinclair doesn't get those facts yet. Especially now, when I'm a fraction away from sucking her dry and saying to hell with the consequences. I turn away before the meager thread of control still tied around me snaps.

"Alec!" She slaps the metal again. "Don't ignore me! Get me out of here! The other cell. *Please.*"

Miss Sinclair doesn't enjoy the smaller space? I keep walking, reaching the door.

"You realize I eat like a human, right? If you want me to stay alive, I'll need more food. One apple won't cut it."

"Suffer. Then you'll know exactly how I feel every single day you and your family live."

I slam the door shut, zipping through the hallways until reaching my office. I stop short outside the door before my fist slams into the wood, creating a dent; one of many that's been placed there over the centuries. At this point, there's more busted wood than there are flat panels.

"Fuck!"

Her blood worked. It fucking *worked*, and never in the history since its creation has there been a report of it not. Or working, and then the newly turned dying shortly after.

There also hasn't been a report of a Sinclair—or any other witch, for that matter—not having their magick.

Are the two connected?

It's with that question I enter my office, my enhanced senses immediately picking up what I was too distracted to in the hallway and zeroing in on the newcomer seated behind my desk. Her feet are propped up on the surface while she twirls the seat back and forth, head tipped back to stare at the ceiling.

It's that witch who took down the barrier around the Sinclair house. Freya, the First Witch.

"You. How did you get in?"

Her head rolls, hair that's now a bubblegum pink rather than white-blonde falling into her face as she circles her finger. "Magick, remember? Your pathetic defenses are nothing. Also, considering I'm the only reason you got to Harlow, the correct greeting was, 'Hi, Freya, how are you? Welcome to my humble abode.' Although *humble* isn't exactly the word I'd use to describe this place."

"You're here to collect on that favour, I assume?"

I cross the room, standing on the other side of my desk. She drops her feet and straightens in *my* chair, sliding it in closer and propping her hands on the surface like she's about to conduct a meeting.

"Not at all. I'm simply here to check in. Make sure she's still alive and all that." She centres her stare. "That's a joke, by the way. I'll know when a witch passes into the Otherworld."

"Summerland."

She tips her head in acknowledgement. "You do know your stuff."

"I make it my mission to learn about my enemy."

"Except you didn't know about Harlow not having her magick," she says in a sing-song voice.

"You did. 'And good luck, Alec. She'll make you wish you had some.' You knew exactly what I was getting into."

"And that isn't even the best part."

"What's that supposed to mean?" I demand, the nerves in my neck tightening.

She shrugs, then randomly starts opening my desk drawers and rifling through them. "One would think a vampire would have more interesting stuff in their desk."

"Freya." Agitation gnaws at me, but attacking the First Witch won't end well. "Back to Sinclair, witch. The cure didn't work— twice. She tried to shove it in my mouth, and later another vampire drank a glass of it. He changed into a mortal, but died while vomiting blood directly afterwards. It didn't work because she doesn't have her magick, correct?"

She finishes searching through my desk and returns with a folder, flipping it open to scan through the numerous deeds for the various lands I own worldwide. I'd inquire about the purpose, but based on her mindless flipping, I'm getting the sense this is Freya being herself and not because she's searching for something.

"Hm, look at you figuring it all out. Yep, that's correct. The cure is magickal; a spell placed on her bloodline by her coven's old High Priestess. Harlow no longer has magick, so the cure doesn't work anymore. It's a part of her, which would explain why the vampire did transition, but the lack of power prevented it from being long-term. As for you, the cure won't affect you. You could drink her dry, and it still wouldn't."

"How's that possible?" I drop my palms onto the desk's surface, leaning closer. "What aren't you telling me?"

She better change what she's announced, because knowing I can drink from Sinclair and not be affected...well, it's a temptation I'm unsure I'll be able to avoid. A moment where I can finally solve the hunger that seems to plague me every time she's around.

She shrugs one shoulder, focused on her pointless task. "You're too old and powerful. If the cure was at full strength, then yeah, it'd work. But given its weakness, you wouldn't complete the transition to human, and it certainly wouldn't kill you."

My fangs throb at the notion of Sinclair being available for my mealtimes, at least for the time being.

"How do I know you're not lying, trying to get me to become mortal?"

She glares up at me. "Believe me or don't; it's only *your* hunger affected. Besides, why would I lie now of all times after everything I've done to help you? Logically, I would have left the protection barrier up, if that were the case."

Fair point.

Moving on, I check, "If she got her magick back, then the cure would return too?"

"In theory." She flips a page, pausing on an island in the middle of the Caribbean Sea. "You seriously own an entire island? Hm, I may have to visit one day. I could use a vacation, especially after dealing with your cranky ass."

Ignoring her, I demand, "How did she lose her magick? Is that common?"

Her eyes flick up from the deed, her expression oddly serious. "It's unheard of. Before Harlow, no witch or warlock has ever lost their powers. She's truly one of a kind." Freya pauses, pursing her lips. "Although, in her case, she gave it up."

"Gave it *up*?" This entire fucking time, *she's* at fault. All while acting like she's broken without it.

Freya turns to a house in Russia I once won in a bet from the reigning Romanov family in the nineteenth century. "She didn't do it on purpose, nor does she realize she's to blame. Her grief was too much at the time."

"Grief?"

Unamused, she glances up again. "I take it back. You truly don't know enough about your enemies. Look into what happened to her parents, Alec, and maybe she'll give you the story."

"They died in a house fire."

"Mhm. But there's more. A lot more. Ask her, because it's not my business."

It's very much Freya's business, but I demand the more important information, the shit I actually care about. "How does she get her powers back?" *Can* she?

"Well, figure out what happened to her family and you'll figure that answer out."

Fucking witch. Slapping a hand on the desk, I reach for the folder, ripping it out from her hold. "No, you don't get to avoid answering. How does she get it back?" I bare my fangs, letting my threat speak for itself.

Freya lifts her hand, and pressure in my gums has my fangs forcibly retracting. She stands, her demeanor nothing like the tiny witch began as. Her bright hair flares a bit, almost glowing as a sense of death radiates from her. "Do not underestimate me, *vampire.* Between the two of us, I am *much* older than you and much more powerful. Because I'm rooting for you, I'll put it like this: grief is the centre of her story. Grief is a heavy emotion. She needs a heavy emotion for it to return."

Heavy emotion...fuck, what even are emotions anymore? The emotions mortals are plagued with don't affect vampires the same way. We lust for blood, revenge, and sex, not always in that order. Emotions involving grief and terror, sadness and love, aren't built into us. We lost those abilities with our transition to an immortal. Something about our kind being descended from a demon—one of the original fallen angels—and demons are soulless creatures.

"More grief then. Or fear."

Freya shrugs again, her expression smoothing. "Sure. Don't really know the trigger."

"You're unhelpful."

Scoffing, she stalks around my desk. "I'm very helpful. In fact, you owe me for quite a few things now. I'm keeping a list, Your Highness."

"Majesty."

She waves her hand. "Whatever. Majesty. Asshole. Dick. Vampire. It all works. Anyhoo, I'm off." She stalks towards the door, throwing it open before glancing over her shoulder. "Oh,

Alec, you're playing with fire. She's more powerful than you assume."

"Powerful. She's power*less*. Wasn't that the point of this conversation?"

Freya winks before shutting the door on all my unanswered questions.

"Wait—" I flit across the room, catching the door before it shuts, but the hallway's empty, the First Witch having disappeared.

SECOND INTERMISSION

Freya

Me again.

Wasn't that fun? Told you, fate's fickle.

Alec Dormer is smart, and not at the same time. He's too focused on revenge and is missing the obvious.

No matter, he'll figure it out soon. Once he—well...I can't give everything away, now can I?

You might be wondering why I dropped by to see him given the Goddess instructed me not to interfere in any way. She sent me another message and said in order to move this along, I had to. Harlow must get her magick back for the rest of the events to pass because we still have quite a bit to get through.

Gotta move this shit along since I still have three more witches to help after this.

Anyway, back to it...after I get a refill of popcorn. Want some?

FOURTEEN

Harlow

I t's dark.
It's small.
It's dark.
It's small.
It's endless.
It's...
It's...
"It's too dark! Help me, I'm scared!"
Words that feel all too familiar echo in my head.
A *feeling* of emptiness that's all too familiar.

Emptiness coupled with a heaviness, in part from the shadows that are making this tiny cell even smaller, heavier, like there will never be light again.

Time slips away over the remainder of the night and into the daytime. I've tried to count the seconds to keep track, but the mounting weight pressing into my shoulders and pinning me into the dirt has long won out.

This cell is smaller than the other one. The walls are closer, the roof shorter. Like he knew about my claustrophobia and wanted to torture me. Him. My captor. The vampire asshole named Alec Dormer.

I wait.
And wait.
And wait.
For the unknown.
For him to kill me.
Drain me.
Torture me.

Hecate, please give me my powers back. Please, please, please, I'll do anything. Let me get out of this space. This tiny, cramped space...

Maybe this is more punishment since I'm behind the blaze that took out two wonderful witches. She's not interfering because She's forsaken me. Maybe that's also why the cure isn't working right. The one feature of myself I've longed to be rid of, I now miss because it could have saved my life.

Maybe Alec will kill me and end my suffering.

Hecate, please. Please. Please.

At this point, I'm no longer sure what I'm even begging Her for. She won't help, because She hasn't so far. Maybe it's time to stop asking. Perhaps it's time to let Her go and beg the devil. At the very least, the one I know.

"Alec." His name slips out between cracked lips, muffled with a sob. It's low, and even with his enhanced hearing, who knows if it carries to him.

"Alec, please, get me out of here."

"Alec, I can't do this anymore."

"Alec!"

Each plea, I raise my voice just a bit higher, hoping it makes it to him, even when he'd probably ignore me. Laugh at my pain.

Harlow.

The voice that once had me thinking I was insane is a reprieve. I manage to lift my head, seeking him even if I know he's not here. I cling to how my name sounded on his lips—inside my head, anyway. The harshness of the H, the purr trailing from the W. Cling to it, begging for a repeat.

"Alec, Alec, Alec...*please.*"

Instead of my name, a sound from far away pushes through the deafening silence, the weight of the room crashing onto me, the feeling of not having enough space, and the endless shadows that taunt me with hisses. It's the sound of metal, I think. Hard to tell, because everything is so muted with my head resting on the ground.

Then there's a new sensation. Something cool but warm at the same time. Something that forces my head up, the touch expanding to my cheek bones and stroking beneath my eyes. I sigh, the weight of them too much to open and allow myself to check who's finally come: my devil or the Goddess. My gaze, blurred from my lack of focus and exhaustion, tries to track the long fingers reaching for my face. It becomes too much effort, and my eyes slide shut once more.

"Sinclair, open your eyes. What's wrong with you?"

Look at him? I can't. Everything is too heavy.

"Hellion, look at me."

Looking at him only gives him more reason to torment me. Haven't I played enough of his games? I wore the pretty dress, attended the master's party on his arm, paraded myself in front of his guests, and gave a piece of myself over to the top buyer. He sold me off, so now he can deal with my suffocating silence. It's no different than the suffocation of this cell.

The cell...how did I forget how small the cell is? Right, it's all in his voice. He's a distraction, as much as he was a distraction in the past, when his existence was a mere voice in my mind.

I should ask him about that.

"Come on, Harlow. I'm demanding you open your eyes."

With the next stroke of his fingers, the slithering falls away, disappearing inside my chest until the next time they want to bother me. With the weight gone, my lids manage to peel open. Eyes as black as the dungeon stare back, his brows furrowing like my panic is a shock to him.

"You came," I breathe.

"You called."

My eyes flutter shut again as his hands come around my body, and for better or worse, he's the safest thing right now, so I let myself fall. He reaches one hand beneath my knees, the other around my back, before pulling me into his chest and standing, keeping me close.

His low murmur breaks through my mental barriers right as he carries me from the cell. "Let's get you out of here."

Even though he grips me tight, he doesn't feel as suffocating as the cell. In fact, it's kind of pleasant to be held by him. His arms feel strong, his body unyielding against mine. And he smells good. Not like death, blood, and destruction, but like a fresh flame once ignited. A campfire after it's been extinguished and the smoke fills the area. Like summertime warmth, which is ironic.

"You smell nice."

His chest rumbles with his laughter, vibrating against my side. "Oh, Hellion, if only you were lucid. You'd hate yourself for admitting that."

"I am lucid," I argue, despite the fuzz covering my mind suggesting otherwise.

"Sure, sure." He sounds amused, but that's also wrong, because asshole bloodsuckers shouldn't be amused by their captives. Defeats the purpose, right?

A moment later, the dungeon door is open and even fresher air circulates through my lungs. While the stairway is dark, it's not as black as the dungeons, and my vision begins to shift.

"Shut your eyes." His gentle command weaves between the strands of my hair, his breath strangely warm against my ear.

I do, obeying him so effortlessly once again. Blame it on my fucked-up senses.

The air rushes around us, and I think he's using his immortal speed to get us through his castle. The angle changes; we're heading upstairs. Then there's another door opening and shutting, more warmth, and then softness beneath me as his arms disappear.

I open my eyes, breathing in air that doesn't smell dank and rancid, in the bedroom I visited earlier—last night?—to get ready in.

Alec's there, pushing me back into the pillows, his body taking up so much space. I wait for that familiar and uncomfortable feeling of claustrophobia to return with his nearness, but it doesn't. Quite the opposite actually.

His gaze is depthless, matched by his equally dark hair, strands falling into his face. He's dressed more casual than I've seen him yet, his plain black tee showing off muscles defined by endless years.

Did I just check out my captor?

"Thank you," I whisper, relaxing into the soft pillows. The bed isn't the best part, even if he probably assumes it's what I'm grateful for. It's the wide-open space. The walls that are easily twelve feet from me, allowing me to breathe properly.

"Harlow—"

It's only my name—one of the few instances he's spoken it— lined with frustration and annoyance, so similar to how he'd say it in my head.

"Why have I been hearing you for months?"

"What?" His hand sweeps strands off my forehead, but they cling to my skin from the sweat. His touch is a balm to the heat. A comfort that soothes. If only I could ask him to continue touching me, healing me. He gets rid of the shadows, and now he's making everything else better too. "Hellion, you're not well. You're not making sense. Stop talking."

My mouth clamps shut, obeying him for some reason. If only so he can continue petting me.

Annoyingly, he pulls back after another few seconds, settling beside my legs and crossing his arms. His jaw is tense when he asks, "What was all that about?"

"Nothing." I glance towards the window, wishing he'd open the curtain and allow the sky inside. *Any* sign of the outdoors, I'll take at this point. Keeping a witch away from nature is torture in itself.

"Do not lie to me," he snaps, his hand forcing my face towards him again. "Was it a ploy to get out of the cell?"

"Damn good acting on my part if it was."

His mouth tugs up on one side. "There she is. Guess you're fine now if that snark that's making my life hell has returned."

"Guess so." I lean back against the pillows, wanting to soak up every minute of comfort before he sends me back to hell. For now, whatever the reason behind this peaceful truce, I'll take the cushion beneath my ass. A mattress versus stone, a blanket versus the hollow chill of what could eventually lead to my death.

"You called for me," he murmurs after a long moment, his tone filled with a sense of wonder and a question I'm compelled to answer.

"Hecate is ignoring me. You're all I have left." Which is sad to consider.

He makes a grunting noise before heading for the door. "We need to talk, so stay here. I'll be back in a few minutes. If you attempt to leave this room, I'll track you before you make it down the hallway." His dark eyes sweep my frame stretched on the bed. "Given your current situation, I doubt you have much fight in you anyway."

In truth, I have little plans to leave this bed. I do go to the bathroom, finding my pyjamas still on the floor where I left them from when switching into the dress. I change back, preferring my own clothes over whomever's dress this is. They're dirty, but no worse off than the dress and much warmer.

By the time I'm climbing back into bed, the door opens again, and Alec returns. "Good to know you're capable of listening once in a while."

"Only when it suits me."

He crosses the room and picks up one of the large wingback chairs beside the fireplace. With one hand, he carries it to the bedside before sitting. On the nightstand, he lays out a water bottle and handful of granola bars that will by no means be enough to sustain me, but they're a start. My stomach growls so loud even I hear it, which means he certainly does.

With a knowing huff, he twists open the water bottle and hands it over. "Small sips, don't fill up. Your body needs a lot more nutrition."

I ignore him and take a long swig before lowering the bottle, not finished drinking, but he's quick to snatch it again, capping it, and rests it beside me on the nightstand out of reach. *Got it.*

"You know a lot about mortal bodies."

"You forget I was once a human." He leans back, spreading his legs slightly and his arms landing on the armrests, like he's settling in for a while. "It was a long time ago, and last night you reminded me of your pesky requirements, so before you die on me, figured I should get you some food."

"And you couldn't have delivered all this"—I gesture toward the food—"last night?"

"Leverage, Hellion. It's all about leverage. Speaking of..." He reaches for a granola bar and rips open the package, shaking it tauntingly. "I have questions you'll answer. For every one you do, you'll receive food."

My stomach growls again, and we both know at this point, he could probably ask me to crawl around on the floor or anything else equally as demeaning, and I would. Food, water, and a bed. The vampire's lining himself up for a world of knowledge.

"I also have things I want to know."

He throws me a look so dirty, it's worse than the dungeon's

floor. "Food or an answer, those are your options. You get one, and choose wisely. I should note, my questions are limited, so before you think to save one or the other until the end, my end may come sooner than you anticipate."

I nod. "Deal."

"What was that down below?"

"Starvation and exhaustion mixed with claustrophobia, which led to a panic attack."

"Claustrophobia?"

"That's a question. You owe me two pieces. It means a fear of small spaces."

Alec rolls his eyes but regardless rips off two bite-sized pieces that I devour entirely too quickly. They wake my stomach up to a painful twist. "I know the definition of the phobia. I was questioning you having it."

"I've had it since I was a kid. Don't recall how it came to be."

He hands over another piece. "Scared of the dark too?"

I shake my head, gaining another bite. There's only one left of the bar.

"Good. Means you and I will get along great." He grins, his tongue flicking against a fang, seemingly mindlessly.

"Because we've done so swimmingly so far."

Ignoring me, he muses, "That didn't happen in the other cell."

"That's a statement, not a question."

"Answer me," he demands.

"The other was larger. I did feel it at first, but was able to pull myself out. Keep myself distracted. That was actually what the runes were for; I suspected they wouldn't work as they are supposed to. The smaller cell, not so much. Water this time."

He hands over the bottle and I down another sip, deciding my next reward will be to ask something in return.

"What happened to your parents? I know they died in a fire. Tell me the details."

The question stuns me into silence, the bottle numb between my grip while visions of flames flit through my mind—and the burning pain associated with each one. "I, I don't want to recount that."

"Captives don't get choices. Answer me." Gone is the teasing from moments ago, the villain back from downstairs instead.

"Alec..." I plead, searching him for some sense of humanity beneath his black soul. Something that'll get him to move on and ask me literally anything else.

"Answer the question, Sinclair, or I'll kill anyone else alive you still care about."

In this, I'll win. Asshole's so sure of himself and his threats. "Go ahead, there's no one left. Your threats mean little, Alec. Threaten to kill me next? I'll welcome the escape."

The vampire leans back, his tongue flicking against a fang again. Only this time, his eyes flash red too, menacingly. "Then I'll transform you into a vampire and force you to live as an immortal for the next few centuries. I'll be right there every step of the way, keeping you alive. So unless that's the future you secretly desire, tell me what happened to your parents."

FIFTEEN

Alec

Very few mortals chase vampirism. Many end up getting turned when becoming victim to a vampire's boredom, loneliness, or when feeding accidentally goes too far.

The case of myself was linked to a larger ploy, so my situation doesn't fall into any of those.

My threat to Sinclair is under the same category. If she pisses me off to the point I'll be forced to keep her around for a few centuries, it certainly won't be out of boredom or loneliness. The thought of dealing with her ass for any longer than fifty years makes me want to rip my own head off.

But I will if she doesn't start opening up about her damned family.

Her teeth nibble on the corner of her bottom lip, making the skin red, and my own hunger increases. She looks away and knots her hands together in the blanket, tugging it a bit higher over her. When returning earlier, I noticed she replaced the dress for her dirty pyjamas, and I wish I had them removed from the bathroom. They reek, for one, burning my nose—not that the dress held up much better down below—but she looked nicer in it.

Nicer? What a strange thought. There's nothing remotely nice about this witch.

She sighs, but it's in no way relaxing as she twists back to face me, her jaw tight and set with a resoluteness. "Fine, you want everything, asshole? To make me relive the single most painful day of my life? One night, two vampires somehow got through my parents' wards. They were fighting them, but their magick and the vampires' abilities were equally matched. My dad told me to run, so I started to. When I was nearly outside, my mom screamed. I couldn't leave them. Couldn't run and save myself knowing it could have been their deaths. I was fully into my powers and Mom had the cure too, so it's not like I was anything special. I stayed to help, channelling everything I had into my attack. But it was too much..." She drops her hands, and I find myself leaning forward. Her next words are a whisper, her tone scraping with the kind of pain only sorrow can create. "My magick took over. Sinclairs, as I assume you know, are fire witches, and I...I accidentally lit the house on fire. It was chaos. It burned the vampires...but also my parents."

Harlow Sinclair and I have something in common, because I, too, killed my parents. Only, I never cried over it.

A tear slips down her cheek, and it's like that little, salty drop punches me in the gut. A cough travels halfway up my throat, the sensation itchy and irritating. A fucking *cough*? I haven't had those since my days as a mortal.

"It was an accident," she whispers. More tears linger by her lavender irises. "I think they tried to put it out, I don't know. It was too much, though."

Two fire witches couldn't put out the flames? I'd never known a Sinclair to get so weak, even during an attack, that they were overwhelmed. With two of them working together, the blaze should have been out instantly.

"The barrier?"

She shrugs, except her shoulders are already so low with grief, it doesn't make much of a difference. "Appeared afterwards. The fire died down, and other than a few soot marks, the house was fine. Magick, I suppose." She attempts to smile, but it's fake, fragile and watery at best. "I was left with two piles of ash from the vampires, my dead parents, whose bodies were burnt beyond recognition, a barrier that erected itself around the property, no magick, and shadows that continue to torture me. I spent days afterwards trying to figure it all out, and the only thing I got is that my fear channelled too much magick—*so* much that it exploded, burned everything, and erected the barrier before draining me. That barrier became my final act as a witch."

I've tuned her final few sentences out, lingering back on her mention of shadows. I do a quick study of the room, noting nothing different. Nothing like she's talking about. Miss Sinclair's trauma has manifested into something greater, I wonder. Something she's imagining.

"Have you tried to get your powers back?"

"In between the grief and ongoing tears and self-hatred?" She scoffs, her sarcastic tone returning somewhat to normal. "Nope. Not until the first night you left me downstairs."

Freya said a big emotion could trigger her magick. It was grief that got rid of it, so grief to return it? That seems counterintuitive.

Or was it fear she felt in the moment of losing them? She was scared for her family and fought back. If it's fear that'll trigger her powers, then it's a task I'm content to take on.

Sinclair continues crying, every once in a while glancing towards the lamp in the far corner when she wipes her face. The tears leave wet lines on her cheeks that make me want to murder something. Despite who she is, seeing her cry seems...wrong.

I toss a sealed granola bar her way, followed by the water she can quench her thirst with. They land in her lap, earning a raised brow followed by another attempt at a smirk, this one a bit stronger.

Before she can ask—and before I can analyze my own actions—I mutter, "You've earned it."

She rips into the bar, eagerly taking a bite, her next words a mumble around the food. My mother would have once had me beaten if I spoke with my mouth full. Everyone in my life was so proper—still is, I suppose. Miss Sinclair is refreshing. She's something.

Something that'll send me to Hell if I'm not careful how I handle her and this situation.

"You're a strange vampire, Alec Dormer."

"You're a strange witch, Harlow Sinclair." A witch without magick. A witch who doesn't look at me like I'm about to eat her. That, too, is refreshing. To be around her and not have her flinching in fear or sobbing constantly. Her fear might smell appealing, but if she cried every minute down below, I might have ended her life to shut her up. Her personality has made her semi-manageable.

She pauses mid-chew. "That's, like, the second time you've ever said my given name."

"I told you what I feel about you and first names."

"Mhm. But then you also go and call me Miss Sinclair once in a while, and correct me if I'm wrong, but isn't *Miss* a title of respect?"

Fucking witch. "Habit, I suppose. Titles were everything in my time." I downplay it while also ignoring the strange sensation this conversation strikes inside me. "You asked a question and gained an entire bar and water. It's my turn again."

She rolls her eyes while taking the final bite of food. "You're in charge, *Your Majesty*. See? Title of respect."

Ignoring everything she rambled about beyond my title, I ask, "Why do you not live with your coven?"

She shrugs, all taunting slipping from her tone. "When we got kicked out when I was a kid, my parents moved us away. Mom said it had something to do with the cure. That the coven feared how many vampires targeted us in their attempt to get to me."

That makes no sense. Her people, Highridge Coven, are ancient and notorious for generations of Sinclair witches, but only this High Priestess has decided to abandon them? Witches are loyal to a fault and will always protect their own above all else, so why wouldn't they want to keep the young Sinclair safe behind their lines, their spells, and their curses? Hell, if memory serves, the Sinclairs created Highridge.

I search for lies, but her expression remains neutral, if not a bit open. Propping my elbows on the armrests, I fold my hands over my stomach and kick my leg up over one knee, adopting a position of ease all while my mind whirls with suspicions and unknowns. There's something more there, and if Sinclair doesn't know, perhaps Freya will be open with information.

"You haven't seen them since?"

She shakes her head, scrunching her nose. "All my training came from my parents. Oh, and Gram's grimoires. Though she died before my birth."

I toss her another bar, finding myself less and less interested in the game where I feed her a bite for information. I've gotten what I need—for the time being, at least. Now, I have to think about how to get her magick returned, and thus the cure.

I should go and consider next steps, but instead I find myself watching her. The way she brushes her hair into her face, as though trying to hide from me. The way she tugs the blanket higher, continuing to ease the shivers caused by the dungeon. So many micro movements. The intake of breath. The double blink before she rolls her lips together. The barely audible sigh.

"I killed my parents too," I find myself admitting, though I'm uncertain why. To ease her guilt by making us equal on one level? That can't be it, because this woman's guilt is her problem and not my concern. "It was after I transitioned. I went back for them; they weren't good people."

She winces. "That's a lot for a newly turned vampire. Traumatizing. If you were in control, would you have still?"

"Who said I wasn't in control?"

"Oh." Her lips remain slightly pursed, her brows pulling tighter together as she realizes that while we both might be the cause behind our parents' deaths, we run in opposite lanes. She misses her parents, and I don't. My only regret is not keeping my father alive for longer to drag out his agony.

"Yes, 'oh.'" I study her expression, searching for that deeper realization that no matter how peaceful this momentary truce may seem, I'm not a good person. I'm a vampire, intent on using her until she dies from old age, blood loss, or when I get irritated by her presence.

"Why'd you tell me that?"

"I don't know." Shaking my head, I stand and start for the door. "If you stayed awake all day from your phobia, you're no good to me now. You'll be too tired for what's next. Stay here and rest. Don't bother trying to escape; the windows don't open and the door will be locked."

She scrambles across the bed, her feet making thumps entirely too loud. "Wait, I have more questions." Her hand wraps my bicep, but I immediately shake her off, glaring over my shoulder.

"Your questions weren't the point of today. Go to bed, Sinclair. That's an order."

"Fuck you." She cuts in front of me, blocking my path, though I can so easily nudge her aside. "Why am I here?"

I sidestep her, reaching the door.

The persistent thing trails me. "What did my family do to you? That's what all this is about, right? The cure is only your means to torment me."

"Two points to the witch. Yes, but it's a story for another day."

"Alec—"

Her attitude's been picking away at me slowly, like a fucking stake being shredded against my insides, but now she's stabbed it into me and I am *done*. I whirl, my movements a quick blur, obviously unexpected given how her eyes widen, hands coming up between us. I stand above her, looming, ensuring she realizes that no matter the semi-pleasant conversation we had tonight, we are far from friends, allies, or even fucking acquaintances.

She is my prey. She is my captive. She is my revenge. She is meant to be hunted, ensnared, and tormented exactly how her family once did to mine.

"Get. To. Bed."

I'm out the door before her next breath, escaping the gnawing that continues ravaging my insides. The feeling *she* causes.

SIXTEEN

Harlow

The door slams shut behind Alec, taking his cranky vampiric ass away. After about ten seconds, I check the door and find it locked, exactly as he said it'd be.

"Well, great," I mutter, turning back to the bed.

In reality, this is better than the dungeon. Not close to freedom, but at least there's a working toilet, a shower, a proper bed, warmth, and no walls that are about to cave in on me. And bonus: Alec forgot to take the remaining two granola bars, so I have those to munch on.

I climb back into bed, my muscles untensing as they melt into paradise. If this mattress is as old as this castle probably is, it's been well preserved, because it feels like a cloud.

I should be planning any escape possible, but for this small moment, I obey Alec's instructions because with barely any sleep over the past three days and now a full belly, my body succumbs to sleep within the enemy's stronghold.

"**M**ommy, save me! Mommy! Daddy! Momm—"

A hand clamps over my mouth, the other looping around my waist, and they lift me off the ground. "Shut it, you little brat. You'll have the entire coven on us."

My screams are muffled against the hand until the second person gestures, and a wall of shimmering blue falls around us. A silencing enchantment, if I remember the High Priestess's teachings. Why would they want me to be quiet?

Why are Mommy and Daddy not coming?

I struggle and kick against the person holding me, but all my efforts are for nothing. They're too strong.

Suddenly, the forest around us disappears as the three of us appear inside a house. There's a door, and I'm being shoved into it with a muttered, "Stay in there and shut up. Hopefully it won't be long."

"Bind her mouth," the other voice says.

The shadowy person gestures towards me, their magick a green wave that falls onto me. When I open my mouth to scream, nothing comes out.

The door shuts, and it's small and dark in here. I slide to the floor, drawing my legs up to my chest.

Mommy...Daddy...help me.

My silent pleas go unanswered, so I pray instead.

Hecate, protect me. I'm sorry I didn't clean my room yesterday when Mommy asked. I promise I will next time. Just tell them where I am.

From sleep, I'm yanked to the top of my consciousness, almost violently. I scramble upright, drawing the blanket closer as the past few hours return in a burst of images.

The cell. The bedroom. Alec.

My dream.

An odd dream. Where would such a thing come from? I've never been away from my parents. Every memory I have is with them.

Which is why I know whatever that was, was nothing more than a nightmare bred from my current circumstances.

I reach up and pull my hair over my shoulder, and some of the strands stick to my skin, plastered with sweat. My hands quiver as I readjust myself back onto the mattress and get comfortable, trying to push anything of my parents from my mind. For now, I can't let grief take me out—again—because crying in front of the vampire once was enough.

It was only a dream. A strange dream. Nothing more.

With a few deep, calming breaths, I let sleep take me away once more.

This time, dream-free.

When consciousness rises once again, it's with a tingling sensation on the side of my face.

I'm being watched.

There's only one asshole who'd be watching me sleep, and since I'm in no mood to begin a verbal battle as soon as I wake, I continue fake sleeping longer.

"Hellion, your heart is beating faster. Stop pretending to be asleep."

Damn it.

With a resigned sigh, I open my eyes. First to the ceiling etched with markings and designs I didn't notice yesterday, and then to the vampire looming beside me, seated on the same chair as yesterday. His legs are parted as he sits low, slouched, like it's his throne downstairs. He's staring at me with no hint of emotion, so who knows which version of him this is.

"You look peaceful when you sleep," he murmurs, his face scrunching slightly, like this fact is a bother.

Only when I don't dream strange things.

"Morning, kidnapper."

"Charming as always, Miss Sinclair. Get up. Use the bathroom for your human necessities, then return quickly."

If he's snappy with his commands, it's for a reason, and getting the sense I need to be equipped to deal with that, I follow his demands. Whatever's coming today, I'd rather not have a full bladder.

When I return, he's in the exact same place. Pretty sure right down to the breath. Given vampires can go a while without moving, this wouldn't be much of a surprise.

His hunter-like attention tracks me back to the bedside, and my hands fist the sides of my pyjama pants, clenching my annoyances into the material. His intensity is scary, and my instincts are screaming at me to stay away, but there's something alluring about it all too.

If I escape from him, I should probably check myself into a psychiatric ward, because obviously my head's all kinds of fucked up.

I stop by the end of the bed, and he tips his head towards it. "Get in. I have shit to do, and you're stealing valuable nighttime hours."

"Why?"

"Three seconds before I put you in bed myself."

"You probably forget this part about being human, but after sleeping for hours, it's nice to stretch the body. Stand. Shit like that. Can't expect me to lie in bed all day and night."

He moves too quickly for me to catch, but suddenly he's in front of me, his hand a stiff vise wrapping around my throat as he propels me closer and spins me towards the mattress. I gasp as he walks me into the bed until it presses against my knees. Between one stuttered breath and my next, I'm horizontal, head on my pillow with him bowing over me. A tinge of red is around his pupils, and his expression is a bit maniacal, like he's minutes away from snapping, his restraint a taut bow I've been yanking on. When he speaks, his breath ghosts over mine in a cool, oddly welcoming breeze.

"Lying in bed all day *and* night is exactly what I expect you to do. It's the bed or the cell, so pick wisely." When I say nothing, my next forced breath pushing against his grip that's just tight enough to be concerning, his fingers lighten their hold. "Disobey me again, and you will not like the consequences." He continues pulling away, his fingers drifting over my skin until contact is broken by distance.

"What's the difference?"

"I gave a command and expect obedience. As I've said, I don't have much time, and dealing with you isn't on my list."

"Then why come here?"

He doesn't reply. "Starting tomorrow, you'll be working to get your magick back. The cure, I believe, is tied into your powers, since at its core, it too, is magickal. When you lost your powers, it faded, which means you need to be at full strength for it to be effective."

He spins on his heel after giving his decree, but I scramble upright, sliding from the bed. The instant my feet touch the ground, he turns back.

"I have zero motivation to get my magick back if it's only for your use." My palms tingle, the inner and deepest parts of me saying something else entirely.

Let him help you. Get your magick back. We miss it.

"Besides," I continue, "it doesn't work like that. You'd think I'd still be without them if I could just *will* them back?"

Although...with magick, I could fight. Alec believes he's in control, but I could burn his precious castle down, him alongside it. I could get free.

"How do you know you can't? You're an expert on witches losing their magick?" he shoots back with a perfectly shaped brow arching into his hairline.

"No, but I'm becoming an expert on asshole vampires."

He smiles once, not taking the bait. "Have a nice night, Miss Sinclair. Don't attempt the door, because it'll be a waste of your energy."

He's gone a blink later, the door's lock engaging filling the bedroom with a loud *click*.

I stare at it much too long before reaching towards the bedside table and taking another granola bar while I plot—unsuccessfully— how to get out of here.

SEVENTEEN

Alec

The Sinclair house is exactly as I left it: desolate, unoccupied, and a grave for two deceased witches.

The door is still unlocked from the night I stole Harlow, but a quick sniff suggests no one's been in here. The neighbourhood, I suppose, seems safe enough. Boring, with a lot of homes that are built identical to one another. For a witch family living away from their coven, they're easy to blend in.

Sinclair mentioned her grandmother's grimoires. Maybe having access to the spells the once-powerful Lorraine wrote down might trigger something. It's a longshot, but a start.

The grimoires are the main purpose for my trip, but I'm also here for Harlow. To unpack more of her strange background and upbringing, which she feels is normal, but I don't. The entire thing is perplexing, most notably the marks on her wrists.

It's unsettling, and I'm sick of the feeling, needing answers so I can return to not caring about every little thing in that woman's past.

I tread through the downstairs, scanning over the family's items while searching for anything suggesting it'd be hiding a grimoire. Right away, I notice the lack of natural objects within the space. There are a few candles and bundles of spices I watched Harlow place around, but nothing else. No pentagrams, no plants. This place looks too...normal. Too human. Like her parents were caught up in the very lie they likely fed to their neighbours.

I pace through the living room, scanning over the many photos the Sinclairs display above the fireplace. Some of her parents, one of their wedding, but I skip over any involving Emily Sinclair to study the ones of my little captive.

In one, she's a child. Five or so, if my recollection about human lifespans is correct. Her red hair is fuzzy in twin braids that rest over her shoulders. She's grinning up at the camera amongst her throne of leaves.

In another, she's older, sitting on a swing, her gaze directed at something far away.

The third picture is her as a teenager, posed in front of a tree, her smile joyful and natural.

The last photo is one taken more recently, based on her features being nearly identical to the woman I have in my castle. Once again, she's seated in a pile of leaves but she's staring down at the leaf in her palm.

Before I realize what I'm doing, I slide the photo from the frame and into my pocket.

Finishing with the mantle, I continue searching the rest of the downstairs, finding nothing useful, so I head upstairs, following the scent of my witch, now slightly faded.

In her bedroom, an empty tote bag on the floor strikes another idea. One that'll get her out of those dirt-crusted pyjamas. I pick it up before heading to her dresser and stuffing clothes into it—a few pants and shirts, another set of pyjamas—before opening the bottom drawer, pausing at the sight of her undergarments.

Fucking Christ.

The initial sight of black lace fills my head with a vision of *her* wearing it—and myself peeling it slowly from her. Swallowing the disastrous image, I grab a handful from the drawer and stuff them into the bag while simultaneously trying to *not* wonder how many human male ilk have seen her in these. Have undressed her of them.

Suddenly, I have a whole slew of new questions for the witch.

Focus. Shaking my head of useless curiosity, I continue searching for a grimoire, peeking under her bed, scanning her small bookshelf in the corner, before opening her closet and revealing complete chaos, junk and clothing strewn in a waist-high pile.

I rifle through it, moving a few bags aside, peeking into a box that seems to be holding nothing but random items, a hoodie tossed to the side—which I add to the bag, realizing she'll benefit from the warmth.

There it is. Beneath the hoodie is a black, leather-bound book, Lorraine's power radiating from the pages like a hot wave.

The book grows warmer when I pick it up and open it. There's all sorts of witchy bullshit spewed within the pages—poetic incantations, jotted notes about potions, lists of herbs and their uses—so I add it to the bag and leave after a final sweep of the room, heading down the hallway to the other bedroom.

The door is shut, and I wonder if Harlow has been in here since their deaths. Inside, the scent is vastly stale and void of her sweetness. Two other faint scents linger, both smelling like the earth. Dirt, trees, and leaves.

The bedroom is basic and as human-like as one would expect. A bed in the centre of the room, the light-green comforter pulled up over the pillows. A nightstand on either side with lamps much too large. Across from the bed is a large bay window overlooking the front lawn. To the left of the swindow, there's a shut door—presumably a closet—and a woman's vanity and floor-length mirror to the right.

Unsure of what I'm exactly looking for—if anything—my search is quick. The vanity, closet, and even beneath the bed reveals nothing interesting. As I turn to leave, the flooring by the door creaks. A light bounce reveals another creak, so I tap my foot, listening for the hollow kickback.

Would her parents really be so simpleminded to hide something beneath floorboards?

I bend and place my fist along the edge of the floorboard. With a bit of force, it pops up, revealing their secret compartment, and I'm instantly more intrigued by it than the rest of the house.

Inside is a shoe box, once again indicating their lack of originality. I lift the lid, taking in the stack of assorted documents. At the very top is a wedding photo, the fact it's in this box compelling me to examine it further. Why would their wedding photos be hidden beneath the floor when they have one on display downstairs?

The couple in the photo is the same, but taken when they were younger, if the lack of age lines on their faces indicate so, as well as the dress's style. But it's not those details that make me pause; it's the deep brown of the woman's hair rather than her signature Sinclair red-orange.

That's impossible.

It's impossible because this woman, the supposedly younger version of Emily Sinclair, the one I left alive to be married and eventually birth Harlow, looks *nothing* like the Emily I knew. Nothing... as in not the same person.

Resting it to the side, I flip through the documents, suspecting what I'll discover before I do. When the expired identification cards state different names, ones not Emily and John Sinclair, I'm partially unsurprised.

Instead, they say Violet and Arthur Hartman.

"Fuck."

Tucking the box beneath my arm, I run downstairs to retrieve the other wedding photo. The one involving the same couple, this supposed Violet and Arthur, older than the one in the box, her hair the same shade as the Sinclair red.

Which means the people who raised Harlow were not her biological mother and father.

Which spurns the question: What really happened to Emily and John Sinclair?

When I return home, there's the faintest unfamiliar scent lingering in the air, and beneath it—

That's when she screams, and I take off.

Because death will be too generous for whoever thought themselves brave enough to go near my witch.

EIGHTEEN

Harlow

A lec doesn't return for the rest of the night, so his task must be pretty big. I've come up with every possible scenario, but have no idea because who the hell knows what a vampire king's duties are.

At some point, I dragged the second wingback chair, the one still beside the fireplace, to the large window to try and figure out exactly where I am.

Other than somewhere not tropical...it's all I got. The castle looks out to a small stretch of flat, grassy land before reaching the edge of a forest; trees consume the rest of the view.

Who knows what country we're in, or even which continent. If we're close to civilization, or if we're on an island.

There's the faintest glow of sunrise on the horizon when the softest click of the door tells me I'm no longer alone. A quiet whooshing noise I'm now associating with Alec comes up behind me before a low thud pulls my attention away from the window and towards the second chair, last left beside the bed and now beside me.

Only it's not Alec settling in it.

A man sits deathly still, his long hair a curtain brushing the tops of his shoulders as he looks entirely too lax for a creature about to attack. Blood-red eyes suck all the breath from my lungs, darting to where my hands tighten around the chair's armrests.

"Don't do it," he murmurs in a grating voice. It's not silk like Alec's, but like he's been screaming for hours. "If you run, we'll be forced to hunt, and then it'll hurt."

We? A prickling sensation brushes the back of my neck as I twist around, taking in the other vampire standing by the base of the bed. With my attention, his tongue sweeps over his bottom lip, drawing my notice to the two piercings there.

Fuck. Where the hell is Alec when I need him?

"We're only here for a bite," the one beside me says, drawing my focus back. I angle my body until they're both in view, even if my place between the bed and the window means I'm trapped between the two monsters. "One bite each, and we'll leave you alone."

"You can't. Your king will—"

"Our *king*." He silences my appeal attempt with a smirk towards his friend. "Hear that, Nikolas? The witch is worried for us. Thinks the *king* will do shit."

"I hear her, Laz," the other one, Nikolas, drawls. "Dormer will learn what it means to keep you from us. We're one of a few coming for you, Sinclair."

So threatening Alec's position didn't work. I eye the bed, debating how fast I can climb over it. It'll probably be a fruitless attempt, but at least I go down fighting.

The one beside me, Laz, moves in front of me, cutting off any meager chance of escape. His hands clench the armrests by mine, long fingers wrapping around the polished wood as he leans in close, inhaling.

"You smell fucking fantastic. Like mortality."

"Mortality sucks. Stay a vampire."

His smirk suggests how my comment failed in its pitiful attempt to appeal to him. He dips down, whispering, "I promise not to make it hurt."

I scream. Pushing every bit into my vocal cords, I yell and shove to my feet, to duck beneath his arm as his teeth barely miss my neck.

Bang!

We both jerk our attention to the doorway and the door that slams against the adjacent wall as it's thrown open, revealing another vampire.

Alec.

Power. Authority. My black fucking knight in this fortress of misery. For once, his presence makes me sigh in relief.

"Shit," Laz mutters as Alec launches himself into the room, passing Nikolas and going for him. For all his words about not fearing Alec, he scrambles away with a second curse.

Alec whirls at the last second and returns to the door to slam it shut and intercept Nikolas's escape with a deep, threatening chuckle that has my stomach knotting. I've heard that laugh before, and it's not good. *No, actually,* I mentally correct. I've heard a similar laugh to that, and it was bad enough. But even when he appeared in my bedroom and chased me through my neighbourhood, he didn't sound this daring. Almost like he's amused by all this, but this version of his amusement will have more lethal outcomes.

Alec glances at me as the monster emerges in a veil of red over his eyes. He assesses me from head to toe with an intensity that unfurls the knot his entrance created in my stomach before facing the two vampires. "You broke into my home, superseded my laws, and dared to go near what's mine. What made you believe you had the *right*? There's a cost to her blood."

The two share a disappointed look before Nikolas reluctantly asks, "What'll it cost then?"

Alec chuckles again. "No price you'll be able to afford, that's for certain. Kill me, and you get to keep her." His eyes flick towards me, emotionless, as his tongue clicks. "It's simple, really. If you thought you could come into your king's home and steal from me, then you must be quite capable. Surely, she's worth the risk?" His question ends on a purr, his lips pulling up over his fangs.

I shift, holding my breath as the two vampires turn to me. Alec will win, though, or else he wouldn't have made such a deal. I hope. For my life, I fucking *hope*, because I'm barely surviving one asshole; I couldn't handle these two.

They share a look I can almost decipher before they head for Alec, two blurs across the room. Alec moves quickly, blocking their path while flitting between them and obstructing attacks. He fights with a deadly precision unlike anything I've ever seen, even at his party the other night. He's silent but violent, like a python, his arms snapping out until something is flung from one end of the room to the other, thumping nearby.

A head, eyes wide open, long hair streaked with blood. Laz's head. I clamp my hand over my nostrils and mouth as the scent of death wafts towards me.

Then everything stops, and Alec has Nikolas held by his shirt, hoisting him a few inches off the ground. "Why are you really here?" Blood coats his fangs, and there's a dark stain on the front of his shirt, but he seems unharmed—a fact I find myself exhaling at.

"Your Majesty...you know why."

"Yes, but I want you to say it," Alec murmurs in a deadly, cool tone that empties my lungs of the remaining air it's clinging to. "In your words, tell me why you dared enter my grounds without permission."

Nikolas's throat moves, and crimson eyes dart my way before he admits, "For her. For the Sinclair witch. We wanted mortality."

"Hm." Alec's silent for a long moment, like he's considering. "But you didn't get permission. I protect my possessions, which includes the witch."

Nikolas's head bobs like a cartoon character. "I, I understand. I'll spread the word, I swear. It'll never happen again, Your Majesty."

"You're right about something tonight, at least. You will spread the word when I place your and your friend's remains by the edge of my property as a warning for anyone else who hopes to meet the same fate."

Alec punches his hand into Nikolas's chest, and, similar to the party, he rips out the vampire's heart as Nikolas takes his final breath, a gasp, his mouth remaining open and forever frozen in a state of shock.

Alec unpeels his fingers one by one, and the body drops with a thump beside Laz's headless one. The heart tumbles to the floor by his feet, and I'm left with one pissed-off, red-eyed vampire who turns towards me.

NINETEEN

Alec

*S*he's safe.

She's not screaming anymore.

She moves a step in my direction, her hands positioned to protect herself should I attack. Charming, but unnecessary.

I glance at the scum who believed they could barge into my home, pushing aside the dismay they succeeded. It's testament to how badly Sinclair needs her powers back, to get the cure effective once more before more try the same. At least she'd be able to fight.

But, for now, their bodies need to be removed from her vicinity. There's a head across the room I need to retrieve, but doing so means going near her, and being near her means I won't be able to stop myself from checking over her body.

"Th-thank you."

She's *thanking* me? Thankful I showed up at the precise time the asshole tried to sink his fangs into her neck—into skin that *no one* will be touching. She's thanking me for nearly having her killed, all because I left her alone, assuming a few hours would be fine.

I underestimated my subjects.

"I mean, I know you did it because I'm some sort of commodity to you, but still...if you didn't show up when you did—"

"They'd still be dead," I cut her off, rendering her misplaced compliments as meaningless. "They'd have mortality for a moment before reaching the same fate."

"Still..."

Still, you'd have been bitten in that outcome.

"Thanks," she finishes, her hands coming together.

I don't know why it's those words that do me in, but I'm across the room in an instant, looming over her as my red-coated vision studies her closer. I've already checked to ensure neither of them harmed her, because their deaths would have been a lot more drawn-out if so. Only when seeing her up close, when confirming she's untouched, does the red fade to a pink, then to black again, and my normal vision returns. I force an unnecessary breath into my lungs, keeping out the scent of the corpses behind me while only accepting the sweet notes of her gratitude. My hands itch to touch her, to *feel* she's alright, but they form fists instead.

"Don't thank me. Ever." *It'll never be in your best interest, Hellion.*

I turn for the discarded head resting by the fireplace, hissing with the sudden movement. One of them managed to scratch me during his attack seconds before I ripped his head off. As much as I'd prefer not to do this in front of her, I need to see what I'm dealing with and lift my shirt to inspect the damage.

The score marks are deep. Injuries to vampires never last long, but ones delivered by a fellow immortal tend to leave lasting marks. It'll take fresh blood to speed up my healing.

"You're hurt," she exclaims, her bare feet rushing over the carpet to my side. A natural warmth radiates from her, despite the chilling scene she endured. But worse is the faint trace of concern. Concern for *me* is the last thing Sinclair should ever feel.

Her hands reach for my side, that very warmth coming temptingly close, but I manage to keep my head on long enough to twist away, my snarl a warning to her and a reminder for myself. A reminder that tonight has changed nothing about my greater plans.

When her arms drop and a flash of hurt crosses her expression, I continue to ignore her and swipe the head from the floor. "I'll heal. Don't get your hopes up." With the head in hand, I grasp his body and hoist it over my shoulder, kicking the heartless one as I pass. "Don't touch him. Stay where you are."

"Alec—"

"*Stay.*"

I run downstairs to drop the corpse by the door before rushing back before she'd have a chance to move. I grasp the second and ignore the sting radiating from my ribs with the extra weight. This time when I exit the room, I lock it, not trusting her to not take advantage of my injury and the recent situation.

I deal with both bodies, placing the four pieces in random places around my property as a deterrent. It takes minutes before I return to the castle and retrieve the items from the Sinclair household where I left them in the foyer when she screamed.

She fucking screamed.

She didn't even scream when I kidnapped her.

She *screamed*, and something inside me wouldn't be stopped until she no longer had anything to fear.

The noise, her fear, it rattled me more than it should have.

I hate it. Hate that it affected me at all. Hate that I had a million and one ideas on how to draw out their deaths but only one became possible: the quickest one. The one that'd protect her the best.

He almost bit her. He almost bit *my* Sinclair witch.

Taking the box, I run up to my bedroom to leave it before seeking the mini fridge of fresh blood bags, all stolen from hospitals. Not because I'm moralistic, but because hunting humans isn't always possible and, given how irritating they are, I don't keep live ones around.

Except her. But she's not food.

I grab two. Downing the first one, my skin begins merging back together, the sting lessening into a mere irritation. With the second one, as well as the bag of her clothes, I return to her bedroom, unlocking it without a knock.

She's settled into a chair but whips around at my entrance. Her heartbeat drives up like a hummingbird's, though immediately slows when she sees it's the familiar monster and not another stranger.

"You're back."

"Always astute in your observations." I lower into the second chair, glancing towards the window, where her attention was before my arrival. She likely saw me run into the forest with the deceased vampires.

"You okay?"

"Unfortunately for you, yes. Blood will heal me quicker." I lift the unopened bag to my mouth and stab a fang into it, sucking the liquid. The metallic taste is a fraction of the faint flavour she gave me the other night, and it's with that annoying thought I glare.

She eyes the bag before facing the window. "Huh."

"Huh what?"

"No human trailing behind you. Not what I expected."

"They're for breakfast. Blood bags for supper. Easier that way."

Sinclair crosses one leg over the other until her body is slightly tilted away. Her spine is straight—too straight—and her breathing slows. I don't know why, but before the lie sits too long and she truly believes my joke, I correct, "Kidding, Sinclair. You should learn to laugh more. It'd do you some good."

She turns her head, hair brushing over her shoulder. It draws my attention to her neck again, to where she was nearly bitten. "So there are no humans chained up somewhere?"

"You're the only living being," I admit. "Humans are too pesky to have around long-term. I don't oppose feeding from them, but only if I seek them out."

Her cheeks lose a bit of that blood as they whiten. "Right. What about the one at your party?"

"Hired service. One willing to be discreet enough." I eye her neck again, wanting to shift her attention to something that isn't my personal life. "Are you okay?"

Some of the colour returns to her cheeks. "Wasn't expecting it, that's all. When the door opened, I assumed it was you. Given who you are, I didn't expect vampires to find me here."

"It shouldn't have happened," I confess, my own apology hovering on the edge of my tongue. Except it's not needed, therefore not happening. If Sinclair didn't lose her magick, the cure would function as normal, and we'd have a lineup of customers paying for sips of her blood.

What happened clearly didn't spark enough to reignite her powers. Which is unfortunate, because it would have been one benefit.

"Their names were Laz and Nikolas, if that helps."

Neither I recognize, but perhaps Cedric can dig something up. He has a better connection with more of our brethren, considering he's so often on the move.

"Should I ask why you know their names?"

"They talked a lot before you showed up."

If they skipped taunting her, I wouldn't have made it back in time. I swallow my dismay around the blood bag, draining it before discarding it on the floor.

"That's it then? You're all healed?"

"Heal*ing*. Give me an hour. Without the blood, it may have taken until tomorrow. If they weren't vampires, it would have been almost instant."

"Oh. You're quite open about your kind."

"Not like you can use the information to your benefit." My amusement fades at the sight of her scrunched brows. With a sigh, I concede, "Ask what you want to. It's all but written on your face."

"Do you sleep in a coffin?"

The random question throws me enough, I laugh. Of course,

this witch would ask that of all things. Harlow Sinclair is as interesting as they come.

"No. I enjoy my bed too much."

"So you *do* sleep?"

"Occasionally. Our sleep needs are much different than a mortal's, or even yours."

"Huh. And here I pictured you getting into a skinny box and folding your hands over your chest."

"If you're referring to that ridiculous movie based on that equally ridiculous book, *Dracula*, you're wrong. Although, the fact you're picturing me sleeping at all might be something we need to chat about, Hellion."

She doesn't take the bait, instead leaning on the armrest, her eyes open in childlike wonder. "So Dracula is just a story and nothing more?"

"Oh, he's real," I confess, thinking of the millennia-old vampire. "But Bram Stoker didn't record his story correctly. Also, no one's seen him in a few centuries."

"Have you met him?"

"Very few alive have."

"That didn't answer the question."

Another sigh. "I have not."

"So Mina's real too?"

"Who's Mina?"

She snorts and leans back. "Guess that answers that. You called the book and movie ridiculous; you'd know who Mina was if you read or watched them."

"One doesn't have to consume something to know it's incorrect."

"Wow." She shakes her head, the hint of a smirk reassuring me tonight's danger has fazed me more than her. "You can't make claims about something you don't know. In the book, Mina was a woman Dracula was compelled by, enough to try to curse her into becoming one of his brides. In the movie, she was a reincarnation of the wife he had during his mortal life, and that's why he was interested in her."

Based on that summary, perhaps Bram Stoker didn't have it entirely wrong.

"Hm."

"*Hm.* That's all you have to say?" Her voice climbs.

"I was thinking. *If* Mina actually existed for the real Dracula, the book version would be the most plausible. He was drawn to her, obsessed over her until he got what he wanted. It's very...my kind." I shift, uncomfortable suddenly with where the conversation is dipping to.

Leave it to Sinclair to probe further. "What do you mean?"

"It means vampires can't love. Most of the mortal emotions stop existing after we're reborn as an immortal. Love isn't possible, but we obsess—*strongly*, fiercely, almost violently. From the outside, it might look like love, but never mistake it as such. Our obsessions run deep, and we'll do everything and anything to sate it. There will be nothing in death or life that'll keep us from the source of our obsession. That's the closest thing we have to love."

"Oh." She's silent for a while, only the rhythmic thrumming of her heart suggesting she isn't finished with this topic. She's analyzing my words, considering what more to say, so it's not a complete surprise when she asks, "Have you ever had someone to obsess over?"

My reply is an unbothered fact. "No."

She finally drops the subject, and we sit in a silence that's unnerving because it's nothing like I've experienced with her. She's staring out the window while I observe her, gawking much too long at the notes of orange mingling with red. The small brown freckles that decorate her cheeks and wrap towards her forehead, a speckling of stars that make Sinclair glow brighter, enthrall me.

A peace radiates from her despite what happened tonight,

almost like she has no idea how close to a different outcome it could have been. The blood staining the carpet behind us is a mere prequel to the pain I could have caused and the horrors she could have witnessed instead. I was gentle—*too* gentle—with their deaths. It happened too quickly to sate my *need*. The very need that has my hands clenching around the armrests before I act and do something so utterly stupid, there would be no turning back.

Then she speaks, no louder than a whisper, and it's a set of words that throws my axis off-kilter.

"I'm glad you're okay, Alec."

TWENTY

"You sounded worried."

Worried? No. Never. Not about him. Even if the marks on his side looked *really* bad. If I'm lucky, when he crawls into bed—*bed*, not coffin—the injuries won't be healed, he'll die from blood loss, and I'll be able to escape.

A senseless fantasy, of course.

"No one knows I'm here, and I'd rather not starve to death. Speaking of, I'm hungry, if you're feeling generous enough to feed me today." I'd eaten the final granola bar hours ago, despite debating holding off until I had the guarantee of more food.

"Apparently I'm feeling quite generous today." I assume he's talking about the fact that he's the reason I didn't become a meal for Laz and Nikolas, but then a bag gets dropped by my feet. "Here. I'm tired of you smelling like the dungeon."

It's an insult and a compliment rolled into one, returning pre-attack Alec to me. There's a comfort in the known, so I'm pleased about his standoffish personality. Curious, I flip open the bag, immediately recognizing it as one from my room. Inside, I find my clothing. Various tops, pants, and even more pyjamas. At first, a sense of gratitude consumes me, but it's quickly replaced by alarm when realizing where he got these.

"You went to my house."

Wordlessly, he reaches beside his chair and retrieves something else before handing it to me.

Gram's grimoire. It was hidden in my closet, placed there after Mom's and Dad's deaths, when I had no more magick and couldn't bear to look at it. It was a painful reminder of learning my powers the first time.

"For that," he explains. "If you're going to relearn your magick, then you need your spell book or whatever that is. Something witchy to connect you to your powers."

His kindness makes sense. He went to my house for himself, not me. Still, glancing towards the bag of fresh clothing, it'll make this hellish situation slightly better—for now, at least.

"The book won't re-spark my magick. Witches are born with their powers and come into them with puberty. The grimoire simply helps with potions and spells. Like a recipe book."

His expression pinches, and he waves his hand. "Then use the book to un-age yourself and redo puberty or something. Do whatever you must until you're able to go bibbidi-bobbidi-boo and make the cure functional."

Yet another no.

Right now, Alec wants my magick more than I do, which means he's vulnerable to making deals.

One of my hands curls on my lap, slightly disbelieving what I'm about to do. The other pushes into the armrest. "Not until you give me something in return."

"Your life isn't good enough?" A brow arches, but he doesn't look away from the window. "Besides, how I see it, I already saved you tonight. You owe me."

Rage flashes down my spine, forcing it straight. "You saved me because you think of me as your property."

"You *are* my property," he snaps, his attention flicking away from the window.

"Fuck you. I want to know *exactly* why I'm here. I want your history and how it links with my family."

Something passes over his expression. His eyes narrow in the corners, his hands gripping the chair's armrests. Then he sighs like I've asked him to slice off a fang.

"Fine," he grunts. "You won't like it, though."

"Was I supposed to enjoy the kidnapping?" I ask sarcastically. "Maybe I'll start accepting shit if I know the reason behind your actions." I never will, but he doesn't need to know that.

"Whatever you say, hellion."

He casts me a look full of doubt, but after a moment, sweeps me into a tale of another time, another world. A history I could never have dreamed up, and a nightmare I'd never want to.

"I lied when I said I was a king in my mortal life, and that I conquered this place. It was always mine to inherit because I was the prince, heir to the throne, son to the ruling monarch. Only, I took it from him much earlier than intended, so in a way, I did conquer it. My father wasn't a good man, even by history's standards—which, I should note, are much different than present. Parents followed different rules. Ethics and laws were crueller. And mine were the cruellest I knew, to both me and my sister, Cora."

A sister? The asshole vampire is a *brother*? Somehow, I don't get that from him. Siblings are supposed to love one another, have a good bond and all that—not that I have personal experience—and imagining Alec having loved anyone, even when love was a possible emotion for him, seems impossible.

"Cedric—you met him at the party—was my best friend...and was very much in love with Cora. Cora returned the sentiment and longed to wed him, but Father always refused the match because he was a stableboy, and too low in station for a princess. No matter how many times I begged him to make Cedric a knight, allowing him to work up to a ranking a bit more suited for her, Father never agreed." His tone sharpens.

"You didn't like that?"

"Station may have been important for alliances, but I wanted my sister happy, and Cedric made her the happiest. Our father got tired of the begging, so he began seeking his own alliance for her. At the same time, wars were breaking out all over the place as sides competed for territory. As humans, we didn't realize the people we were fighting were witches—didn't know witches existed. The one particular coven giving us issues housed a certain family."

"Sinclairs," I fill in the gap, and he nods. "Wait. If you were battling Sinclairs, that means this castle—*us*—is near—" My mouth clamps shut, though I've already given too much away. *Fuck.* I shouldn't have said that, should have held on to what little hints he's allowed slip.

Alec chuckles. "Highridge Coven? No, that was before the coven inhabited Banff. Don't read more into this story, Hellion. As if I'd give you anything that could help you escape."

I study his face, seeking whether it's a lie or not, but after who knows how many centuries alive, he's either a really good liar or telling the truth.

"To end the fighting between our kind, Father offered Cora to the coven as a peace treaty. An arrangement, since that was how so many mortal disagreements were solved. For that, station no longer mattered to him. Nor Cora, and I feared for her safety. Mother and Father packed her up and sent her off." Alec pauses, his tongue sweeping his bottom lip in a way that momentarily makes my brain stop functioning. Only for a moment, because the vulnerability seeping from him makes me feel...well, empathetic. "In truth," he murmurs, "I think Father was happy to be rid of her. My parents only intended to have me, the heir. A daughter was never part of his plans.

"I was there when the transfer happened. Was there to see Cora scream and cry for Father to return her home." Alec's hands fist the armrests again, this time the metal crying beneath the force. "He walked away without a backwards look, so I planned an attack to get her back. Cedric joined me, and the next night, we went armed to where the coven made camp."

I lean forwards, captivated by his story. So far sad, and I'm suspecting it's about to get worse. "You failed?"

"In part. We succeeded in getting Cora out of the tent, but that's all. Turns out, the Sinclairs had deals with vampires—a species we'd only heard about. Back then, the world was more faith-based, and there were rumours of a devil's child running around, drinking the blood of humans, though nothing had been confirmed until that moment. The coven sent the vampires after us, and our mortal speed was no match for theirs." He stops, wiping his hand along his mouth. "To this day, I don't know why the group changed us instead of killing us like the coven instructed. But when we woke up the next day, all three of us were in transition, and instincts told us how to complete it. The coven disappeared, and with our transition, we were all filled with a bloodlust I simply can't explain. It was more than a need to kill. It felt like I'd die if I didn't get revenge. I had it the worst, more than Cedric and Cora. I blamed my parents for what happened. Father, for giving Cora to the coven and not allowing her to wed Cedric, and Mother, for doing nothing to stop it. So I returned here, slaughtered them, and took the castle for myself."

His callous words, spoken with a chilliness the beginning of his story didn't have, make me flinch. No sign of regret or dismay; just cold facts. I open my mouth, uncertain how to reply.

His smirk is a twisted coil of no regrets. "Like I said yesterday, I, too, killed my parents, only mine deserved it."

"What happened after that? You began hating Sinclairs?"

"Yes, because they, too, were at fault, considering they sent the vampires after us, but my hatred for them didn't really spark until much later. You see, a few things had come from our transition. My parents were no more, and Cora and I were free. Cora and

Cedric got to be together while I ruled in my father's place. We fed on anyone and everyone, won every battle. Life was fucking *good*." A sense of peace that makes my bones cold crosses his expression. "We were *gods*," he continues. "Powerful and unstoppable. Cedric and Cora lived here for a while, but eventually went off on their own.

"During that time, wars between vampires and witches were mounting because neither side had ever gotten along. All over the world, the two sides fought...and we were no exception. There were challenges up north, so I left here to assist and met up with Cora and Cedric. One night, Cora was hunting in the woods, and your ancestor, Elizabeth Sinclair, captured her. Killed her in retaliation. Cedric and I were close but out of reach to save her in time. He stayed with her body while I hunted Elizabeth through the woods. I ripped her throat out."

He looks my way, his eyes tinged red in anger, or the memory of the kill. A feeling that isn't fear courses through me, and it's one I could never have guessed I'd have towards this man—this vampire.

Sympathy.

"I'm sorry."

He huffs. "It's not your apology to give, now is it? No, Elizabeth stole my sister from me. That was *twice* your family condemned mine...so I condemned yours. From then on, I vowed to end every generation of Sinclair witches, leaving only one female alive to carry on the line. Of course, they then invented the cure to vampirism and made it a part of you, a twist that sometimes got themselves killed before I had the chance."

I stare at him, my body stiffening with every passing second I forget to breathe. But it's in those passing seconds that the small sliver of sympathy I felt only a moment ago disappears. Fades with the resurgence of hatred for this creature. With the end of his story, he's reminded me of every reason why I can't let my guard down. Why I hate Alec Dormer, no matter what's happened today.

"That's why you came for me?" My question is a whisper, quieted by dread and understanding. "You're going to kill me."

It makes sense. Mom told me Gram's sister died in her early twenties, but not how. Mom was an only child. I'm an only child. Our family stopped producing more than one child every generation because of *him*.

This is...this is so messed up.

He shakes his head, not paying attention to my near-breakdown. "Your family has tried to best me, but I'll always win. Your death would end the game, and I'm not ready for it to be, so I've changed the rules. For the rest of your life, the very thing that was designed to protect the world from my kind will be the very thing that'll condemn you. As I mentioned the other night, immortality is ongoing, and you're my newest entertainment. For now, at least."

What?

No.

He's saying—

What?

I'm up and out of the chair before my next breath, pacing as far back as the room physically allows me. And even so, when my back hits the wall, I keep pushing, willing myself to go through it while determining the likelihood of making it over the bed.

"You know, for a moment, I actually felt *bad* for you. For your sister. You really are an asshole."

Alec watches me with a slight tip to his head that makes his hair shield his face. "You're not in danger, Sinclair, sit down."

"For now." But how long until he tires of selling my blood, of seeing the reminder of his sister's murderer before he decides to wipe me out?

"Maybe forever. You're the most entertainment I've had in a long while."

Forever? Forever can burn in fucking Hell before I even *consider* letting him stick his fangs in me.

"You're unbelievable. Sorry for what my ancestor did to your sister, but that was *long* before I was born. You've killed dozens of my family for what...one death?"

"My *sister's* death."

"Again, I'm *sorry*, but my life—I'm not at fault. And neither are you! Let it go—Cedric obviously did." I think about the vampire who approached me on the dais, and how there was no hatred in his expression. "This revenge plot of yours is pointless because *I* did nothing to you or Cora. You've decided to punish me for a crime I didn't commit."

Every ounce of self-preservation is gone, and words fly without considering consequences. At this point, I don't even know what'd be better: to stay alive and hope to escape or to piss him off enough he ends my life and saves me both from this future and my misery.

Alec is a blur streaking across the small space. His shadow encompasses mine as he bends down, strands of hair brushing my cheek. "Say it," he growls, pulling back enough I can see his face. When I'm forced to watch his lips part and his fangs slide farther from his gums—and ignore the way heat flashes between my legs. "Say it," he commands again, his tone low and velvety, like satin gliding over my skin. "Say what's on your mind, Hellion. Say how much you hate me."

"I hate you." It's a weak whisper, driven by apprehension and none of the intended malice. "You're cruel."

He reaches for a clump of my hair, twirling the strip around his finger as he muses, "I'm a vampire, and it's best you remember that. Cruelty is my very nature. I fear you may have forgotten that today."

I did, but won't ever again. "So be crueller. Or show me mercy, depending how you look at it." I turn my head until the hair slides from his finger. His hand doesn't move, though, and my cheek brushes against the same finger. "End my life. I'd rather meet death now than be dragged into your torture for some unknown length of time."

"So you've said before, which is a mistake. Hint for if you ever invent a time-travelling curse and return to the past to change this present: Never tell the kidnapping asshole what you desire. Because now, I'm able to use it against you."

Damn, he's right. I'm an idiot.

"You see death as a freedom, and we can't have that," he continues, his words so low, I'm practically reading them from his mouth. His finger brushes my cheek, creating a path of heat as he reaches for the same clump of hair and pinches the ends. "It's interesting how easily you greet the concept of death. How when you learned what I intended for you, you feared it, and yet you begged for it too. Very confusing."

"There's a difference between choosing my fate and having it chosen for me."

He chuckles darkly, his breath cool against my nape and icing my veins. "Yes, that there is. Or is this your horrendous way of surviving *me*?"

"We all do things we have to, to survive. Even you."

"That wasn't a yes." He smiles, his teeth a threat on their own.

"Fuck off."

He loops my hair around his hand, the slight tug on my scalp a taunt. "Are you sure you wouldn't enjoy immortality? You'll die, as you're so eager to do, and get to continue living all at the same time. You'll be stronger than ever. Human emotions will no longer faze you. That grief you cling to? Gone."

"Like yours?" I counter with a raise of a brow. "Because you're the fucking poster child for managing grief."

With a growl, he wrenches my head back until I'm staring at the ceiling. Pain flitters over my scalp, my hand going to where he has me, but he's unyielding even when I claw at him. "Your attitude is something else, Hellion. Be careful how you speak to me."

"Go. Die."

"I'm already dead," he replies before jerking away. My head thumps against the wall, and I rub the small ache as he stalks away, pausing by the fireplace. "When I return tomorrow night, these logs better be on fire." His eyes rake over me, not shielding his disgust. "And you'll be changed into something more respectable."

"When I get my powers back, I'm burning you alive."

"There she is. Keep it up, Sinclair. Anger looks good on you."

He's gone from the room, door locked and shut, before my next blink.

Twenty-One

Alec

What the fuck was that?

It's the question plaguing me all the way down to the kitchen because, before retiring in my room for the day, I couldn't not hear the way her stomach grumbled for food. I retrieve more of those bars she seems to enjoy, mentally noting to find something more substantial for her to eat soon.

I take the long way back to her room, and on arrival, open the door without knocking.

And stop.

And stare.

And *feel*.

She's on the other side of the bed where I left her, wearing nothing but panties and a bra—both from the bag. It's that damn black lace I fought like hell *not* to imagine her in.

She screeches, but the noise sounds no louder than an echo from downstairs for how my senses tune everything but her out. My hands tighten until the food crumbles while my cock twitches for the one woman I should never crave. My gums ache, my fangs demanding to come out and suck the vein between her thighs.

"Alec!"

*She's...*yeah. I can't even let my thoughts formulate, to admit what the rest of me knows.

Creamy skin that's undoubtedly pure velvet to the touch is all I see. Splatterings of freckles cover her arms and legs, now freed from those hideous pyjamas. There's a sudden desire to rip the lace from her and explore every curve, to trace the path of those little freckles.

"Alec! For fuck's sake!"

Take.

That fucking inner voice urges me to break my old promises and determine exactly how loud I can make the witch scream.

Sinclair.

Witch.

Prey.

I recite everything she is to remind myself of everything she isn't.

"Alec!"

This time, her screech successfully pulls me from my haze, but it doesn't clear it. Suddenly, I'm by her side, tossing the granola bars to the side. Her hips fit my hands perfectly, and I spin her around and push her onto the mattress.

Her hands come up to cover her chest, which is an effort long overdue, because I've already seen everything she has. Nearly every tantalizing inch. "What the hell are you doing? Get out!"

"You forget whose room this is. Whose castle. But by all means, I'll return you to the dungeons if you'd prefer."

I'm pissing her off only to make the redness in her cheeks expand to the rest of her body, chasing it with my gaze. Imagining the same kind of redness from her blood coursing from her neck and between my lips, *finally* able to drink the flavour that's teased my senses since day one.

"Alec," she repeats, my name a growl in her throat. It's cute, if not a little pathetic, how hard she tries to hold her ground. "Get out."

Her heartbeat quickens, and I'm pleased. She can get a sense of what I felt when entering; the world tilting on its axis.

While I doubt this will be the thing to spark the buried emotion that'll unlock her magick, everything must be tried and tested, right? I'd be doing her a disservice by backing away, by allowing her fear to subside.

"Why would I knock when this is the sight I'm greeted with?"

She pulls her bottom lip into her teeth to utterly torment me. I reach for her, pulling her lip free before she accidentally damages herself. A lifetime of control will unravel if she makes herself bleed.

When she speaks, her lips brush against my finger. It's a sensation I can't help but marvel at. "Because I'm related to the people who killed your sister. You can't separate me from my ancestor to rationalize your actions, so this should be no different."

She's right, but it doesn't stop me from leaning closer. From inhaling the sickle of apprehension. Her comment brings a smile to my face, this one unthreatening and genuine.

"You're learning to twist facts to your benefit. That's good. But you forget, vampires are inherently attracted to flesh." I shift my hold to her wrists, and her pitiful mortal strength resists when I go to tug them away from her chest. I allow her the modesty and stop pulling, even if any effort on my part would break her hold.

"I, I...you hate me."

Releasing her wrists, I shift towards where the bra straps rest on her shoulders, petting the skin towards the curves of her breasts. "That may be true, but I can still appreciate your beauty."

My strokes continue over the curves of her arms, over her stomach—which she caves in as though to avoid. I follow the line to the edge of the very panties I envisioned her in, pausing when she sucks in another breath, wondering exactly how long it'll take before she breaks it.

"Get off," she whispers, catching my gaze once more. She swallows roughly, her plea caught between her fake bravado and fear. Another scent rises, this one sweeter than anything else. Like blood and sugar and everything dark.

Her desire.

"Make me," I taunt, trying to use the conversation to keep me focused enough so my fingers don't slip beneath the edge of lace and discover for myself what Miss Sinclair tries so hard to hide. "What's that human saying? You got yourself into this, you can get yourself out." I pause, fake considering my words. "Yeah, that's it. If you want me off you, use your magick."

"You're an asshole."

"So you tell me constantly."

She drops her arms from her chest, only to push me away while angling herself upright. "I'll repeat it 'til you agree with me." She manages to duck beneath my arm, leaving me crouched alone on the bed, and I let her. She dips towards the floor and snatches a plain tee from her bag, scowling. "That's all this was then? Your fucked-up way to somehow spark my powers into returning? Newsflash: If they haven't come back during all the other hell you've put me through, or what happened earlier, they wouldn't for whatever the fuck that was."

I twist until I'm seated on the edge of the bed, crossing my arms while observing her yank on jeans, her movements uncoordinated and jerky. "Is that your way of saying you didn't hate it?" The scent from between her legs answered that long before she opened her pretty little mouth.

"Leave. Sun's up. Don't you have a coffin to crawl into?"

"You know the answer to that. Didn't realize you care about my sleep habits."

With a glare, she throws her dirty shirt at my face, but I catch it. "The first chance I have, I'll be watching you burn in the sun, so no, you're confusing annoyance with concern."

"In my world, they're the same."

Her pants come soaring through the air. "Go away. Die. Burn. Sleep and never wake up."

With both articles of clothing in hand, I turn for the door, not because she's demanding but because I never intended to stay as long as I have.

"Always pleasant chatting with you, Hellion."

"Asshole," is her final grumble before shutting the door. I linger for a moment, listening as she crosses into the bathroom before locking her in and heading to my own quarters.

Inside, I drape her clothes over a wingback chair that's beside the shoe box, as well as the picture of Sinclair I stole from the mantle, before heading into my ensuite for a hot shower to wash off the lingering blood on my arms and chest I didn't get to earlier.

The water does little to burn away the flames licking through my blood after that match with the witch. The *need* to return and finish what I started, first with my fangs buried in her neck and then my cock in her cunt. I might have only been fucking with her for my own entertainment and her torment, but it took centuries of control to keep myself intact.

It also does nothing to quell the other source of my rage—subjects disobeyed laws long laid about entering this castle uninvited and believed they could take her.

If I was a minute too late...

I'm toweling off when my nose picks up another intruder. This one is becoming familiar, which is concerning on its own.

Tightening the towel around my waist, I leave the bathroom and return to my room, barely sparing Freya a glance as I cross towards my walk-in closet.

"How did you get in here?"

"You truly have no idea how much I can do. I'd start listing the ways, but we'd be here all night. *Although*"—she whistles—"I might make an exception if you don't put on a shirt."

"You're not my type, witch."

"Because I'm a witch or because my hair isn't red?"

Ignoring the jab, I quickly dress and find Freya sprawled sideways across the wingback chair, her legs tossed over the armrest. Her hair's different again, this time a shade of light purple that matches her eyes.

"You should pick a hair colour and stick to it. You're exhausting to keep up with."

"What's life without whimsy?" She tugs on Harlow's pyjamas hanging beside her. "This is disturbing, Alec. We should probably talk about your newest obsession."

Her word choice hits a bit too close for my liking, especially after my recent conversation with the other witch. Harlow Sinclair will never be my obsession because I'll never allow it. She's passing entertainment while working toward a grander plan.

"Putting aside your invasion into my home, why have you come?" There have been too many uninvited guests today.

She gestures to the shoebox resting on the opposite seat. "Because the Goddess gave me permission to explain all this to you. So before you run around with your head cut off, chasing your tail and all that jazz, trying to figure this out, we'll save you a step."

"So you know what that is?" I nod to the box.

"Question is..." She kicks one leg over the other, propping it straight up into the air because...well, I'm learning Freya is weird as fuck. "Do you?"

I cross to the box, lifting the lid and retrieving both IDs and the wedding photo. "When Lorraine Sinclair birthed only one child—Harlow's mother, Emily—I left them alone. Then Harlow was born. I've been following the Sinclairs close enough to know this"—I jab my finger into the wedding photo—"is not Emily. Never in history has a Sinclair witch been born with anything but red hair."

Freya barely spares the photo a glance before she makes an

unamused noise. "Recent generations of the Sinclairs have a grim history."

"What does that mean?"

"Why, Alec? Sounds like you care."

Fisting the IDs hard enough they bend under pressure but don't crack, I state, "Anything to do with Harlow is my business. Who are these people?"

Freya swings her legs to the side to sit up and reaches for the IDs. Reluctantly, I hand them over. She glances at the names, her lips pursing, a seriousness settling over her that I didn't realize her capable of.

"Witches are supposed to be there for one another. There are few things witches value above all: their coven and their magick. What Violet and Arthur Hartman did was a betrayal unlike anything our community has ever seen. They turned against the Highridge Coven, killed their own, and kidnapped that girl when she was only eight-years-old."

"So they're not her birth parents?"

Freya shakes her head and flicks the tip of one of the ID cards. "No," she murmurs, "they're not, but they raised her as such after murdering Emily and John, then stealing their identities before disappearing into the human world."

Shit. I don't know why I care...but I do. This is...*fuck.*

"Why doesn't she know any of this?"

"They wiped her memory of everything before she was eight. That was right after binding her magick, something they continuously did over the years, to ensure she could never overpower them."

A rage settles in the base of my stomach with the picture of my little witch as an even younger witch; a child, terrified of being taken from her real family and then forced to forget them entirely.

"She had her powers, though." Enough to burn a house.

Freya smiles sadly, shaking her head. "Not all of them."

I drop into the second chair. "Tell me everything."

At the end of Freya's story, everything makes fucking sense. *Everything.*

Her confusion over the marks on her wrists. *They did that.*

The shoe box. All their hidden secrets.

Why Harlow doesn't live with her coven; they never kicked her out.

The fact her "parents" weren't able to save themselves from the fire. They were never the powerful Sinclairs they feigned being.

"They were earth witches."

Freya blinks. "Yeah, how'd you guess?"

"Smelled it in their room. When Harlow told me what happened, I found it strange that two fire witches couldn't put the blaze out."

"You're better than I guessed you'd be. Yeah, most trained witches *can* do other elemental magick outside of their own, but it's typically weak. The Hartmans knew enough to keep the show up."

My gaze returns to the shoe box. If Harlow knew all this, it'd kill her. Half her life was a lie. Her memories constantly stolen. The people she knew weren't who they claimed. Her magick being forever weakened from her true state.

Her magick...

Again, I look at the box, but this time with different considerations. For her to learn the people she loved were the villains in her story, it'd make her angry. Viciously angry.

Angry enough to spark the match her magick needs.

Hell, *I'm* pissed.

For her. I'm pissed for my Hellion. That she was deceived and the people who called her their daughter and earned her affection when they didn't deserve it. If they weren't already dead, I'd rip them apart limb by limb myself. I'd burn them alive again. I'd allow her to throw the match and revel as she danced on their ashes, letting her take charge of her own story for once.

"Your fangs are peeking out," Freya states in a sing-song voice. "So much emotion for the witch you hate. It's interesting."

"Your point?" I press into the chair, rubbing my tongue over my fangs until they ease the ache. "Surely this would spark a deep enough emotion to trigger her powers?"

Freya lifts a brow. "That's a choice you need to make. Do you show her the evidence, knowing it'll probably hurt her more than their deaths? Certainly anything more than you've done to her. All to trigger her magick, and thus the cure. Or do you save the pain, but possibly never gain the cure back?"

First one. Obviously.

I think.

Harlow will have to know, because the effect will be enough to meet my needs.

For Cora, I must.

But I don't want to harm Sinclair that way.

There's a strange notion of protection twisting me up, of wanting to keep her from this. It pulls on parts of me I didn't know to exist. Parts that want to soothe and protect her from the pain, to save and comfort her and allow her to cling to the positive memories she has. The Hartmans are gone and she's alive, and that's all that matters. Regardless of which set of parents were her real ones, *she's* living with the outcome, and her continuously drawing breath is all that matters to me. That she's *okay*—as much as she can be.

Freya gets to her feet, slapping her thighs. "Anyway, I'm off. You really are a pain in my ass."

"Wait." I snatch her arm before she can pull her disappearing act. "You knew, even back then. Why didn't you help her?"

She doesn't meet my eyes when she replies, "Because fate sucks.

I can't interfere in witches' lives when it happens for a reason. That past had to occur so the present can pass as it should."

"What does that mean?"

By the time I finish my question, my hand is gripping air, the First Witch gone.

TWENTY-TWO

Harlow

I have to get out of here.
 I pace towards the right side of the room.
 I have to get out of here.
Towards the left.
I have to—

On and on my laps go, my pace quickening after the first three.

For all the temporary peace that seemed to have been present between Alec and me when he shared his story, that's all it was: temporary. His kindness is nothing more than an act, a ploy to get me on his side.

Do I want my powers back? Obviously. But not to be a blood-sucker's revenge.

Which means needing to figure out how to get my magick back, if that's possible, but not tell him. Or to escape.

I stop in front of the window, staring at the afternoon sun. The very sun that'll burn Alec to death, which means if there's any hope of freeing myself, daytime is crucial. At the very least, hours would pass before he figured it out, and by then, ideally I'd be far away.

With a deep sigh, my forehead falls onto the glass. If only I had a way. I'll have to convince him to trust me enough that he starts keeping the bedroom door unlocked, but how long will that take?

Probably years of scheming, and even longer to have it unlocked during the daytime.

No, I decide. *This ends, and soon.*

My hand comes up to touch the glass, imagining the fresh air beyond it. It's that singular act that makes me realize what's right in front of me.

The window.

Making a fist, I knock on the glass, its echo telling me it isn't too thick. Breakable.

I twist, scanning the room in excitement. With something to break it, that could be my answer. The bed's too large to drag over and, even if I tried, I probably only would manage to get it a few inches by the time the sun sets and the vampire comes stalking me. That'll be a last resort. The bathroom? I could possibly rip the towel rod from the wall and stab it through the glass. That's only *if* I get it off the wall...

My gaze lands on the two chairs occupied by Alec and me earlier. They're very movable, large, and heavy. With enough force, I could potentially push them through the glass. At this point, anything's better than dying on his terms.

I head for the nearest one, turning it until the back is pressed against the pane. That's when I stop, when doubt creeps up. What am I thinking? This room's at least three storeys high. Jumping will be my death. I'd need a way to get down from this height.

Another scan of the room takes me to the bed again—and the blankets. A method used so many times in movies, where stunt people make it possible. It's a cliché...but a cliché that could work. It's a king-sized sheet and should, at the very least, cover one storey of the castle. Maybe?

Alec will wake up to find me splattered on the grass below.

But it's something. Right now, my only other plan is to somehow gain his trust, which would take years. It's now or never. While Alec is tucked away for the daytime, I *have* to do this, because nighttime when he's prowling isn't possible. Besides, running aimlessly over lands I have no clue how to navigate will be easier with sunlight.

With my potentially painful death now planned out, I head for the bed.

"Hecate, give me the damn strength. If you're still watching over me, make this work."

The pillows land on the other side of the room before I strip the bedding. First the top sheet, then the fitted one, tying them together with a million knots. I probably lose a few inches of material doing this, but I'd rather fall the extra few inches than have my rope unlink midway down.

With the two sheets tied together, I head for the second chair and loop the material around the leg in a tight knot. A firm yank proves it's tight, hopefully enough for my weight.

Weight. I'll need to weigh this chair down, or else it's falling through the open window with me, and my rope ladder will be useless.

I toss Gram's grimoire onto it, the thick and heavy leather-bound book a start, and then top it with the bag of clothing. In the bathroom, I grab every towel possible, adding it to my stack. Nothing besides the book is overly weighted, but hopefully all together, it'll be enough; they're my only options. There's nothing heavy in this place, annoyingly enough. Plus the weight of the chair itself may help.

And now, for the grand finale...

I again line the empty chair up to the window and walk backwards, all the way to the bed, for a running start. I don't let myself breathe or think, just push off and shove the chair against the window.

It successfully cracks the glass, a crooked line running down the centre.

"Yes!"

Feeling energized by the possibility of escape *right there*—that my stupid, maniac plan is actually working—I reposition the chair to repeat the process. This time, it makes the crack expand, the splintering of glass music to my ears, before tumbling through, taking most of the window with it. The sound of freedom whooshes in, followed by the smell of escape. Euphoria runs through my veins, and I bounce on the balls of my feet, happy *something* in my life worked for once.

Taking one of the towels from my weighted stack, I clear the shards of glass still around the window to avoid injury when I climb through. Once satisfied with the cleaning, I push the chair beside the wall, hoping the corner will help keep it in place.

"I can't believe I'm about to do this," I murmur to the empty room. To Alec, who's tucked away in his quarters, wherever those are. I wonder if he heard the noise, if he'll be here soon.

Just in case he will be, and before I question my sanity a moment longer, I toss the tied-together sheets out the window, watching them fall the length of the castle's siding. It stops about a dozen feet from the ground.

Grasping my end, I sit on the edge of the window and carefully inch myself out, twisting until my feet are on stone and I'm somehow successfully propelling myself down.

This is actually working. By some miracle, the chair hasn't moved, everything seems to be going as planned. I begin to slide down faster, spurred on by freedom being *so* close. Just a few dozen more feet to go.

Halfway down, the sheet slides me a few inches farther down.

"Shit." My gaze darts above me, spotting the chair now on the edge of the window and not where it should be.

Gotta hurry before this gets bad.

My hands move faster, but my jerky movements cause the chair to inch closer to the sill.

"Fuck."

Suddenly my grip is useless as it all comes crashing toward me, chair included.

"Fuck, fuck, fuck!"

The ground rushes toward me, my arms scrambling to retain a pointless grip on the sheet.

This is where I die. Goddess, save me.

Clenching, I brace for the impact, trying to angle my body in a way that'll be the least painful. Back or feet, I haven't decided yet, but I have mere milliseconds before it's too late and—

The air freezes. The chair hovers above me, the sheet suspended midair.

I'm the only thing still moving, but now at a much slower rate. My back meets the grass, and I scramble out of the way of the suspended items right before everything unfreezes and comes crashing down, landing around me, my clothing and Gram's grimoire scattering.

"Thank you, Goddess," I breathe, pushing to my feet.

I scan the castle's side, all the way up to the window I managed to escape from. It worked. It *actually* worked. A bubble of laughter explodes from my chest, the mingling of pleasure and excitement that I'm free is overwhelming.

Free as long as I can get the hell away from here.

"See ya, Alec Dormer. It's been fun."

I turn and take off down the grassy field, not sure where I am or how close I am to civilization. I might be running towards nothing or everything. I might be running for a while before finding humans. But I'll keep going, running as long as he's hunting me.

By the time I reach the edge of the treeline and immerse myself in the forest, the sun is lowering. There's only hours until nighttime.

That's when Alec will come.

TWENTY-THREE

Alec

I didn't mean to rest, considering it was only the other night I had. Clearly, dealing with Sinclair's antics is exhausting enough it drove me to.

When I get up, I grab the shoebox of lies that'll hopefully spark something so big in her, it'll be a few flames. With it, I head towards her room, sending a rapid knock against the door, disbelieving my own actions. Although I have no qualms about seeing her undressed, we have bigger things to deal with than arguing.

After a moment, there's still no answer.

"Sinclair, I was warning, not asking."

I slip the key into the door at the precise second my senses pick up on two things: the whoosh of wind and the slightly faded scent of my witch.

I'm inside instantly, the box dropping to the ground in my rush towards the destroyed window.

She can't be that stupid...

I peer through the glassless, damaged opening, spotting the two wingback chairs on the ground, one with its legs broken, and the scattering of her clothing, towels, and her grandmother's book.

She is. She's *that* stupid.

Tricky fucking witch. I'd smile if I weren't so pissed. Could appreciate her determination and creativity if I didn't dislike it so much. Her determination truly would make an excellent vampire, if she didn't have so much of that witchy cunning.

I step from the window, the ground and my feet coming together in a slight *thud* with impact. I study the items all around me, and then the grounds bathed in nightfall.

Sinclair knew precisely what she was doing. She planned and waited until I would be unable to come for her, but all she's done is piss me off. No matter how far she's run in however long it's been since her daring escape, I *will* catch her. And when I do...

A few different outcomes flit through my mind, each one more inviting than the last.

Finding her is my first task. Punishing her will come later.

Hunt.

Chase.

Kill.

Hunt.

Chase.

Feed.

My senses attune to her. My eyes shut for a moment, picturing the direction my scared little witch took off to. My nose picks up her trail on the wind, as though the very nature witches pray to is on my side rather than hers. My fangs lengthen, readying to attack, and my eyes are taken over with a bloodred coating as the monster is released from his cage.

Harlow Sinclair is no longer revenge for my sister's death. She's my prey.

And I'll soon remind her why running from a vampire is a bad fucking idea.

It's dark with very little light seeping through the treetops. It's cloudy tonight, so the nearly full moon is mostly covered. It's appropriate that the darkness is on my side, which has me wondering how she's faring with vision equivalent to a mortal's.

Her trail zigzags through the forest. Crafty witch, but smart too, as she's obviously trying to confuse my tracking abilities by not running in a straight line. At one point, she doubles back before taking a different direction. All these tricks are costing her; she won't be as far as she could be without the detours.

Scurrying scared, knowing eventually I'd figure out her ploy. Probably getting tired by now, considering her body is no better than a mortal's, and without magick, she has no advantage. Between us, I'm able to go all night, while at some point, she'll collapse.

Hunt.

Chase.

Kill.

Her scent is stronger near a tree, and I suspect this is where she took a break. Without water, surely she won't be able to go on much longer. I continue in the direction her scent continues, pushing through thick shrubbery.

In the branches, blowing with the wind, are strands of orange-red. Hair that's evidently been ripped from her scalp during her determination to go the most difficult route. Chuckling, I unloop them from the branches and release them into the wind. They blow behind me, in the direction of my castle, exactly where Sinclair will be locked within when I catch her.

After the hair disappears from view, I dart off again. With every step, her scent intensifies. I've doubled what she ran in hours in mere minutes.

Yet she believed she could escape me? I'll prove why that was a stupid idea.

Hunt.

Chase.

Kill.

I suck in a breath through my mouth, swallowing the scent of her fear. It prickles the roof of my mouth. Have I ever craved a being's blood as much as I do hers? No, and I doubt there will ever be anyone else who makes me so ravenous. And it *is* her—all her. I'd been around dozens of Sinclairs, and not one of them had me dreaming of draining her dry in every manner possible.

A lifetime of self-preservation demands I don't believe Freya's claim that I'm too old for the weakened cure to be effective. But the short few days of craving my witch wipes away all that sensibility and demands I consume.

After another few steps, my ears pick up something that suggests I'm close.

Her tiny pants. Her breathing is ragged, lined with exhaustion and fear.

I smile.

Continuing at a walking pace, I catch up quicker than she can escape. Through the tree trunks, I spot her, hair streaming behind her. I match my next few steps to her heartbeat, memorizing the sound as it ricochets through my brain and sanity, demanding I feed.

I flick my tongue against a fang. *Soon.*

I can't fucking wait...but only after I play with my food. After all, that hunt passed too quickly. She made the rules for round one, so now, it's my turn to design the second round.

Unfortunately for her, I don't play fair nor easy.

I let her run a few more feet, wallowing in the sense of satisfaction that she's managed to escape. It's thrilling, seeing her believe she's a winner in a game I've been playing since before her birth.

Silly little witch doesn't even peek behind her as she flees. So confident that she has this. She pushes between two trees when I streak by, my steps cracking on nearby twigs.

She gasps, spinning, but I'm already gone, shielded by the shadows of trees too far for her weak eyes to pick up.

Once she starts sprinting another direction, I do it again, and she yet again stops, scanning the trees.

"Alec, stop fucking around! I know it's you."

It could be the wolves and bears that also roam these woods, but unfortunately for her, I'm the most dangerous hunter on her trail.

She starts running again, her feet making all sorts of mess in how they kick up sticks and leaves. This time when I catch up, she slams into me, face in my chest, her curse disrupting the silent woods.

Once regaining her footing, she stares, finally understanding what she's done. "I, I had to. You would have too if you were in my position."

She doesn't wait for my answer before bolting, this time towards the right. Now it's adorable defiance, because the game's up. I've caught her, so she seriously can't believe she'll escape now?

By the next tree, she glances over her shoulder, but I haven't moved. I wait for her to face forward before robbing her of escape once again.

"You've fucked up, Hellion, and now you have to pay the price of your carelessness."

She backs up, blown eyes darting around as the perfect little prey. For every two steps she takes, I take one. Her attention scurries to me like a scared bunny when sticks crack beneath my weight.

"Y-you can't attack. You can't drink from me. You'll die."

I tilt my head, focusing on her pulse. "Sounds like you care."

"I don't. It's a warning."

A warning that not only will I ignore, but I'll gamble my immortality on if only for a better taste than the one she forced on me the other night.

"I have a warning for you as well." My chin lowers, lips lifting until she can see exactly how extended my fangs are. How hungry she's made me. "I have your scent memorized. You can run all night long, but there's nowhere you'll hide that I won't be able to find you."

She licks her lips, her nervous energy only feeding my hunger that much more. "I only have to make it 'til sunrise."

I glance between the trees and towards the horizon. "Night fell not even an hour ago. You have a long night of evading me if you wish to make it until morning."

"Then that's what I'll do."

I chuckle, the sound slithering through the trees and wrapping her in my taunt. "Please do, Miss Sinclair, and make it fun for me while you're at it."

"F-fun?" She jumps a few more steps, almost tripping on her ass.

"Fun," I repeat, continuing my slow but steady pace towards her. "Vampires are natural predators, and you, little Sinclair, are my prey. You made yourself so the second you thought to escape my home. So please, run, and allow me the thrill of the hunt, because when I catch you, you'll regret every step you've taken during this ridiculous attempt."

I pause, waiting for her to rush off, but she continues watching me with the same intensity I am her. Guarded, her back stiff, hands rubbing on her thighs. Clearly she needs more incentive.

"Run, Hellion. *Run.*"

This time, she obeys, streaking through the forest, cutting between trees and foliage, her pants music to my fucking ears. Her heartbeat lays the precise path I'll soon follow—but only after a few moments. When she gets far enough away she believes she has a shot, that's when I'll go.

Her scent eventually fades, as does the sound of her attempt. I check my phone, expecting minutes to have passed since letting her go, but nearly a full hour has instead. Time passes so quickly when a thrilling hunt is on.

No matter, because the farther I have to track her, the tastier victory will be.

The hungrier I grow.

I take off in the direction she did, trailing her scent. This time, it's a straight line because she assumed I'd be close behind her. She got decently far, I'll admit, but I catch up in mere minutes, spotting her bent over between the trees.

Now, now, you shouldn't have stopped running. You make it too easy.

Like she's heard my thoughts, she begins sprinting again, but this time I don't let her get far before I'm on her, arms wrapping her waist and taking us both to the ground. I spin so I'm beneath her, cushioning the fall so the forest floor doesn't hurt her, but quickly roll us both over until I'm crouched above her on my hands and knees.

The faintest streak of fear flits through her gaze at the same time her scent alters to something spicier, something forbidden—lust. I wrench her head to the side, clearing the path for me to make the single stupidest, and probably most fatal, mistake of my immortal life, but unable to stop myself either.

Without rhyme or reason, without a counter to every reason I shouldn't, I jam my fangs into her neck and begin drinking.

Euphoria races through me.

Bliss.

Thirst—and the answer to it.

Feed. Drain her dry.

And then something else. Another feeling—another sensation. One as unwelcoming as everything else Sinclair has brought to my life.

Protect. Care for her. Keep her safe.

Immediately followed by the sensation of being pushed off the edge. Of being no longer myself. Of being ripped apart, shredded from the inside out, all by this woman.

No…no, it's impossible.

A word slices through me, clearer than anything else, awakening instincts I've never before felt.

Bride.

My Bride.

My mate…

THIRD INTERMISSION

Freya

Remember when I said fate is a fickle bitch? Well, this is her coming through.

Let's recap: Alec, our lovely resident vampire king—who doesn't act how a king should, but what do I know?—is mated to Harlow Sinclair, the youngest of the exact family he vowed a lifetime of revenge and retribution towards.

Fate sucks, doesn't it?

The biggest kicker is that vampires cherish their Brides—their term for mate—above all else. Mating amongst vampires, a creature who's naturally solitary, is very uncommon. Not quite to a rarity, but certainly uncommon. So when one finds their Bride, there's nothing in Heaven, Hell, the Otherworld, or Earth they won't fight to protect them from.

Hatred and his protective instincts will be a bitch to deal with. For Alec, anyway.

Shame, eh?

I, meanwhile, am enjoying the heck out of this. So settle in, because the drama is *long* from over. We still have to see a certain witch regain her magick and a vampire learn to utterly despise himself.

More popcorn? Maybe candy this time? Hm, choices...

TWENTY-FOUR

Harlow

Math was always my shittiest subject, but even I guessed the odds of tonight going as planned were not high. Successfully escaping from the castle alive and unbroken; I was only about thirty percent certain that would work.

Getting far enough away in the hours until night: fifty-fifty, considering I couldn't be certain how far away civilization is or how large this forest is.

But once he caught up to me? Told me to run in a voice I felt within the deepest part of my core, where a nearly forbidden desire bloomed? Zero fucking percent.

I had my shot—*did I, though?*—but once he found me, I knew there'd be nowhere I could run fast or far enough that he wouldn't catch up again. Which is why when the strange silence is shattered by the single crack behind me, I know the game's up.

He's found me. Again.

Arms wrap around my waist, yanking me towards the ground. I think I scream, but the sound's too tangled in utter fear over what Alec is about to do.

He scared me from the beginning, when he appeared in my bedroom, considering he's a vampire intent on hurting me. But that fear was only background level, mingling with a curiosity of the unknown. When he paraded me in front of his friends, I wasn't scared, not really, despite the numerous bloodsuckers who'd kill me without a second thought. Because I knew he wouldn't let any of them touch me.

I think tonight is the first time I've felt complete terror towards him.

This isn't him being mean or playful in my room or the cell, where all his games have been pointless taunts. No, this is pure danger in its most basic form. His fangs are longer than I've ever seen, his eyes a bright, eager crimson. Desperation drips from him— desperation to feed on *me*. He doesn't seem bothered by the fact that my defective cure will make him ill and kill him.

Alec slides his body beneath mine to take the impact of the fall, which I'm grateful for. The moment we're down, his legs bracket mine and, in a flash, he's crouched over me. I'm still, motionless in both anxiety and uncertainty as I take in who—what—is above me.

A monster. A literal monster, who doesn't seem to recall the numerous times he's reassured me he wouldn't kill me. No, this is Alec in his ruthless form. It's the ultimate reminder he isn't human. He'll hurt me without blinking, without an ounce of sympathy. He'll do whatever he feels will serve his revenge needs.

I'm utterly *fucked*.

Alec smiles the faintest bit, but it's nothing friendly. It's the smile of a victor. Of the predator whose prey got caught in the snare. Of the shadows right before they encompass the light.

He bends, his lips brushing along my neck as his hand wrenches my head to the side. Panic spikes, my mouth opening to yell out his name or something to get him off me, but before the words form, I feel *it*.

Twin fangs imbed into my neck, right over my pulse, and blood gushes from my body into his mouth, a river of crimson releasing all the parts of me that have been hiding. Alec's uncovering them all sip by sip, stealing them for himself, baring me in ways no one else has ever been able to.

The initial sting quickly fades into a calming sensation, and I understand what he meant by feeding being sexualized. I may have been terrified seconds ago, but with every pass of his tongue, I'm willing to be whatever he wants me to be so long as he doesn't stop.

A moan builds in my throat, but releasing it admits what I can never admit.

And then, he stills and stops drinking. A line of blood runs down my neck and over my collarbone before meeting the ground, and slowly, his fangs unhook from my neck.

I should be thrilled, should push him away and take off. Maybe he's feeling the effects of the cure he assumed he was above. Maybe, for all his talk about punishment, he's satisfied with only this.

Eyes veiled with red but tinged with black—with restraint threatening to return—stares back, wide—shocked.

"No." The whisper sounds more guttural around his fangs, coloured with my blood. More slides from the corner of his mouth towards his chin, and I find myself reaching up to smudge it, a trance-like sensation sweeping me away.

He flinches before I make contact, scrambling off me before he's a blur across the space, pressing his back to a tree. The only movement is the subtle flare of his nostrils.

I sit up. "What is it?"

He twitches, his fingers splitting the tree's bark. "Impossible. What the *fuck* have you *done,* witch?"

Did he transform? He seems very much a vampire still. I touch my neck, covering it with my palm to ease the bleeding.

"What have *I* done? You were the one attacking—"

"No," he interrupts in a growl. "No, this isn't possible. Your fucking coven *cursed* me. This—you—is all some ploy, isn't it?"

I stand, getting the sense I might be fighting for my life soon. "What ploy?"

He growls, red consuming the little bit of black he's regained as he stalks forward before abruptly stopping. "Stay there, don't move." He moves, though, in another step before once again stopping. "Actually—no. *Run.* Go! Leave."

"So you can chase me again? Game's up. I realize I'm not getting away from—"

"Leave!"

I freeze despite the command. He sounds so...so desperate. That's when I notice what I didn't earlier; the quiver in his arms and his fangs digging into his bottom lip. The way his entire body vibrates, the way he continues pacing towards me but stops despite every nerve and muscle wired to keep going.

Oh, Goddess. If I felt like prey before... No, *this* is...this is bad.

"Run north. You'll find a road."

He's letting me go? This isn't a game? Too unlikely.

Still unsure what's going on, I let my eyes sweep over him, silently saying goodbye before turning the opposite direction. Hopefully I'm angled north, or at least somewhat close enough I'll figure out the way.

A final peek over my shoulder shows him still in the same spot. It's too dark and I'm too far away to see where his eyes are, but I feel them. My neck throbs under the memory of his teeth, my core tightening with desires unnamed. With a force I shouldn't tempt again.

This better not be another cruel game and he's actually letting me go despite everything that just happened. His strange behaviour has me doubting the truth behind his words.

Another glance before he disappears from view. He's still there.

I run for a few minutes, obsessively checking behind me. Heart pounding and feet aching, I continue. I've been on them for too long, my body dragged down with exhaustion.

A wall appears out of nowhere, feeling like I've run into literal bricks. I don't need to look to know who's caught up, the bloodsucking *liar*. The liar who seeps desperation and fatigue, like he hasn't slept in years, shadowy marks etched beneath bloodred eyes and a jaw clenched so tight, I'd believe he could break his own teeth.

"Harlow."

My given name on his mouth causes me to pause. He spoke it like I would when calling on Hecate; with reverence, a gentleness so opposite from his usual malice. I miss the moment when he grabs me, backing me against the nearest tree, gaze trained on his bite from before.

"Alec..."

Ignoring me, he forces my head to the side, and his teeth slide into the holes he's already made. The sting is so minor, then I'm right back to being swept away. Only this time, I cling to a shred of sanity that *something isn't right*. I buck my hips and push against him, but he only pins my arms.

"Stop fighting me," he mumbles into my skin before gulping deeper.

"Y-you told me to!"

He lets up again to repeat words already spoken. "You've fucked up. If this is a trick meant to trap or deceive me, you're out of luck, Hellion, because now you won't be going anywhere."

"You're insane." I shove him, trying to twist my head from his impossible grip. I'd sooner break my own neck, I think.

"Not yet," he replies darkly. "But you're about to make me so. You're going to be good for me. You're going to let me taste you."

Do I have a choice? Those didn't sound like questions but rather facts.

Before my next breath, he drinks, only a few sips before he forces my head to the other side, impaling the skin there. Stinging pain flutters away for pleasure, but it doesn't slow the survival instinct having me fight, kick, and push against him, making no more progress than if I were fighting a wall.

Come on, powers. If there's ever a time for you to return, this would be it.

"Alec!"

He growls before his fangs slide from my neck, but I'm anything but successful when his eyes clash with mine. They're a red so dark, they're depthless. A void I'll lose myself inside. One hand comes up to my face, strangely tender, another revere.

"You taste fucking *divine*. Like my greatest sin. At least, that's what you're about to become."

Before I fully comprehend his words, his mouth slashes against mine. He kisses as angrily as he drinks, dominating in his claim. His tongue slides over mine as his hand delves into my hair to control the angle. His fangs slip against my lip, but he's careful. He releases my hair to instead rest his palm on the base of my neck. It's there he feels my breathy moan, and his kiss grows frenzied—too frenzied—and for all his caution, one of his fangs nick my bottom lip.

He swipes his tongue along the stinging cut, blowing ragged breath against me. Him being so close shows the drops of perspiration on his forehead, the skin taut around his eyes.

Sweat. *Did* he begin the transformation?

"I fucking *hate* your kind." His harsh words contradict his gentle hold right before he kisses me again, his tongue pushing blood inside my mouth. It's sour and metallic but not gross. It's almost *right*, like kissing Alec shouldn't taste like anything else.

He releases me, and the tree disappears. The air grows increasingly cold, my head a convoluted mess of blood loss and overtiredness as my vision completely blurs. I'm about to reach for him, beg him to stop, tell him I'm passing out, when I'm abruptly a lot warmer, the sky is darker, and then my back meets softness.

I look around. Stone walls. Above, there's a black canopy. An unlit fireplace along the far wall.

"My bedroom," he explains. "If I'm going to damn myself more than I already am, then I want your blood soaking my sheets when I do."

Busy making sense of our environment change, the fact that he just ran through the woods at some crazy insane speed, I miss when he grabs my shirt by the collar and rips it.

He's quick, and suddenly my bra is gone, torn at the centre, and his mouth descends towards my chest, sucking a nipple into his mouth.

Fuck, this feels like heaven.

Regardless, it shouldn't be happening. I push his shoulders, but my fight only spurs him on. His tongue massages my nipple, sweeping me away to a place where right and wrong no longer exists.

"Alec...stop."

Shockingly enough, he listens, but not without obvious effort. He rises on shaking arms. It's then I realize he's *not* meaning to harm me. His next words, a whispered breath tinged with distress, solidify the revelation.

"Fight me, Harlow. Tell me you don't want this. I won't be able to harm you."

I'd scoff if he didn't sound so sincere. "Since when?"

"Since you've cursed me."

"What are you talking about?"

Ignoring me, he reaches for my pants. "I mean it. Fight me. Right now. Fight me and run."

"Why? So you can chase me again? I'm tired of your fucked-up games, Alec."

"This isn't a game." In a flash, he's above me, his fingers pinching my cheeks until my entire focus is on him. He breathes out once, his exhale warm against my skin. His brows lower, a tortured plea for me to really listen. "I mean it. I can't—*won't*—hurt you, but you *have* to make your intent known. If you don't...you're damned. As damned as I am."

Confusion clouds me alongside exhaustion, blood loss, and

desire. I *shouldn't* be lying here. I should be begging him to release me. But tell that to my libido, who's apparently making every wrong choice.

Alec releases my face to trail down my body, his teeth nipping but not breaking skin. He chuckles into my stomach before his nose presses into the edge of my pants. He inhales deeply, his rumble filling the room's silence.

"If your blood is divinity, then your pussy will be fucking nirvana."

He wrenches my pants down my legs, and my feet move to help, not quite sure of my own actions. It's only when I'm left in nothing but panties that the fog momentarily clears—the realization of where I am and who's with me—and I push myself upright.

He goes stiff, watching me the way a snake stalks a mouse before striking. Slow and calculating. "Say it, Hellion, or burn alongside me."

"What is happening? What have you done to me?"

"What have *I* done to *you*?" He laughs again, running a finger through the blood on my neck, smearing it. He gathers a few drops before drawing a circle around a nipple, my body heating with his sensual touch. "What the fuck have *you* done to *me* is the better question. Was it you or your ancestors who thought to curse me?"

"I still have no idea what you're talking about."

"That's the problem." With a gentle tap to my chest, Alec knocks me back to the mattress. "You don't know, and you haven't run. You haven't begged for your freedom." Two fingers stroke over my panties, heat building in the base of my stomach as my insides come alive. He nudges them aside, finding me ready. "For freedom, for me to stop...you haven't pleaded to the side of me that'll protect you above all else, which means I now get to act on my basest desires. The instinct that demands I *claim* you."

I'm still processing his words when he shoves two fingers inside me, and my back arches off the bed.

TWENTY-FIVE

Alec

*T*ake her. Claim her. Make her ours.

Instincts consume, battling with my inner demons—the desires that have driven me to this point.

Kill her. End her. End all this.

If only I didn't bite her, I'd never know what I believe I've suspected all along. Looking back, it all makes so much fucking sense. The way her blood—cure aside—smelled so delectable. The way I couldn't truly harm her. The numbness I felt when finding her lethargic in the cell. Reflexes buried knew I had to protect her... even if I didn't understand why.

My fingers sink inside her, and her back bows with a guttural sigh. She's unbelievably tight. A virgin? Fuck, I hope so. To find out my Bride will know me and me alone satisfies the basest parts of the monster within. And to taste virgin blood...that would be a first.

Even the thought makes me groan, my hunger for her never to be satisfied.

"Beg," I command, stroking two fingers inside her core, stretching her.

Beg me to stop.

Beg me to save us.

"Please," she murmurs, not at all understanding I needed her to beg to end this.

Hatred and lust pour into my touch as her legs fall farther apart. It's like this I study my Bride; the blood painted across her chest, the bite marks on her neck, everything declaring her as *mine*. Everything that'll ensure she never leaves.

Fuck, I hate you. Even thinking the words makes my head ache, because the drive to keep her safe and protected won't allow me to hate her. But it's not *her* I hate. Not anymore. Maybe not ever. She's always intrigued me above all others of her family.

"Say no."

Her shattered breathing tells me *yes*, which only pisses me off.

"Tell me no," I demand. *Tell me no so I can stop this before you hate me. Before you believe I've forced you.*

"No...don't stop."

Damn you, Hellion.

An emotion weaves through me, one that's new, drifting along the connection—the bond—that's fragmented but slowly linking into place between Harlow and me, like a ribbon being laid, a spell being cast. Slow and steady, the mating bond forms.

From it, emotions that are not my own drift towards me. It's her—her feelings that, when I focus, I'll be able to feel as though they're my own. The link that'll allow me to sense her, to know when she needs to be cared for or protected. For now, only one-sided.

I search through the wave coming from her unknowingly into me, seeking distaste, hatred, or some other negativity, but find nothing. A fact as troubling as everything else. Uneasiness, uncertainty, but not fright as her craving grows as strong as mine is.

That, too, satisfies me. Last thing I want is for her to be with me out of fear.

"Alec, please." She bucks into my hand, and I'm utterly fucked. The sight of her, all sprawled open, her skin darkening as the blood rushes through her body...it's heady. She's beautiful, her expression twisting as she chases pleasure.

So I stop thinking about the past and present that got us here, the bond being positioned between us. Stop considering anything but *her* and her pleasure. And my own desire to taste her everywhere.

"Please what?" I ask, settling into position. "You asking to come, Hellion? Is that what you need?"

"Yes."

Ducking down, I swipe my tongue over her clit, ending her hissed response. The liquid flowing from her pussy is greater than divinity, as guessed. There's nothing on Earth, besides maybe her blood, that is more appealing. There's something mystical to the flavour, as though invented in Heaven by the angels themselves, except Heaven is so far out of reach for us both.

"Your fucking taste..." My mumble remains unfinished, no words quite able to describe it.

I lick her while fucking her with my fingers, my other hand resting on her hip to still her movements. I have to maintain dominance over her before she makes me lose myself entirely, as my control is getting shredded with every little gasp, moan, and cry she releases from her pretty little throat.

I *must* claim her, that much I'm aware. If I don't fuck her and satisfy the mate bond, it'll remain unfinished and eventually drive me to madness.

Unless she fights me. Tells me no. It's a fine line, because no matter how much I need to claim her, the monster inside me won't be able to hurt her. In the end, my Bride has the ultimate choice.

And she's choosing wrong...

I swipe my tongue over her clit again as my fingers slow, teasing her insides, not letting her come yet. Not until I get my fangs in her thigh. I nuzzle the area until her breath hikes before piercing her skin and sliding my teeth cleanly inside.

"Yes," she groans, her thighs clamping around my head, but I force them back to the bed.

With her juices on my tongue and her blood in my mouth, my cock is painfully hard, eager to bury itself inside her. But she has to come like this. Just like this. I *need* it.

Once again, I press into the sensitive spot inside her, and she bucks into my hand, her thighs pushing against my grip. Her moan fills my room, a sound my immortal memory will savour for days, months, even years, to come. Her cunt clamps down as I finger-fuck her through her orgasm. I drink harder, my tongue massaging her thigh as blood flows freely, a part of me demanding I stay right here for the rest of the night.

She's panting when I unhook my fangs and slide my fingers from her. I rise up, needing to see for myself she's okay, and am greeted with a tentative smile.

"That was...um." Her cheeks go red. Harlow's almost too beautiful for her own good.

Harlow.

From the moment I realized what she is to me, she stopped being Sinclair.

She's my Hellion. My Harlow.

I can't respond. Words refuse to formulate into sentences that'll actually be comprehensible to her.

I move off her and the bed, stripping my clothes quickly, the material an irritating barrier between our bodies. Longing pulses through me, my gaze bouncing between her face and her pussy, my cock twitching at the sight of both. But utterly undone when she bites her bottom lip.

Take her.

Claim her.

My Bride.

Once stripped, I rejoin her on the bed—*my* bed. She's the first in centuries to ever be here.

And the last.

I readjust her body farther up the mattress, and the monster inside rumbles in contentment when she doesn't fight me positioning her arms above her head. My fingers stroke against her scars, a fresh hatred pouring into me, more intense now than when Freya explained them.

She *needs* to stop being so perfectly submissive before both our lives are forever changed.

No—she must submit. She needs to let me take her. She has to become mine. Fully, completely, utterly mine. I must devour every part of her. Every tear she'll ever shed. Every smile. Every laugh. Every drop of blood.

All.

Fucking.

Mine.

"You okay?"

Her question nudges my consciousness, and my teeth, pressed together so tightly, slowly unclamp as I return to the present. Return to *her*. Always her. Forever her.

Fuck, I can't do this.

"Yes," I manage, while begging her to *see* inside my head. To feel my emotions as I do hers. Her curiosity, her desire, her nerves. It's all too much.

Stop me, Harlow.

Submit to me, Harlow.

The two thoughts battle one another until there's a clear victor. Until my grip tightens and I position her arms even higher, making her back bow. She's completely subservient, the monster inside me thrilled to be able to take her, consequences be damned.

And there *will* be consequences. A whole fucking load of them.

I position myself between her legs, my cock brushing her wet core, but I don't enter her. Not yet. Not until I look her in the face and see her thoughts for myself.

She stares back expectant—hopeful.

I'm undone.

I'm fucked.

We're fucked.

Stroking along her pussy again, I coat myself in her cum before nudging my head inside her. Her breath catches. She's tight but stretches, her shoulders rolling into the pillow, tugging her wrists.

I grip tighter, my teeth snapping. "Submit, Hellion."

She immediately stops moving, and I search the bond, finding apprehension as her eyes eventually reopen. "Are you going to kill me?"

"No."

"Are you planning on releasing me?"

Never. But I can't tell her that. She has to stay close, protected, and in my bed for the rest of eternity.

I bottom out inside her, pulling out only once to coat my cock. She takes all of me easily without threat of a barrier, which makes me want to kill something—*someone*—whoever's been inside her in the past.

For now, I thrust, bouncing her head against the pillow, and her pile of red hair spilling everywhere captures my attention. She looks *right* here, like this bed was made for her.

"Fuck, you feel fantastic."

She only moans in response, pushing her hips against mine and matching me stroke for stroke, her own thrusts getting harder, quicker. She's perfect.

I bend over, grasp her neck, and haul her upright, taking her mouth in a single rough kiss. She kisses me back before I pull away and slide my teeth into one of the bite marks on her neck. Her pussy clamps down tighter, her head falling back with a whine. She's limp in my arms, thighs bracketing mine as I continue pushing into her.

Nails scrape my lower arms, the faint pain urging me to suck harder, urging more blood into my mouth. There's never enough, and there will never *be* enough.

Mark me, Hellion. Make me yours.

I drink faster, harder, my orgasm creeping closer, and that does it for her. She goes stiff in my arms, her pussy clamping tight.

"Alec...*fuck*. I'm coming, I'm coming...I'm—"

I remove my fangs from her skin to speak. "You're doing so good, Harlow. You feel amazing. Can you come again, my beautiful witch? All for me. All fucking mine."

She has no idea what she truly agrees to when, in between heavy breaths, she manages to nod. Blood trickles from her throat over her shoulder, and a drop plummets to the sheets, laying her claim upon this bed as surely as her soul has to mine.

I flip us over, sitting on the edge of the bed with her on my lap. Her hair tumbles over her shoulder, but she's quick to push it away. My hands tighten around her waist, pulling her down on me while I thrust up. Like this, the normal lavender of her eyes darkens with lust, and her lips part as she tries to speak, only for her attempt to be quickly stolen by a low gasp.

"You're deep," she finally manages to whisper.

"Mhm." Not sure I'm capable of speaking as my gaze latches onto her neck and my numerous bite marks. I want more. I want her blood as she orgasms around me.

I fist her breasts, bringing them up to my mouth. She watches, breathless, as I flick my tongue against both nipples and drag a fang along one, teasing the possibility.

"You want this?" I pause, waiting for her response, half expecting a *no*, except a breathless little *"Yes,"* comes instead.

Keeping her gaze, I take a nipple into my mouth, lapping the nub as my fangs score the upper side of her breast before pushing down. She gasps, her eyes clamping shut in pain. Her hips stop moving, but I finish my bite, sucking very little blood in my mouth as I wait for her pain to pass.

"It's good," she whispers after a moment, a nod encouraging me to continue.

I have to be careful. Between her escape, sex, and the blood I've consumed from her, she's bound to be weakening soon.

But until she shows signs, I suck, my tongue flicking her nipple while drinking. I keep an arm around her waist and hold her tight, fucking her as deep and fast as her body will take.

My Bride.

It's a marvel. *She's* a marvel. The entire fact she's my mate.

But it's also the worst thing that could have happened to either of us.

"I hate you," I murmur into her skin, the pressure building at the base of my cock.

But I don't hate her. I hate Elizabeth Sinclair for murdering Cora. I hate whichever Sinclair witch made Harlow become my downfall. I hate Violet and Arthur Hartman for lying to my Bride and murdering her real family. I hate this situation...but not her.

"I hate you too," she murmurs in return. "It's why I ran."

I lift from her breast to look her in the face, to admit as much as I'm able to. "You fucked up when you did. You have no idea what you've done. If you didn't run, I wouldn't have attacked."

Her hips still, her body leaning backwards into my arm. "Are you *seriously* blaming me?"

My free hand weaves through her hair, keeping her in place should she attempt to leave. "Yes, because you were placed in my life to wreck everything."

"Wreck every—" Her words cut off when I slam her down harder. "What...did...I...wre—"

Her body bows, this time interrupting her own question. Her hair brushes the back of my arm as she goes motionless, her body tense and convulsing around my cock. With her orgasm, mine won't be held back any longer.

I bury my head into her shoulder, tongue laving over a bite

mark as I shoot inside her, groaning into her skin. Marking her inside and out with *me*.

No one will ever go near her.

No one will ever look at her.

No one will ever touch her.

She's mine.

All. Fucking. *Mine.*

Now and forever. For eternity.

As my orgasm slows and she's coming down from hers, her body going lax in my arms, I drag my nose up the column of her throat, smelling a combination of me and her. Of the cure, nature, everything forbidden in the world.

For the first time in centuries, I relax, turning us to rest against the pillows. It's my little Hellion's new permanent place, even if she's unaware.

I have to tell her.

Now. Soon. Eventually.

She looks utterly disheveled. A mess from her run, from being attacked in the woods, from our fucking.

She looks like *mine*.

The one in this blasted, eternal world who can end my immortal soul by a single act of her own hand.

The one who's now forced to walk in the shadows with me for the rest of our lives.

The one whom my entire body is attuned into. To protect, care for, be whatever she needs from me.

Fuck. My head thumps. Seeing Harlow—a goddamn Sinclair— in my bed is everything wrong. It's everything right...but it's also everything that should never be.

Only bliss comes through the bond as she smiles up at me. Her happiness is too much. She should hate me. Hate me so I can actually hate her in return and attempt to end this fucking connection —if such a thing is possible.

Protect. Keep her.

Has there been a situation of a vampire ending a bond with their Bride? I haven't heard of one, but it must be possible. *Must* be...or I'll go mad. I can't keep her.

Even considering the possibility of breaking the bond makes my insides churn, a feeling I've never had during my life as an immortal. But she makes me weak.

She's also a weakness I'm stuck with.

Harlow

He's staring at me like he's never seen me before. As though *he's* not the one who acted so fucking odd tonight.

Kidnapping me—that made sense. He's a vampire while I have the cure. I rationalized his reasoning.

Locking me up—again, from his perspective, I get it.

Selling my blood—not right, but I've processed his reasoning.

Chasing me through the woods—he was pissed I escaped. It was expected.

But everything after that? The taunting, the biting, the sex. The way he seemed to be fighting himself every second of the way until I gave him permission.

Alec studies me as intensely as I am him, but for once, he doesn't seem like he's the hunter. He looks terrified, if I didn't know better. His expression is taut, body wound tighter than a rope.

"What was—"

He gets out of bed, retrieves his pants, and heads for the door.

"Alec!" I scramble upright, a wave of dizziness washing over me. Maybe he drank too much. I mean—he had *a lot*, but I couldn't stop wanting it. I get it now, how sex and feeding go together for vampires; there's a depravity in it. A recklessness, a hedonism I found myself craving. Not that his cock wasn't impressive, but I think half my orgasm was because of him drinking.

"Stay." He glances over his shoulder, his eyes reverted back to black, mouth in a snarl. "I'll return later. Rest. Your body went through a lot tonight."

"Yeah, no."

Since when has he ever cared? I slide off his insanely tall bed and cross the room towards him. Something flashes across his face, making me aware of the blood staining nearly every inch of my skin. Even between my thighs, mingling with our combined cum.

"Not until you explain what that was out there." I gesture to the window, indicating the forest. "After you first drank, you changed. You were different."

He laughs humourlessly. "You have no fucking idea how right you are."

"So tell me."

His jaw works back and forth. "You won't enjoy the answer."

"I already hate you, so it can't be any worse." Although, Alec's never hidden his evil from me, so yeah...I think it might be worse and he's about to call my bluff.

"That's your first mistake."

Hating him is a mistake? I think it's the rightest thing in the world. "What'll be my second?" I challenge, crossing my arms over my naked chest.

"Trying to leave again."

I don't dignify that with a response. Running through the woods is a no-go; I see that now, but I *will* come up with a new way to get out of here. Sex released the pent-up emotions we both had from tonight, but it's nothing more. Sex doesn't change the fact that he wants my magick returned only to make the cure work as it should, to make him a profit for his messed-up revenge ploy.

When I say nothing, he turns for the door. I'm quick to cut in front of him, placing myself between him and it, half-surprised when he doesn't just knock me out of the way. We're both aware he could get by me without effort if he wants to.

"Tell me," I demand.

Alec scans me, trailing over the marks all over my body. His eyes soften from a depthless black to something else. It's a moment so brief, I'm convinced I imagine it.

"My marks look good on you." It's a barely there whisper, like he's talking to himself. "Your family knew exactly how to tear me down. I wonder if they planned for you to be the sacrifice, or if it was shit luck."

What is he— "Alec, my family's done *nothing* to you. In recent years, at least."

"If only you were in on it, but you're so fucking innocent, you don't even know the facts of your own life."

My own... "You're making no sense!"

"I know." His jaw slides forward before he sighs. "Fine, but you'll regret asking. What do you know about Brides?"

"Um. White dress. Weddings. One half of the couple undergoing a marriage ceremony, usually the half identifying as female. Why?"

"No"—he shakes his head—"not in the human sense. What do you know about a vampire's Bride?"

Nothing. Didn't know that was a thing. "Um. Black dress? Gothic wedding? One half of the vampiric couple—"

"No," he interrupts, his tone sharp and irritated. "A Bride is our term for a mate, the one made for us. They're uncommon, and not every vampire is destined to have one. For many, it's something that doesn't exist, so no one goes searching for them. They might choose to take mates on their own accord, but it's the equivalent of mortals picking their spouse. Even those aren't common because, generally, vampires are happier alone. It takes a lasting connection in which two vampires can stand one another for decades or centuries. But a

Bride is a *true* mate. Someone destined for us. Someone who becomes our ultimate obsession. We recognize them by blood alone, and the connection is nearly instant. A vampire's Bride is usually another vampire; it's just how it works. As for the specifics, no one knows. Some believe in fate. Personally, since we're descended from one of the Fallen—angels who fell from Heaven alongside the devil, becoming the original demons—I think it has something to do with that. Something celestial rather than otherworldly."

"We recognize them by blood alone, and the connection is nearly instant." His behaviours changed after his first bite.

The only thing that prevents my stomach from bottoming out is the other fact he mentioned: *"A vampire's Bride is usually another vampire."*

"What's that have to do with us?"

"A vampire can't harm their Bride. We're wired to care for them above all else. Acts of possession are all we know, the only way we'll act. A bond forms between the mated pair, allowing them to feel one another's emotions. After it's in place, the Bride becomes the only being they'll ever feed from again. Their immortal lives become entwined with one another's in every way." He pauses, repeating in a firmer tone, "*Every* way."

A chill runs down my spine, but I force my question out. "Again...what's this have to do with us? Why are you telling me this? A Bride is another vampire."

"I did say that, didn't I? That's the fucking cruellest part. The *one* fucking family I've vowed to destroy—and one of their own becomes my goddamn Bride!"

Me? Sense and sanity bend until they're a mingled mess in my mind.

My arms drop by my sides, and I stagger against the door behind me. "What are you talking about?"

He growls, taking a step towards me. I question his claim about not harming me any longer, because he looks slightly crazed. Angry.

Well, pissed, actually. "You really need me to say it? You're smarter than that, I know you are. It's impossible for a vampire to have a Bride from another species—or so I believed—yet that's exactly what you are to me, Harlow. There's only one explanation that makes any sense, and it's that over the numerous generations of hunting your family, they caught on and cursed me with *you*." He spits out the final word, his body inclining toward me. Despite not having any heat, and this conversation not exactly being warming, there's a magnetizing fervour to him.

That would hurt if I cared even a bit about being a bloodsucker's mate. "How do you know it wasn't the cure making you feel something? How do you even know that's what this is if you've never experienced it before?"

He laughs harshly, rubbing a hand over his hair. "It's really hard to fucking miss when each one of my instincts shifted from wanting to hunt and slaughter you to caring for you, to fucking you... claiming you."

"*Claiming me?*" I jerk, my head thumping on the door. "I'm already trying to get away from you as it is, I don't need more motivation."

"That's the thing. You *can't* leave. Not now, not ever. Not any longer. I won't let you."

I have a billion and one arguments to that statement, but I hold them in, knowing it'll accomplish nothing.

"Still, this could all be in your head."

Suddenly, he's right there, his chest against mine, his fists coming up on either side of my head to trap me in. "I wish it were, but it's not. The moment I drank more than a few sips, my every thought attuned to you."

The memories of earlier flit through my mind. The way he went from drinking to throwing himself against a tree and demanding I run away. "That's why you freaked out."

"Wouldn't you?" He turns his face, his nose trailing up my neck as he inhales. My thighs clamp together, logic taking a backseat to desire. "I couldn't believe what my body was telling me. Still can't. I was stuck between wanting to rip your head off and wanting to keep you close."

"You told me to run."

He lifts his head, seeming almost apologetic when he utters, "I wouldn't have been able to let you go."

Well, you will one day.

"You said you wouldn't hurt me when you almost...you didn't rape me."

Flat black meets me, as though offended by the statement. "We're wired to protect our Brides, but we're also driven to claim them. Blood and sex, I've told you, are key, especially to mates. Sex left my scent all over you so other males know to either stay away or risk death."

Yeah, that we'll be getting back to later. A possessive vampire boyfriend isn't what I signed up for.

"But if you didn't want it, and I forced you, it would have hurt you, and to hurt you would be like tearing my own head off. It was the loophole you could have used."

My gaze finds the bed behind him. "You seriously wouldn't have forced me?"

He shakes his head, his lips thinning into an unsatisfied line.

"What would have happened if we didn't fuck?"

"Once we find our Bride, we're compelled to claim them. If we don't, we'll go mad until we do."

"And if I always denied you?"

"Then I would have gone crazy until finally succumbing to death. Waiting would have weakened me. It'd be a slow, painful process, probably taking decades, but at some point, my body would give up."

Oh. "'Kay, but how do you know all this if Brides are so uncommon? I'm getting the sense you don't have a handbook on all this."

Exasperation lines his face, and in this moment, he seems more human than ever. "When you're around as long as I am, one hears things. Learns things."

Hm. Well, ideally he learned incorrectly. "And if I don't want to be your Bride?"

He smiles, but it reminds me of his predatory one from the forest. It's not friendly or kind. It's the smile of a winner before snatching his prize. "That's too bad. When I said you fucked up, I meant it. If you never ran away, I wouldn't have had to chase, and I wouldn't have bitten you. I would never have known."

Is he serious? I cross my arms, pushing them into his rigid chest, trying to gain a few inches of space—and failing. "You're seriously blaming *me* for this? Let's not victim-blame here, and don't bite me next time!"

Ignoring my point, he murmurs, "You know how impressed I was when I saw the broken window? Pissed as hell—still am—but impressed. You were inventive, and I'm truly shocked you managed to get to the ground without harming yourself."

I won't be telling him that, somehow, magick helped.

He scans my body clinically, ending at my feet before a determined set of his jaw has him saying, "Speaking of, you're exhausted. Your body went through way too much for someone who's no stronger than a human."

Abruptly, the air changes and the door at my back is replaced with the bed again as Alec rests me on it, tucking the blanket over me. There's a different edge in his eyes, one that solidifies everything he just told me. His movements are gentle, his touch caring. The complete opposite of everything he seemed in the conversation.

Oh, Goddess, help me. I think...I think he's telling the truth.

"What happens now?" I whisper as he pulls away.

"You stay."

"You really were telling the truth when you said you wouldn't kill me?"

"I can't hurt you without hurting myself. You're safe. You're the safest woman in the world."

Except that's not how I feel. "You can't keep me here forever."

He gives me his back. "We've had this conversation before. Yes, I can. Whether it's for the cure or for your protection, Harlow, your life became mine the moment I took you from your house."

Harlow. Oh my fucking Goddess... Yes, it all makes sense now. His voice in my head. It's always been there. Something was pulling me towards him long before he came for me.

"Your voice," I blurt, my revelation refusing to be kept from him. "Do you think that's why I've been hearing you?"

"Perhaps."

Silence stretches between us. My hands knot in the blanket, torn between getting out of bed and following or staying here. It's in the space between us, I understand. Everything he's said, it's not a lie, even if I wish it was.

"I hate you," I whisper.

"I hate you too."

And then he's gone.

TWENTY-SEVEN

Alec

eelings I never once imagined to exist now own me. Instincts I'd rather tear from my motherfucking throat than return to my bedroom and see her there. Making her my Bride doesn't mean we have to *like* one another; eternity living together while being apart sounds fine to me.

Except for the fact she's my new source of life. My reasoning. Everything preventing me from dropping her in the dungeon where she'll be safest from anything that can harm her—and thus me— and throwing away the key, forgetting about her presence. That would be the most ideal situation.

No, ideal would be not being mated to her.

Fuck. Me.

I slam my palm into my office door, the wood cracking beneath the force. It snaps open, crashing against the adjacent wall. A physical manifestation of my anger but nothing near enough what I need.

"Nice night?"

Of course she's fucking here. She's *always* here.

"You." I'm across the room instantly, lifting Freya up from where she's perched on the edge of my desk, pinning her to the

windows behind it by her throat. "This whole time, you knew what she'd be to me."

"Yep." In a quick flash, the witch is gone and my palm lands, now empty, against the glass. I whirl, finding Freya behind me before my feet are lifted off the floor and I'm pressed to the spot I had her seconds ago, held by the invisible force of magick. She ticks a brow up and lowers her hand, keeping me in place. "I'll let you go as long as you don't try to kill me."

"I *should* kill you, you conniving bitch."

"I think you mean witch." She shrugs, uncaring about the threat I'll more than happily deliver. "I had orders to not interfere."

"Except that's entirely what you've done."

Another wave of her hand, and my feet thump to the ground. "No less than what I was instructed to. Besides, if I told you she was your Bride, would you have bitten her?"

"Fuck no." I would have stayed far away. Maybe even sent her back home. Without tasting her, the monster inside would never have discovered its mate, and I'd return to going through my entire life never knowing wiser.

She clasps her hands in front of her. "Exactly why I couldn't. So ask your questions, because I'm sure you have some."

"Can it be broken?" The question immediately makes my insides churn, threatening to puke up her blood. The instinctual part of me would prefer to cut off its own head before losing its mate, but the rest of me...I *need* her gone.

Freya smirks and retakes her seat on top of my desk, propping her feet on my chair. She's in some ridiculous pair of ripped jeans and flat-bottom shoes I believe are called Converse, if memory serves correctly from the numerous ads I've passed about them over the years. Her hair's a bright green this time, and she fiddles with the ends as she responds.

"Maybe by death, but you know what'll happen if she dies."

I'll perish too. And I'd never be able to be the one to kill her myself.

"Next question."

"This is the Sinclairs' doing, isn't it? It's the only way a witch could be my Bride."

"Hm, not sure if I can say..." Freya's haunting purple eyes flick to my ceiling where she stares for a long moment. "Turns out I can. No, the Sinclairs didn't do this. Fate did, if you'd believe it. Assisted by something else I can't say."

I don't. Not at all.

"Why?"

"Harlow's one of the most powerful witches alive, even if she's unaware of this, and you're one of the vampire kings. Sounds like a kickass match made to me."

It isn't. Not at all.

"I can't hurt her. That's why you were never worried. You knew at some point this would all come out, and why you helped me retrieve her that night."

Her tongue rubs across her teeth as she nods. "Good little vamp putting it all together."

"It's also why I can drink her blood, isn't it? It has nothing to do with my age." Her blood was made for me and *only* me. Cure or otherwise, the bond began linking us together from the very beginning, being the reason behind the strange sensations I got around her.

"Man, you're smart. I see why you're king."

"And you're a smartass. Don't you have somewhere to be?"

She looks up from fiddling with her nails. "Oh, I'm sorry, was answering all your pressing questions *not* helpful? I'll go if you have no more."

I have many more, and yet none of them come to my mind.

How do I break the bond without killing myself?

How do I live with her?

How do I keep her when she wants nothing to do with me?

How do I keep her when a part of me wants nothing to do with her?

She slides off the desk, approaching. "She's a gift, Alec, so treat her as such. Be smart about this. Your sister is long dead; don't kill your future by trying to save your past."

"I'm not trying to save my past, as you put it. I understand Cora is long dead and won't be returning."

A sad smile graces her lips. "Thing is, yeah, you are. You'll never appreciate Harlow as your mate if you don't move on. Cora wouldn't want you to throw away what could be between you two."

"Harlow hates me," I argue instead of responding to her spiel, her statement about my sister stoking a rage inside me. Cora would want revenge as much as I do.

Would she, though? Cora was a peacekeeper.

"For now. Anyhoo, I should be off. More vampires to torture and all that. More witches to help."

"What *do* you do every day?"

"Oh, I'm here and there. Helping my kind when needed. The vampire comment was a joke, so don't be getting jealous. You're my only bloodsucking pal." She pauses, her head ticking to the side, eyes glinting with mischief. "Although, how I hear it, you only suck the blood from one being. The very being who..." She trails off, turning towards the door.

"Who what?" I demand when she doesn't finish.

She holds up three fingers "Wait. Three..." She lowers a finger. "Two." Another finger. "One."

At the end of her countdown, the ground beneath my feet vibrates enough I'd believe it was a hurricane if we were in the general path of one. Centuries of a firm foundation is rattled by a force so deadly, it staggers Freya, her hand catching on the doorframe.

She *knew* this was coming. "What the fuck was that?"

"That would be your Bride getting her magick back."

TWENTY-EIGHT

Harlow

Shortly after Alec leaves, I do too, refusing to be in the vicinity of anything of his. No matter what he claims, no matter what freaky instincts he has, I don't share them.

"Fuck this. Fuck fate. Fuck the bloodsucker. Fuck everything."

After stealing his shirt to dress in—because, turns out, there's one thing of his I need—I leave his room, realizing I've never wandered the castle alone, which means having no idea how to get to the room he's been putting me in. Walking down the hallway and past a window helps determine I'm on the same floor, so I keep walking until something seems remotely familiar.

The place feels dismal. Lifeless, with such low light streaming past the thick curtains hanging over the windows. To be so far away from nature, so disconnected from Hecate, makes me shiver.

It's the physical reminder why Alec's claim makes no sense. This castle is grim and dark, full of hatred and pain, the vampire king no better than a beast ruling within its walls. And apparently *I'm* his mate? Vampires are Dark creatures, while witches and their energies are Light. We'd never fit.

Eventually I reach the end of the hall, being met with two directions. I choose the right by random guess, hoping it'll take me to my room.

Finally at the end, I do find it, the door still parted from when Alec was in here and found me gone. The window is a gaping hole with the nighttime breeze blowing inside, adding a chill to the air.

Maybe another room for the night. Surely if I head next door, it's another spare room.

Halfway turned, my gaze catches on something on the floor. Something that wasn't there before.

A box. A shoe box, if the logo from a popular company is any indication.

But why is it here? Is it a gift? Finally proper shoes to battle the endless stone in this damn place.

I crouch and lift off the lid, half-expecting a pair of sneakers, but it's not that at all.

There's paperwork. Documents. Pictures. Plastic cards upside down.

I lift the top picture, attention drawn to the familiar faces of Mom and Dad.

My heart practically sings in sorrow at seeing them. Since being taken, I've forced myself not to think about them or the grief, because I couldn't handle it plus fighting with a vampire. Focusing on the present for once, rather than the past, in order to survive.

But seeing them...all that pent-up emotion crashes into me, heavy and suffocating, like an intense pressure in my chest, squeezing my heart until there's no blood left in it for it to beat.

The shadows slither around my neck, reminding me what I've been preventing myself from reliving. They've stopped bothering me over the past couple days, Alec's presence keeping them away, as though I'm being given a reprieve to deal with one shitty thing at a time. Or if the shadows are linked to my grief, then being sad again has welcomed them back.

The sensation yanks me back to that night. To reliving the house fire, the final image of Mom's and Dad's faces is all I have before everything went dark. Until I woke up on the grass outside my house, human paramedics bent over me, firefighters standing around bewildered by the blaze that died on its own.

The picture is different than any I've ever seen, the colour a sepia rather than bright. Mom's in a wedding dress and ceremonial white cloak and—*wait*. This is different from the one on the mantle. It's an older style with more ruffles and lace, long sleeves and a high neck, while Dad's suit is a light blue instead of black. They look younger, and Mom's hair isn't red. She must have dyed away the classic colour.

Were they wed before? They never mentioned the picture in the living room being their second ceremony. I suppose stranger things have happened, such as why this box is here. Alec must have found it in my house and—what, decided to torture me with the memories?

I rest the photo to the side, stroking my finger over Mom's face before reaching into the box and retrieving the two cards, flipping them over.

Identification cards.

My attention goes to the name on Dad's card, his picture a much-younger version of the man I knew, and the name...

Arthur Hartman.

What the fuck?

I look at Mom's card. Violet Hartman.

Those are not my parents' names. Not even close. Not the first, and especially not the last.

Heart thumping, I rest them to the side and reach deeper into the box, grabbing the next thing. It's a sheet of paper in Mom's handwriting. A letter—no, a journal entry I read over and over until the words make sense.

Harlow had a dream last night about being handcuffed to a wall. She woke up crying, saying her magick would no longer work. I calmed her down, explaining it was a bad dream, but I think her memories are returning. Arthur will wipe her mind again later tonight, and hopefully the memories remain trapped for longer. Feels less and less time passes between each wipe, and I'm growing worried one day, erasing her mind won't be possible.

The paper flutters from my hand, my gaze dropping to the scars on my wrists. Handcuffs—exactly what Alec guessed. Exactly what my mind was trying to recall this whole time in those little flashes.

The feeling of aloneness, fear, of the walls caving in while my arms are chained to the wall behind me, and I'm unable to get free. No matter how many times I yell for Mommy and Daddy, no one's coming. The days are endless, the nights forever.

"Oh my Goddess…"

This whole time, Mom and Dad were wiping my memories. I glance towards the other IDs—the other names, the fact oh so obvious but unsaid within my mind. Unaccepted beneath my grief and horror.

I reach into the box for the next item, pulling out a set of birth certificates, both with the same names as the IDs, only Violet's has a different surname; her maiden name, presumably.

No Sinclair to be found.

The next thing is another note, again in Mom's handwriting, this one dated months prior from the last.

We fucked up. It was never supposed to go this far. And now, Harlow will be raised as ours for the time being. My mistakes are ones I need to live with. The coven's hunting for Arthur and me, but I think my plan will get them to stop trailing us. We'll disappear and raise Harlow as our own. It'll be fine. Sloane is angry, but instructed us to do what we must.

Sloane? Who the hell is that?

Another note, this one dated between the two others.

Harlow's magick is manifesting as strong as we always guessed it'd be. She's untrained and unpredictable. She needs her coven, but we can't take her back. Arthur has an idea to help control her, and I hope it works.

On and on they go, small flashes of my life, of memories returning only to be stolen by Mom and Dad.

No—*not* Mom and Dad.

Strangers. A Violet and Arthur who've been parading as my parents.

It's the last note that breaks me for good, this one dated earlier than all the others. Found at the very bottom of the box, the first written in this miniseries of my life's tormenting past.

Emily and John Sinclair are dead. We had to.

My breaths are heavy, mingled with disbelief. Shock. Anger. Fear. Confusion. Every feeling blends into a turbulent storm until my hands are shaking, my body quivering, heat shifting into a pain that's quickly eased as well. Heat that burns but warms. That destroys and protects.

But it's more than heat.

It's a chill. It slithers alongside that very warmth, coating me. It's a pleasant sting that wakes me in ways I've never felt before. It constricts around my arms, my chest, my thighs, tightening and loosening over and over like a hug. Black tendrils are in the same places, gliding over my skin like silk. My old, familiar shadows hover above me, bathing the room in night until they move abruptly, joining the wisps around my body.

And then a voice, one new, not Alec's from all those months ago: *We've been waiting.*

Beneath me, the castle vibrates. I barely register the sensation as everything settles into place. Truths that were right in front of me this entire time, locked behind memory-wiping charms and an evil I've never known to exist.

The people who raised me were not my parents. In another case, that might have been fine—adoption and foster homes—but this wasn't the same. I wasn't given up by my birth parents. They were *murdered*, and I was taken from them, trapped within my own body. My memories, my magick, all for whatever sick games these people were playing.

They killed my real parents, then lied to me for a decade. I *grieved* them—grieved people who never deserved my love, my affection, my fucking *anything*. I wept in the home I shared with them— another lie—after my powers accidentally took them out, when I should have been killing them this entire time. As a kid, I was horrified by the thought our coven didn't want us, when they *kept* me from my real home. Friends, family, all of whom I have zero recollection of.

My entire life shouldn't have happened like this.

I was lied to. Deceived. Mocked. Forced to play dress-up into whatever they designed me as.

Everything pours out of me then.

The lies found inside the box.

The deaths of my real parents.

The lies fed by my fake parents.

The grief I had over them.

The ignorance about my life.

The horror of being kidnapped by a vampire.

The distaste of becoming his mate.

Every feeling ever had won't be contained, not any longer.

Every tear shed.

Every plea to the Goddess.

Every spell I know.

Every scream ever yelled.

Every time I said "I love you" to my parents.

Every good memory shared with them.

Every banter, good and bad, with Alec.

Every.

Thing.

Do it, the voice whispers in my ear. The tendrils coil around my arms, nudging my palms open. *Feel what you must. Embrace it.*

Everything emerges, bundled into a deafening scream that's almost immediately drowned out by the roar of fire exploding from me. The tendrils remain where they are, nudging me to my feet as flames create a wall around me, but not before burning the box to ash, taking with it every document detailing two people's treachery.

The castle shakes again as I step over the flames, welcoming the pressure in my palms. The heat that says *welcome back*, except it feels stronger. Almost like it's welcoming me from time well before months ago when I lost them. Power like I've never felt courses through my body. The tendrils slowly fade, slipping beneath my skin, becoming friends with my fire.

My magick is back.

I wave my hand, testing my control. The flames sweep in an arc, singeing the carpet and blood stains. Smiling, I close my palm to extinguish the fire before practicing a few other wordless spells: sliding the curtain over the broken window, turning on the bathroom taps, lifting the bed a few feet off the floor. Little things to ensure I'm truly as I should be.

I'm free, and this time, Alec will be unable to stop me.

Staring at the ashes left from the items *he* obviously placed there, I send a silent thank-you to them. If not for the truth, then my magick would still be lost within grief.

"Harlow." From the doorway, my name is breathed like a prayer. A whisper barely audible over the roar of fire burning beside me.

I face Alec, my mind and heart confused. Despite everything, I don't want to hurt him, not really. I hate him, though. Maybe. Something bright lingers within me, but it's masked beneath rage and heartbreak. Beneath feelings without labels.

Attack. He trapped you. A chill runs over my neck and down my arm, urging my palms open. Not for my fire, but for the tendrils that slip from me and dart towards Alec, catching him off guard.

His body lands with a thud across the hallway, and by the time I step from the bedroom, he's getting to his feet, reaching for me like *I'm* the problem.

My heart thumps. I don't want to hurt him—not really—but I can't care about him either, and have to do what I must.

I walk away.

"Harlow!"

"Don't stop me, Alec. I'm leaving."

Fight him.

No, I tell the voice. *No, I won't hurt him. I don't* want *to hurt him.*

I make it to the staircase before a streak of colour blocks me. Before hands descend on my shoulders and my magick prickles, urging me to throw him off me.

"You knew," I murmur instead. "You *knew* they weren't my family. I suppose I should thank you for placing the box in my room."

He curses, his gaze darting towards the bedroom. "That's how —You can't go."

"Watch me." I step around him, making it all the way down the staircase before he's a blur in front of me again.

His hands latch onto my upper arms and I'm swung around,

my back pressed to the nearest wall. He feels like everything both right and wrong. Everything I could have but everything I shouldn't. A monster who kidnapped me but one who's also taken care of me.

"Let me go," I demand. "Don't make me hurt you."

Do it, the voice urges, the slither an unwelcome chill down my spine. I want my fire—*only* my flames. The tendrils are new and worrisome.

They're not. They're your potential.

"You can't hurt me," he says, his voice pulling me from the imaginary argument I seem to be having. Exactly like all those months of hearing his voice, I'm momentarily backed off the edge. "You're my Bride. The bond between us won't allow you to harm me."

"Witches don't have mates. I might be yours, but you're not mine."

My words smother the tiny ember that's been slowly igniting since the moment we met.

They're necessary words because, for once, I'm the victor.

TWENTY-NINE

Alec

She's right. This is why we only bond with our own. But she's also wrong. She's proved it in the way she looks at me, the fact she was hearing my voice long before we met. The bond was always meant to be, even if neither of us were aware.

A vampire doesn't exist without their Bride. I will have no choice but to follow her if she goes, forever craving a thirst only she'll be able to quench.

I pinch her chin, aware at any second my powerful witch can throw me across the room. While I have her, I'll keep her until the very last moment.

"Stay."

She tries to jerk from my hold, her jaw tense beneath my palm. "Fuck you. You've said time and time again you only planned on using my blood for your own gains."

"You know it's not like that anymore."

"Me being your Bride doesn't mean you care about me. Doesn't mean you'll love me."

As though you'd love me after all this? "Told you, vampires can't love, but that doesn't change anything." Emotions don't matter within mate pairs. She's mine, I'm hers, and she must be protected.

Something passes through the bond from her to me. A sense of uncertainty, of fear and longing.

"You'll be targeted if you go out there." I'll lock her in the dungeon before I see her harmed because of the curse in her blood, which should now be effective once more.

"If they attack, I'll kill them. It's been fun, but bye." The purple in her eyes flickers to a deep lilac and—no, even darker. Almost black. It's the telling sign of an attack, but I'm quicker than her, and I lock my arm around her waist and run her away from the foyer.

"I won't let you go. You forget, you're mine now."

The words are barely out of my mouth before a burst of heat flashes through her body and breaks my hold. She lunges back the way we came, strangely quick, and her arm juts behind her.

I jump as a spell narrowly misses me and chase her down the hallway, poised to do whatever I must to keep her here. By the door, she whirls around and casts a line of flames between us, stopping me in my tracks as it roars hot and tall enough to prevent me from jumping it. Her breaths are heavy when she glares over the orange, shaking her head.

"As I said before, witches don't have mates. If you think I'm yours, that's your problem. I'm leaving."

"I'll follow you." I edge as near to the flames as I can, eyeing the height.

"Don't."

Regret filters from the bond, which tells me everything. "You don't want to do this."

Her shoulders cave in a fraction, another sign I'm correct, but she remains rigid in her reply. "You have no idea what I want. Nor have you ever cared."

"I know *exactly* what you're feeling. Fear. Grief. Uncertainty. Regret. I feel you as though they're my own emotions, Hellion."

Her expression ripples into pain, until she abruptly shakes it off.

Her lips move in a murmur, the language unfamiliar, the words quick and low, but I react regardless, knowing the sounds of a hex.

Before I make it two steps, my body is flung into the air like a marionette, crashing against the stone at least a dozen feet above us. If I were mortal, the impact could have broken my back, but as it stands, I brush it off and fight against unmovable binds.

Harlow stares, head tilted to the side. She's a mix of the woman I've come to know and someone else. There's something different about her. Not bad, but different. An air to her I find even more compelling but can't place.

She turns away.

"Harlow." My tone changes. It's guttural, threatening—*daring*. "Don't do this."

"It's already done." By the door, she glances over her shoulder. The blankness in her expression breaks for a second, and the tiniest bit of sorrow comes down the connection.

"I'll find you," I vow. "There's nowhere on Earth you can hide that I won't be able to get to you."

"I'm sorry, Alec." She gestures my way, hitting me with an invisible pressure that sends me catapulting toward darkness.

But right before sleep consumes me, I'm forced to witness my Bride walk away from me...alongside the shadows hovering around her.

I come to, finding myself on the stone floor with someone above me.

"This isn't what I expected to find." A familiar voice cuts through the fog, and a hand stretches down. My next blink clears the remnants of Harlow's spell until Cedric looming over me becomes clear.

"What are you doing here?" I ask, pushing to my feet and

shaking off the last thing I remember. My Bride walking away from me—*leaving* me. The moon is visible through the large window in the upper corridor, meaning hours have passed, the sun has fallen, and Harlow is who the fuck knows where.

Cedric cuts into my vision, reminding me of his presence. "You haven't answered any of my calls. I've been in the dark since the night of your party. Where's the witch?" He eyes the charred stone from where her flames created a barrier between her and me. "Don't tell me she overpowered you?"

"She did more than that. She—" I stop, rubbing a hand over my face while debating how much to tell him. If there's anyone on the planet I trust, it's Cedric, but admitting this feels wrong. Like Harlow must be protected from everyone and everything, herself included, and that means ensuring no one knows what she is to me, even Cedric.

"She what?" he prompts.

Then again, he has as much reason to hate the Sinclairs as I do, if not more. For a while, he and Cora were mated, and her death left behind a hollowness in Cedric that's never faded. If I don't admit everything, there's no telling what he'll do to get her back out of some misplaced feeling of being helpful, and no one, not even him, will harm her.

"She's my Bride."

Cedric's expression flicks through a few emotions at such a quick rate, a mortal would miss them. Shock, dismay, intrigue and something else. Something extremely fleeting that makes me tense.

Rage.

Understandable he'd be angry that a Sinclair has now become untouchable, but it's an emotion I'll need to pay particularly close attention to.

"That's impossible," he finally whispers.

"I thought so too, but I can't ignore what my body's screaming at me."

He blinks. "That means you drank from her. You risked it?"

"She ran and triggered my hunting instincts. I couldn't help it."

"Fuck." He blows out a breath and swipes a hand over his hair as his attention goes to the shut front doors. "I won't say I'm happy about this. Just...confused. What now?"

Me too. I don't admit that part, don't let him in on my own uncertainty. "I'll go find her."

"She left?"

"She has her magick back and overpowered me. That's why the cure didn't work—that's what you saw. When her parents died in the house fire, she lost her powers, but they're back now."

His mouth parts in an *ah* motion. "That'd explain..." He trails off and gestures towards me before glancing at the ground.

"She's strong."

"Would you expect otherwise? She's a Sinclair."

I watch him, seeking that flush of rage beneath his friendly tone, but it seems faded. "She's unexpected, that's for certain. I didn't— Cora—"

"Would be happy for you. She always whined about you having no one."

"And you?"

His stance remains lax when he replies, "If you took her as a mate because you liked her or something, I might have concerns about your well-being, but the stories always stated the Bride bond is unbeatable. You have no choice about having her as a mate, which means I have no choice but to accept it. We have too much history—centuries of it—for me to be pissed at something like this."

His words should bring some measure of relief, but they don't.

They're also not something I need to concern myself with right now, so I shove away from the wall, slapping his shoulder as I pass. "Stay here, will you? Make sure no fucker shows up. The other night, two targeted her."

"I found them. Pieces of them, anyway. The head by the southern border?"

I shrug. "They should consider themselves lucky that attempt happened before I discovered what she is to me."

Cedric trails me to the door. "Your people are expecting you to provide information on accessing the cure, but no one's heard from you since the party."

"Her being without magick nullified the cure's effects, so I couldn't risk it. Anyway, doesn't matter anymore. Plan's done. Anything that'll harm her, even her mental well-being, is off-limits. *She's* off-limits. Make sure that point gets passed along." I'm the only one who'll ever enjoy her blood from now until the end of eternity. The moment I bit her, the plan changed. Disappeared. Revenge isn't as important as her life.

Cedric makes a noise of agreement. "All your years of work, gone like that."

"Yes." My tone is sharp, ensuring he knows not to question me. I pause by the doors and look back at him, my statement a threat as much for him as anyone. "No one touches her. I'll keep you updated when we're on our way back."

"Good luck," he calls after me.

I won't need luck. Just a bond to follow.

THIRTY

Harlow

I walk through the same forest I ran through last night with much less fear. If another vampire happens upon me, I'm better prepared, my magick just a flick away.

The night is silent while the light between the trees shifts from dusk to dawn, the early morning glow a tease on the horizon. By the time I reach the edge of the forest, the sun's more visible, making me suspect it's about five in the morning.

Even if Alec has woken, the sun will keep him away. While I might not have a particular plan in mind, I'll be far gone by the time the sun sets.

Exactly as he said last night, by the edge of the forest is a cemented road. It stretches far ahead and behind, giving no sign of a location, but it's a start. By following it, eventually I'll get somewhere. Unfortunately, it'll be by foot as I never grasped the concept of magickal transportation methods, like being able to pop myself from one place to another with only the location in my mind's eye.

So, I walk on, hoping someone drives by and takes pity on me.

Hours pass without a sign of life. I'm nowhere far enough from Alec's castle that he wouldn't catch up with me. Now, the sun is high in the sky, about midday, which means I have maybe another six or so hours until he comes.

I take a bend in the road when a cracking noise echoes behind me and the ground ruffles, the signal that the peace of nature that's been my only form of entertainment for hours has been disrupted.

And then there's a voice. More like a breathed whisper carried towards me on the cool afternoon breeze of early fall.

"Harlow Sinclair."

My palms tingle with the beginning smolders of a fireball ready to form, to defend, while I recall the silent incantation for a protection spell, should I need a shield between me and the intruder.

I slowly turn, coming face to face with a woman. A woman, whom for all accounts I don't know, but a familiarity has me lowering my hands, the warmth dissipating. Dark hair is bound up in a bun, keeping her face clear, but still she swipes at the few stray hairs hanging, moving them out of the way from wide eyes that fade from brown to purple, the telling sign she's another witch. She stands tall, confident, but with my spin, breaks into a gasp that has her stumbling forward, reaching for me.

"You're alive. It's actually you."

"How do you know my name?" I prepare to run because there have been enough unfriendly people in my life that I don't need another, even if there's still something comforting about her.

Her brows fuse together and she rocks back on her heels, coming to an abrupt stop. "You don't remember me?"

"Should I?"

"What have they done to you?" she asks in a low whisper. "My name is Morgan Hargrove, and I'm the High Priestess of Highridge Coven...and your guardian."

Home. It's a word that catapults into my head. A word that sounds right and familiar. Highridge coven *should* have been my home, but according to the people I called Mom and Dad, they got rid of us because of the ongoing vampire attacks.

"You kicked us out." Even as I say it, my chest clenches with the falseness in that argument while something else probes the back of my mind.

A memory...or something.

"Morgan, look over here!"

"I see you, Harlow. Great job!" The woman turns, her smile kind—

And her face is the same as the one in front of me.

"Kicked you out?" She—Morgan—practically chokes, rapidly shaking her head. "My girl, no. I'm getting the sense you've been lied to, but no more than I have been as well."

Morgan paces forward another step, lifting her hands, seeking permission, which I give by not backing up. She completes the final step before her palms rest on my cheeks, cupping my face, her touch as cool as the breeze.

The sensation quickly dissipates into something else: a series of visions that slip through my mind.

Morgan hugging me tightly. "Happy birthday."

Morgan standing in a kitchen between two other people, a man and a woman. She glances over at my entrance and waves.

Morgan standing beside a child, holding her hand as they cross the yard towards me.

"You're truly alive." Her voice snaps the images away, and I jerk, trying to chase them. To bring them back. She takes my movement wrong and lowers her arms with a frown. "Sorry."

"No, it wasn't...did you do that?"

"Do what?"

"I think I saw..." I reach down for her hand, bringing her palm back to my face, willing the images to return. The feeling I know something—that this woman is telling the truth. "I *saw* you. You were hugging me. You were walking across a yard."

Morgan's lips part, and her face scrunches as though in pain. "Fuck, they really—no matter." She lowers her hand again. "We'll get it sorted, I promise. For now, I'm still trying to realize this isn't a dream. That you're alive and here."

"You keep saying that."

"You shouldn't be," she murmurs. "You died. Your magickal signature faded. After you disappeared, I spent months searching for you until the mortal police called with the report of your death. I saw the accident for myself, and yet here you stand." She scans me, pausing on my neck before nudging hair off my shoulder. "You've been attacked."

The need to hide what happened between me and Alec has me batting her hand away and bringing hair back over my shoulder. "Forget the bites. What do you mean, I *died*?"

At first, I assume she'd heard of the house fire, but her mention of an accident suggests there's more to Violet and Arthur's deception than the box let on.

Her attention remains on my neck, and it's obvious she doesn't want to let the marks go, but with a deep sigh, concedes. "Seems we have a lot of catching up to do. How would it sound to go home after all this time? Your *real* home."

What is home anymore? Maybe subconsciously, home—the last one I knew before Alec kidnapped me—was where I was heading to. Back to where my stuff is. Back to what became the grave for my powers, my family, even my self-worth.

Except it doesn't feel like home anymore. It's the source of pain, of losing the people I loved. It's the place where they spent years forming me into a being for their own gains, isolating me from a coven. It's a reminder of the shadows that once weighed me down, and of the night Alec came for me. It's my past.

If I go with Morgan, if I trust her, then I get to see where I came from. Get answers for everything the box didn't give. Unlock the secrets of my past and determine what exactly happened with Violet and Arthur Hartman, and why Morgan thinks I died.

And hide from Alec.

I take her hand in mine, and it's like I'm home. Magick swirls from my palm to hers, our powers recognizing one another. She smiles before the ground disappears from under my feet.

The air is different. Lighter, if that's possible. The sun feels brighter, like we're closer to it. And behind me aren't trees anymore—except there are certainly a lot of those in the distance, covering the incline of stone that consumes my entire vision. It's magnificent and beautiful. Nature at its purest, its finest.

I spin, taking in the mountains, the cloudy sky blanketing much of the blue, and the crispness in the air. It's a place without smoke and exhaust. Without the bustle of a town, or even the openness of the countryside.

It's Banff. The place Highridge Coven calls home.

The houses Morgan and I are standing nearest are cabin-style, their sidings covered with a varnished wood that's obviously for decoration only, covering the thick building materials needed for houses this far north to survive a winter that's always one nip away. They have a sense of modernity too, with large windows both in the upper and lower floors, overlooking the cobblestone street we're on.

"Banff," I breathe.

Morgan nods, tugging me into a walk. "Very good. It's where we've lived for centuries. The Sinclairs created Highridge, did you know that?" Her eyes cut towards me, as sharp as her frown before she mumbles the presumed answer to her own question. "No, I suppose you didn't. But it's true. This is your legacy, Harlow."

My throat is thick as I'm tugged along, mind repeating what she's said. Banff was more than only home then. More than just a coven. Violet and Arthur took me from the place my family lived for centuries. Anger flushes through me, but I quickly tamp it down with another glance towards the unearthly mountains all around us while forcing air into my lungs.

"Still in Canada then."

"Excuse me?"

"I've been living in a small town in Ontario for as long as I can remember."

Morgan abruptly yanks me to a stop, her nostrils flaring with her sharp inhale. "Days. You were only *days* away from us this entire time? Nearly seventeen years and you—" She stops, her grip tight around my fingers. "I'm sorry," she says after a moment, loosening her hold. "It's difficult to learn you were so close this entire time. Had I known, I would have come for you."

"I believe you." And I do. I feel it. My magick recognizes Morgan. Though the memories are vague and blurry, my heart does too.

"There is nothing I can ever do to make up for how I failed you. Other than returning you home."

I want to tell her it's fine, that there was nothing she could have done, but is it fine? At this point, I don't even know what's up anymore.

"Where did you find me?" I ask instead, wondering precisely where Alec has been hiding me.

"Just over the U.S. border, in Montana. Come." She turns up the street, her knitted cardigan swirling around the backs of her thighs.

Montana. Close enough Alec will find me, *if* he's able to track me here. He didn't exactly give details on how the supposed mate bond between us works.

Morgan gestures to some of the houses we pass. "This is the area of the town inhabited by the coven. We prefer to stick close to one another." She continues, turning down a skinnier road, and I fall back, inspecting the homes and realizing with a punch to the gut that the people residing in them could have been family. They should have been witches and warlocks I grew up alongside.

The churning in my stomach travels up, prickling my eyes with the beginning formations of tears. For years, I hated how the coven abandoned us, never giving me the connection every witch desires. As much as I loved my parents, two witches aren't enough. Not when knowledge is passed from coven member to coven member, each learning from one another's experiences, getting to practice other elemental magick, reciting a variety of incantations. My coven consisted of only two, and I now understand why I know nothing beyond fire, or why I used to obsessively pour over Gram's grimoires —which I now realize were probably stolen from my real family.

The prickle behind my eyes travels back down, this time in my veins, igniting the very flames they spent years teaching me. Anger stirs. Arthur and Violet Hartman, whoever they were and whyever their reasoning, kept me from my true potential.

"Harlow," Morgan calls softly, doubling back when I've made it no farther than the street's corner. "We're almost to my house where we'll talk, but I'd like to show you something first. I understand it must be confusing."

You don't, though. You have no idea what it feels like to learn you had an entire other life at one point. That the life you had was a well-orchestrated performance.

I force my mouth into a smile, because it's not her fault I'm mentally spiralling.

It is her fault, that slithery voice returns, making me shiver uncomfortably. *She's High Priestess. She is to blame for everything.*

"Harlow?" she calls again, and I shake off the sensation while ignoring the unwelcome voice and follow her up the road, this time staying beside her until she brings us to a stop in front of a house.

Similar style as the others. Two storeys done with polished wood, a wraparound porch that covers two-thirds of the house, and a large bay window overlooking the polished yard. A stone path connects the sidewalk to the red front door and is decorated with various kinds of flowers.

"Do you recognize it?"

"Should I?" I ask, even knowing I should and why she's wondering. The house might seem unfamiliar, but an energy pulls my feet from the sidewalk to the pathway, an invisible wall of power urging me forward. Parts of me know it, even if I don't.

Morgan's hand wraps around my wrist. "We've taken care of it, never allowing another to reside in it. Perhaps deep down, I hoped for this outcome, that you'd come back to us one day."

My throat and heart swell with a newfound ache, only this time it's welcoming too. Pressing my lips together, I nod and duck my head to follow her, unable to formulate a reply. To return to the place I once called home is...unlike anything I could have ever dreamed, but it's also nothing I've *had* to dream of. Something that I didn't know was possible until recently.

Morgan leads me to a similar-looking house and through the grey front door. The modest foyer immediately opens to a sitting room, a fireplace along one wall and a couch facing away from the window overlooking the front yard. She passes by and down the hallway lined with pictures—my attention unable to land on any one long enough to make out the people in them—and into the kitchen filled with modern appliances and a granite U-shaped countertop.

This is nothing compared to the mortal-looking home I grew up in. Mom and Dad seemed determined to hide anything cultural, while Morgan's home seeps nature and magick—*life*.

Candles cover many of the surfaces, and there are various kinds of plants hanging from doorways and walls, wrapped around posts. A wooden pentacle hangs on the kitchen wall, and beside it, an ankh—the symbol of love, life, and reincarnation. Paintings depicting the numerous versions of Hecate are scattered around the downstairs. Herbal scents emit from every room, welcoming, delicious, and easing to the mind, body, and spirit.

My magick sings. This is more than before the accident, before I lost my powers, before their return hours ago. My eyes flutter shut as I take it all in. The *life* that pours from its walls. The soul awakening mine.

This may not be my house, but I'm home regardless. Whatever Violet and Arthur did, they raised half a witch—and Alec got the outcome of that. The scared, powerless, and weak version of me. The witch never truly connected with nature how I should have been. No wonder Hecate abandoned me. I wasn't *me*, not really.

Inside the kitchen, a woman turns from where she's pouring hot water from a kettle into a mug. At our entrance, her mouth slips lax, as does her hand. The kettle crashes onto the counter, sending hot water surging from it. She would have been burned if not for the spell Morgan casts its way to suspend it midair—and the speed the woman darts away from it and towards me.

"There's no fucking way." Her purple eyes flick between Morgan and me, pausing on Morgan. "Mom, this isn't real, right? This *can't* be real. She isn't...you're—" Her hands come up to cover her mouth, one layered over the other while her talking continues, now an unidentifiable mumble.

Morgan slides by my shoulder before heading towards the counter. "Harlow, meet my daughter, Carina. Re-meet, I suppose."

I study the woman in front of me, seeking some recognition in her. In the shine of her brown waves, in the flicker of her eyes, in the softness of her face. But she—Carina—remains a mystery to my wiped memory.

Carina drops her hands, her mouth still doing this gaping fish movement. "There's no way. You—you *died*. We were supposed to play outside the day you—oh fuck." She spins on her mother. "This isn't fake?"

"No." Morgan retrieves two new mugs and begins filling them. "I know you have a lot of questions, but I'm going to ask that you make yourself busy elsewhere until Harlow gets settled."

Carina pouts, obviously not enjoying being kicked out, but truth is, I'm thankful she is. I don't know how I can get the entire story out to one person, let alone one who'd likely react dramatically to the details.

"Of course," she agrees after a moment. "Goddess, you have no idea…" She reaches for me but drops her hands at the last second. "Welcome home, Harlow. I've missed you."

And then she heads down the hall. The door clicks shut behind her, and I take a breath.

"You two were best friends as kids," Morgan comments, carrying over two steaming mugs towards the round table in the corner of the room. "Come, please sit."

The table's beneath a window that overlooks the side of the house and down the road to the home she said was mine. If Carina and I lived this close to one another, I imagine we'd still be close. Like sisters, perhaps. A friend through everything. A witch going through all the same changes I did. I faced puberty alone, but understanding my ever-changing body *and* my powers with a friend would have been nice.

I choke down the grief with a tentative sip of the herbal tea, singeing the edge of my tongue as I do. It's a welcome sting, distracting me from everything else.

Morgan wraps her palms around her mug and shifts in her chair, leaning as close to the table as she can. "I've dreamed of being able to speak with you again so many times, and now that you're in front of me, I don't know where to begin."

"Maybe I should go first. I, uh...I'm aware the people I called Mom and Dad weren't my birth parents, although I only learned that this morning. Long story, but I found journal entries written and apparently, they were wiping my memory. That's why I don't really remember anything."

With her mouth in a flat line, she says, "Alright. Tell me everything you know, and I'll fill in the gaps." Her attention goes to my neck, where evidence of Alec's bites makes me bring my hair over my shoulder.

I wonder what he's doing right now.

I wonder if he's coming for me.

I wonder what I'll do when he does.

THIRTY-ONE

Alec

Leaving Cedric behind, I streak through the woods, following my Bride.

Every nerve inside me is hardwired to her scent. To *her*. To ensuring we get her back and can keep her safe, protected forever, shielded from anyone who'll do her harm.

Her scent travels in a straight line through the woods. This time, she didn't try to make it difficult on me.

Because she wants me to find her.

Logically, I know it's because she was in such a hurry she didn't bother with stealth, believing her powers will be enough this time.

My eyes remain peeled for signs of a struggle between her and any other who'd seek the cure, but the scents remain clean and bloodless. It's almost unfortunate, because I could use a fight right now. To not show mercy and release the frustration that's been knotting my insides since the moment Harlow left the castle. I need to kill something in rage, because it certainly won't be her. Never her.

I'll rip out my own intestines before I harm her again.

Right after I'll do anything in my power to apologize for the harm I *did* cause.

The closer she gets to the edge of the forest, the less traces of urgency can be found in her scent. She exited the forest and followed the road for some time, making it impressively far before stopping.

There's another scent mingling with hers that sends panic scorching down my spine. There's a sickly natural trace to the newcomer, suggesting only one thing: a witch was here.

I'd be concerned about Harlow's whereabouts if I didn't have a pretty good idea where this witch had come from—and where they took her.

I turn north and start my way towards the Canadian border, and eventually Banff, Alberta, where Highridge Coven, the coven every Sinclair up to Harlow has been a part of, makes camp.

No need to chase the bond. I've been to Banff numerous times over the years. They often have a protection barrier around the town, forcing me to wait until the inevitable time when the Sinclair I was hunting left safety.

This time will be no different, only I'll be keeping her.

THIRTY-TWO

Harlow

"A few months ago, two vampires attacked the house. Mom and Dad fought them off and told me to go, but I couldn't leave them and stayed to help. My magick exploded greater than I've ever felt before, and it lit my house on fire. It was chaos. The vampires burned, and it was all I saw before passing out. I woke up outside with paramedics over me. The house was fine, but my parents were dead."

Morgan's frown of sympathy is hidden by her sip of tea.

"After that, there was a protection spell around the property, except I no longer had access to my powers."

"Magick is driven by emotions, which explains the barrier," she remarks. "Your magick used the last bit of itself to keep you safe. As for losing them...I'd never heard of such a thing."

"For the following couple months, I fell into a depression that only broke when I had to survive, when Alec came for me."

She sucks in a breath. "You wouldn't mean Alec Dormer, would you? The vampire who's been after your family ever since Elizabeth Sinclair."

"That'd be the one." Of course, the coven would know about him. "He captured me, locked me up, and later revealed his history with Sinclairs, except with me, he wanted to sell the cure to other vampires." I skip over the party and other details of my time with Alec.

Her gaze goes to my neck. "So he's not the one who bit you?"

"Uh, I'll get to that." I pull more hair over my shoulder, ensuring the marks are well covered. "The first vampire who bought the rights to my blood drank from a goblet." At her paling face, I quickly add, "It was fine. Fine as it could be, anyway. Didn't hurt. Once the vampire drank, he transitioned into a human. It was really miraculous to see—he was my first. But the change didn't last long. He started puking up my blood and died. Alec determined that because I didn't have my magick, the cure wasn't at its full strength."

She lets out a grunting noise but leans back in her chair, tapping her fingers along the mug. "A *vampire* pieced that together?"

I shrug, not really knowing how he came to the conclusion, nor caring. With my powers now functioning, it no longer matters either.

"He was really determined for me to get my magick back. But he wasn't all that bad." At her lifted brows, I add, "He was pissed and locked me in a smaller cell than the first, but when my claustrophobia got bad, he took me from there. Gave me a bedroom. A really comfortable one." My cheeks warm with the memories of everything that occurred in that room.

"A bedroom doesn't make him a good person."

"I know." The heat flashes hotter in embarrassment and defence. "Besides, once I learned why he was doing all that, I was more determined than ever to escape. So one day, when he was locked up away from sunlight, I used the bedroom's furniture to break the window and escape."

"You are a Sinclair," she murmurs dryly, affectionately. "Wouldn't expect anything else. That's when he caught you?"

"I got away...kinda. He caught up and bit me." Hiding the fact I'm his Bride might not be the wisest in case he comes here and has an entire coven battling him. I don't want to see him dead, no matter what.

I don't want him to get killed. A fact as striking as everything else I've learned in the past twenty-four hours, but one I push aside for later.

"He claims I'm his Bride," I finally admit, her reply the distinct thud of her nearly empty mug landing on the table.

"You're *mated* to a vampire? Oh, this is bad."

"How's it possible?" I lean onto the table, hoping this woman, this High Priestess, knows things. "He says vampires typically mate with their own kind."

Her eyes flick to the ceiling. "Only She'd know." Her tone is sharp when she checks, "You're absolutely sure?"

"He's acting like it's the truth." Images of Alec flit through my mind. The way he chased me from my room to the front door. His expression, the betrayal and hurt when I slammed him against the wall. The threats he made.

"I'll find you. There's nowhere on Earth you can hide that I won't be able to get to you."

"Also...I think I've been hearing his voice in my head long before we met. Like even before my parents—Arthur and Violet, I mean— were killed."

"That's not possible. Witches don't hear voices."

"I can't deny what happened. I'm telling you all this because I think he might come for me, if he can track me here."

She laughs once without humour. "Oh, he'll come. He won't be able to resist his instincts to be close to you."

Which makes me a danger to this entire coven; I can't be certain what Alec would do if I'm kept away. It's a fight between him and me, and the coven shouldn't get in the middle. "I can leave so no one gets hurt by accident."

Ice freezes her gaze. "*This* is your home. We are your coven. I'm welcoming you back to the place you should have always been.

Banff is protected by a spell, and we have deals with the shifter pack by the base of the mountains. He won't get to you, or any of us, for that matter."

"He'll try."

"He'll fail."

The thought doesn't make me relax, because I truly don't know what to do about Alec—how to feel. What his claims mean long-term. My entire focus so far was getting away, but I never considered after.

"Why would you risk the coven?" I ask, using the conversation as a distraction from my unknown emotions.

"You *are* the coven." She reaches to rest her hand over mine. "We protect our own here. But please, finish your story, because I have my own to tell."

Although my worries are an uncomfortable nagging sensation, I force myself to continue. "After returning to my room, I found a shoebox of stuff. An old wedding portrait of my parents when they were younger, and Mom didn't have red hair, which I found strange. Stranger were the IDs labelled as Violet and Arthur Hartman, and letters she—Violet—wrote. Letters about me. Kidnapping me. Wiping my memory so I don't remember my life before them. Binding my magick to make me weaker." As panic constricts my throat, my words come out quicker. "I realized they weren't my real parents. *Nothing* was real. The people I loved—the people I called Mom and Dad—were liars. What...?" Anguish makes my eyes heavy as I focus on her, pleading for the rest. "Morgan, what happened? What happened to my real parents? Why wasn't I raised here? Why did you assume I was dead? Please...I need to know."

She squeezes my hand tighter, a gesture I feel is more for her than me. "I *hate* what I'm about to say, but I hope it provides clarity." With a sigh, Morgan pushes her mug to the side to slide her palms flat against the table. "You were seven when they joined us.

They escaped their old coven because their High Priestess practiced black magick."

That term has only popped up once in my lessons—within Gram's grimoires when she wrote warnings about it. Black magick is believed to be the ultimate form of Darkness a witch or warlock could fall into. It's spurred on by death; to receive the abilities, a sacrifice must be made. The more murders, the more powerful the practitioner grows. Those who remain on Hecate's side are considered Light, but those in the Dark lose their souls and turn away from the Goddess and everything She stands for.

"Inherently, witches don't know how to properly function with black magick," she continues. "We're not Dark creatures, not like vampires, and when our powers get caught up in it? It's evil, and for that reason, forbidden. When Violet and Arthur came to us, we took them in. They refused to tell us which coven they'd come from, which should have been my first clue, but my mother, who was High Priestess at the time, believed their resistance was only from their fear. She allowed them into our coven, our circles, and our family. All was well for a while...until it wasn't. Until after a full moon ceremony, when we often gather. Your parents loved them and often were the last to leave—which you were always pleased about. You and Carina got to hang out with Jasper—Carina's cousin—and the other children."

Jasper. I wait for the name to spark a memory, but like Carina, nothing comes.

"I don't remember him," I admit.

With an affectionate smile out the window, she replies, "I anticipate my daughter is at Jasper's with news of your arrival. You'll see him later. Your parents didn't hang around long after that particular ceremony. No one really saw them leave, and feeling it was unlike them, I stopped by on my way home." Her jaw moves back and forth before her whisper slips out, one so full of grief it slices across the table and into my own heart. "What I found—they were dead.

And you...you were gone." Her eyes flash away from the window. "I'm so sorry, Harlow, for not doing more. For not checking five minutes sooner. For doing *nothing*."

My chest constricts. Is it possible to grieve people I don't remember? To grieve what was? What should have been? The couple who lived in the house nearby, never able to grow old together or see me grow up.

"Violet and Arthur turned away from Light like the rest of their coven. Seems they were only here on orders, but they hid that part of themselves well. To this day, I don't know what their exact commands were, which coven they came from, or the reasoning behind their actions, but we suspect it had something to do with you, because you were what they took. We went after you, of course, following your signature."

"Signature?" She mentioned that before but never explained its meaning.

"Every witch's magick leaves a trace typically only their coven's High Priestess can recognize. As a Sinclair and the creator behind the coven, yours has the strongest signature compared to, say, mine. Your signature was still active, so we knew you were alive, and never stopped searching. Two days later, my mother stopped feeling you. That same night, the human police called about a car accident and traced the last registered address of the licence plate to us. Three bodies, no survivors. Two adults—a woman and a man—and a...a female child, Harlow. *You*. The girl had red hair. She was your size. Your magick disappeared. Everything lined up. We had every reason to believe you were dead and had no choice but to give up."

My back falls against the chair, unsure how to process this. Violet and Arthur murdered my parents, kidnapped me, and then faked my death. Seems like a lot of work if they were following orders, especially considering I never met another coven growing up.

Unless those memories were stolen as well.

"They murdered innocents," I realize with a strike to my heart. "You said there were bodies, but it obviously wasn't us three." Who was in the car, then, if not me and the Hartmans? Who did they use in their cruel games?

Who *were* these people? The people I called Mom and Dad? The people I *loved*. The people I nearly died for, whom I wept and grieved for fucking *months* over.

They were a lie.

They might have fed me, clothed me, taken care of me. Were there through every life stage, cheered me on and held me during bouts of sadness. Taught me enchantments and to control my powers.

But did they love me?

They were strangers who stole me from my family, my coven, and kept me for themselves. They killed my parents, deceived the coven, and murdered innocents in a cover-up.

"That's why you assumed I was dead."

"We mourned you all, Harlow. Held memorials. Your parents' bodies got buried. The coven wasn't the same after the betrayal. Years passed, and whomever's orders they were following, no one else ever came. It was like a nightmare that never really happened. Until mere hours ago." She huffs in partial amusement. "I was convinced I was imagining it, but for the first time in years, I *felt* your magick. The signature, the heat...it's the same. I thought there's no way, it's a trick of the mind, but *had* to check. Followed the trace until finding you wandering the side of the road. And now, here you are. Home."

Home. This still seems like a fever dream.

"If their orders were to kidnap and fake my death, to what end? I don't recall meeting any other witch as a kid."

She shrugs, pursing her lips. "You're one of the four most powerful bloodlines to exist, Harlow. You're also the holder of the cure to vampirism, and vampires are our enemies. You have a lot of value, and perhaps they wished to capitalize on that."

"Maybe..." I replay what she just said. "Wait—one of the four?"

Morgan leans back in her chair, her lips curling in disgust. "Don't tell me they didn't even give you a proper education?"

"I'm guessing not."

"Hecate, give me strength," she mumbles, rubbing a hand over her face. "Seems we have a lot to catch up on, but for now, to answer your question, the hierarchy goes as follows." She lifts her hand, gesturing with each name she lists, moving it down the invisible column. "Hecate, the Goddess of Magick, Witchcraft, and Earth; Freya, the First Witch as Her representation on Earth, and then the covens made up of witches and warlocks. Amongst them, we're all descended from one of four bloodlines. Four humans that were given the gift of elemental magick, becoming the first group of witches answering to Freya as their High Priestess. The Brooks, the Deverauxs, the Yarrows, and the Sinclairs. Freya led them through all the teachings of witchcraft, elements, nature—all things Light—while identifying who revealed a stronger connection to which element. Your descendant was gifted fire."

Damn. I stare at my palms, where centuries of fire magick course through my veins. Descended from one of the first witches is...wow.

"What were Violet and Arthur's magick? I only ever saw them use fire."

"Earth. Had you been raised here, we would have trained you on the basics of the other elements. They obviously had enough knowledge of fire to fake it."

That'd explain Mom's enjoyment of gardening, though it's strange she never decorated with plants.

"Did I learn this history before? I mean, before I was taken?"

She offers a small smile of empathy. "The history of the witches is something you would have been taught when you were about twelve."

There's too much unknown, blocked within years of charms. So much I'd like to know, especially being back with the coven. Even if it became too much after a lifetime without a coven and I opted not to stay, I'd be doing myself a disservice by not giving every honest attempt to become the witch I should have always been.

"Do you think I'll ever get my memories back? I'd like to remember my parents, and what my life was like."

"I promise, Harlow, I will do everything in my ability to get them returned to you. And I have an idea on how we can do that."

THIRTY-THREE

Alec

By the middle of the night, I pass the border into Alberta, and the remaining stretch up to the Rockies is quick and familiar. All too soon, I reach the small picturesque tourist town of Banff, nestled between mountains. Given the time, tourists are tucked into their hotels while residents remain in their homes until morning, when it'll be another day of dealing with the masses and selling overpriced tourist shit to them.

On the very edge of town, farthest from the main core, is the set of roads the members of Highridge Coven live on. It's there I feel the pulse in my stomach, the invisible cord tugging me towards the last house up the slight incline.

I pass the Sinclair house without a glance, scenting my Bride by the walkway but nowhere near the building.

By the final house, the flood of power is nearly visible—if one knows what to look for. Witches have a tell. The florals, the candles, the sickening natural fragrances wafting from the wood-sided house, but it's the one beneath all that owning my focus.

After running all night, Harlow's scent rocks my core, my gums reminding me I'm hungry, despite only drinking yesterday. She left me, though, and the monster must be reassured we have her back.

I pace up to the house, following both her sweet scent and the bond. There's another witch inside, but she won't be an issue as long as she knows not to keep my Bride from me.

Her feelings prick at my nerves. She's happy. Apprehensive and nervous, but pleased, and it pulls me to a stop, my irritated snarl spooking a bird chirping on a branch nearby.

I have to be smart about this. She'll be defensive, even if there's nothing she can do to hide herself from me. Nothing that'll prevent me from taking her.

Not even herself.

It's with the bond I reach out to her, testing something I've only ever heard about occurring between mated pairs. With her not being a vampire, and not having drank my blood to complete the connection on her side, I can only hope it works even a fraction.

Harlow.

THIRTY-FOUR

Harlow

The sun has long dipped behind the mountaintops by the time we finish talking, and it's all so much to process.

Morgan takes our mugs to the counter to get more tea, leaving me with my thoughts. The most pressing is the sun has set and Alec's probably on his way.

Morgan returns to the table and slides me a fresh drink. Her thoughts were obviously where mine are, if her comment is any indication. "Sun's down. Your vampire will be here soon, I imagine. How would you like us to handle him?"

"Us?"

"He won't broach the town, so we can ignore his presence, but I worry for the innocent humans in the area and what he may do. Or I can take the coven and we'll deal with him."

Oh. No, I don't want that. Not at all. Alec's strong, but against an entire coven of fully fledged witches? He'd likely lose, and that isn't what I want.

"Um, I don't know, but I don't want him harmed."

She gives me a curious look over the rim of her mug but says nothing. The steam floats from the dark liquid, tangling with the air when I blow on it before testing a sip.

"How many coven members are there?"

"Twenty. Not counting the four babies born in the last couple years."

That's twenty people she'd ask to protect me if I wanted her to. That's also twenty powerful people who'd overpower Alec, and it's with that thought driving up my panic I repeat, "If he comes, I'll deal with him."

Another strange look, and yet again, no comment. The room falls blissfully silent as we both sip our drinks. It feels like only moments later, Morgan slides her mug away, gaining my attention.

"When was the last circle you participated in?"

"Years ago," I reply, my heart aching with a low pang. "It was the night before my eighteenth birthday."

"That's *six years*!" Her exclamation rocks the table, my tea sloshing up the side of the mug. "For fuck's sake, they made you mortal."

"I suppose so, yeah." There weren't many growing up that I can recall—but then again, who's to say how confident my memory is? When I turned eighteen, we never did them, despite my few requests. Thinking about it, Mom always seemed uncomfortable when I asked, and it was that reason I never snuck the supplies to do it on my own.

No wonder Hecate hasn't been answering me; I abandoned her before she abandoned me.

"Mom and Dad—I mean, Violet and Arthur, we didn't hold many ceremonies or anything like that. They didn't seem to enjoy them."

A shadow encompasses her expression as she gestures for me to stand and follow. "Those who play with black magick often avoid honouring nature and the Goddess, so I'm not that surprised."

By the door, she waves her hand and sends our mugs flying into the sink, the tap briefly turning on to rinse them. Violet always limited magick usage in the house, fearing humans nearby would accidentally spot us. Living in a tiny town only surrounded by fellow witches certainly has the benefit of not hiding.

"I take it, then, it's been some time since you've participated in a Full Moon Ceremony?"

"That would be never."

She stops short in the entrance to the living room, and I crash into her back with a low *oomph*. "I'm sorry, Harlow. Fuck, it's not fair how much you missed out on."

"If it helps, I didn't realize how much I missed out on, so I never really missed it."

Her glare suggests it doesn't ease her guilt, but it's true. I'd read about some of the ceremonies within Gram's grimoires, but when I broached the subject as a child, it was often met with disinterest. One can only beg so many times before learning to give up asking, so by the time adulthood came, the patterns my parents had became mine. Besides, I had no idea how to run a circle or a Full Moon Ceremony, or if they'd even work if I was the only one in them. The grimoires conveniently left out the instructions.

Truth is...hearing everything I could and should have experienced stings. Yeah, I miss having a group of twenty witches and warlocks I call family. I miss the ceremonies. The connection to Hecate. Only, I never realized until now I miss those things.

"Sometimes on the full moon and holidays, I'd light a candle in Her honour. Say a blessing. But that's it."

Morgan's expression would be calmer had I told her I murder people daily.

"Well, by happy coincidence, tomorrow is the full moon, which means the entire coven will gather. If you'd like, you can not only join us, but it'll be your official introduction. You can watch or participate; up to you, since I understand this might be overwhelming."

"I want to join," I reply instantly and without thought. "I won't know what to do, but I'll figure it out." I think.

Morgan clasps my hands between hers as her shoulders lower with her deep breath. "You have no idea how happy that makes me. It's strange having you back." She reaches up, tucking a strand of hair around my ear, her touch gentle—a mother's touch. "It's like having your mother again. You look so much like her, you know. When I first saw you, for a moment I thought you were her."

"You two were close, weren't you?" It's how Morgan speaks about my real mom that suggests it.

"The closest. We grew up as best friends. Your parents made me your guardian. Your godmother would be the mortal term, in case you weren't taught terminology. In the case of their deaths, it was up to me to protect you, and while I've failed so far, I won't any longer."

What do I say to that? What *can* I, when it feels like she's ripped me off the bit of stability I was clinging to, all to move me to a larger and more stable platform.

"Thank you."

"Never thank me for doing what's right," she replies, turning into the living room. "Would you be interested in a circle right now? I know it's late, so it doesn't have to be much."

Despite the exhaustion that made me ragged earlier, it feels like I wouldn't be able to sleep even if I tried. Not when she's offering me a lifetime of catch-up.

"I'd like that."

Morgan shows me the chest of extra candles, purified crystals, and bundles of herbs in the corner of the room. She lays out four candles and places obsidian and quartz— crystals intended for protection—on the floor with herbs between each one, connecting them in a circle large enough to consume most of the floor's space, about four feet wide.

She gestures to the green candle nearest me. "North, representing Earth. It's air, fire, and water, going clockwise." She points to each one as her finger rotates in the air. "Four elements, four directions. Calling the elements in ceremony deviates from the pentacle's design. The elements' positions, for one, and also the exclusion of spirit. Spirit, in my opinion, encompasses everything. All four elements, all four directions, and anyone involved. It's inside us, and thus, inherently part of the ritual." She holds out a hand for me. "Join me."

I step into the circle with her, careful not to mess up the unlit candles and other ingredients, and position myself nearest to the candle representing fire, directly across from her.

She gestures for me to lower to the floor, and I get into a kneeling position like she does, trepidation and excitement running through me. It's been so long since I've felt this connection with the elements, and we haven't even begun.

"Ready?" she checks, and only with my deep breath and nod does she throw her hand towards the candle facing North and begin the incantation.

"Spirit of the North, I summon you.
Bring forth the essence of Earth to deliver us."

The flame ignites instantly—but not with a flame. Rather, a wisp of tiny, green leaves swirl in a circle, no higher than a candle flame.

Whoa. The last circle Mom and Dad held, the candles were lit by flames, not the elements. Though, whether that was a proper circle now remains to be seen.

Morgan steps closer to the candle positioned to the East and repeats a similar incantation before lighting the final two candles, all while I remain in awe.

"Spirit of the East, I summon you.
Bring forth the essence of Air to connect us.
Spirit of the South, I summon you.

Bring forth the essence of Fire to purify us.
Spirit of the West, I summon you.
Bring forth the essence of Water to heal us."

One by one, the candles ignite with their respective elements: a mini tornado, a warming flame, and a large water drop that dances the same way as fire.

All at once, I *feel* them in ways I haven't before. The invigorating scent of earth, the welcoming brush of air, the warming comfort of fire, and the cool wash of water. They combine in the circle, wrapping me in their fold, taking my mind and soul away from my body and to a better place. A place without worries and stress, without old plots and deception. For now, it's me and Morgan and the spirits. Nothing more, nothing less.

Morgan sits across from me and holds out her hands, palms up, for me to take. I slide my hands into hers, holding her as she does me. Her eyes shut but mine remain open, compelled by the swirls of power radiating in the space.

"The circle is now open. Blessed Be, Harlow."

"Blessed Be, Morgan," I reply, the words strange on my tongue. The last time I said the traditional greeting to my parents was...*have I ever?*

"Hecate, I thank you, Goddess of Life and All Things, of Witchcraft and all we hold dear, for returning Harlow to our arms. We promise to love and protect her for all the years she spends on your sacred earth but ask for your blessing as well."

The spiritual flames above each candle flicker out and then back on, and a hypnotic enchantment falls upon the circle, making me gasp. A brush of a hand that isn't Morgan's, a whisper of words unspoken and unheard—She's here.

I want to cry. Weep and apologize for every instance I assumed She's forsaken me.

"Do you feel that?" Morgan murmurs with a smile.

"Yeah. It's...I can't even describe it."

"I understand."

My eyes flutter shut to chase Her caress, but then a coolness falls on my shoulders and Her touch is suddenly gone. Something invisible slithers around my neck, and that menacing voice from earlier interrupts. *You're mine*, it says, chasing away the Goddess and everything good.

I gasp, ripping my arms from Morgan, trying to make sense of what that was, how to describe what happened when I hear another voice, and just like that, the safety the circle gave me zaps away, even though Morgan hasn't closed it yet. Too soon, reality returns like a wall crushing everything I hold dear.

Harlow.

He's here. Of course, he's here.

"Morgan—"

The door crashes open, banging against the wall, and Morgan leaps to her feet, hopping over the candles in her rush towards the hallway. I run after her, throwing myself between the two enemies before either gets hurt.

"How the fuck did you enter the town, vampire?"

He's here. The fact he got through the wards Morgan claimed were around town becomes unimportant compared to the sight of him, which I can't help but drink in. His hair, blown back and windswept, presumably from his run, and his black eyes that are entirely focused on me while ignoring the witch who's a much greater threat. His chest rises and falls with breaths he doesn't have to take, his nostrils flaring as he studies me from head to toe, a rumble filling the hallway.

I force my back to him, his gaze caressing my spine with the same pressure his hands would. My body is hyper-aware of his presence, like everything existing between us before yesterday no longer matters.

But it does. A lot.

"Don't," I warn Morgan. "He won't hurt you. He's here for me."

"You're protecting him?" Her hands lower. "I thought...no matter." She shakes her head, focusing on him again. "The barrier is designed to keep any witch, vampire, or shifter not born of Highridge Coven out. How did you get through?"

"Walked over the town's line," he replies, his voice a dark rumble I feel in the base of my stomach. "Not my fault your spells aren't up to par."

Morgan stares considerably at him before glancing at me, back and forth as her conclusion is drawn. "He drank your blood. He has some of you inside him. That's how."

"I'm only here for Harlow. Then I'll leave."

"That won't be happening." Morgan slips her arm around my waist and yanks me away from him before I can properly react.

Alec's eyes flash a threatening red, and he narrows in on where she's holding me. I've seen this look before. The look before attacking, like he had at the party and my room. If he thinks I'm threatened—

I push away to place myself between them, shaking my head to ask her to stop fighting—and him to not attack. "I'll speak with him, it's fine. We won't go anywhere."

Her lips fold together as she debates what she doesn't truly have a say in before finally coming to the same conclusion with a resigned sigh. "If that's what you want. Not in here, though. I won't have a vampire inside my home. Go around back so no one sees him." To Alec, she adds, "You harm her, I'll be coming for your fangs."

"I'd rather rip them out myself if I do," he replies, his words echoing around the confused and empty cavities of my heart.

Ignoring the turbulent sensation, I step outside and scan the area to make sure we're alone. Given it's the middle of the night, most of the nearby homes have their lights off.

I lead Alec around the side of the house towards the small,

fenced-in area, passing through the waist-high gate. It's too dark to make out anything but the single thick tree in the corner and a few planter boxes towards the other side.

The moment my feet cross the backyard's threshold, the wind picks up. No, wait—that's because hands grip my hips, turning me around, and then my back's against the tree after having been rushed across the yard, an imposing body trapping me there.

Defend yourself. He trapped you. Took all your choices. He's the enemy. A coolness wraps around my wrists, tempting the shadows to return. *Remember how good it felt claiming control of your destiny yesterday, when you pinned him to the wall? Think about—*

Alec's rough, dizzying kiss silences the voice, claiming every ounce of that very control for himself.

FOURTH INTERMISSION

Freya

One overbearing vampire.

One formidable coven of witches.

And one pissed-off woman who's been betrayed by almost everyone in her life, that vampire included.

I'm taking bets. Want in?

And for a snack to get through the next bit, I'm thinking... hmm...poutine? We are in the tourist trap of the mountains, after all. Gotta eat like the locals do.

Oh, don't worry, the drama between our lovebirds is *far* from over. So many answers and questions still to go.

It'll get better and worse.

They do gotta hurry up, though, because while the vampire is fun to mess with, now that we're in Banff, I've scoped out the next guy.

Wolves have a temper.

Alec needs to move this along so I can go pet my next animal friend. Think the soon-to-be alpha shifter would prefer a pink or purple collar? I'm thinking pink; it is my favourite colour.

Oh! I should dye my hair bubblegum blue for the next bit.

Pink collar, purple leash. Decision made.

Although. I should probably leave the wolf-taming to his future witch. Your thoughts?

THIRTY-FIVE

Alec

y Bride.

Safe and in my arms.

And seconds away from being tossed onto my back so we can return home.

My hands travel the length of her body towards her thighs, where, with little effort, I hoist her into my arms, using the tree to trap her. Her legs tighten around my waist and her arms around my shoulders as a tentative intrigue echoes down the bond.

I slide my fingers into her hair, and grip her tighter, kiss her harder, telling her with my mouth exactly how I feel about her running. How the monster inside is demanding I show my Bride why taking off was a bad fucking idea. It craves ripping her clothes off and taking her right here, witchy audience be damned.

She breaks from my mouth for a much-needed gulp of air, and the moment she has it, I haul her back to me, a hand on her neck to keep her submissive.

It's been nearly twenty-four hours since I've been inside her, and the bond wants a repeat. Wants to be inside her for as long as she'll allow me to be. To tie her to my bed and keep myself sated on her blood and cunt while pampering her until she wouldn't possibly consider ever leaving. We can spend eternity in my sheets, drinking and fucking.

She'll pull away soon. I know Harlow, and the hate she felt for me hours prior didn't vanish with her reuniting with Banff. So while I have her, I take my fill, the bond a cruel, prickly reminder this won't be enough.

Almost on schedule, her hands push into my shoulders and her head turns, breaking the kiss. Her lips are swollen, and her eyes are a dark shade of lavender, begging me to kiss her again.

"You can't—we can't. How did you find me?" She ducks her head, as though to hide, which will never again happen. Her legs loosen, silently asking me to put her down, but I tighten my hold, denying her request.

"I warned you there isn't anywhere you can run where I won't be able to find you. As my Bride, we're connected. I tracked your scent through the woods." My nose slides up the side of her neck, enticing a groan as I take in what I've been forced to go without. "Until you disappeared, when I picked up another witch's scent. It was all too easy to guess where you were headed, but even so, I followed the bond between us."

"What bond?"

"The mate bond. Biting reveals who our Bride is—if we're given one—and between drinking your blood and sex, a connection forms, allowing me to track you and feel your emotions. There are rumours of other abilities, but obviously I haven't been able to test them before now."

"Whoa, wait." She leans against my hand, creating as much space as my arms allow for. "Put me down and back up. You can *feel* me? Like reading my mind?"

I only listen to one of her demands. "No, it's a sense of your emotions, like they're brushing against my own. It's how I knew you were concerned about me when I appeared in front of that witch." The memory tugs at a smile, that when the witch would have attacked, Harlow cared enough to block it. "Or when you were in my room, I felt what you felt. And right now, you're scared. But not of me—although that's only an educated guess. Your emotions don't indicate the purpose behind them. You're scared because I'm here and you have no idea what it means. Minutes before I entered the house, you were calm." As much as I've always been attracted to her fear, I can't deny her tranquility intrigued me on another level.

"Why can't I feel you then?" She tries to mask it with her blank expression, but beneath her apprehension, she's annoyed, which is intriguing considering what she's saying.

"It's only a guess, but probably because you didn't take my blood in you. Blood-sharing is the ultimate act between mates. Bride or chosen partners, it's *the* act that links a couple together. If you were a vampire, I'd imagine the bond would be completed on your end." Or it wouldn't exist at all, because she's not a vampire.

She stiffens in my arms, sniffing. "Don't wait around for that 'cause it'll never happen."

"I'd expect nothing less, Hellion." The familiarity of our banter is a welcome greeting.

"Is it always like that? Mates aside, if you drank from another, would a bond form?"

"If it did, we'd all be connected one way or the other by now."

She's silent, digesting the news. The skin between her eyes is wrinkled, and I can't help but reach up and stroke it smooth. When our skin meets, she jerks, jamming her elbows into my arms.

"Nope, too much. Put me down."

I don't.

"Alec," she says in that warning tone of hers, and while it's cute, it doesn't work how she wants it to.

"First, I want to try one of the rumoured abilities."

"Which is?" She drags her tongue over her bottom lip, teasing me with the taste I haven't had my fill of quite yet.

I stare at her, mentally verbalizing what I want to, urging her to hear me.

Harlow.

She gasps, her eyes blown wide and slaps my shoulder. "No, no, no! Not this again. I won't fuckin' deal, not again." Her palms press into the sides of her head as she shakes it back and forth. "You knew, this whole time, why I've been hearing your voice! Did you know I'd be your Bride? Was this yet more fucking lies, another person deciding my future?"

Using the tree as leverage to keep her upright, I manacle my hands around her wrists and tug them away from her head. "No, I didn't know. I wouldn't have bit you had I known." Although she doesn't visibly show it, her emotions flinch with hurt. "I've never heard of mated pairs being able to hear one another before bonding. I don't know why you did, but perhaps it's a result of being a witch. When I called your name before barging into the witch's home, that was the first time I've ever consciously attempted to mentally contact you, so anytime before today wasn't my doing." Deliberately, anyway.

Her fight ceases, shoulders slumping. "Fuck. Wow. Okay. Wow." She swallows her rambles, finally managing a few coherent words. "On one hand, cool, but on the other, I'm already trying to get away from you as is. I don't need more ways for you to torment me."

"Every hour since biting you has been torment, Hellion, so I don't see how this is any different."

Her eyes flash with something unspoken, and the bond reveals nothing. Whatever it is passes for determination as she narrows her eyes, looking intent enough to scour my soul.

After another moment, the expression breaks for a puffed breath and, "Nothing?"

Smirking, I reply in her head. *If that was you attempting to speak to me, I heard nothing. Assuming for the same reason you won't feel my emotions. Not until you drink my blood.*

"So never."

If that's what you want.

"I want you to put me down."

This time, I listen, allowing her body to slide against mine, feeling her soft curves against the hard planes of my body. I remain where I stand, and when she tries to cut to the side to regain space, my arm comes up, blocking her.

"We're not finished."

"Was me slamming you against the wall not a good enough hint?"

"My Bride is powerful. Why would I be upset?"

"Yeah, well, your *powerful Bride* is getting annoyed and has another hex ready if you don't back the fuck up and let me go."

"Why would I do that when we're moments away from heading back to the castle?"

"I'm not going anywhere with you. I *ran* from you. If you forgot, you kidnapped me. You were going to use me and then kill me."

There's no denying the past, but there's also no denying how the future is vastly different, and that *she's* my future. She'll be who I go through life for. She'll *be* my life. While I don't believe in fate, her kind does, and somewhere along the way, she became my fate. For that reason, I'll protect her above anything—myself included.

"You're my—"

"No." She shoves her hand over my mouth, cutting me off. Her skin is a bite away, but I limit myself to only a brief lick, pleased when her cheeks flush pink and she doesn't pull away. "Without the title," she continues, her voice a bit unstable, and lowers her hand. "I know what I am to you, but the fact remains that witches don't have mates. The *only* reason you want me at all is because of the bond. Otherwise, you hate me being your mate. Hell, you hate *me*, so why should I want to be around you? Give me one good reason."

Battles and wars where so few survived to be victors were simpler than dealing with this woman.

"I've wanted you for a while, but my hate blinded me."

She freezes, mouth parted. A squirrel nearby squeaks, and Harlow returns to the moment. "You're lying."

I wish I were. That I keep to myself.

"You've been my obsession longer than I realized you were."

"That's not the same. You were obsessed with using me, not getting to know me."

"Yes, and somewhere along our time together, that changed." Maybe even before I bit her. "Something out there wants us together. Must be for a pretty good reason, so it's our duty to see it through."

"Oh my fucking Goddess," she mumbles, tipping her head back until she's staring at the sky. With another sigh, she pushes by me, and this time, I let her go, sensing her need to walk the rage out. "First it's a bond, now it's our duty. It doesn't work like that, Alec!" She whirls, her foot sliding on the grass, but I dart to her side to keep her upright. She yanks away as fast as she's stable, shooting me a scathing look before continuing her march towards the house.

I intercept her path. "I don't have a choice, Hellion. My entire being demands I'm by your side, whether or not we like each other. Which, I do, by the way. Like you."

"What are you, twelve?"

"Believe me or don't. Your beauty was one of the first things I noticed. Your resilience was the second. Your humour, the third. You know how many Sinclairs have put up such a good fight? None." I pause, searching her face, imploring her to understand the truths I'm revealing. "They fight back, sure, with curses and other witchy shit, but they always lose. How is it the witch without her powers beat me?" Her heartbeat thrums louder, inviting me nearer.

"I didn't beat you. Not until I got my magick back."

Another step, and her pulse jumps in excitement. "Oh, you beat me, Hellion. No other Sinclair would have survived me the way you did. You destroyed my will the moment you cried in that cell."

"I survived because you let me. You would have slaughtered me that first night if not for your plans."

That may be true.

"Ever think fate was the driving force behind my plan change? After generations of Sinclairs, only when it's *your* turn did I alter my course. Why's that?"

Her breath catches on the wind. "Thought vampires don't believe in fate."

"We don't, but I'm starting to. What other explanation is there?"

Her gaze darts to the near-full moon in the sky, presumably looking towards where her deity would be, seeking answers neither of us will ever get.

"I'm not a vampire," she finally whispers, tipping her head back down. "I have a coven again. Putting aside both of us and feelings and bonds and whatever else you've thrown my way, I'm a witch who's finally home. A witch who barely knows how to be one, if today was any indication. I don't know how to be a vampire's Bride."

"From what I've experienced, you know how to be a witch very well. And there is no lesson on being a vampire's Bride, other than the fact you're mine." I snag her wrist, keeping her pinned to the spot. I catch when my words invoke a reaction urging her to run. My thumb traces the steady beat of her pulse, making small circles. "That's your lesson. You. Me. The end."

"I'm not leaving. This is where I was meant to be. Violet and Arthur murdered my parents and kidnapped me, forcing me to live half a life. One day with Morgan and I want more. I *need* more. I need this."

Centuries of being immortal has trained my expression to remain flat, to not reveal I knew all this after Freya told me her story.

It's all the stuff I meant to tell her, but then she escaped the bedroom and it was one thing after the other.

I despise the flash of grief coming from the bond.

I hate her trepidation more. I didn't plan to stay; I planned on snatching her up and running back home. She'll hate me if I do that, and hours ago, it didn't matter. Her feelings about me or mating were secondary to the fact that she needs to be safe and protected.

Until now. Until she's looking at me like she's seeking permission when we both know she's not. Until she looks at me with wide, violet eyes that are sprinkled with something I've never seen from her. Not distress, not anxiety, not rage. Pure bliss, happiness...hope.

Hope is something every immortal loses over their ongoing life. Hope becomes nothing when, with our powers, you can have anything. Why hope when we take? Hope is also a curse when wanting something that's impossible. Why hope for an out to this life when there are so few methods?

But Harlow's hope? It's fucking beautiful.

"Then I won't either."

"Alec—"

"I don't have a choice. Feelings aside, the bond won't allow me to leave."

She rolls her lips together before conceding with a nod. "Okay... just don't die. The coven will be pissed to see you hanging around."

They'll be more than pissed; they'll be deadly, but I let her cling to that faith. "Didn't know you still care."

Expecting a quick quip, she unbalances me when she murmurs, "I didn't know either, but I don't want to see you hurt. Bond aside."

Good, I inject into her head.

"Good," she murmurs back, twisting to face the house again with a sigh. "Look, I don't know what's next, but in a few hours the sun will be up. Which means you need a place to stay."

"Worried for my well-being again, Hellion? A man can get used to this." There's caves and shit all over the mountains, and it won't be overly difficult to find one, not that I'd like to be so far away from her.

"A bit," she mumbles, twisting to face the house, the single light on downstairs. The witch is observing us through the back window, her face concealed by tricks of light—presumably for Harlow's benefit, but I'm able to see. "I can ask Morgan if she knows somewhere safe."

"I'd appreciate that." Even if we're both aware this Morgan witch would rather see me burn in the sun than help me. "She's by the back door."

Harlow heads for the door and enters, peeking back before the house swallows her up. The moonlight is at an angle that reveals her small smile. A smile I'll cling to until tomorrow night, when I'll get to see her again.

The door shuts, and she talks quietly with the witch, their conversation audible with the help of my enhanced hearing. It's a quick exchange where the sound of Harlow's plea distracts me from the words being said, and then the door's opening and the older witch is stepping outside, crossing towards me.

"Alec Dormer, is it? You've made yourself quite known around these parts."

I watch her, not in the mood to get into this. The witch will demand I leave, and the only thing preventing me from ripping out her throat is Harlow's obvious affection for her. The quicker the conversation finishes, the quicker I can start seeking shelter.

"Because of you, I now need to modify the spell on the border," she muses. "Honestly, I never foresaw one of my own getting close enough to a vampire to make this an issue. Your kind creates a lot of problems, and when one member holds the very thing many vampires crave, you understand why I'm cautious about you being on my land."

"Because you want to protect Harlow. Except you didn't in the past."

She flinches before the hurt slides off her, replaced by fury. "You know nothing about the past, vampire."

"I do, actually." And then I summarize everything Freya told me the other night, about Harlow's fake parents joining the coven under false pretenses, getting close to everyone before murdering the real Sinclairs and taking Harlow for themselves.

The witch—Morgan, Harlow called her—straightens, observing me from beneath her nose despite being shorter than me. "Hm, I should ask how and why you know all that, but I'm getting the sense it doesn't really matter, does it? You're here for Harlow, and you're right; I didn't protect her well back then, but I'm vowing to do better this time."

No one can protect her better than me.

"When news spreads she's mine, my brethren will cease coming for her. Those who think to go against me will meet their deaths. She doesn't need you."

"But she wants the coven, doesn't she?" Her small question throws me, snarky, reminding me a bit of Harlow. "If she didn't wish to rejoin us, she'd be running back with you."

"She claims to want this," I agree, "but time will reveal how this all plays out."

"In that, we're in agreement, vampire. You care for her, so I hope you'll help me protect her from the next threat."

"Threat?" If I had a heart, it'd be pounding. The single word unlocks the monster within me, the part demanding I break into the witch's home and snatch Harlow away, bundle her up and take her home to keep her safe from everything, even a fucking paper cut at this point. "What are you talking about?"

"There's a reason Violet and Arthur kept her for themselves, and I fear it's not good." Her gaze travels to the sky, scanning over the nearly full moon. "Something's out there," she murmurs. "I felt it the moment I felt Harlow's signature. Something's coming...and since she's your life and death in physical form, you'll protect her. I fear our joint efforts will be required."

I don't like what she's saying. That a threat is coming, unknown at this point.

If Freya pops around, the witch has a few more questions to answer.

"For now, you have a problem." She glances towards the south-east region, the snow-capped mountains in the distance. "Sunrise is in a few hours. She requested I help you get somewhere safe, so—and I can't believe the words that are coming from my mouth—I'll permit you to stay inside my home, warded in my basement. It's windowless, so no daylight can enter. The enchantment I'll place on the door will only permit Harlow or myself to enter, and I'll let you out at sundown tomorrow. *If*"—she juts a finger into my face—"your fangs even think about coming near me or my family, you'll lose them, and I'll send you on a one-way vacation to the sunniest, hottest place you can imagine. Understand?"

"My fangs will only ever be near one witch."

Her nose wrinkles as though the very thought is abhorrent, but she gestures for me to follow inside. She leads me down the hallway, stopping by the door across from the kitchen. Before entering the lightless basement, I tilt my head towards the ceiling, listening for the telltale scraping of feet or breathing from my mate.

Morgan smirks knowingly. "She's upstairs in a room directly above us. Probably already passed out. In you go so I, too, can get to bed."

On the top step, a dart of my hand stops her from shutting the door. I stare at her, her purple eyes similar to Harlow's, but wrong too. A telltale sign of a witch, but Harlow isn't my enemy any longer, while this woman technically is.

Which is why I speak two words that grate at my throat, the

wrongness of saying this to her a scalding brand on my neck, but meaning them regardless.

"Thank you."

She bobs her head before shutting the door, hiding her flash of surprise. Her spell work is a murmur before the wooden door fizzles with a white coating that soon fades into nothing, and her steps pace away.

THIRTY-SIX

Harlow

As I'm sliding into a bed owned by a practical stranger—Carina—Morgan knocks on the door before poking her head in.

"Hey, wanted to make sure all is good."

I'm not even sure what "good" is anymore, but I force my mouth into somewhat of a smile, even if it ends up more as a grimace. "I appreciate the bed. Carina's okay with it?"

"She's sleeping in Jasper's spare room, which isn't anything new. She uses the place to get away from me. You'll see her in the morning, because I doubt she'll be able to stay away much longer."

"Looking forward to it," I say, and it doesn't feel like a lie. "Is he...?"

"He's down in the basement. It's windowless, so he'll be safe."

"Thank you." I shouldn't care about the vampire who would have sold pieces of me for his own amusement, but a part of me does. There's no name for it other than Stockholm syndrome. It's the part of me that isn't sure whether to hate him or not. The side of me that latched onto him outside, craved more, *wanted* to believe his claims.

"Have a good sleep." Morgan's yawn tapers into a sleepy chuckle. "We've all been awake too long. Night."

"Night," I reply to the partially shut door. A second later, her feet tread down the hallway towards her bedroom, and I recline against unfamiliar pillows, settling into Carina's bed.

For weeks now, all I've done is sleep in unfamiliar beds. Ever since Alec took me, it's been cells, a spare room, his bed, and now Carina's. At some point, I'll need to return home to clear it out and sell it; Morgan will eventually expect me to move back into my family home, where the last bed I had would have been a child's.

My teeth press into the side of my cheek, biting down on the emotions threatening to take over. It won't do me good stressing about any of that, especially with how tired I am. The bed is comfortable, and sleep is but a moment away.

It's sweet of you to care about my well-being, his sarcastic voice echoes around the chambers of my mind, and like that, I'm awake again. I completely forgot about this nifty (irritating) development.

"I don't," I whisper into the room, since I can't reply in his head, assuming his hearing can catch it.

Liar. It's okay. Your resistance was always one of the things I enjoyed about our time together. Breaking you down, getting you to realize.

"Realize what? How much I hated you?"

How much you tried your damndest not to see a man beneath the monster.

"You are a monster."

Yes. You know, even before our bond, I could pick up a sense of your emotions. Your heartbeat is quite telling, and mortals often release scents of fear and desire, so I had an idea. There was more than one time you looked beyond my revenge.

Maybe. Like when he told me about his family and, for the briefest moment, I felt bad for him. Before he ruined it with more truths.

Or when he took me from the cell after it got too suffocating.

Although, that one was all his fault, because if he never put me down there to begin with, it wouldn't have been a problem.

Or when he climbed on top of me in bed and for a second, I forgot I hated him. Forgot anything but how much my body craved his.

Sitting in a witch's basement isn't how I pictured this day going. Then again, everything with you has been unexpected.

"If you're looking for an apology—"

I'm not, he interrupts, the sharpness of his mental voice as cutting as his real one. *I'm stating this isn't* anything *like I ever pictured happening. Sitting in the basement of a witch's home, not as a captive, while my Bride is in someone else's bed. You should be in mine.*

The possessive growl attached to his words makes my stomach tingle. Stupid body.

I know you hate me, Harlow, and truthfully, I hate myself too. Outside, you were right about the bond pulling me to you. But that wasn't only it, and what I said was also the truth. From the moment we met, there was something different about you. Something alluring that sparked a feeling besides hate. But you were wrong about something as well. When we met, my obsession with you began. Prior to that, I was obsessed with revenge. Nothing more, nothing less. I didn't view the Sinclairs as people, but tools towards my goal. But you...the moment you ran through your neighbourhood, I couldn't get enough. You think I would have visited just any prisoner? No, I never intended on dropping by your cell until the party. You think I would have cared about your claustrophobia? No, but you've been casting a spell on me since that moment, long before your powers returned. It's a different kind of magick; I feel it. You screamed my name, and I didn't even think, I just knew I had to get to you. Had to ease your agony. I couldn't—can't—stay away, Hellion, bond aside. I don't understand the connection between us, but it's solidified the fight I was having with myself every fucking day. The side of me that demanded revenge versus the other half, becoming so addicted to you, not wanting to see you harmed, even by me. I couldn't see you broken—can't see you break. It's why I hated you more when the cure didn't work. You wouldn't fit in the little box I had prepared for you. Instead, you couldn't suit my revenge, but I also couldn't dispose of you like I would have anyone else.

My heart pounds wildly, my eyes unfocused as I try to imprint every syllable from his speech into my head permanently.

"Why are you telling me all this?"

Vampires are known predators, and no matter what he claims, I'll always be the prey. That speech...it's simply one more example of the hunt he's putting on. It's a method to lure me in, nothing more.

Because, like it or not, we have eternity to figure this out, and I'll be there every second of it trying to make you see reason.

"What if reason isn't enough? What if I want love one day?"

There's silence in my head for a moment. And then another. I stare at the alarm clock on Carina's bedside table, watching the numbers tick two more higher before his mental sigh comes through my head.

As if you'd love me after everything I've done.

Could I? If I gave this an honest shot, could I change my emotions from hate to love?

Haven't they already begun to? Shifting from hate to like, at the very least. If I truly hated him, I would have ended his life in the castle rather than knocking him out. I wouldn't have cared that he's safe from the sun tonight.

Before I can come up with an answer for both myself and him, he murmurs, *Sleep, Hellion. You're tired. Sleep...because we're far from done, you and I, and you need your energy. I'll stop talking.*

I'm about to scream with frustration, but instead obey his command without a secondary thought, pushing away everything today has brought forth in exchange for much-needed rest.

Alec keeps his promise and doesn't bother me for the rest of the night.

An hour later, I'm still awake wishing he would.

I sleep until mid-afternoon, my body catching up on its lost rest. The clock reads 1:02 p.m. when I wake, stretching my leaden body as I slide from the bed and peek between the white curtains.

For half a second, I forgot where I was, but the sight of the Rockies brings it all back. It's so lovely here, open and natural. What a sight to wake up to each day.

I could get used to living in Banff for sure, I think, letting the curtain fall back into place.

Morning, Hellion.

I ignore him and head out of the bedroom, all but running into Morgan as she's exiting the bathroom across from Carina's room.

"Good morning! Afternoon, I should say. I placed a fresh towel in the bathroom if you'd like to shower. Figured you might."

Considering I can't recall my last one, yeah. It was sometime before bolting through a forest from a maniacal vampire, getting fucked within an inch of my life, and then my successful escape.

"That'd be great, thank you."

She slides past me and heads for Carina's dresser, pulling out jeans and a long-sleeved black top. "You're about Carina's size, so these should work. Incant them to adjust, if need be. I'll have breakfast prepared when you're finished."

"Thanks."

I wait until she disappears down the stairs before entering the bathroom, spotting a towel folded on the edge of the sink.

After a hot shower, it feels amazing to put on clean clothes. With a quick fix of magick, they fit. Then I head down with my dirty clothes wrapped inside my used towel and find Morgan in the kitchen, frying something on the stove.

Movement from the table catches my attention seconds before Carina's head lifts from where it was buried in her cell. "Harlow, hey!"

"Carina," I greet, shifting foot from foot, feeling awkward in front of the woman who apparently was once my friend, but having no memory to confirm this. "Sorry for stealing your room last night."

She waves her hand. "Jasper's been wanting to beat my ass in video games for a while now, so it worked out. He's excited to see you."

"He better not have too many hopes considering I have no memory of him."

Keep it like that.

I tip my head towards the basement door, biting down on my smirk before Morgan notices. I wonder what she'd do if she knew he could get in my head. It feels like a secret I shouldn't share with anyone else. Nor do I really want to.

Just because you're back with the coven doesn't make you theirs. This Jasper will learn that, or else I'll rip the magick from his body and make him choke on it.

I cough, hiding my laughter behind my hand. It should be a horrifying thing to hear, but the image of Alec literally trying to rip a witch's magick from them, which is impossible, is amusing.

Carina sips from her mug, pulling my attention back to the kitchen and away from the vampire in the basement. "He'll live. Anyway, I'm sure it's strange being back, but I thought maybe I could show you around town? There's a reason Banff is so highly visited, and if you're going to live here, it'd be a shame for you to not do all the touristy shit first."

"That 'touristy shit' keeps the town thriving." Morgan flicks her fingers towards her daughter, scowling. A spark of blue flits from her fingertip and taps the back of Carina's head, who only rolls her eyes in return.

"Says the woman who owns a crystal shop downtown. Besides, she'll be busy setting up for the ceremony tonight, so I figured you and I could hang out. If you'd like."

I want to, a lot. I'd want to more if I didn't feel like reality was about to slap me in my face.

Morgan nods her agreement, flipping something from the pan onto waiting plates. "She's right. I have a lot to prepare for tonight. Not that I wouldn't be thrilled having you around as I do so, but seeing the town would be much more fun. Also, feel free to drop your clothes by the basement door. I'll have them washed later."

Both options sound appealing, but they're right. The little I've seen of Banff is breathtaking, and I want to take it all in. There'll be other full moons I can observe the setup for.

"I'd love to."

"Great."

I slide into one of the free chairs as three plates float from the counter, dropping lightly on the table. They're filled with eggs, toast, and pancakes, and my stomach growls painfully at the sight.

Fuck, I can hear that. The deep rumble chimes through my mind.

Next time, don't starve me. Even if he can't hear me, it makes me feel better having said it.

My first bite of eggs makes me groan. It's been entirely too long since I've had something more than granola bars or an apple. "Real food. You have no idea how needed this is." A statement for every being in the house.

I have better ways of making you moan.

I choke on the same bite, earning concerned glances from Carina and Morgan that I wave off, wishing I could tell the voice as easily. Maybe it'd be worth sipping his blood so the playing field is even and he can be forced to endlessly argue.

"Thanks for the food...and everything. And keeping Alec safe." I glance towards the window where the deadly-for-some-beings sun radiates.

Carina's head whips up from her plate, her widened gaze darting between her mother and me, but it's Morgan who responds, shaking her head. "Between us, Carina. No one can know we're harbouring a vampire, not even Jasper. Swear it."

"He won't hurt you," I add quickly, feeling the need to defend Alec to them.

Only if she hurts you. Otherwise, I'm past killing witches.

"Oh, it's not that. I think vampires are cool, that's all—not that I've ever met one, so I can't wait till dusk."

The uncertain look that crosses Morgan's face suggests she's not a complete fan of the idea. "My daughter enjoys dangerous things that make my hair turn grey."

Carina rolls her eyes. "A simple enchantment removes signs of aging, duh."

Chuckling, I comment, "He can be a bit prickly. I'm still in the process of training him."

Carina spits out her coffee, giggling, while the rumble inside my head threatens violence.

You haven't trained me. You've just unleashed another level of me. One even I didn't know existed.

Why do I like the sound of that so much? I've seen what he can do when he's being protective.

You're intrigued. I feel it.

Ignoring him, I listen to mother and daughter discuss the ceremony tonight while we finish the delicious meal. Carina disappears to shower and change while Morgan cleans the kitchen with a wave of her hand, magick doing all her work.

"I have to go to the shop, but you'll be okay, right?" Morgan stops by the table. "Once Carina's ready, you two can head out."

"I'm great," I tell her honestly. "I'm thrilled you found me yesterday, truly."

"I'm glad." She smiles and disappears into the hallway. A moment later, the front door shuts behind her, and I stand from the table.

Upstairs, the shower still runs, telling me I have a few moments, so I walk towards the basement door, pausing with my hand on the knob. Morgan's enchantment shimmers, letting me know it's still active, but when twisting the knob, it turns for me.

Wondering if Alec has sucked out my sanity alongside my blood, I descend the steps into the vampire's lair.

THIRTY-SEVEN

Alec

I hear her before I smell her, and I smell her before I see her, and I *felt* her even before she touched the door. She saves me from the conversation I've been having on the small electronic device I despise so much.

CEDRIC
Find her?

ME
Yes. With her family's coven.

CEDRIC
Are you remaining in Banff?

ME
For the time being.

CEDRIC
YOU'RE going to stay around the coven?

ME
Yes.

CEDRIC
Why not give this up? Get her home? Do what you always intended.

Cedric isn't so involved in my plans usually, and I wish that was the strangest thing about his behaviour.

After a moment of restraint, Harlow's standing at the bottom of the wooden staircase, her weak eyes scanning the dim, windowless basement until finding me seated on the ground.

Conversation with Cedric forgotten, I'm quick to my feet and even quicker to her side, the magnetizing sensation sucking me into her realm. "Oh, how the tables have turned." My chest presses close as I loom over her, craving any inch of her skin she's willing to give.

"What do you mean?" She rocks towards me, her scent filled with everything I desire.

"Once, it was I who visited you in the cells, and now I'm the one locked up."

"Don't see it like that. Morgan's doing us a favour."

Us. What an interesting way of looking at this.

"I'm aware." My voice vibrates against her back, and I lower my head to speak into her neck, my breath warming her skin where my bite marks remain visible. Knowing she's about to leave the house and see an old friend named *Jasper* makes me only more eager to remind her again whom she belongs to.

The scent of her prods at my hunger, my gums aching for what I wanted last night after my journey.

"They're lucky they obviously care a lot about you. I wouldn't be sitting in just any witch's home."

She twists away, putting herself a foot away, which simply won't do for long. Her eyes sweep the unlit basement. "You're okay down here?"

"You care?"

"I mean…"

"It's cozy," I say dryly. "So cozy it got you to visit." I tug her away from the stairs to keep her to myself as long as I'm able.

Her skin flushes the most delicious shade of red as I lift her onto the washing machine, stepping between her legs.

"You came down of your own will."

As her eyes adjust to the low light, they scan me, and slowly—agonizingly slow—she reaches up, caressing her fingertips along my cheek and up to my eyes. Her touch feels fucking amazing, and my hands press into the washing machine beside hers, letting her retain control for now. When her thumb passes again, the metal cries beneath the pressure, forming indents.

"You look tired, and I never thought I'd say that about a vampire."

"I expended a lot of energy travelling. I was in a rush."

She frowns. "You didn't stop for a snack?"

"Like I said before, mated pairs don't feed from another, whether it's a vampire, human, or animal. You're my sustenance."

Her tongue sweeps her bottom lip and, whether she realizes it or not, she leans towards me. My fingers dig into the machine harder.

"And if you don't?"

"After a few decades of starvation, of no other blood being enough, I'll fall into a coma, more or less. If you want me gone from your life, you can starve me. Otherwise, from here on out, my life is literally in your palm."

Her lips form a small O. "Sounds painful."

"Not that I have experience, but I'd imagine so."

She chews on the inside of her mouth before ending in a sigh, her head dipping until hair falls into her face and restricts my view. The machine gains a reprieve when I reach for her, tucking her hair behind her ear. With my brief touch, she holds her breath, the usual rise and fall of her chest non-existent.

"Can't have you die after convincing Morgan to save you." She lifts her wrist towards my mouth.

Her offer means she cares, at least a little bit.

Holding her gaze, I part my lips, and my fangs lengthen from my gums. Her pupils constrict, and her fingers flash white when she begins curling them into the machine, inches from where my indents lie.

Bringing her wrist closer, I continue holding her attention as my fangs pierce her skin. She flinches a little before the flash of pain transforms into a sweeter scent of longing, and her lids flutter shut.

I won't point out her reaction, not willing to give her more reason to be defensive over something she's slowly coming around to.

Her blood—fire and ash—ignites on my tongue, and what begins as a gentle sip quickly grows as my other hand comes up to hold her hip steady. Her lips roll together by my third gulp, and by my fourth, the slightest moan slips out.

I drink enough to hold me off for a day or so but not enough to make her weak before unhooking my fangs and laving my tongue over the injury, healing it.

Thank you, I push into her head.

She's about to reply and I cling to it, until a loud voice from upstairs calls her name, making Harlow stiffen in my arms.

"I have to go." She nudges my chest and, even being reluctant to release her, I lift her off the machine. "Coming!" she hollers, reaching the steps.

She disappears upstairs, leaving me grinning.

My witch came to see me because she wanted to.

She just won't admit it to herself.

THIRTY-EIGHT

anff is a lovely town with too many tourists packing the main strip that remains blocked off to cars. Carina shows me all the quaint shops and points out the best places to get snacks from, including BeaverTails; something I've never actually tried because my hometown—or what I believed was home—didn't have any locations of the popular restaurant chain. The fact, when I mentioned it, was met with absolute horror before she dragged me along, ordering three cinnamon-sugar-covered ones. "The best flavour," she described them being after the cashier rang her up.

"Hungry?" I eye the second BeaverTail she keeps after handing mine over.

"Nah, it's for him." She gestures to a nearby table where a guy waits, playing on his phone. He's bent over the table, head leaning on his hand, hair that's a combination of blond and brown covering his eyes.

He looks up at our approach, and his eyes, a masked vibrant blue, flash purple in recognition as his mouth slips open. "Shit, it's true. I assumed Carina was fuckin' with me."

"Why the hell would I do that?" She scowls, rolling her eyes.

Feeling his scrutiny, I manage a small smile that's meant to be reassuring. "I'm real."

He offers his hand in a shake, standing to pull out a chair for me. "It's surreal to see you, but I'm sure you don't want to talk about all that now."

"Hey, I'll get my own chair, thanks. Dick." Carina slides the BeaverTail in front of him. "And here, I went out of my way to get you a snack, and how do you repay me? By calling me a liar."

"I mean..." For that, he earns a flick of magick that neither seems to care about mortals possibly noticing. He ignores his cousin and gets to asking me how it is being back and where I've been.

Sitting with them becomes natural. While they're both lost within my locked-up brain, they feel like home. Like childhood reimagined.

Carina has sarcasm to rival Alec's, and though Jasper is fairly stoic, he's nice. My anxieties seem to melt away with every passing minute Carina walked me around town, and now with Jasper, it's like none of them even existed.

As they argue back and forth about one thing or another, my mind travels back to the house and the vampire hiding from the sun in the basement, and it's with a heavy pang to my heart, I realize Alec will never get this. He'll never be able to see Banff during the afternoon, with the sun lighting up the wall of mountains on either side and all the shops open and vibrant with business.

Maybe I could take him around during the nighttime. It won't be the same with everything closed, but it's something.

Why am I trying to have a date with my unwanted vampire kidnapper-turned-stalker?

This debate brings another thought to mind. That Alec will forever be limited to the nighttime, while my life in the coven spends much of it beneath Hecate's sun.

It's like I'm lost between two paths, unsure which one to walk into the future on.

"Harlow?" Carina snaps her fingers, jerking me from my daze.

"Sorry."

"Yeah, and sorry to snap, but I called your name a few times."

Not wanting to admit where my mind was, I say, "Busy admiring the town."

Jasper glances to his right, towards the mountain most visible and imposing. "It gets old real fast. One day, you'll long to get away."

Carina shoves his shoulder, scowling; a face I'm learning is her norm towards her cousin. "Big shot here thinks he's too good for the coven."

"Never said that." Jasper shifts his hand over the table, and a swirl of white smoke flicks Carina in the nose. "But now's not the time to really talk about that, is it?" He scans the area, and it's then I notice how the street is a bit less busy, tourists beginning to hole themselves up in their hotel rooms or return to their campsites.

"Ceremony soon?" I guess, crinkling my wrapper to toss away.

Carina gathers the three to take to the garbage nearby. "Nah, not for another five hours or so. We'll start close to midnight."

"Speaking of"—Jasper gathers his phone, shoving it into his pocket—"I need to get going. I agreed to meet up with Colton, Jackson, and the others beforehand. Want to come?"

And meet more people? Morgan said she'd introduce me at the ceremony, and I'm not sure I'm mentally prepared to meet anyone prior to that.

Thankfully, Carina senses my anxiety and saves me. "Your asshole friends will drool all over coven royalty, so hell no. Besides, Mom's kinda hiding her until tonight, doing it all at once."

"Colton's been asking about you," he comments to his cousin, who immediately scrunches her nose.

"Been there once. Actually twice. I'm good. Not again."

Jasper chuckles. "Suit yourselves. I'll see you both later." He tips his head to me in goodbye and walks away, getting sucked up by a family walking nearby.

"Besides," Carina starts once he's out of earshot, "it's nearly dark."

The sun is a barely there crest. By the time I get back to Morgan's, it'll likely be set. The enchantment on the basement will be lifted, freeing Alec, who'll undoubtedly come for me.

"I can walk you back, if you want. Or we can keep exploring town. We have hours to kill."

Although I don't want to be rude and turn down the continuation of her tour, Alec will interrupt regardless. I still don't understand his moods, and I wouldn't want Carina to be caught in the crosshairs.

"You mind if I go back?"

"Sure thing." She stands with me, her mouth opening and shutting twice before she begins walking away. She doesn't ask whatever she obviously wants to, and curiosity starts gnawing at me.

"What is it?"

"I get you don't remember me, so I didn't want to pry. Just wondering how it works, that's all. A vampire and a witch. Does he...you know?" Her eyes flick towards my neck, which is hidden by my hair.

Checking to ensure no stray humans are close by, I slide my hair away from my neck and remove the enchantment on my wrist so she can see both marks.

"Shit," she curses, but stares with curiosity over disgust. "Did it hurt?"

"No, it felt...nice." *Pleasurable. Sexy. Blissful.* But she's right. Considering I don't know her, going into details like this feels a bit much.

It shouldn't have been.

If life were different, Carina and I would probably be very close. Talking about personal things would be normal. My chest twinges, wishing we were like that. Being homeschooled and kept away from anyone but the neighbours on either side of us, I learned to entertain myself and hide any personal issues. Not that there were many, considering what in my life could have led to drama? I wasn't given the chance to have typical, human, high school experiences.

"Huh." Her curiosity breaks out into a smile. "Can't wait to meet him."

"You could come with me," I offer. "He won't hurt you."

"That sounds—" She stops when her phone vibrates and glances down at the incoming message with a groan. "Actually, Mom needs a favour. I gotta get materials from the shop." She thumbs behind her. "You can come, unless you're still stuck on seeing your vampire boyfriend, which honestly I'd choose over chores."

I laugh, finding Carina's easy personality infectious. "Thanks, but I'll go make sure he's okay. How should I get to the ceremony later?"

"You have a phone?"

"Somewhere. Left behind when Alec kidnapped me."

"Okay, be at Mom's house at 11:30 p.m., and I'll come get you from there."

"If you give me directions, I'm sure Alec can find it by scent. A gathering of witches in the forest probably won't be hard for him to miss."

Her brows fly into her hairline. "Never thought of that. Kinda cool." She rattles off decently descriptive directions, gesturing through them. "If you're not there by 11:45 p.m., we'll find you. Tracking one of our own in a place this tiny isn't hard. You good to return to Mom's alone?"

"I think I got it." But just in case, I point in the direction I think I need to take, recalling the path Morgan took me on. Carina confirms and we split, her heading deeper into the town while I head towards the residential area.

By the time I turn onto Morgan's road, the sun has finished setting and a blur streaks toward me, stopping only a foot away. There are numerous reasons I shouldn't want to see him, but after a day of so much newness, Alec's familiarity is a welcome sight.

Also...I missed him.

"Good rest?"

"Not at all. Fuckin' hate daytime. What did you do?"

"Carina showed me the town. It's really beautiful. So picturesque and quaint. And I met her cousin, Jasper, who's apparently an old friend."

His gaze drops down to my right hand, and he grunts. "That explains the stench. He touched you."

He could tell that? Fuck, his senses continue to surprise me. "He shook my hand." My words don't seem to register. He grabs the same hand and lifts it to his mouth, his tongue dragging over my palm. For every reason, it should gross me out, but there's a sensuality to it as well.

His black eyes flash red for a brief moment before he releases me. "Better. Can't stand the scent of other males near you, let alone *on* you."

In all the time I've known Alec, he's never outwardly looked uncomfortable, but I can't deny he is now as he stares at the ground and shoves his hands into his pockets.

"You actually mean that."

"If you want your precious coven to not toss me out, then yeah, I do. It's hard to ignore the instincts that have suddenly been controlling me."

Sympathy rolls through me. After centuries of unfeeling, I'm sure having a Bride all of a sudden *would* be different. Alarming to have your feelings controlled by something uncontrollable.

"I'm sorry."

His eyes flicker, and his smirk shows the tip of one fang. "I'm not. But have you noticed where you stopped?"

I face the house I stopped by once so far. When I passed it earlier with Carina, I kept my head down and refused to look.

The Sinclair house.

Alec's cool fingers slide between mine. It's unlike him to be so touchy, and the sight distracts me enough that I miss when he begins walking, my body pulled behind him as he approaches the start of the path.

"Wait, what are you—Morgan didn't give me permission."

He glances over his shoulder, one brow hiked. "It's *your* home. You don't need permission."

"It hasn't been mine for a while. Alec, wait!" I jam my feet into the cement, nearly tripping when his immortal strength continues dragging me. "We can't go in. We don't have a key."

On the porch, he taps the black mailbox hung beside the door. "Says *Sinclair*, does it not? What's your name again? You have every right to enter, key or otherwise." He pauses, turning to me. "It's up to you, Hellion. Ready to face your past?"

"I think Morgan has a plan later..." I trail off when his expression says he doesn't care.

"Fuck Morgan and anyone else. Harlow, this is *your* home. Your history. Do you want to go in?"

Do I? This home belongs to strangers. To the version of myself that is a stranger. The house, according to Morgan, is as it was last left, which means a bedroom that knows which toys I enjoyed, while I don't. A living room that recalls the sounds of family time, while I don't even recall the people involved. A kitchen with the scent of meals lingering, while it's food I no longer remember the taste of.

It's a home once owned by strangers, and while I hope after tonight they won't be as unknown to me, it doesn't change that my experiences with them were limited to eight years of life.

Maybe this will help trigger my memory.

Alec strokes his thumb over the back of my hand, his touch

gentle. It's ironic in a sickeningly wrong way that I'm about to enter the Sinclair house with the vampire who murdered most of them, but it feels right. Like he should be nowhere else.

Not sure what that says about me.

I nod, finally answering his question, and Alec reaches for the knob before I can second-guess my decision and twists abruptly, breaking the lock.

"I'll have it replaced another time," he murmurs, pushing the door open to the house that last knew ghosts. Two dead witches and a kidnapped child.

Alec steps to the side to allow me to go in first, but I can't move. My knees are locked, body not cooperating no matter how much my mind is telling me to take a step.

So simple. Move a foot, then the other. A fucking baby can do this.

But a baby wouldn't be aware of the weight of these steps.

"You're safe." His voice, gentle as the wind, cuts through my anxiety. "We don't have to do this if you don't want to."

"I do."

I do, I remind myself, lifting one foot over the threshold while the other drags behind. Alec follows, tightening his hold on me as he reaches over to flick on a switch.

The entrance opens to a small area, a double-door closet to our left and a mirror hung on the wall to our right. In front of us is a small Y—stairs that go upstairs or the doorway into the rest of the main floor.

I lead the way past the hall closet and towards the attached door, walking by a small built-in office with a U-shaped desk, an old computer dating the kind of tech this place saw.

I continue through the house, inspecting the décor. The paintings, the mirrors, the lights. Every wall is covered in something, giving an insight into the kind of home my parents liked.

It's the far wall in the living room, across from what was probably a large TV for the time, that numerous portraits are hung. Even from a distance, the three people—two tall and one short—are clear.

I should approach, see the details of the faces. *See* my parents for the first time.

But I'm stuck. Just like outside, except then I *knew* I wanted to enter...I don't know about this.

Harlow? A hand squeeze.

"I, I...I thought I was ready. Tonight, later, I might see them. I can see them now...but it feels like a lot."

Alec makes the decision I can't and tugs me the opposite way, returning the way we came and back towards the entrance.

Thirty-Nine

Alec

As an immortal, emotions have become easy to ignore. The finicky things that mortals trouble themselves with no longer hold the same meaning, whether it be feelings, laws, or beliefs.

As a human, I was forbidden from feeling things like empathy towards my sister's cause to be with Cedric or anything beyond my father's approved list of behaviours. "You are a prince, act like it," he'd often recite. As an immortal, I'd forgotten what it is like to feel at all.

As a human, prince or not, laws were followed. The laws of men, of life. Laws limiting how we should act, where was right to go or not. While the world was different, and being a man gave me a sense of immortality, in truth, I was far away from where I am now. I was still governed by my own morals, what's perceived as right and wrong. As an immortal, human laws no longer direct me. I can steal whatever I want, break into anywhere, murder anyone without fault.

As a human in the old world, Christianity was the prominent belief system in my part of the world. God ruled us, decided which laws were to be followed and how we should serve Him. God was the purpose behind the wars my father initiated to conquer land, though we all knew that was bullshit. God gave a "reason" behind people's actions, an excuse. Now, being an immortal, I'm aware Celestials—God and the devil, angels and demons—are real, but it doesn't mean I follow any particular deity. Or that they give two fucks what we all do.

Which is why I can't understand Harlow's feelings on the level I wish I could. An empathetic level, in which walking through her childhood home where parents she has no memory of were murdered would mean more than nothing to me.

Correction: It means a lot, because it means something to her, but I don't understand the emotions pouring from her to me through the bond.

It's a stomach-clenching discomfort caught between need and denial. A feeling of intense sorrow and contentment. It's confusing, reminding me how difficult it was to be human and saddled with such emotions.

It's the same feeling she sometimes gets ever since the night of discovering she is my Bride.

My hand is wrapped around hers in a hold more intimate than I've ever given another being, but there's a sense of rightness to it. As I lead her away from the wall of pictures—that intensified the ache so harshly, it felt like bile was coming up *my* throat—I keep looking at our hands twined together. The bond doesn't instantly strike feelings or even make us *like* one another, and I haven't quite decided what to feel about Miss Sinclair. What I do know is how her emotions, tonight in particular, strike a deeply rooted pain in me.

I enjoy the feeling of her touching me so innocently. Her hold is strengthened by her growing trust, the support she's allowing me to provide. Even that I don't mind.

I pause by the staircase, inspecting her blank, desolate expression, wondering how much more she'll be able to take before making the decision for her and tugging her towards the stairs.

She nearly trips on the bottom one when realizing where we're headed. It's the second when her grip turns cold.

"I, I don't know about this."

"Nothing will hurt you," I reassure her. "Not even your own emotions." Because I won't allow them to.

For once, the bond isn't sensing danger and a need to rescue her, but I do. And I don't fucking like it.

I walk her slowly up the stairs, scanning the house that's been modernized over the centuries. Before the coven was smart enough to put a barrier around the town, I had access to the Sinclair house and have been inside on the odd occasion. The walls weren't finished back then, and the floors were an old, stained carpet. The windows couldn't open and were often frosted. Heat inside was limited to whatever the fireplace provided.

The landing is now covered in a soft carpet our shoes track dirt over. The railing is a glass that overlooks the downstairs, melding into the white wall that carries into a stretch of hallway with three doors.

We stop by the first, the pink comforter on the bed catching my attention. A doll's house, nearly as tall as Harlow, consumes one wall, and a bookshelf filled with picture books is beside it. A dresser on the other side, its drawers partially open with clothing spilling out. The scent of Harlow is faint—*extremely* faint—in the air.

"Oh my Goddess," she breathes and steps by me, releasing my hand to tread inside the room. I remain in the doorway, ready to catch her should she fall victim to her own emotions again.

She walks around the room slowly, brushing her hand over every surface; along the books' spines, the roof of the dollhouse, the bed's headboard, along the edge of the mattress, the windowsill, and finally the top of the dresser. She completes a full circle before she looks at me, her eyes rimmed red.

"I, I don't...I don't remember any of this."

And then she sits—crumples, more like it—her knees digging

into the soft carpet. I'm right there, grabbing and positioning her beside me. Her side presses into mine, her skin hotter than usual, and she seems to have no control over her limbs, letting me move her how I want to.

I take her hands between mine and sit, waiting for her to speak first. Her breath hitches with every inhale before it's harshly blown out between her teeth, like breathing is physically painful. Through the bond, there is no more sadness. No more grief. Only confusion.

"I hoped by coming in here, it would spark something. A memory—*something*. I mean, I lived here. Slept. Played. Why can't I remember?" Her teeth slide together, the grinding sound making me wince.

"The mortal mind is delicate, or so I've heard. The enchantment the Hartmans used, combined with your body protecting itself, is likely why."

She twists her head until it's on my shoulder and she's looking at me. "Insightful for a being who hasn't been human in how long again?"

"A while."

She doesn't move away, and I find myself shifting my body to make her more comfortable. My arm curls her into my side while my free hand strokes through her red strands, satin gliding through my fingers.

"Bet when you took me you never thought you'd be sitting in my childhood bedroom, of all places."

"No," I agree, keeping my voice soft for her, "this wasn't in the plans."

"Life's funny. From what Morgan's told me, it sounds like everything was on track for me to have a normal life...until it wasn't."

I press my fingers just a bit harder into her skull, mimicking a massage while trying *not* to think about how she was robbed of everything she deserves and how I'd love nothing more to end the lives of the Hartmans if they weren't already dead. "Life is unique," I correct. "It's one thing I've learned over my time. It continues to evolve. Sometimes for the better, and sometimes not."

"Do you enjoy your life more now than you did as a human?"

"Yes." It's not even a question. The only thing that gave my mortal life a slight edge was my sister being alive.

"Do you enjoy your life more now than say...one hundred years ago?"

One hundred years ago, I was ruling from my castle, waiting for the living Sinclair to be bred, and passing time with whatever came along that sparked my amusement. I was bored and not thriving. A century ago, I never imagined having a Sinclair in my arms, let alone *wanting* her to be there.

Time passed quickly then. The world was modernizing. Cars were becoming mainstream. It was the time between World War I and II, and the world was coming out of what was referred to as the Great Depression. Mortals were so wrapped up in each other as even the cities grew from small villages with lots of farmland to massive cities of buildings that strove to reach the clouds.

I remained at home for most of it, missing the world that once was while dreading what was to come. Cedric was in New Orleans at the time, fucking and drinking everything that moved in one of his mindless rampages that he'll go on every few decades when he realizes how long Cora has been gone from our lives.

There was nothing to do. Nothing to live for. No one to obsess over.

Until the witch in my arms came to be.

"Life is immensely more enjoyable than it was back then."

"Which means you're definitely older than one hundred years, which means you saw everything my history books would have taught me. Plenty of wars, the Roaring Twenties, the Titanic—were you on it?"

"The concept of being stuck on a ship in the middle of an ocean sounds horrendous."

She freezes before whipping me with her hair when twisting towards me. "Are you afraid of water?" Her lips spread in a slow smile, like she's figured out all my secrets.

I stare at the space she's created between our bodies like it, too, is another secret I can't decipher. While temperature doesn't bother me, she was warm. A kind of warmth I *did* feel...and I want to again.

So as I talk, I tug her back, and she resettles without comment. "Vampires are not cats, so no, I'm not afraid of water. Had I been on the Titanic, I would have lived no matter if I made it into a lifeboat or not. But I've always preferred having the land beneath my feet and not restricting myself to ships, or even air transportation."

She leans her head against my shoulder and laughs. "You know, you're not so bad, vampire. I still don't like you, and I still think you should go home and forget all this Bride stuff...but you're not so bad either. When you're not out to murder me, that is."

"You're not so bad either, Sinclair." It's disturbing that I mean it. Before Harlow twists back around, I drop a kiss onto her forehead, resting my lips against her warm skin for a moment and drinking in all she is. It's a touch more tender than I've ever given another being, but it feels like I need to. Maybe it's the location, her feelings that have gone from upset to calm, or maybe it's my own craving to be close to her.

I do know it isn't the bond.

She melts under my touch, and I can't help but stroke the skin beside her eyes, murmuring, "Once I would have killed anyone with eyes like yours. Now, I find myself enthralled by them."

"Nice try. You're pulling out centuries of sweet-talking women to try to get me to accept the bond."

I wish that were the case. I keep that to myself and instead make light of it. "Is it working?"

She only winks before glancing towards the window, the old, faded-pink curtain pushed to the side. The moon is full above, a precedent of the ceremony she's about to have.

"What time is it?"

I slide my phone from my pocket. "Ten."

"Then I have at least an hour more." She glances around the room before staring at the door. "I should probably finish looking around this place."

"You don't have to. If it hurts, it's not worth it."

"That's the thing, it doesn't hurt. It's just...I don't know." She shrugs. "It feels empty, if that makes sense. Everything here is unrecognizable. The child who once slept in this room was a different version of me. Someone innocent and happy, who had the world. I should feel sad about not remembering the people who slept down the hall. Instead, I'm confused."

I sweep a hand over the back of her neck, gathering her hair on one side and allowing my fingertips to trace her skin. It's getting increasingly difficult *not* to touch her. "You have no memories of this place or your parents. I think it's natural you're not sure what to feel."

"Says the guy who can't feel anything."

"Never said I can't feel *anything*. Besides, it's simply logic. You feel like you *should* be sad, but it's hard to be upset over something you can't recall."

She makes a noise in her throat, pulling her legs in closer. "Maybe you're right. Maybe the ceremony will help. Morgan says she has a plan to get my memories restored. Or, at least, enough so I have some image of the past."

"You're perfect how you are, Hellion. Memories or otherwise."

She doesn't reply to that, and I don't push her to say anything more. My touch continues over her back, tracing imaginary designs while fingering the ends of her hair. It becomes a game of pushing her hair to the side and watching it swing back towards me.

After another twenty minutes, her head falls onto her knees. I listen for a sob or the feeling of grief to finally hit her, but only find contentment.

My Bride is pleased. And that's enough for now.

Another few minutes pass before she sighs. "Feels good."

"It's meant to."

Without lifting her head from her knees, she turns her head. "Thanks for this, I guess. Even if Morgan gave me a key, I'm not sure I would have done this. Especially not alone."

"My pleasure."

She watches me. "You mean that."

"I don't often say things I don't mean. You'll learn that eventually."

Her spine decompresses into my hand as I continue petting the back of her neck and down, completing loops until she sighs again, this time in resignation.

"We should go."

"Scared for the ceremony?"

"More nervous."

"It'll be fine." I stand, offering my hand to help her up.

She accepts it and stands, her chest close to mine. Her head falls back to look me in the face. "How do you know? You're an active viewer of witches' ceremonies?"

"Because I'll murder them all if it's not."

She snorts as I take her hand to lead her from her old room, and then the house, except I wasn't kidding.

FORTY

Harlow

I give Alec the directions Carina gave, and he tosses me onto his back with a wicked grin, walking me down the path, past the mailbox with my name, and out onto the street without a peek back at the house that's mine but not really mine.

"Close your eyes. Or don't."

The wind picks up, and colours become a muted blur of grey, black, and green lit only by the moon above. He's moving much too fast for me to make anything out, and I think I scream his name, but that too is eaten up by the wind.

A moment later, it all dies down, and Alec stops in the middle of the forest. He crouches slightly and releases my hands so I can slide off his back.

Very few of the smiles Alec has given me have been genuine. Most were sneaky, the smile of a victor, which is essentially every-thing he's been. But this time, there's a lightness to his midnight-coloured eyes that makes the stretch of his mouth seem perkier. While his fangs are visible, his lips aren't curled back, purposely trying to be threatening.

"Fun?"

"It was...something." Something cool, if I'm really honest.

He points between the gathering of trees to the people mingling around in black cloaks, and all the happiness I was feeling dissipates for anxiety. I'm about to have a coven meeting for the first time ever. People will meet me. They'll know I was gone and that I'm back. They'll ask me questions. They'll demand answers. They'll—

Two hands come down on my shoulders and pull me back into his otherworldly body. His hair tickles the side of my face as he dips into my neck, making me shiver at the telltale ghostly sensation of his fang sliding up my neck.

Relax. You'll be fine.

"It always throws me when you do that—speak in my head."

Worked, didn't it? Got your mind off your stress. Say the word, and I'll take you away.

"No. I want to do this. I've been looking forward to it all day." Even if present feelings indicate otherwise. I step from beneath his hold and toward the—*my*—coven. When I'm between two trees, I whisper, "Thanks, Alec."

My pleasure, Hellion. Go kick ass.

I step from the treeline, scanning the crowd for Morgan or Carina; people I know, while hoping everyone else doesn't notice me. There are dozens of people gathered in mini groups, talking amongst themselves.

A woman breaks away from a group, immediately followed by a guy holding a black cloak in his hand. When realizing they're Carina and Jasper coming to mob me by the treeline, only a dozen feet from where Alec waits, my lungs breathe easier. They position themselves so others don't have a clear line of sight.

"Hey," Carina greets. "Mom mentioned you might be overwhelmed if we start approaching everyone, so if you wanna stay back here for a bit, we can. She understands. They don't have to realize you're you until she begins the circle."

"That'd be good." I cast a grateful glance towards Morgan, who's off to the side speaking with two other women but watching me from the corner of her eye.

Jasper hands over the cloak, which looks like a smaller version of the one he's wearing. "Here. It's yours to keep. Every Highridge Coven member needs a ceremonial cloak."

"Thanks." The material is thick and heavy, but soft. I find the top and loop it around my neck, tying it together.

"Look at you, all grown up and ready for your first coven ceremony. Aren't you so proud?" Carina blinks wide, dramatic eyes up at her cousin, who merely shoves her arm, chuckling.

"You're an idiot, Car. Harlow, you look great. Fits you well."

You're beautiful, Hellion. His voice slides down my spine, softer than the material of this cloak.

I fight the urge to turn and call attention to his presence when Jasper's head whips up, eyes narrowed on the exact place I left Alec waiting. "Shit," he curses at the same time Carina demands, "Is *that* your vampire?"

Jasper's palms immediately light up white—air magick, I learned earlier, but I reach out to block any impending attack.

"Don't," I plead, right as Morgan crosses towards us, a warning look aimed at her nephew. "He won't attack. He's with me."

Thankfully I'm saved from the questions when Morgan forcibly shifts her nephew and daughter to look another way. "Stop calling attention to him," she grits. "I'm aware he's here, Jasper. It's like Harlow said. We can trust him for now."

"Besides..." Carina winks. "He's only interested in eating one of us."

And I'm fucking ravenous, and not only for your blood.

Jasper throws me an incredulous look but obeys his High Priestess, who's now walking in Alec's direction. Hopefully not for anything bad, but I resist looking because I'm noticing others glance our way. Instead, I debate lifting the large hood over my head and hiding from the coven.

"I want the story later," Jasper mutters. "And ignore Carina. She enjoys romanticizing our enemies. She's a bit obsessed with sneaking down the mountain to check out our resident shifter pack."

Carina scoffs, putting her hands on her hips. "'Kay, enemies or not, have you *seen* the alpha's son? That man is something else. I'll overlook the wolfy part of him for the rest."

I perk at the mention of creatures I've had no passing with. "Actual shifters?"

Jasper chuckles. "There's a lot to it, but it's a story for another time."

Morgan passes by, gesturing for us to follow, so Carina takes my hand and leads me forward. I twist to wave at Alec before merging with the ranks of the coven, who all stand in a circle with Morgan positioned by what I assume is North. They spot me immediately, a low buzz of conversation filling the area.

Ignore them.

Hard to ignore the confused and excited exclamations of my name being tossed around, but Morgan calls them to attention.

"Sisters. Brothers. Welcome to September's full moon. As you see, we have a new witch amongst our ranks, but it's a member we'll be welcoming back. Harlow Sinclair, so it seems, never died. I found her yesterday and brought her home, and I ask that we use tonight to thank Hecate for her safe return."

Safe? For once, I agree with Alec's scoff. After learning what I had, was I ever safe?

"Is she truly Harlow Sinclair?" a man on the other side of the circle calls. "She could be an imposter."

Alec growls in my head. *Disrespectful fuck.*

"I felt her signature," Morgan replies. "I feel her as though she never left. The accident that led to us believing she died did not involve her or the Hartmans."

"What happened to them?" a woman asks, casting a nervous glance my way.

"They died," I answer before Morgan has to. "They won't be coming back."

The witch opens her mouth with a follow-up question, but Morgan waves her down. "Afterwards, I will answer any questions you may have, but for now, I would prefer to celebrate her return. I also request we use tonight's full moon to call upon combined energies and help Harlow retrieve memories that have been stolen from her by Arthur and Violet. Harlow has no recollection of anyone here, nor her childhood with the coven."

Or my real parents. Everyone here would know Emily and John more than I ever will.

What will these "combined energies" consist of? His possessive growl vibrates through my mind, but this time, I use the sensation to calm my racing heart.

There's an agreement that runs through the circle and Carina squeezes my hand, reminding me she's still holding it. Jasper takes my left, and I notice how everyone's now holding hands.

Morgan breaks away from the circle to begin calling the elements using the same incantations she spoke inside her house. There are no candles this time, but regardless, the elements make themselves known.

With Earth joining us, leaves circle the area before forming a ring behind everyone's feet.

With Air joining us, a gust of wind snakes around us.

With Fire joining us, a heat blankets the group.

And with Water joining us, my anxiety is momentarily washed away.

"Harlow," she calls, stretching her hand towards me. "Join me in the centre please."

Another squeeze from Carina before I release her and Jasper and walk towards Morgan, failing to ignore the intense attention from everyone around me.

Morgan clasps my hand to position me in the centre of the

circle. "We need to focus every positive thought toward Harlow. Recall your memories of Emily and John. Remember any and all, no matter how brief, interactions you had with Harlow as a child. Focus on the fateful news we received and how the absence of the Sinclairs felt to us individually and as a whole. Control those thoughts and redirect them to one another, to a collective consciousness we can send to Harlow. I feel—I hope—we may help her retrieve memories long concealed."

Alec's voice rumbles in my head. *I don't like this.*

I'm not sure I do either.

Morgan rejoins the circle, taking the hands of the witches on either side of her. "Are we ready?" Her question is for the coven, but her attention remains on me.

A murmur of agreement goes through the group, and I'm forced to nod.

Hellion...

I stare through the coven at him, hoping he recognizes from the distance what I'm trying to tell him. To remain hidden before we have a bigger problem. To not worry about me, because Morgan won't let them hurt me.

I also look his way to seek comfort.

If you're harmed at all, I'll rip them apart. That's a promise, not a threat, so tell them to consider how much voodoo shit they're about to do. Your well-being isn't up for debate. The memories, your past, nothing matters more than your present.

Strangely enough, his deadly promise eases me, even if I remain silent to the coven who's trying to help.

"Begin." Morgan's demand circles the group and, one by one, witches and warlocks shut their eyes.

The clearing falls silent.

No wind. No animals. No sign of life.

It's not working. They can't do it.

Realizations crash upon me.

Arthur and Violet fucked me up too bad.

Morgan murmurs something I don't catch.

And then—*pain.*

Blinding, agonizing pain that slams my knees to the ground, hands gripping my temples as throbbing pressure assaults my head. I bow over the grass, screaming into the earth, begging it to help me. To save me from this.

Harlow!

The murmurs around me grow louder, and though I'm not looking at any of them, sparks of blue and white fill the area, the combination of air and water magick swirling around me but not touching.

Stay away! I mentally yell at Alec, though he can't hear me.

It's all I manage before my mind gets yanked viciously to another time and place.

FORTY-ONE

Alec

I fucking hate this ceremonial shit. Nothing ever good comes from witchcraft.

Except Harlow. She's an exception.

Being a part of this is what she wants, so I won't interrupt, and if I'm honest with myself, it's what she needs. But I still hate it.

Her red hair is a mini flame lit by the full moon when she joins two others, a witch and warlock. I assume the witch to be Morgan's daughter, Carina, and the male must be whom I smelled on her earlier. He hands her a cloak that she ties around herself. It swirls nearly to her feet, the hood wide across her back, her hair tumbling over it.

She's so lovely, and it's with regret I realize I've never told her that.

You're beautiful, Hellion.

I remain in the treeline, watching, and then suddenly, all three are looking my way, the male's voice rising at the same time his palms light with magick.

Morgan rushes towards him with a strict warning, and then cuts across the field to me. She casts a spell over herself but, seeing as nothing's changed, I don't know what she's done.

"Glamour," she murmurs, though I didn't ask. "No one should

notice me over here. I see you figured out how to get out of my house."

"No thanks to you leaving instructions."

"I've made the choice not to mention your presence to the coven yet. They need to adjust to Harlow being home, and her dragging along a vampire mate might be too much for them."

If anyone breathes shit to her, they'll answer to me. A fact I doubt this High Priestess would enjoy hearing.

"If you insist on being present for our ceremony—our *sacred* ceremony, I should note"—her emphasis not masking her annoyance over my presence—"then you need to remain out of sight. Afterwards, we'll have a small gathering when I'm sure many of the coven will be distracted greeting Harlow on a more personal level. No matter how much your vamp instincts are demanding you take her away, you can't interrupt."

My gaze goes from the witch to my Bride. Standing amongst her own kind, her beauty only made more obvious by the shadows of the night, it's impossible not to view her as a witch. Despite the attempts to get her powers back, I suppose it's been easier to view her as a weak human up until now, but now she exudes power that makes me hungry.

Not to destroy, but to worship.

For the first time in...well, *ever*, I want to bow to another person. To be *her* loyal subject, forever and always.

"I understand," I murmur to the waiting witch, not taking my eyes off Harlow.

Morgan heads back to the coven, but I'm too preoccupied watching my mate to grant her any more of my attention. Harlow's hands make nervous flutters by her sides, and the bond reveals a mix of nerves and excitement.

I prop myself against the tree, cross my arms, and observe from the shadows. The place I'm forever destined to be while Harlow will remain in the Light.

As Harlow is led towards the waiting coven, she glances my way and smiles. It's simple, but rocks me to my core. It's as blinding as the sun that'd burn me.

Morgan begins by announcing her presence to the coven. A few ask questions and, while reasonable, they piss me off, and I throw quips into Harlow's head.

Eventually, Morgan starts her witchy process and leads Harlow into the centre of the circle. She starts explaining to the coven how they'll collectively get Harlow's memories back, something I never realized could be the coven's focus. For Harlow, I want this to work, for her to know the people who truly loved her rather than the deception she was raised with.

I don't like this, I tell her, because it sounds precarious at best. It sounds like something that'll make Harlow dream of possibilities to get them yanked away from her. *Hellion...* She hasn't looked my way, and if I were to ever feel nerves, it'd be now.

Answering my silent demands, Harlow stares at me, her purple eyes saying what she can't mentally.

Too bad for her, I don't give two fucks about her empathy towards the coven.

If you're harmed at all, I'll rip them apart. That's a promise, not a threat, so tell them to consider how much voodoo shit they're about to do. Your well-being isn't up for debate. The memories, your past, nothing matters more than your present.

Then they start, every coven member shutting their eyes. Low mumbles I don't make out come from each individual.

For long minutes, nothing happens.

Through the bond, Harlow's hope wanes, and for every bit it ticks down, I'm feeling a fraction more murderous.

Morgan murmurs a final command.

Pain ricochets through the bond from Harlow to me, assaulting my own head as surely as hers is. She slams to her knees and bows over, her scream tearing my every nerve.

Harlow!

I push off the tree, intending to get to her. Fuck the High Priestess. Fuck every witch and warlock who'll raise their magick against me. They can chain me to a tree for all I care *after* I save Harlow.

Two steps from the treeline, an invisible force slams me back.

No! With a growl, I throw myself at it again, forced to witness the air shimmer white.

"Let me through! Witch, look at me!"

The High Priestess doesn't.

I *need* to get to Harlow. Need it more than blood. More than anything.

A crack beside me has me momentarily distracted, Freya landing on the grass.

"Remove this!" I flash my fangs. First Witch or not, I'll rip her fucking throat out if she doesn't help.

"Morgan put it up to keep you both safe."

"Safe? She's not safe. Let me get to her!"

Freya shakes her head, grimacing as Harlow screams again, her cry echoing through the deepest parts of me. The parts that are burning in their own personal hell.

"Then why the fuck are you here?"

"Because they're about to see a lot that'll raise questions, and the High Priestess will need guidance towards the right path."

The right path. The right *fucking* path. She's speaking about witchy bullshit while my mate is in fucking *pain?*

I run into the barrier again and again. I'll never stop fighting until I get to her.

When she screams again, my insides shred apart.

FORTY-TWO

It drifts from my mind, hovering in the air like a projection screen for the entire coven to view. Their gasps seem so far away, lost amidst the throbbing of my head. It's only the projection that compels me to lift my head, my fingers knotting around the blades of grass in my vicinity as I try to focus on what's being unleashed.

"Mommy!" I dart towards the woman across the yard, wrapping my arms around her knees.

My mother lifts me in her arms, swinging me back and forth in that way she knows I enjoy before instructing me to head inside and get changed for bed.

That vision fades, and a knife-like scraping sensation against my brain physically yanks another one forward. And then another. And another.

"Make it stop, make it stop..." My hands clench my head, each scraping more painful than the last.

"Mom, it's hurting her!" a voice screams. Carina, I believe.

In the distance—or my head, I can't figure out what's what anymore—Alec bellows in rage.

On and on they go, flashes of my parents—my real parents. Mom's hair is vibrant red, and I see now how weak in comparison

Violet's hair was. There are images of her telling bedtime stories with the smoke and shadows made by her flames, and it is nothing like how Violet would tuck me into bed.

Alec screams my name. I wonder why he hasn't come yet. I want him to save me.

"Carina, over here! Let's play hide and seek. You first." Carina bolts down the road from her house to mine.

Memories of early childhood flit through the numerous scenes, but I need them to stop. I'd rather be lost and deal with the unknown.

"Stop...please."

The pain doesn't stop.

Alec yells again.

Then there are memories of Violet and Arthur. First at coven events, and then speaking to me. Asking me simple things about myself. Favourite foods. Activities I enjoy.

It's the last memory that makes my insides rattle the most as the image appears in front of us all.

I'm sleeping when I'm woken by a bang downstairs, a yell, and then a, "Get Harlow!" I think it's Daddy yelling at Mommy.

I push the blanket off my body and rub my eyes before sitting up, staring at the door, and wondering if I should get out of bed.

I'm in the middle of deciding when there's more yelling, more banging. I slide out of bed and rush towards my closet, my hand on the knob when my door flings open. I turn, expecting Mommy or even Daddy, but it's not them. It's a woman with dark hair. I've seen her at coven events. She has a pretty name, named after a flower. Violet. She's nice.

But she shouldn't be in my house right now. "What are you doing here? Where's Mommy?"

My question goes unanswered as a flash of green fills the room.

The memory fades, quickly replaced by another one. The same

one my consciousness dredged up in Alec's cells, only this time, it's the full scene.

Alec. He's still yelling.

My head is still being scraped by a knife.

And no one's listening to me as I beg them to end this.

"Stop, stop, stop…" My voice fades, dry from the pointless begging.

A cool slither wraps my hands where they're clenching around the grass. *Make them stop. You can do it.*

How? I ask whatever the voice is as an image continues playing in front of me.

Cuffs weigh my arms down, and no matter how much I yell, scream, and pull on them, I can't get free. The skin around the cuffs stings, sliced and bleeding, from the amount I've yanked on them.

"Mommy! Daddy!" I yell and yell, but no one comes. For hours, I'm crying. I'm hungry, tired, and cold.

But no one helps me.

Mommy always told me she'd be there for me. So where is she?

It feels like days are passing, where every minute is more pointless hope. I wish I was older and had access to my magick, but Mommy says I'm too young. That my powers will come in alongside something called puberty, but she hasn't told me what that fully means.

Finally, the door opens, and the first thing I see is the moon. It's full. Next, a figure blocks the beautiful glow and my connection to the Goddess, whom Mommy said to always pray to if I need anything because She cares for all her children.

"Plans changed. You'll be coming home with us for a while, Harlow."

That vision fades as well, leaving a question to float through the coven: What plans?

More memories surface. Memories of my years being raised by Violet and Arthur, referring to them as Mom and Dad. Memories in which I'd wake up asking about the woman in my dreams and the mountains we used to live near. Later in the day, I'd forget every-thing all over.

Memories that were taken from me, resulting in me losing hours of my life. Over and over.

"See this?" Mom points to a grimoire that I've been using to help master my new magick. She's pointing to an incantation, but it's one I don't recognize. Not that I know many spells.

"What is it?"

"A special kind of power that's very strong, called black magick. You can be like the Goddess herself with it."

"Seriously?" The concept of that much power is intriguing, consid-ering all I can do right about now is dry my own hair.

"Yes. Memorize it. I need you to know it deep down, even if by tonight you'll have no recollection of learning it."

Gasps come from the coven, but another memory replaces that one. This one grim and masked with magick.

One that depicts the numerous flashes of Arthur wiping every black magick enchantment and curse they forced me to learn.

Another where they cast a curse over me, and I leave the room with the fire inside me much duller than when I walked in.

Another one where I snuck around the house one night and overheard a conversation that wasn't meant for me:

"She's growing too powerful, Arthur. Her Sinclair blood is too strong. It's getting harder to bind her magic. One day, we might not be able to taper it."

"Maybe we let it then."

"If we allow that, it'd undo all the work we've been doing to make her Dark."

"Unless she's meant to master both."

"You have a plan; I can tell by your expression. What is it?"

What are they talking about? I lean closer to the door to hear better, but the floorboard creaks. I freeze, hoping they didn't catch it.

Steps pound towards me, and I'm not fast enough when running back to my room.

"Make it stop!"

The memories flash through more recent years, pausing on the night of the fire that took everything from me.

The force of my magick flings my limp body out the door, and it lands in the middle of my backyard as the house continues burning.

Mom...Dad...my mind won't stay focused.

But right as my eyes slide shut, a darkness envelops me. Shadows hover above my head, prodding my chest but unable to enter. They don't seem bothered by it, though, remaining around me like a depraved hug.

Then there are memories of Alec in my room, of him kidnapping me. Of the cells, the party, the bedroom, and the forest. Every intimate moment between us laid out for the coven, all going towards the recent event of getting my magick back.

This time, *all* of it. Finding the box, my emotions, and the surge of fire that consumed me, burned me from the inside, my *true* powers returning, no longer restricted by Arthur's deception. At the very end of the most recent vision, the shadows I believed for so long were all in my head, fucking with me out of sick amusement by the Goddess, slip inside, mingling with my elemental power.

More gasps.

Alec is fighting to get to me.

The slithery feeling. The voice urging me to do things. The way it hurt Alec.

The flashes of anger I've had since—

The murmurs break. Hands release one another. A blast knocks a few members back.

The scraping on my brain ends, and while my body demands rest, I force my head up, seeking Morgan's guidance while my lungs work overtime, trying to stabilize.

Morgan's staring at me open-mouthed, her arms still out by her side from where the witches on either side of her released her hands.

Murmurs travel around the coven, few words louder than everything: "Black magick. They made her Dark."

Anguish fills Morgan's eyes, and she drops to her knees, mirroring my position. "That's impossible..." she breathes, so low I'm surprised I hear her. "Black magick requires killing. They—"

I killed my parents that night. I tried to *protect*, but I instead *destroyed*.

I opened myself up to Darkness.

I scan the group. The stares. All unwelcoming, terrified, horrified.

Carina looks puzzled.

Jasper looks dazed.

Morgan looks disappointed.

Unable to suffer the weight of their judgement for a second longer, I lunge from the circle and streak into the woods, bushes and low-hanging branches tugging at the cloak tied around me. The string pulls taut around my neck until I undo it, letting it flutter to the ground behind me, a black stain on nature.

Exactly as I am.

Hellion.

I ignore him and keep running.

Harlow, stop.

A command I also ignore.

This entire time, I drained myself of my fire magick only to allow the shadows to slip in and fill the gaps left behind. A cold and unwelcome pest, taking over slowly, bit by bit.

For a fucking *second*, I thought maybe, just *maybe*, I could forgive the people I called Mom and Dad. That after all they'd done to my family and this coven, the love I felt for them growing up would decide everything. Like kids who get adopted; it's the family they know who matters more than the family they had.

But no. Every hug, every moment, was all for show. Whatever their reasons, Violet and Arthur *used* me. Created me to be something I'm not—shouldn't ever be.

The whoosh tells me who's incoming before the body appears in front of me, dark eyes covered by dark hair, a creature of Darkness himself, standing amidst the dark forest...in front of the witch forced into it. Like a fucking match of fate.

I nearly laugh, but instead voice my thoughts. "It all makes sense now."

"What does?"

"You. Me. My attraction to you. Me being your Bride, despite not being a vampire. It all makes sense! From the minute we met, I felt something different with you. Something I've never felt towards another, and I assumed it was some weirdness pulling us together, considering I was hearing your voice long before we met. But no." I huff, partially annoyed I'm admitting all this to him when I've barely processed it myself. "No, it's not that at all. It's because you're a *vampire*, descended from a demon, and I'm tainted with black magick. We're both creatures of Darkness!"

He hauls me to his chest, his arm an unbreakable band around my waist. "Do not say that. Black magick hasn't tainted you."

"But I *am* tainted," I argue. "You can't deny that, because you know it's true."

"Fine, it is true," he agrees, his hand coming up to the back of my head, his fingers wrapping around the side of my neck until they brush his bite marks. "You are tainted—tainted by *me*. I could think of nothing better, because you're a fucking gift that I'm *pleased* to have, and it has nothing to do with the magick you control—Light or Dark."

"You don't get it." I shove his chest, twisting to get away. "Black magick *destroys* witches, Alec. There's a reason it's forbidden. You saw everyone's faces back there. I'm dangerous. The coven I've just rediscovered will kick me out because I'm unsavable. And you...you need to get away from me, because if it doesn't destroy me, it'll destroy you. And I don't want that, okay?" I don't. At all. Because like it or fucking not, by some sick twist of fate, we're connected enough that I care what happens to him. Regardless of the past, Alec doesn't deserve to be brought down by me.

His eyes glisten beneath the full moon. He's a natural predator, but for once, between the two of us, I might be the more dangerous one. He releases my body to grasp the sides of my face, walking into me until I'm forced backwards. "Black magick cannot destroy me, because you have already annihilated me, Hellion. Since the moment we've met, I've been breaking down piece by fucking piece, never to be whole again."

Another step.

"It won't destroy you, because I will conquer every level of Hell, Heaven, and whatever Otherworld there is before losing you. Death would never dare touch what I've claimed. Death is not possible, because the sorry soul who tries to steal you will have *me* to deal with."

Another step.

"As for the magick...you think I care? As you've said, I am a creature of Darkness, so your Darkness is now my Darkness. If you submerge yourself in it, I'll be there to catch you. If you want to fight it and remain in the Light, I'll be the shadow at your back, an obscurity forever trailing you. Either way, Darkness is a part of us both, and I don't give a fuck."

Another step, and my back hits a tree trunk with a low gasp. His hands curve around the sides of my face, fingers digging into my jaw until he tilts my head.

"I *thank* the imposters who raised you, because they made you fucking perfect. Perfect for me. Perfect in every way. Light, Dark, or a mix. And if your asshole coven wants to toss you out, then they're missing out on a powerful witch who'd damn well strengthen their ranks."

"Alec," I whisper, my throat tight with the many other things I want to say. To deny. To argue about. "It's not the same," is what I manage. "This kind of magick is bad. I'll fall into it the more time passes, even if I fight it."

His lips part, showing his fangs, as though merely threatened by my words. "You don't know that for certain. Besides, have you not listened to a fucking word I've said? It doesn't matter to me, and it shouldn't to you. Morgan cares a great deal about you; I can't imagine her kicking you out over something you had no decision in. The coven might be able to help you. I watched something truly miraculous tonight. Maybe they can do it again."

"You don't know that for certain." I use his own words on him.

"You're right, I don't. But once again, I don't really care, because there will never be a future where we're not together. No matter how much you fight me, it's you and me now. While you're busy fighting me, I'll fight your demons, banish those shadows. Whatever you need, Hellion."

I reach up to cup his face, still not sure how to voice every-thing in my head. "The shadows don't bother me when you're around. I've always appreciated that about your presence. Although, after tonight's revelations, what I've been thinking of as a good thing might not be. Might be one more reason to stay away."

His eyes flicker, intense pools of endless ocean during the night. "It only proves my point. Between the two of us, I'm much more encased in Darkness, which means you won't have to worry about harming me. I'll battle it for ownership over you."

"That doesn't exactly sell me on the concept. What if I make you worse?"

"Worse," he repeats, amusement tingeing his tone. "Hellion, I will drown in everything wicked, immoral, and Dark if it means you get to rise up and break free from the shadows. I'll remain the villain if you get to be the hero. Never doubt that."

His offer makes my heart skip a beat. "What if I don't want you to?"

He ducks, his whispered reply imprinting on my lips. "When have I ever asked what you wanted? This time will be no different. I'll do whatever it takes to save you from everyone and everything, even yourself. The fact you don't want me to is all the more reason I will."

"Alec..."

"Shut up, Hellion." His low growl is all I hear, all I feel, before his lips take mine in a kiss so overwhelming, so sweeping, I'd believe it alone could resolve the battle between Light and Dark inside me.

FORTY-THREE

Alec

Darkness isn't choosy. We all have it, and it's a fact I learned early on during my mortal life. But until becoming an immortal, I didn't understand the true meaning of evil.

Evil is a spectrum, and we're either tipped toward being bad or full-on depraved. One's decisions determine the level.

Harlow's concerns over becoming evil aren't possible. She has too much potential in her to go completely Dark, even if I'll accept her regardless of which end of the scale she ends up on.

She has to embrace herself, no matter her chosen path.

I force her head back and tear at her clothes, ready to prove why being evil isn't such a bad thing. Why when the coven tosses her out, I'll make her my queen.

Once I have her bare, her clothes a torn mess on the forest floor, I lift her in my arms, winding her legs around my hips.

"Alec, what are you—"

Before she's able to think, to wonder, to be swept away in her own doubts, I shut her up with my mouth, my fangs nipping at her bottom lip. Her blood elevates the kiss to heights only meant for Heaven, a place far away from us both. My tongue sweeps over her lip, gathering the blood to push into her mouth, forcing her to taste how fucking delectable she is.

Using the tree to keep her suspended, I undo my pants and stroke my cock before lining myself up with her heat. I spread her with two fingers, my thumb stroking her to life, and thrust inside her in one hard move.

She moans, head thrown back into the tree. So natural, so beautiful. It bares her neck, and I don't deny myself from tasting her. She's getting swept away by the sensations while I'm lost in her taste, the feeling of her, and the bond growing stronger.

"Do you feel it?" I murmur, unhooking from her neck.

She turns her head, trying to catch my gaze. "Feel...what?" Her normally vibrant purple eyes are unfocused.

"Me inside you. A creature of Darkness inside his witch, a creature of Light."

"Mhm."

"If you allow me inside you, why can't you accept your own Darkness?"

"It's not the sa—"

I thrust harder, my fingers bruising her hips as I push her down, effectively ceasing her disagreement.

"Until you give me the answer I want, you're not leaving this spot. You're not coming. As long as it takes, Hellion."

"Alec, I won't be able to stop." And just as her core follows her own words, her orgasm nearly about to yank her into the abyss, I slide from her, leaving her empty and wanting. She gapes, whining. "That's not fair."

"It's perfectly fair. You don't get to come until you accept yourself. Until you realize how fucking magnificent you are—*precisely* as you are. Darkness and all."

"Then we'll be both celibate."

Bet you we won't be. I push back inside her, slowly this time, watching as I hit the deepest parts that cause her eyes to roll back. *That's it. You were saying, Hellion?*

"Fuck off." But it's lost so much of her normal venom. A fight from a woman who's lost hers.

Light or Dark, you're perfect.

She moans, her nails digging into my shoulder. Even undressed, she'll never be able to penetrate my skin, and for the first time since learning she's my Bride, I wish she were a vampire so she could truly unleash the full depth of her anger.

Not that trying won't also hold its intrigue.

I release her hips to shrug out of my shirt. "You're angry, Harlow. You need someone to hurt. Something to take your rage out on. I want to be that for you. Give me your rage, however you wish to deliver it."

Her hand flattens over the place my heart once beat. "I don't want to hurt you."

"That right there, that you don't want to, is the very reason you won't."

Grasping her hips, I spin us away from the tree and drag us to the ground, settling beneath her, her pussy clenching as she comes down on top of me. It's a position I've never been in for any other woman because it'd mean giving up my control. But Harlow can have every bit of it, and I roll my hips into her, urging her to claim it for herself.

"Not now, but after this, what if the black magick fucks with my fire? You heard what happened; they were binding my magick. I'm stronger now than in the past, and with the Darkness..." A slashing emotion—pain—slices down the bond, and it's the only reason I let her remain still atop me. And then it's her whisper—a sign of that caring nature of hers I've come to love. "What if my magic explodes again? It's fire, Alec. It'll kill you."

"Then you'll be free. If you die, I die, but since the bond is one-sided and incomplete, you'll get everything you want."

Anguish stares down at me in the form of masked feelings and potential heartache. "What if that's not what I want?"

"Then you won't kill me. Hellion, you're talking like you'll have no control."

"I won't! You and I both have no idea what'll happen."

"Yes." Seized with irritation, I sit up, my arm clenching around her waist to keep her still, my cock buried deep inside. "You're right. Neither of us know what'll happen, but you're pissing me off. You're giving up before you even try. Where's the Sinclair I kidnapped, the one who ran for her life? The one who sat in that cell and never once gave up? You sharpened a rock, for fuck's sake, to defeat me. *You*, Harlow Sinclair, *my Bride*, you don't give up. Ever. Don't worry about me, because no matter what happens, death won't keep us apart. Death would give you a chance to move on, and I've decided I'm too obsessed with you to allow that. Now..." I fist her hair, yanking her head back until her back arches and her perfect, budded nipples consume my view. Before I lose myself to them, I demand, "You're angry, Hellion. You're confused. You're hurt. You're scared. And don't lie, because I feel every single one of your emotions. Before we return to the coven, you need to work this out, and I want you to do so on me. Magickally or otherwise, unleash yourself." I dip my head, tracing a nipple with my fang and whispering, "Please, Harlow. For me. For yourself. Let it out. Let yourself go."

My tongue swipes over her nipple while my fangs dig into the flesh, but just like every other bite, I do not go gentle. I devour her like I would prey I didn't care for. I drink in heavy gulps, urging her to fight me.

A moment later, she does. Heat comes through where her palms are on my shoulders, and it's with a genuine flinch I pull away, yanking my teeth from her skin to meet her smirk seconds before she grasps my neck and angles my face up to hers.

"How do you know what I need?" she whispers against my lips.

Because I can feel you better than you feel yourself.

"Thank you."

And then she takes over, and it's a beautiful thing, letting go to her. Seeing as she comes up on her knees until only the tip of my cock is inside her and then sinks back down, burying me as deep inside her as she can. She does it twice, taking her time, her body twisting with pleasure.

Do it, Hellion. You know you want to. Just feel.

She moves harder, faster, and I thrust from below, helping her towards the finish—helping her *let go.*

Her back arches with her cry, birds and bats fluttering far away as she disrupts the sliver of peace around us. My little nature disruptor. My piece of Darkness, all for me.

Fucking beautiful.

And that's when it happens. When her eyes flash with something dangerous and alluring, when the purple of her eyes flicker to a midnight black, the same colour as mine, and her nails dig into my skin. She won't break it, but she tries, riding me into a near-oblivion.

"Feel it. Let it out. Let yourself be who you are."

Her eyes flash to mine, purple again but tinged with fear. "I don't know who I am."

"Then we'll figure it out together."

I wish my skin wasn't so impenetrable that I'd bleed for her. To see her hard work pay off the way it should and—a sharp sting disrupts my own thoughts, and like my plea was answered, small beads of blood drip from her nails and down my abs.

She throws me a wicked grin and comes down harder on me. "Magick."

Fuck, this witch is perfect. It's a thought meant for myself, but I let it go to her too so she understands where I stand.

I push myself into a sitting position and grip her hair, arching her into me as I force her down, her legs tightening around me. Her nails glide from my chest to my shoulders where she digs in again, breaking the skin. Blood paints my skin, not nearly as lovely as the artwork I created on her chest.

She looks down on me, her hair creating a wall between us. "Feels good."

"It's meant to. You can't break me, Harlow. If you want to control the Darkness, let me be your outlet. When those shadows' voices are becoming too much, this is how you release them."

Her mouth opens to reply, but it's cut off by her silent scream, her gasp, as she stiffens in my arms, her core clamping tight. Her nails sink even harder, and I swear she's taking my skin with her this time.

But I don't care. Skin or blood, she can have every part of me.

"They're here," she whispers, her breathing still uneven.

I lift my head from the veil created by her hair, disturbed I was so wrapped up in her I didn't hear anyone approach. My arm tightens around her hip, ready to shield my Bride's naked body from the intruders, except no one's here.

No one...but then I understand what she meant. From behind her, the air is thicker, darker, more obscure. The trees disappear in a blur of grey, melding with the shadows emitting from her.

The shadows she's always spoken about. A physical manifestation of her Darkness, dancing in the air behind her, likely called by my bleeding.

She's mine, I tell them. *I've already claimed her soul long before you.*

Can they hear me? I don't fucking know.

But by the time Harlow unhooks her nails from my shoulders, they fade away, leaving us alone.

She looks at me with a mixture of apprehension and bewilderment, like she's unsure what to feel. Her attention slides to my chest and shoulders, where the blood remains, but the cuts have already resealed themselves. Before she does something stupid like try to apologize, I kiss her.

I kiss her until her heartbeat calms and when I know for a fucking fact the shadows understand my claim on her.

I kiss her until the tear sliding down her cheek dries up.

I kiss her until I understand the sensation ravaging my insides.

I kiss her until she pulls away with a small blush and a bite of that bottom lip. I pull it free, admonishing her with a shake of my head. "Bite too hard and you'll make yourself bleed. I won't be able to focus."

She slides her hand up the side of my neck, tracing my hairline. "Maybe that's the point."

"Except tonight's about you. You okay?" Asking another's feelings is unusual, and frankly, *wrong*, but nothing ever feels wrong with Harlow.

"Honestly...no. But you're making me better."

"That's what I'm here for." I flip her over, rising above her as I inch down her body, intending to continue making her feel *better*. Better only comes when she can no longer remember her name.

My thumb circles her clit, swollen and red from our fucking. She releases a low whimper, biting that lip again as her hands fist the ground on either side of her.

"I'm a creature of Darkness, which means my touch is too, yet you accept me so easily."

She hums, her eyes shut to the earth. "It's not the same."

"Tell me how it isn't." I wait until she starts speaking the first syllable of whatever pointless argument she's about to present before flicking my tongue against her clit.

"Not fair."

"Very fair." I lick her again, my hands clenching her thighs to keep her spread open and needy. She tries to buck into my mouth, but I keep her down, sliding my tongue as deep as I can to fuck her with it.

She's on the verge of coming, the sweet scent of her cum returning tenfold, her heart skipping a beat, but she suddenly stops her rocking attempts, lowering her hips to the ground.

"Bite me."

The bond prickles with desire, no fear, so I slide my tongue from her, dragging my lips over her core and towards the inside flesh of her thigh. She trembles under my hold but doesn't fight as I pull the skin taut and sink my teeth in.

"Holy fuck." She bucks, but my free hand keeps her immobile, wrapping around her thigh until she's hugging my head.

Her blood is thinner here and ignites on my tongue. Combined with her cum, it's a taste I could very well bottle and live off of forever.

And I intend to. Live off it forever, that is.

My thumb massages teasing circles along her clit as I drink deeper, harder, her blood making my cock hard all over. God, she tastes so fucking sweet. I'll never be able to stop, not until she kicks me away, even though I know I'll never be able to hurt her either.

My Bride tastes perfect.

"Alec."

It's with my name on her lips and her blood in my mouth that she comes again, her hands fisting my hair as she forces me down. I don't let her, not completely, ensuring my teeth don't dig too hard into her. I let her believe she has control, and when her arms drop limp to the ground beside her, I slide from between her thighs and crawl up her naked body, smudged with blood and dirt, to place another kiss on her lips.

"Everything I'll ever hunger for is between your lovely thighs. I'll spend eternity down there."

She throws me a playful smirk. "I never agreed to be with you forever. I still don't even know if I *like* you."

"Oh, you like me, Hellion. From that first night, you desired me. You forget." I tap my nose, indicating my enhanced sense of smell she'll never be able to escape.

"Lust doesn't equate to deeper feelings."

"No," I agree, "but it's a start."

Giggling, she pushes into a sitting position and scans her body. "I'm a mess."

"You're a vampire's Bride. You've never looked more the part."

She laughs again and looks towards the forest in front of us. I see the moment it all returns, seconds before she curses. "Shit, the coven..."

"The coven can burn for all I care. I know you think you're home, but if they look at you like that again, I'll have no qualms about ripping out every single one of their hearts. *You* come first. They failed you once by allowing those people into their coven, so I'll be making sure they don't fail you again."

The only sound of her reply is her rapidly beating heart.

Harlow

"Can I show you something?" Alec asks as he zips up his pants. He places his shirt on me, skipping my own clothes, wherever they got thrown to, and buttoning his up, then rolling up the sleeves.

"Show me what?"

He takes my hand, pulling me closer to him, and my insides jump like he *didn't* just fuck me on a forest floor and let me use my magick on him. "Trust me. I think it's what you need."

With a wary look, I climb on his back, adopting a similar position to when he ran from my parents' house to the forest earlier. Knowing what'll come, I lower my head to hide from the sharp sting of the air that'll be created by his speed.

After a few moments, the wind dies down and I'm being lowered to my feet in front of a small expanse of ground lined with a metal fence about hip height. Beyond, sticks wrapped with coloured ribbons are scattered in neat rows, about two dozen back.

"What is this?"

Wordlessly, Alec takes my hand and tugs me through the gate, down the centre. A path, based on the flattened grass. He stops in the last row, leading me to a spot where the ground is more raised than the rest.

He releases my hand and steps back, allowing me to crouch and read the inscription—no, the names—on the two orange ribbons tied to the single stick.

And that's when I understand where we are, what this place is, and why this stick in particular Alec led me to.

The ribbon is orange to represent the fire magick of my parents.

For Emily and John Sinclair, their names written in neat, black block letters.

"Oh..."

I haven't been able to understand grief as an emotion in a very long time, but I am sorry, Harlow. I'm sorry for what happened to them. And I realize it might be ironic coming from me, but regardless, you didn't deserve to grow up with murderers.

Other than my own paced and disturbed breath, the cemetery is silent. No birds flutter. The wind is calmer than earlier. The immortal behind me is noiseless, his only words ringing in my mind. And me...I stop breathing because I don't know what to feel. Stop thinking because I don't know how to process this.

I tilt my head back to catch the clouds moving over the moon, as though Hecate is telling me the night of the full moon is passing, and the ceremony I learned all the truths from is over.

That the past remains in the past.

My fingers dig into the grass by my knees.

"I, I saw you tonight," I whisper to them, not even sure they can hear me. "For the first time I can recall, I got to *see* you, but it feels empty. Like I was watching a movie. I, I don't know how to feel... Mom. Dad."

A tear slips down my cheek. I don't speak again until it hits a blade of grass by my hand.

"Your murderers raised me, and it's the worst kind of fucked up because I don't know how to feel. They were Mom and Dad to me. I loved them. But they're the villains in this, and I hate them for what they've done. And yet...I miss them. They held me through every illness, taught me to control my magick, took me to the movie theatre, and dressed up for the silly human holidays. For better or worse, they were my parents."

Another tear slips down my face, this time filled with guilt over what I'm saying to the people who gave me life, who should have been the ones to do everything I listed.

I lift my head, rereading the names on the ribbon. Near-strangers, no matter what tonight has done.

"They're dead. I, I killed them. By accident, and it is something I've had to live with, but I'm happy they're gone—happy *I* killed them. The price of black magick was their deaths, and although I didn't realize at the time I was avenging you, I'm kinda pleased it worked out like that, that their plan—whatever it was—failed in the end.

"They turned me Dark. Taught me forbidden magick. The shadows that tormented me for months were because of *them*. Because they introduced it into my life. They're why I am how I am. Why I can *feel* it festering inside me. It wants blood. It's angry. It wants—" I cut off when the slither wraps around my neck again, taking me back to when I was riding Alec and it was more than thrilled to be called upon. It craved his blood, his pain, and I gave it.

Behind me, Alec kneels. His hand strokes my hair, brushing it off my shoulder. It's then I realize, when it clings to my cheeks, exactly how many tears I've shed. "I feel your pain."

"Then why do I feel empty?"

"Darkness. It's why vampires lose their ability to feel most major emotions." He shifts until he's on the ground and pulls me into his lap, adjusting his shirt so it covers my thighs.

"Do you miss feeling things?" I tilt my head until I can see him.

"Sometimes. Other times, no. Emotions are pain, and feeling yours right now tears me up inside. I haven't felt grief since Cora's death, and even then, it was probably a fraction of what I would have felt had I been mortal. But lately..." He sighs, a low rumble that spreads a warmth through me different from my magick. "Lately, I've had this sentiment inside me that goes a bit above any obsession I've ever lived with. A feeling I only get when looking at you."

My palms are sweaty despite the cool air, and I rub them along my thighs. "That sounds dangerous."

"It might be." His thumb sweeps mindlessly over the scars on my wrists.

"How do you feel about feeling?'

"I'm coming around to it."

"It's the magick between us."

"Maybe." Black eyes flick to mine. "Or maybe not. But talking about this isn't why I brought you here." The wind catches in his hair as he focuses on the grave in front of us. "I know tonight's a lot between your house, your memories, and now this, but I thought if you had a piece of them, it might help come to terms with earlier."

"How did you know this was here?" I ask before remembering *whom* I'm speaking to.

"Sure you can figure that one out." He shifts me off his lap and back to the ground before crawling forward, pacing over my parents' grave. It's odd, not only to see him crawling around the ground but to have him so close to the family he once took so much from.

The other orange ribbons dancing in the breeze catch my attention. How many of them are in the ground by Alec's hand?

Alec moves aside stray leaves that fell onto my parents' grave and is murmuring something I don't catch to them. It's low and spoken with sincerity and keeps me relaxed. He returns to my side, sitting cross-legged and pulling me into his lap.

As he plays with my hair and strokes the side of my neck, murmuring small words of encouragement in my ear, I share stories of my life with both my parents and him. To the clouds that uncover the moon above and Hecate, who's gazing down on the scene.

I'd like to say She's smiling too.

FORTY-FIVE

Alec

At some point during her storytelling, Harlow passes out in my arms.

People don't sleep in places they feel unsafe. Which means at some point, she's decided to trust me enough to relax around me.

Given the night she's had, I shift until she's lying down and using my thigh as a pillow. Her hair streams over my lap, and I stroke my fingers through the strands that were once soft but now are mixed with dirt and broken leaves from our time on the ground. I pick out any that I find, even if I kind of like her like this.

Like that, in the cemetery with the souls from witches past— many I've put here myself—I hold one of their own, thankful a witch's magick seems to fade with their death, or else I'd be fighting an invisible army.

Hours pass and, besides the occasional squeak from a squirrel, chirp from a bird, or gust of wind, all is silent. But too soon, the time nears sunrise.

I wake her slowly with a few caresses to her cheek, enthralled by the fact this witch is all mine. She wakes slowly, yawning in a way I find captivating. I haven't yawned since my human life.

"Hellion, you have to get up. Sun will be rising shortly."

She yawns again, and I help her sit upright. She stretches, arching her back, her nipples hard through my shirt. More than anything, I want her back in my bed where I can spend every waking minute ravishing her body, especially after the bullshit from the coven last night. She'll want to return to the High Priestess, I'm sure, but I'd be more than thrilled to carry her away from here.

"Sorry, I fell asleep." She tries to stand, but her body, laden with sleep, does her no favours.

I duck, lifting her bridal style and tucking her into my chest, her head on my shoulder, exactly how I carried her from the tiny cell when she called for me. After readjusting my shirt so it's covering her bare ass, I begin walking.

"You didn't have to carry me. Pretty sure you did your duty long enough being my pillow."

"Don't have to, but I want to."

She hums, her body loosening in my arms, accepting what she needs. "Well...thanks." Once I'm out of the cemetery and through the small gate, walking in the direction of the High Priestess's house, she sighs. "I almost don't want to go back. I still don't know how to feel about everything."

"Say the word and I'll keep walking. You don't need to have everything figured out."

I spot the argument even before she speaks, her forehead rippling with last night's anxieties. "Hecate will turn against me with black magick, if She hasn't already."

"This is why vampires don't have deities. The devil, maybe, would be the closest thing, but we certainly don't pray to him. If your goddess no longer cares, then she's missing out on an incredible witch."

She watches me, those purple eyes of hers sparking with words unsaid. It's another few feet before she murmurs, "Sometimes you really surprise me, Alec. Last night, for example. You were really nice. I never thought I'd say those words. There's still so much I don't know about you, and it's confusing."

"Ask whatever you want to. Good or bad, I'll tell you anything."

Unfortunately, we reach the High Priestess's house, and given the sun is less than an hour away, I don't have the time to wait for her questions.

By the front door, I place Harlow on her feet and readjust my clothing so it covers everything before we enter, immediately being swarmed by three people who rush from the nearby living room.

Morgan's on her instantly, yanking her in a tight hug while the other two remain back. Carina's staring at Harlow while the male watches me, distrust in his eyes, like I'm supposed to give a fuck. He's lucky I'm allowing him so close to my Bride when she's naked beneath my shirt and still smelling of my cum and marked with dirt.

"Fuck, Harlow," Morgan exclaims, thrusting Harlow back to examine her. "I spent half the night searching for you before realizing you probably didn't want to be found. I sensed you were still in Banff, though; your signature was within the town's lines."

"I'm okay." Harlow waves to the other two before crossing her arms, covering her chest. "Just tired. I know we have to talk, and I'm sorry you guys stayed up all night waiting, but we should all sleep."

Morgan rolls her lips together, obviously wanting to argue it, but agrees with a nod. "Yeah, I think rest will be smart before talking about...everything." Her eyes flick towards me. "Feel free to use the basement again."

"And you can take my room," Carina interjects. "I'll sleep at Jasper's again."

"It's fine. I'll be sleeping downstairs with Alec. Thanks, though." She walks past them all, ignoring Carina's subtle wink, Morgan's gaping mouth, and Jasper's frown. At the basement door, she turns towards me, no comment required before I join her.

She doesn't speak until we're safely downstairs. "I don't want to be around any of them right now. They'll want answers I don't have. And you make it all better. You won't demand the same things." She watches me head for the corner of the basement, searching for any spare blankets or towels in a few of the boxes down here that she may be able to use for warmth since my body temperature isn't helpful. "You've always made it better," she murmurs in a considering tone. "I've been hearing your voice for months, and sometimes it kept me sane. The shadows gave me a reprieve from the second you appeared in my bedroom. They returned that night in the dungeon, but went away during your visits. From the beginning, we've been linked. The signs were there all along, but we never knew to look."

I'm looking now.

I'm looking, and I *see* her.

Harlow isn't the Sinclair I always assumed her to be. She's just my Hellion. My obsession.

And if she's right, then her shadows always knew not to fuck with what's mine. Black magick may be a part of her, but it won't beat an actual creature of Darkness, a descendant of one of the first demons.

"I'm glad you have access to black magick," I state. "My body still remembers the way it was thrown against the wall. You'll be able to defend yourself if anyone comes close—and for dealing with my ass when you get pissed off." And she will get pissed at me at some point over the years.

"I didn't want to do that." Her steps make small clicking noises over the stone as she approaches. "The shadows, they speak to me, encourage me to do things, like defend myself."

Well, that's a new one.

"You were newly recharged. and I deserved it after everything." I drop to the ground, the cool wall barely noticeable against my skin, and gesture for her to approach. "Can't find a blanket or anything. You can go up and ask for one?"

"It's fine."

She lowers herself, one thigh on either side of my leg and situates herself on my lap, just like she was earlier in the night when my cock was buried inside her. She shivers and leans into my chest, curling her hands between our bodies for warmth.

The same kind of warmth that spreads through my body at the feeling of this—of my mate on my chest. Not because she'll fall asleep like this, but because she's chosen to be on me.

It means everything in a time of my life when I'm only just learning the definition of *everything*. It's synonymous with Harlow.

I stoke a hand through her hair, never able to get enough of her. She needs a shower after our adventures outside, but I'm not recommending it until I've gotten my fill of her.

So never.

Her head lowers to my chest, ear to the place the organ long dead once thumped. If there was any chance of it beating again, I think it'd happen at this moment right here.

Being immortal, sometimes life can blink by in an instant. Yet there's never been a time where I've been more content to just *be*. Where contentment *is* being still and holding this scrap of a powerful and intriguing woman in my arms.

Her breaths are warm along my side, comforting and paced. While I don't require breathing, I choose to match my inhales and exhales to hers while my hand continues its petting. She should be able to sleep like this, but instead she speaks.

"Before we came inside, you said I could ask anything about you."

"Only if I get to ask my own in return."

She lets out a low huff, almost a whisper. "You know everything already."

"Not everything."

"Like what? Actually, don't answer that. My turn first." She lifts her head and straightens on my lap but leaves her hands on my chest, her fingers creating small, rhythmic circles. "You never told me how old you are."

"I'm old. Old vampires mean strength, power. Next question."

Her smirk is a slow climb. "Is someone self-conscious about his age? Fine." She rolls her eyes playfully, and I'm struck by how much I enjoy the relaxed, spirited side of Harlow. "You claim you're one of the kings of vampires, but what does that entail? 'Cause from what I've seen, you haven't done all that much except show me off to a bunch of vampires." Her gaze flicks to the corner of the room as her expression falters, another question unspoken across her face.

No one's getting your blood, I reassure her. *They'll have to go through me first. The cure will remain in your pretty little veins, never to be used again.*

Her chest visibly decompresses, giving me a better peek down the opening of my shirt. "Good. Now, answer the question."

"Royalty in vampire communities is slightly different from human monarchies. We don't follow laws like mortals do, but someone needs to have some authority over the others in case they slip up, like go on a rampage and destroy cities. Essentially, I put fear into others."

"How do you become a king?"

"You take the role, of course."

"Which means anyone can challenge you for it and become the next one?"

It's happened in the past, but they didn't succeed. "They'd have to beat me, but yes."

"And there's multiple?"

"I monitor the North American vampires. Europe has its own leader. Australia. Russia. We take territories to not only rule over, but to protect."

She nods, seemingly digesting it all. "Your turn."

I ask the first thing that comes to mind. The thing that's been on my mind since the moment I ran her back to my bedroom and fucked the mate bond into her. "I thought you were home-schooled."

"I was."

My hands clench her thighs, imprinting my touch and erasing all those who came before me. "Give me the names of the mortals who've ever touched you. You weren't a virgin."

She laughs loud enough that half the house could hear her if they were still awake. "A jealous vampire. Charming."

"You think I'm joking?" I slide her closer, fingering the collar of my shirt, tempted to rip it from her and show her how *not* joking I am. "You have no fucking idea how pissed I was to realize someone touched you before me. So who's the mortal whose head I'll be placing on a spike in my office for touching my mate?"

She laughs again, a tear sliding from her eye that she wipes away, only for another to follow. Only amusement comes through the bond, so I don't believe they're tears of sadness.

"I was homeschooled, but not a nun. There were two before you. When I was seventeen, I lost my virginity to my next-door neighbour. Arthur and Violet were very protective—which now I get why they were so psychotically anxious all the time—but my neighbour was the exception since we grew up beside one another. He was basically my only friend."

Her neighbour will be easy enough to track down.

"But," she rushes to add, sprawling her palm across my chest, "he's moved away since then, and *no*, I'm not telling you where."

Cities keep deeds of previous home owners, so it's a matter of getting his family name and pursuing.

"The second?"

"A few years ago. He was a co-worker, but has long since moved on. I'm also not handing over his name."

"It won't be hard to get ex-employee records, Hellion."

"Don't hurt them, Alec. I'm serious. I'll be pissed as hell and slam you against the wall if you go after them. Besides, since we're sharing past experiences, what about yours? Maybe stick to the past fifty years or so, though, or we'll be here all day."

Chuckling, I return my hands to her thighs, tracing invisible lines up and down, enjoying when her skin breaks out in goosebumps. "There's been no one worthy enough remembering."

"That sounds like avoidance." Her tongue skates over her teeth before asking, "There must have been someone in your past life who you cared for?"

"As a human, my future wife would have come to me in an arranged marriage, and at the time of my death, none had been set up yet. The first while as an immortal was spent drunk on blood, sex, and power, but I couldn't remember the names, let alone the faces, of anyone." That time was a blur of centuries long past and not caring. "Vampire women are tedious and power-hungry. Mortals are fragile and dull. There isn't anyone of note."

"My body's basically mortal. That mean I'm fragile and dull too?"

My hands grip her hips, pushing her down on me so she feels how non-fragile and dull I think her. "You're everything opposite of dull, Hellion. You give me life in ways no one else ever has. I believe it's now your turn."

"You mentioned transitioning to a vampire in the past. How does that happen?"

"A mortal needs to consume enough vampire blood before dying. When they go, they die a human death, but a vampire's natural healing qualities revive them into reawakening as an immortal. How they die doesn't matter, only that they do so with a few sips of vampire blood in their system. Once awake, they need to drink the blood of a living creature within a few hours or they die again, this time for good. It's like a trade-off; deceased blood transforms, living blood revives."

She traces a line down my abs, getting close enough to my waistband that my cock takes it as an invitation. "Have you ever turned anyone?"

I tip her head up, wanting her to see my face when I reply, "There's never been anyone I've wanted to be around for eternity."

Her gaze drops to the space between us, and her hands slip off my chest to knot in her lap and rub at the scars on her wrists. "What'll happen to me? Witches live long lives, but not *that* long."

"The moment I chose you, our lives got linked. You die; I die. If you complete your side of the bond and I were to die, you would as well. As long as I live, you will too. Whether that's another century, a millennium..." I trail off as the blood drains from her face. She says nothing, but her heart goes off like a butterfly's wing—and it's as fragile as one too.

"You didn't choose me, though. Fate did."

"No, Hellion, *I* chose you. If I truly despised you, I wouldn't have followed you here. I would have allowed myself to wither without your blood and eventually fall into a coma."

She leans away, putting entirely too much space between us. "So you chose me over death? That's not exactly selling me."

"Harlow, I have given you every reason to doubt me, but I vow to spend the rest of forever proving to you I want you for reasons beyond whatever it was exactly that made you mine and me yours. You're my equal, and I apologize it took me a while to realize it. *You*, everything about you, drew me in from the beginning. How I see it, this entire time, you've been the predator between us, not me. It's why I'm here. Why I didn't immediately seek ways to break the bond. You're scared, and I can feel it. Take the time you need, because I'm not going anywhere. We have eternity, you and I, and I plan on using every second of it."

She's staring at her lap, but I feel her tear on my hand as though she's sobbing. To me, one tear is one too many, and I wipe her cheek, my hand lingering when I don't want to stop touching her.

She reaches up, tracing along my cheek and towards my lips. I part them as her thumb brushes my bottom lip, and she slips inside my mouth, lightly brushing one of my fangs. They extend, responding to her touch.

"Are you hungry?"

"For you, always. In general, no."

"They're sharp," she murmurs, stroking the tip again before reaching for my hand. I let her control it, curious when she brings my index finger up to my fang and pushes it against the tip, the skin breaking after a moment of bated breath—hers. Blood swells in a small, red bead.

She brings my finger to her mouth and sucks the tip.

FORTY-SIX

The taste of Alec's blood bursts on my tongue. What I guessed would be disgusting, or at least not remotely tasty by any means of the word, isn't. It's metallic in that familiar blood way, but so much more too. A vibrancy that ignites my taste buds, tingling with saltiness that makes me want more. But beneath the coppery taste, there's more. A flavour I can't place, but something inside me is becoming increasingly familiar with.

As it slides down my throat, melding with my saliva, another sort of burst happens, this one in my stomach and chest. Suddenly, things are clearer than ever. My mind opens to every possibility between Alec and me. A connection forms, seen only through my mind's eye, that connects him to me exactly how I've been to him since the night I ran from him. It's a smoky grey, a darkness making him mine, but nothing like the shadows that spent months stalking me. No, this grey feels like home.

Like I'm coming home.

The bond.

Alec jerks beneath me, his eyes shifting a ferocious red. A growl vibrates through his chest, and I suck harder. The slithering sensation circles my neck, the black magick within me waking to the taste of him. Darkness meeting Darkness.

Suddenly, I'm flipped onto my back, the chill from the cement floor rendering Alec's shirt useless. It gets hiked to my waist as he slots himself between my legs and rips into his own wrist, blood dripping from his arm and onto my chest, an offer silently presented around eyes as wild as the night he first drank from me.

I open my mouth, accepting the decision I've made, and he shifts his arm until blood drops onto my tongue, mini explosions going off. My hips rock into his, chasing every sort of feeling he'll give me as I bring his arm down, mouth latching on the bite he's made.

A ticklish feeling tingles my mind seconds before his voice, as clear as if he verbally spoke the words, filters through. *Do you understand what you've done?*

I knew what I was doing the second I pricked his finger with his fang. What completing the bond on my end will mean for us—for me.

I don't love him, that much I know. Is it even possible to go from loving someone who, only weeks prior, kidnapped and meant to use me in his fucked-up revenge games? Probably not. But what I do know is I feel stronger for him than anyone else in my life, past or present. He's accepting what I am without judgement. He's one of the few who have never lied to me. He's *here*, and this whole thing proved that no matter how much I fight it, fate brought us together and, for some reason, made me his mate. We're together forever, and eternity will feel painfully endless if I remain determined to limit him to the vampire he was rather than the one he's becoming for me.

It's with little focus, an almost instinct driving me, to push my reply into his consciousness, now able to do what I never was before. *You accept my Darkness, so why should I keep avoiding yours?*

He tugs his arm away and traces my mouth, smudging blood over my lips and chin. *As fucking fantastic as that feels, your body isn't meant for blood. Bride or otherwise, I don't know if it'll make you sick.*

Probably not, considering the cure doesn't work on you.

I'd rather not risk it. Verbally, he murmurs, "There's no greater pleasure among mates than blood-sharing."

I tilt my head to the side, offering my neck for him to drink. And he does, my body unfurling like the final wisp of smoke from an extinguished fire.

Is there really no greater pleasure than this?

He shakes his head without detaching, his hair brushing the side of my face. His gulping is more relaxed than in the past, as if savouring every drop. He lowers his body onto me, his cock hard against my stomach.

Proof. You have no idea how much I want to make you scream, Hellion.

So do it.

He pulls his fangs from my neck, tongue catching a spare drop of blood on the corner of his mouth. "Not here," he murmurs, stroking his finger down the side of my face. "Not where people can hear you. I want you all to myself. Besides, your nap in the graveyard wasn't long, and you need more rest."

Even the mention of a nap makes me yawn, the sound tapering off into a small giggle. "Maybe you're right."

Alec flips us again until I'm back on his lap. Blood trails down my neck and into his shirt. He traces the path with his thumb before gathering a few drops and licking them from his finger, his eyes fluttering shut with a low moan.

"I never knew it could be like this. Your voice is like music in my head. I never want to go without it."

I look up at him, meaning every syllable when I say, "You won't."

He smiles briefly before reclining against the floor and shifting me on top of him, my legs falling to the side, my arms tucking close to our bodies to retain the warmth and avoid the cool ground.

Sleep, he commands. *I'll wake you in a few hours.*

He pets my hair and he begins humming a tune I don't recognize. One filled with heartache and ecstasy, of pain and pleasure. Of enemies and lovers, of descent and growth.

It's the story of him and me. Of us.

Alec is perfectly still beneath me, having held me in the same position all day, and I wake first with a sleepy stretch that bumps my head against his.

When he doesn't move at first, I slowly readjust to look at him, catching his shut eyes and unmoving chest. His face is paler than usual, but there's a contentment I don't recognize as he sleeps.

A sleeping vampire. Not a view I expected.

I reach to move a curl off his forehead, and his eyes flash open, finding me instantly.

"You were sleeping," I comment before he can speak.

"Told you I do."

"You were tired too?"

"No." But he offers no more as I shift off him, coming up onto my knees and stretching. "Everyone left the house a few hours ago, so you can shower undisturbed if you'd like."

"That'd be nice." My body is a combination of blood and dirt, and I can't even imagine what I look like to him. Hair unbrushed, mouth not having seen toothpaste in over a day.

You still look beautiful. Exactly how I plan on keeping you for eternity. His smirk reminds me of the ones he'd use as a part of his mask when he visited me in the cell, only this time there's an underlying playfulness to it too.

He's right about the house being empty, not that I

doubted it. I head upstairs to use their shower and pilfer through Carina's clothing for more, hoping she doesn't mind. I should get Alec to retrieve what I wore yesterday from the woods.

Is there a limit on the distance of this thing? I ask him, slipping on a pair of jeans.

Wouldn't know. You're my first Bride. Haven't exactly had much experience.

Other vampires haven't mentioned it?

Having a mate, Bride or chosen, could be a weakness. No vampire would discuss the specifics of the bond in fear it'll be used against them.

So I'm a weakness for you?

His low growl vibrates through my mind. *You're my only weakness, Hellion. If I ever bow to another, it'll be at your feet or to save your life. You're the only thing that can ever hurt me.*

I know you're joking or whatever, but if I can't control black magick, that might very well be what happens.

I've already told you how I feel about your magick, so I refuse to argue about this again.

Accepting me doesn't mean I'm unafraid, though. I finish dressing and head downstairs, planning for a brief stop by the kitchen for water when a note taped to the wall across from the basement door catches my attention, unnoticed earlier.

Harlow, I'm at the shop, if you'd like to come talk when you're awake. -Morgan

Taking the note, I slip it into my back pocket and head for the door, bracing for the inevitable conversation needed to be had. Perhaps I'll pass coven members between here and town's main core, but I wonder how they'll react seeing me. If they view me as an enemy now because of the Darkness inside me. The notion makes my chest burn.

I'm heading to Morgan's shop. Not sure if I'll be back before evening.

I'll find you if you're not. Don't take her shit, Hellion. Say the word, and we'll leave this place.

I don't reply, because I'd rather not put the possibility of a negative conversation out into the universe. Good vibes and all that follow me down the road, past the Sinclair house, and into the main core.

Testing the distance, I send down the bond.

I hear you. He sounds amused.

Does it weaken if I don't drink regularly from you?

Not sure.

Why didn't I hear you right away when you first drank?

Because I didn't send anything to you. Couldn't have you freaking out before I arrived.

That makes sense.

The main core of Banff is—as usual, from my short time here, anyway—filled with tourists walking in no decipherable patterns. Kids scream for ice cream, BeaverTails, and other sugary treats after supper in one of the numerous restaurants; gift shops have their typical lengthy lines; and people mingle everywhere, photographing the giant mountain that serves as a backdrop to the strip.

The bustle is crazy, but welcoming too. Ever since my fake-parents' deaths, I holed up in my house and exclusively had food delivered when I decided not to starve myself to death. Then it was Alec's castle, where he and I were the only signs of life. This feels normal. Like the old version of me, even if that version has long been killed.

That version was also a lie.

Morgan's shop comes into view, and the sign is flipped *Closed*.

After a quick test of the knob, though, it turns. Strange, and even stranger is the shop being closed.

"Morgan?" I call out, wandering towards the path between the glass countertops that presumably leads to the back room. "Carina?" I try when her mother doesn't respond.

All is silent, so I head behind into the back room, scanning the desk, numerous file cabinets, and boxes of inventory.

"Morgan?"

Crack.

Awareness is a cold dose of reality that instantly unsettles me. I need to get out of here...

A body materializes when I step back towards the back room's entrance, a man as tall as he is wide. I don't catch his face before a heavy hand covers my mouth, his other coming up in a series of motions. A black cloud encompasses me before my vision turns fuzzy, the realization of what he's doing being my final moment of consciousness.

Black magick.

"I'm sorry, Harlow."

That voice... It's...

Dad.

FORTY-SEVEN

Alec

A while passes before the thinnest feeling flits through me, through the bond.

Anxiety. Panic.

It's the same dreadful sensation as when she was locked in the dungeon and suffering from claustrophobia. It has me on my feet and across the basement.

Harlow, what's wrong?

I wait and wait but get no response. Have we reached the maximum distance that the connection can reach and we're unable to hear one another? While possible, I *feel* it isn't that.

Something's wrong.

Hellion, answer me.

More silence.

Nothing through the bond. No feeling. Just emptiness.

My Bride is in trouble, and it's probably those fucking witches. They're doing something to her, and it'll be their final acts before I rip their heads off.

I'm coming.

I'm at the top of the stairs quickly, fists slamming and cracking into the door, but the enchantment the High Priestess covered the basement with shimmers, telling me it's not dark out yet.

Fuck. Even if I broke through her spell, I can't go outside.

I *must*. Harlow's in danger.

Fuck, fuck, fuck.

While I'm aware of all these facts, it doesn't stop me from seeking the bond again, for a feeling she's alright.

And never getting a response.

FORTY-EIGHT

Harlow

I'm woken by the clasping of metal around my wrists, and, like a veil has been lifted off my face, I'm instantly alert, searching for anything telling about where I am.

The space is dim, but not as bad as the cells Alec kept me in. It's small—suffocatingly small—and only deep inhales keep me focused on the fact I'm fucking chained, which is a much bigger problem than my claustrophobia flaring up. Cuffs are latched around my wrist, connected to chains bolted to the wall.

No, not the wall. But something... It's dirt, like a small cave, the ceiling dripping with roots. There's a familiarity in this too, like I've been here before.

Been here in my nightmares, in the flashes of concealed memories discovered last night.

I've been here in the past.

Fuck. Fear can't take hold just yet. Not if I want to survive. Swallowing through the short breaths and clammy skin, I grab onto the chains, yanking on them until determining my mortal-level strength won't do shit against them. The metal around my wrists align so well with the old scars there, and it all comes crashing down.

The similarities. The small space. The handcuffs.

Wherever I am, this is where I was kept when I was eight and stolen from Banff the first time.

Something scrapes nearby. I'm not alone, but the cave is too dim to make out the obscure blob coming towards me, the length of the cave stretching farther than I initially believed; the peek of light, of nighttime, far away.

Alec! I call through the bond, hoping and praying he hears me, while yanking on the chains as I try to channel every ounce of my power into something tangible. Something that will free me.

No response.

Hecate, find him for me. Please.

"Give up. The cuffs are enchanted so even your magick won't be able to break them."

That's impossible.

The blob splits apart into two. Two people approach, one having casted a small fire in the corner to light up the cave.

Nothing's changed between then and now. Not the cuffs, the cave, or the people behind it.

They're strangers. Their expressions are blank and nothing like the affection I knew. Everything about them is a premonition of events to come.

"Mom. Dad."

I'd like to believe they're ghosts haunting me—if ghosts were real. Witches go to the Otherworld, Summerland, to be with Hecate or get reincarnated— usually determined by whether they have unfinished business. Human spirits pass on to Heaven or Hell, decided by their life's deeds, and vampires go nowhere, their bodies left for nature to reclaim.

But these aren't ghosts. They're real, unfortunately. They're the people I once loved, who called me theirs.

Everything, what they hid from me, is so much clearer now. Perhaps it always has been and I just couldn't see it, but clearer than ever are their own shadows clinging to them. Darkness, as thick and as poignant as mud, and as suffocating as this cave is. They're so encased, it's taken the red hair I knew and the brown from the picture and transformed my ex-mother's hair into a deep black.

"How? You died." *I killed you.*

Mom—Violet—steps forward. "You believed you did because we wanted you to."

"But your bodies—"

"Weren't ours," Arthur, the man I knew as Dad, interrupts. "You did exactly what we'd hoped."

Rocks settle in the base of my stomach, because if the burned bodies weren't them, then—

"*Who* did I murder?"

"Mortals; no one important."

"But why?" I let my eyes travel between the two of them before jerking against the cuffs, my current predicament more important than deaths they may never tell me the truth about. "What am I doing here?"

Violet waves her hands, and black smoke materializes two chairs. They each sit in one facing me, as though conducting an interview. "I'm sure you have questions, and we'll be happy to answer them while we wait."

My blood freezes over. "Wait for what?"

"The reckoning, of course," Violet replies, making zero sense. She crosses one leg over the other, her hands resting primly on her knees. Even her mannerisms are so different from the woman I knew. "You're about to become even more powerful than you already are, Harlow Sinclair."

While so many questions arise, her saying my surname—the one they claimed as their own for so long—distracts me, forcing another thought instead. One whispered with the weight of our history.

"You killed my parents."

"We needed you," Arthur chimes nonchalantly. "More than they ever would. You're meant for bigger things."

"Like utilizing black magick," I guess, willing it or my fire magick to function. Anything to help me out of here. Instead, I'm left with a pitiful attempt at yanking the chains, my skin reminding me of the last time I did this and the marks I got to show for it.

Violet watches my attempt with pursed lips. "They're charmed to not break. And yes, Darkness is a very big part of your future. You should be thanking us."

"You're monsters," I spit. "Murdering monsters who kidnap children and steal identities."

Violet uncrosses her legs to lower her hands, woven together, between her knees. She leans closer, her depthless eyes taking on a near-familiar flicker. "We work for a higher power. A war is coming, and there are a few key players to ensure witches are on the winning side. Unfortunately, the winning side is not the one *Hecate* insists on aligning Herself with." She speaks the Goddess's name like it's poison. "Hecate has chosen the side of good, when we must follow a different path. Earth will be in danger, and if we wish to survive, we need to become soldiers. Light magick will not save us."

Higher power. Coming war. Soldiers.

"You're crazy."

She shrugs. "I'm not. Something's coming, and we have to be ready. The man we work for needs you at your best."

I scan them, noting what "best" they mean. "You've been teaching me black hexes for years and wiping my memory of them. Wiping my memory of *everything*."

"Yes," Arthur continues, "you were much trickier than we expected. Our original job was to kidnap a Sinclair descendant, which is why we tricked our way into your coven. Your mother would have never turned Dark, but you? At eight, you were untapped, not yet come into power, which meant we could shape you into anything. We took you, as per our orders, but then instead of handing you over, we were asked to raise you, teach you the better ways. The vampirism cure in your veins was created from black magick—don't know if you ever figured that tidbit out—so you had great potential already. Essentially, you were halfway there."

I stare down at my hands, as though envisioning the cure. Logically, it makes sense. Magick like this isn't natural, nothing gifted by the Goddess. But it also means the High Priestess who put the cure in my veins dabbled in it. It's a fact no one's ever mentioned and I never put together.

Arthur chuckles. "Your coven has quite the history with black magick. Why do you think it's taboo now? When your powers came in, you were stronger than anticipated, though it shouldn't be entirely surprising. Sinclairs are some of the original witches, and with the cure, you're a level above the rest of us."

A slither coasts around my neck and, for once, I'm happy to have the Darkness; I might need it to fight theirs.

"As a result, we had to bind your magic," he continues. "As you got older, you got stronger. Every time we taught you a spell, your fire responded to the Darkness, even before you had the capacity to use that kind of magick. We knew it was only a matter of time before locking it wouldn't be possible—which ended up being for the best. The cure may be infused with Darkness, but it's not nearly enough. You at full strength? Your element mixed with Darkness... you'd be the ideal weapon—once activated."

If my stomach could drop lower, it would.

Darkness snakes down my spine, reminding me it's still here, its low hissing voice urging me to destroy them.

I jerk. *It's still here.* The cuffs are supposed to render my magick useless, but they're not. At least not all of it.

I drop onto my hands, pretending exhaustion has taken me out, but I dig my nails into the dirt, aiming to fill myself with every kind of power I can pull upon.

"Activated?" I repeat, wanting the rest of the story and to keep them talking so they don't pay attention to my hands.

"Murder creates Darkness. You needed to kill, but we knew you, Harlow. You were a Sinclair through and through, no matter how much we tried to alter that. You wouldn't do it willingly."

Then, no. Now...it's debatable.

"We planned the attack with help from vampires. Bloodsuckers had no idea they wouldn't make it out alive and believed they'd receive sips of your blood—the cure—by the end. When they came, we fought to make it look realistic but knew you'd never leave your parents behind." Arthur's smirk turns mocking, my hate only growing that much more. "And you didn't, not once disappointing us that night. What we didn't expect was your magick to be *that* strong. We underestimated it after years of hindering your abilities. The explosion took us by surprise, but we got out of there in time and popped back to drop the drugged humans we had waiting. They burned in your fire alongside the vampires, and you were never the wiser. Pulled you from the wreckage and went into hiding."

"Of course," Violet says, "we never foresaw the possibility of you extending yourself so far that your magick faded. What you gained with the murders was almost immediately expelled, though hung around. Black magick is similar to elemental magick in that it's almost alive, so it recognized everything you were, are, and could be, and lingered, waiting for the time you'd get your abilities back. Which was only a matter of time; no witch could live long without them. We've been brainstorming how to help you retrieve them— without making ourselves known—when that vampire showed up and took you away. Our orders changed once again, and we watched and waited."

"He'll come for me. The instant the sun sets."

"We'll be gone by then," Violet says. "Your mate will end his search shortly after he begins."

What does that mean? The words stick to my throat, because I'm also not entirely sure I want to know.

If black magick chose me, then I need it to choose me again. To *protect* me. To defend. And I focus all my energy into channelling the very semi-living power I have no clue how to control while also trying to keep them talking.

"What mate?" I ask, downplaying the effect of her words.

Arthur laughs. "You always were a shit liar. Our alliance is partners with a vampire, so we've been let in on all your new secrets."

Another vampire knows about Alec and me?

"Why me? That's the only part I don't understand. You could have stolen *any* witch."

"The four mortals who were given the gift of the elements became the first four witches in existence. A Sinclair being one of them. You are the remaining heir of that bloodline, so you are one of the four chosen."

Thank fuck for Morgan's recent lesson in witch history. But if I'm *one* of the four, that means three other bloodline heirs are in danger. Or will be. Or have been.

"Who are the other three?"

Silence from them both, though it's not entirely unexpected.

Arthur goes on, "Once all four of you are Dark, there is a ceremony our High Priestess will complete to inject the combined power through all witches."

All...they're planning on turning everyone away from the Goddess.

"So what now?" I tug on the chains. "We sit here until I fully turn to your side?"

"You already have." Violet huffs. "We've been at this for decades, so don't think us stupid. When you regained your magick a few nights ago, Darkness infused with your element. You are the exact witch our cause needs. Now, we wait for sundown, when you'll be retrieved and brought to another place to be kept safe until the time of the war. That's when we'll need you."

"Which is when?"

She shrugs. "In a few months, or years, perhaps. Until then, you'll continue developing your powers under new teachers."

"You still sound crazy."

"You're the lucky one, Harlow. The other three witches, while we need them, are less important. You, as the only vampire cure in current existence, are a very valuable commodity, and our boss wants you all to himself for an insurance policy. If the war doesn't turn out the way they think, you might be their plan B."

"And you? When this war doesn't go how you want, you'll die for this supposed cause?"

"Yes," both echo at the same time. It's Violet who continues, "We're doing this *for* witches. When the four bloodlines join, our High Priestess will be performing magick to save everyone. Everyone will understand eventually."

"You can both fuck off."

The tunnel behind them suggests how low the sun is getting. Now dusk, the trees barely filter any light through. If sundown is coming, I need to get out of here before then.

So I focus. Magick is ruled by emotions, and I'm about to feel stronger than ever. Emotions greater than what I felt when supposedly killing them.

This time, I won't miss.

FORTY-NINE

Alec

The moment the sun falls, the enchantment does too, and I'm out of the basement as the High Priestess walks through the front door, arms leaden with shopping bags. It's sickeningly normal and humanlike, but the lack of Harlow behind her only confirms my suspicion.

In the past few hours, there have been a myriad of emotions from her ripping my insides apart. Shock, panic, concern, betrayal, and curiosity. It's a jumble making no sense.

But this witch *will* answer for all of it.

I'm in front of her instantly, my hand around her throat. Her shopping bags slip from her arms and crash all around us, items spilling out.

"Where's Harlow?"

She struggles, nails scratching pointlessly at my skin. "With… you…"

If she thinks Harlow's with me, then it's either a good fucking lie or something is worse than I believed.

My grip loosens slightly, but I don't let her down. "She went to your shop."

The witch's expression goes deathly pale, and her reply guts me all over. "My shop is closed today."

I haven't felt fear—true fear—in a long fucking time.

"So where is she?" I ask, but it's a question more for me than her before I take off to town, uncaring if humans out mingling late notice the inhuman blur. I track Harlow's scent to a small shop, following it to the back room.

Morgan, in all her witchy abilities, manifests in front of me. "Smell anything?"

"Yes." My Bride's scent, tinged with fear, enticing my fury, and the others overlaying it. "Two witches."

If witches were involved, Morgan's the most likely suspect, but she ignores me, instead closing her eyes and holding up a finger for me to wait.

"Magick leaves signatures; it's how I found Harlow the other day." The sudden silence is deafening, a *tick, tick, tick* from across the room telling me how little time I might have. After an agonizing moment of planning two deaths, Morgan opens her eyes with an irritated huff. "They're not anyone from the coven, which means they're outsiders and I can't sense them. It's Dark, though. And strong."

"So she was taken?"

The thought shifts to the primal side of me. The side where every thought shuts down, leaving me with a very basic focus: to hunt the bastards, destroy them, and reclaim my Bride.

Harlow. Hellion, answer me. Be okay.

The bond is silent. No emotions. No thoughts.

Fuck.

It unlatches the final switch, freeing the monster within—and his determination to kill.

Whoever thought to take my Bride is fucking *dead*. They'll be destroyed, ripped apart, and I will be *merciless*.

I head out of the back room. I'll trace her scent. I'll follow the bond. I'll find her.

The witch calls after me, running to catch up, but the monster doesn't care. She's a witch, and any witch besides Harlow is the enemy.

"I'll contact the coven. We'll find her. We'll get her back."

I don't reply, my mind already gone, searching.

By the shop's entrance, utter and complete loss punches me in the stomach. Grief without an explanation, a cruel twist of the empty cavity where my heart once beat. Now, a useless organ long inoperative and only brought to life by its mate.

FIFTY

Harlow

Every flash of my childhood flits through my mind. I focus on the way I felt during them—happy—and the devasta-tion when learning they were a lie.

Darkness slinks up my spine, curling into me.

The memories the coven pulled out come up. The *real* memories with my *real* family. I focus on the relief of having them returned, on reclaiming the past and realizing the present I should be having, and my rage towards these two for taking that from me.

Darkness coils around my neck like a weighted necklace containing all my possibilities.

I recall Alec finding me, hunting me through my hometown, and how terrifying it was being chased by a killer.

Darkness twists down my arms, towards the cuffs.

Then there are memories of a similar hunt, this time before claiming me. The way I was both turned on and frightened.

Darkness manifests into a slimy, slithering, snake-like substance, wrapping my arms with sleeves made of tar.

I focus on the feeling of learning I was his Bride.

Darkness unlocks my fire, and my hands warm, responding to the storm of emotions about to take me out.

"That's impossible." Not sure who says it, but the two words simply add to the feelings coursing through my body. The *victory* is oh so close. The way it drives me to prove myself to be the monster they insisted on creating.

And now they'll have to deal with their creation.

Both kinds of magick, black and elemental, twine, working together and fusing into one thing—one *powerful* sensation overwhelming my mortal body, my arms now vibrating.

No, wait... It's not only me. The entire room vibrates. This little cavern they've dug out, likely utilizing their earth magick to create a holding cell for a terrified eight-year-old child.

Destroy them. Save yourself

That voice glides through my ear, the tar around my arms constricting. For once, I no longer fear the possibilities. For once, I'm in control. Balanced.

Vicious. Violent.

And soon to be victorious.

"Harlow, stop!"

I don't recognize my own voice when I ask, "Why should I?"

Alec would be proud of me, I think.

It's thoughts of Alec—the way he touches me, holds me, fucks me—fueling my fire. The cuffs melt off, leaving marks from where they dug in because they were too small, sized for a child. The marks are near duplicates of the ones left in the past.

More evidence they're the real monsters.

Freed from the cuffs, I stand, fire encasing my hands while Darkness hugs my arms. It moves as I do, tightening in places as it travels down to the rest of my body. My stomach, my thighs, even my feet.

"Harlow, you are not in control."

"I feel more in control than ever, so thank you. *Mom. Dad.*" I spit their names, the final time they'll ever hear me refer to them by those titles. "You truly did what you set out to do."

The two stagger away from the chairs, hands up. Their own

black magick forms to protect them, but it's much smaller than mine. Much weaker. An interesting fact.

They're aware of that too, based on their expressions.

I take a step, the entire cave rumbling.

"Harlow, stop! We'll help you."

"Help me?" I spit. "You've only helped me to save yourselves. You murdered my family, stole me as a child, held me captive *here.* You raised me to love you, made me feel loved in return. I grieved you when you died. I *blamed myself* when it was all some fucking game." I laugh, my chuckle vibrating violently down my stomach. "But I'm done playing."

Violet raises her hands, Darkness emerging from them as though to attack. I'd be more concerned about losing, considering they have years on me mastering the power, but her fear says it all.

"We did love you. Despite everything, we raised you most of your life. We truly cared for you."

"Liars. I don't think you know how to care for another. Not unless it does something for you."

The cave rumbles beneath my feet, but my Darkness flicks forward, grabbing both witches by their necks. Fragments detach to link their hands together, palms facing one another, rendering their magick useless. They're hovered a few inches off the ground, heads close to the cave's ceiling as more dirt falls from the trembling earth.

"Harlow, please, let us go."

"Give me one reason." I pace towards them. "Darkness is bred with murder, right? You have no one to blame but yourselves for this. And now...I'm feeling generous."

Hope blooms across their expressions, and it only serves to feed me. To do what they've done to me my entire life and deceive them.

"To the Darkness, of course. It's hungry, dying to come out and play, and I believe your souls will be enough."

The cave rumbles again, chunks of dirt falling from the ceiling.

Panicked eyes flick up, Arthur shouting, "Free our hands! You'll take this cave down on us all."

"And?"

"You'll die too! Harlow, free our hands. We'll cast a barrier; we'll protect you too. Don't die because of us. Kill us if you must, but don't be stupid. I'm begging you as your father."

"I was stupid for ever loving you. You're not my father, so don't grant yourself that title."

Darkness tightens around their necks, cutting both airways off, their eyes bulging in their final few seconds of life.

"Fuck. You."

The strands tighten, lives snuffed out.

The cave rumbles beneath me so hard, the roof begins caving in.

It creates a resting place for the two earth witches who turned Dark.

And the final Sinclair.

FIFTY-ONE

Alec

It's the feeling of being burned alive and having my head chopped off. It brings me to my knees, the ground coming towards me much too fast. The witch's steps rush forward, an exclamation filling the room. Even with my enhanced sense of hearing, she seems far away, like she's yelling from down the road and I'm a mere human.

The void in my chest expands upwards until something bursts and blood sprays from my mouth. *Her* blood, my blood. The mated liquid lands on the ground, creating a design of pure cruelty, a taunt of what was and what isn't anymore.

"Alec!" The witch rests her hand on my shoulder, the chill of her magick coming through my clothing. What she's attempting to do is beyond me, but it'll fail either way. Because even without fully understanding what's ravaging my body, even without having felt it in the past, I *know*.

Every part of me knows.

Every drop of blood that's been signed over to its Bride.

Every vein. Every pointless breath. Every*thing*.

Gone.

Fragmenting apart. Stolen by fate—the very thing that gifted my witch to me.

Gone too soon. Lifetimes stolen.

Harlow.

There's no answer. Of course, there isn't.

"Har..." I try to say around the gurgle of blood, to tell the only person here what's happening.

So she can give up searching.

My insides shatter with *her* final breath. The bond so taut, stretched beyond distance, terror, and fate, snaps, this time stretched by death.

Taken by death.

Her death.

The Sinclairs once stole what was precious to me, so I took their lives. Somehow, I suspected it'd all catch up with me eventually, and now it has.

I destroyed many of them... but they've *annihilated* me.

I'd say it was the cruellest thing they could have ever done, but it'd be a lie. Because nothing is crueller than making me fall in love with her and then taking her from me.

It's my final thought before my life, after countless lifespans, also ends.

FIFTY-TWO

Harlow

FIFTY-THREE

Alec

FIFTH INTERMISSION

Freya

Um.

Yeah.

What. The. Fuck?

Excuse me while I interrupt this depression-fest.

Confused? Yeah, you're meant to be.

Although, *I* shouldn't be. Yet I'm so fucking lost, it's not even funny anymore.

Hecate has shit to answer for, because this is *not* everything She disclosed. Deviation happened today and I *will* get answers! Maybe it's Her obsession with free will. Maybe it's something else. But once Harlow and Alec get their happy ending—wait. Will there be a happy ending for them now?

Shit.

There's supposed to be. If they don't, then everything else falls apart.

Harlow was supposed to lose the black magick, not accept it. I didn't foresee any of this. Hecate left so much out, so who the fuck knows what else She's hiding.

I despise being in the dark. And yes, that was meant to be funny. Punny. Ha-ha... No? Dead crowd.

'Kay, oops. No, that time it wasn't supposed to be a pun. Insensitive, I know.

I'll shut up now.

Her death—and his...that's new.

Fuck.

I'm too anxious for popcorn this time.

FIFTY-FOUR

Harlow

…

…

…

Everything hurts.

…

…

…

I should be dead.

…

…

Yet it hurts.

…

…

…

More than anything, my gums ache.

…

…

…

"Hey, I got you, you're okay."

Alec?

No, but it is a voice I vaguely recognize. Like *very* vaguely.

"This isn't what I expected to find."

Right. Arthur and Violet mentioned a vampire would be on his way. Is this him? Which means, any moment now, I'm about to be drained dry, right? For the cure.

Shit.

"You need blood, Miss Sinclair, and fast. And then, you and I will wait for the real show."

Blood? Show?

I'd ask, but everything feels so weighted, and blackness envelops me again.

FIFTY-FIVE

Alec

...

...

...

My eyes open.

Black encompasses my vision, but it quickly fades for colour, making the witch hanging over me, her mouth in a frown, clearer.

Everything comes back in a rush that causes my chest to clench. Including why this witch is above me. Why I'm lying on the ground of some tiny shop in Banff.

Harlow died.

My Bride is dead.

Which means I should be too.

But I'm awake. I search for the familiar buzz of the bond. It's present. Shattered, but not absent.

She's alive.

It's a thought driven by hope...and possibility. Harlow consumed my blood before leaving the basement, and if she did die—

I stare at the witch, sitting up until I'm too close for either of our comforts. "Did you bring me back to life? How much time passed?"

"No, and less than five minutes. I've never seen a vampire pass out like that."

"I died."

She follows me up when I stand. "Randomly?"

"When our Bride does, yes."

"Harlow's dead?" Her screech is too much on my ears, and I turn from the shop, tiring of the conversation that's preventing me from getting to Harlow.

"I don't know," I admit, half-distracted. "I assume she's alive now. I can still feel her."

Without another word, I take off, heading towards the Banff outskirts, letting the bond direct me. I run through the vast forests and numerous small bodies of water decorating the land, passing the territory reeking of a pack of shifters.

There's no scent trail, but I listen to the fragmented bond that, with every step, grows stronger. I don't allow hope to take over— not yet—just follow it by instinct.

Harlow, I test after a few more feet, only to receive more silence.

So much silence. *Too* much silence. I never want to go without her voice in my head again.

I won't fucking survive it.

The pull takes me halfway between Banff and Calgary, and I dip deeper into the woods, a faint scent catching on the breeze. It's not Harlow's, but the two others' from the shop, which means I must be coming up to the right place.

The scents lead me to a large pile of dirt where they grow extremely strong, tainted by a third.

By Harlow's.

"No, no, Hellion, you're okay. You have to be." I leap onto the dirt, senses seeking every molecule of Harlow's trace, seeking the exact place her body is or the direction it goes if she made it out.

It's challenging to distinguish any one thing, because her scent is all over the place. At the very centre, there's a hole about waist height dug out. It's empty but reeks of Harlow.

Hope blossoms, finally unshackled from the binds I've placed it in since waking. If she's alive, if she transitioned, then she's somewhere in these woods, probably terrified. Ideally, she's attacked an animal because if she doesn't drink soon...the thought causes me to search for a trail faster.

I won't think about my witch possibly being one of my own until I see it. Until I find her.

Lingering with her sweet scent is another—not the witches who kidnapped her. It's a familiar trace I've been around for centuries. From another vampire who would have known she's in Banff.

But he shouldn't have known to look for her *here*. Why is he in the area?

Whatever his reason for being here, he has my mate.

And when a flash of her panic hits me like lightning, I know it's for no good reason. I should have fucking known from the moment I admitted what she is to me and he seemed off.

I take off, following their mixed scents even if I don't need to. If this is what I think it is, then there's only one place nearby he'd take her. The place he's never moved on from.

When I finish with him, I'll ensure he's forever separated from his own mate.

FIFTY-SIX

Harlow

For the second time tonight, I wake in an unfamiliar place and on the ground. It's like everyone's read the same *How To Be Bad* handbook. Alec and the dungeon floor. My ex-parents and their cave. And now this.

"Wake up, Sinclair. I have blood for you."

Blood?

Groaning, I take in the space. It's a building, the stone walls crumbling and the ceiling barely stable, only maybe a human's height above. It's small, with evidence of a fireplace once present.

In the very far corner, a spider spins a web.

Wait. How is it possible to see that? I blink hard, scrunching my eyes together, this time begging my body to wake up entirely and get out of its dream state, but when I open them again, the spider is still spinning.

I sit up, my nose prickling with the sickly scent of this place. Like death and gore had a battle and lost. It smells like mold and garbage and anything that is sour and vomit-inducing.

How is it possible to be picking up on all this?

A cup is waved in front of my face, stealing my attention. Whatever's in it is sweet—sweeter than a candy store—and my teeth ache.

A heat blazes through me that sparks me into movement, quickly reaching for the cup, only to have it yanked away.

"Ah, ah, Miss Sinclair, we have some talking to do first. Can't have you at full strength quite yet."

That voice again...

I stare past the cup to the man holding it.

He's dressed casually in a pair of jeans and a hoodie, contrasting the first and only time I've met him, when he was the only vampire to approach Alec at the party.

"Cedric?"

He flashes blinding white teeth, two fangs pointedly elongated. "You remember me."

"What are you doing here? Where's here? How did you find me? Where's Alec?" What was I even doing? Flashes flicker through my mind like a movie reel. Arthur and Violet cuffing me to the cave. My magick melting the cuffs and beating them. Strangling them. The cave coming down on all our heads.

How am I alive?

"My, you ask a lot of questions." Frowning, he crosses the room to rest the cup on the edge of the crumbling fireplace. He leans on the wall beside it and crosses his arms, regarding me like I'm an animal in a zoo. "Since we have some time before Alec finds us, I'll answer them. I'm here because of you. This is my old house. It was once a cottage. I found you because I was on my way to you anyway. Alec may still be in Banff, or he's on his way. I can never predict his moves these days."

My head thumps. There's too much he's said, too much to make sense of. "You were...on your way..." Recalling what Violet and Arthur said, I slide my feet towards me to stand, suddenly realizing he's not being a friend to Alec by helping me out of the broken cave. "You were the vampire they were waiting on."

"Very good, Miss Sinclair." He tips his head.

"Are they alive?"

"That's your next question?" He blinks, frowning. "No, they're not."

Good. While I don't know what the hell's happening, at least that part of the nightmare is over.

"You made a very grave mistake back there," he remarks casually.

I move to stand, the ground and ceiling coming much too close for comfort, and I stagger, catching myself on the closest wall. "What's happening to me?" A wave of dizziness nearly knocks me off my feet again, reminding me of that time I had a fever as a teenager and thought I genuinely died and moved to the Otherworld.

"You're transitioning. Not sure if Alec ever explained the process, but until you get blood, your body is stuck between human and vampire."

Transitioning because of Alec's blood.

I'm becoming a vampire.

In the cave, I gambled on the bit of blood I'd ingested.

Which means I'm no longer a witch. Once again, just like that, my powers are gone and Hecate has forsaken me. Or, this time, I have forsaken her.

"If I don't get blood?" Alec mentioned the transition would fail, but I need to hear it again, when it's become relevant.

"You'll die. Again. Since you already have, death will catch up with you. If anything, I'm surprised you're still standing. I wasn't sure you'd make it with the cure in your system. Turn yourself human before you fully transition." He shrugs, so uncaring. "Not that it really matters anymore. You were supposed to remain a witch, Miss Sinclair. You're meant for so much more, but how can it work now that you're on your way to being a vampire? If I allow you to drink that, anyway." He nods towards the cup beside him.

"Alec will kill you if you hurt me."

"Alec killed me a long time ago, so turnabout is fair play."

"Is that why you're working with witches?"

"The witches were useful. They have their own plans, and believing I was the mastermind behind everything was one of them."

"So you weren't the one giving orders?"

"No. But the coven your fake parents belong to and I are working towards the same goal."

"Violet and Arthur explained why I'm important, which means you can't kill me," I say, overconfident in my role. "I'm one of four heirs they need Dark for their ceremony. That hasn't changed. I'm still a Sinclair."

I'm bluffing, because who knows what I am anymore.

His lips curl up, and he makes a humming noise. "You do know your stuff. Yes, you in particular are very important to the cause, being you're the cure to vampirism. Others wish to harness that, to control you, to ensure no more vampires turn mortal. We need all the soldiers, you see. That's why I attended Alec's little show-and-tell. For show, but also to gain an idea of anyone interested in mortality so we can remind them why Darkness and immortality are our future."

Is it still possible to puke as a half-transitioned vampire? Because I feel sick. "So you believe in all that war stuff too?"

"Believe it?" He chuckles. "There is no believing what's a fact. It's very real. A few decades ago, I was approached by a group who's been hearing rumbles from the Celestials. I joined them; Alec did not. He doesn't understand we must stand with our side."

"Your side," I interject. "None of us have anything to do with the Celestials." The angels of Heaven and the demons of Hell come to Earth for their own duties of maintaining Earth's balance, but their charges are humans, not us. They exist in a different realm, and we all abide by tentative truce on the planet in which they don't bother us and we don't bother them.

"Anymore. But you forget, vampires are descended from a

demon. From one of *the* Fallen—seven angels who fell with the devil to Hell, so we are driven to obey him. Of course, the faction I'm part of wants a backup plan, which is where the witches come in. The kind of magick that will be required in this war isn't your elemental magick; it's too focused in Light—on Heaven's side. That's when we infiltrated a coven and convinced them to join us. They were driven by the temptation of black magick and everything Dark. The coven has their own plan to get the entire witch species Dark—you being a key player in that. For us, we don't give two fucks how it's done, so long as by the time war comes, we have black magick on our side."

So this isn't a partnership like Arthur and Violet explained. I was being used by them, they were being used by the vampires, and the vampires may or may not be being used by their demon father— that part I'm still confused by.

"You're his friend," I whisper, switching to a more personal topic and away from the supposed war. "His longest friend. I'm his Bride. Difference of opinion or not, how could you betray him like this? All for a war that may or may not happen."

His eyes flash red in a warning I have no strength to battle. "When the orders came that this generation, *you*, were to be their chosen Sinclair representative, the first of the four to lead the other witches into black magick, I said nothing to Alec. I knew what those witches were planning to do. That they'd turn you Dark by faking their deaths, whisking you away to their coven, and Alec would forever be searching for the final remaining Sinclair to continue his pointless journey to ease his guilt. But then he decided to keep you alive. Made some ridiculous plan to use you for profits. I kept tabs, of course, eventually planning to steal you from him. The witches said the Darkness didn't take, so new plans were being formed, but then Alec tells me he mated you. That you were his *fated* Bride." Disdain drips from every syllable.

"Our mating wasn't his fault, or choice," I murmur. "I know you lost Cor—"

He's across the room in an instant, my neck in his grip and fingers pushing against the airways my life still requires. "Do *not* speak her name. You don't know anything, so don't fucking pretend to."

"I know..." It comes out strained, trapped in his grip. "I know you loved her." Or was she his obsession? Would the love they felt in their human lives transfer to the so-called emotionless immortal lives Alec described?

"Loved?" he repeats, fingers curling around my neck. "Cora was my everything, and Alec *took* her from me. *He* fucked up the plan that night and caused the vampires to chase us. Then, years later, it was *he* who decided to stop in Sinclair territory when we were passing through. Cora was hunted by the coven because of *him*."

She made her own choice to go hunting that night, I want to say, but since I value my life, I won't point out how he's blaming his friend for events that were really no one's fault.

With another look of disgust, he uncurls his fingers from my neck, and I crumple to the ground. This time, I don't have the strength to stand. Between using my powers to save myself and then dying, I have little hope without finishing the transition.

"So that's what all this is about," I mutter as Cedric reclaims his spot across the room. "Revenge. Alec took the woman you love, so you'll take his Bride."

"Originally, no. Not until I saw you killed yourself. Like I said, I was meant to collect you and hide you away from Alec until the coven was ready to use you, but then you went and killed yourself. Suddenly the only options became to allow your transformation to progress or to ensure it doesn't, and you die. And this is just too good an opportunity to let pass by. Alec doesn't deserve to have you as his vampire Bride for the rest of immorality."

This is so fucked up. "Too bad for you, he doesn't love me, so it won't hurt him the same way."

The look Cedric gives me asks if I'm really that dense. "When you die, so will he. That's why we're waiting, you and I. When he arrives, he'll be alive just long enough to witness your death before the bond forces him to succumb."

"Which is why you haven't let me drink."

"Having you weak is best. Like this, you're no threat. You're too drained for your magick."

My weakened limbs would sadly agree with him, but I counter, "I've been holding off to get through this riveting conversation before attacking."

His gaze suddenly darts towards the right before his lips curl in a grin. "He's arrived. Time for us all to have some fun."

And then he's across the room to stand beside me, and Alec appears in the crumbling doorway.

FIFTY-SEVEN

Alec

The scents track to the abandoned cottage he once lived in with Cora. It's a disintegrating mess after centuries of lack of care, but the one place he always returns to, trying to keep her memory alive.

I'm not surprised this is where he brought Harlow.

I enter the cracked doorway slowly, catching their quiet hum of conversation. Of him announcing I've arrived, taking away any element of surprise—not that I believed I'd get one with him. Centuries of friendship allows him to know how I move, act, and think.

Harlow resting against one wall knocks against my empty chest cavity, just the sight of her filling what hasn't been alive in a very long time. But the feeling quickly dissipates when I take in *how* she looks. Her skin is pale beneath the smudges of dirt, her normally vibrant hair lies limp around her shoulders. The wall seems to be keeping her upright. Her eyes flash between her witch purple and vampire red, confirming she's in transition.

You're alive, I throw down the connection, praying it's fused together enough she can hear. It's packed with desperation she never leaves again and relief at finding her alive.

Not without difficulty.

My witch tries to stand, determined to be strong even now, but she doesn't have to prove shit. The fact she's made it this far speaks volumes. In her attempt to get her feet beneath her, her hair shifts to the side, and I catch the faint imprint of five fingers around her throat.

Murder runs through my veins, but it's centuries of self-control that keep it tamped down while I take in the other person here. My oldest friend. My brother in every sense of the word.

"Alec," he greets in a friendly tone. "Took you long enough."

"Cedric. Thank you for unburying Harlow. I saw the destruction left behind." I go for cordial, hoping—fucking *hoping*—this isn't what it seems.

"I was on my way there anyway." He clamps his hand on her shoulder, fingers digging in until she flinches, but I hold my ground until a prime opportunity. "Had business with the witches."

I tried, her voice comes through. *I tried to fight, but my body is weak. The magick I used, dying, it's too much.*

I got you, Hellion. Just hold on a bit longer.

"Hope it got completed," I say to him. "I'll be taking Harlow now."

He smiles, but it's nothing like the ones I've gotten from him over the years. It's the one he gives his prey right before devouring them, when he's always chasing the freshest blood, no matter whom he destroys to get it.

"Oh, but she's part of my business, old friend. It's simple, really. You murdered the woman I love, so I'll be taking your Bride."

Of course, it's about Cora. It's *always* been about Cora.

My eyes flash to Harlow again as I step deeper into the room, keeping my distance. I know Cedric. The way he hunts, tortures, and plays these kinds of games. I know how he fights, what his weaknesses are.

But he also knows mine. And he's presently holding on to my newest and biggest one yet.

You'll be okay, I tell her.

"You're punishing me because you blame me for Cora's death, but you think I haven't been paying for it every second of eternity? She was my *sister*, Ced. My baby sister, whom I did *everything* to protect."

"You protected her until you didn't," he says cryptically, his grip on Harlow making her flinch. Her transitioning strength is meager compared to a vampire with centuries of power within him, and if it wasn't bad enough, he makes it worse by dragging her in front of him, placing her on her knees facing me.

It hurts. Everything hurts. My throat is like a desert. My gums sting.

"Let her go, Cedric. You know what'll happen if you don't."

Her eyes flick to the fireplace across the room. *There's blood in the cup.*

You'll be okay, I promise. We'll get you out of here, and we'll get you blood. Do you have magick?

A witch transitioning into a vampire is something I've never heard of before. Witches generally avoid getting attacked, and vampires couldn't be bothered. If she is the first of her kind, then everything's on the table. Everything's unknown.

I don't know. I've tried to call on it, but I'm too weak.

"I could," he muses. "Or I could force you to witness her slow demise as she dies without the ability to complete her transition. She'll die as neither a witch nor a vampire, and we both know an unchanged vampire's death is slow and excruciating. Hours filled with agony. Or"—he slides his hands around her head, touching *my* mate—"I can snap her neck and be done with it. You'll remain alive just long enough to witness her death before succumbing to your own."

"It's a lot of effort to go after her when you had a lifetime with me."

"You're right," he replies, his tone slow and thoughtful. "You fucked it up the moment you decided to keep this one alive. Then you went and mated her and…" He chuckles. "I can't let you have your woman."

"I don't deserve her, yes." I test taking a step nearer, forcing my attention onto him rather than Harlow, though it fucking pains me. "We've had spats before, brother. We can figure this out. Let her go. Let her drink."

"Brother." His lip curls. "You lost that right when you chose her over Cora." He releases Harlow with a hard jerk, and she catches herself, her hair whipping over her shoulder when she twists to glare.

He's an asshole.

Stay down, I command her. *Play weak. Bow your head.*

She follows my instructions, but not before sending a quick defiant look my way.

"I'll do anything, Cedric. You want me on my knees? I'll get on my fucking knees. You want my crown? It's yours. Castle, lands, title, everything. She's all I want."

"And Cora's all I wanted."

"I know." I step forward again, this time shifting my feet slightly, preparing to attack. Cedric thinks he's winning, so he won't let Harlow go. I see that. "If you were anyone else, you'd be dead already. The deep history between us is too important, but this is your only chance, Ced. Let her go, or I won't have a choice."

"No."

Stay low and move away.

She doesn't ask why, doesn't look at me, but ducks and rolls out of the way mere seconds before I'm on top of Cedric, taking us both to the ground.

Leave! I command, begging for her to run, escape, and find blood before she collapses.

Her steps scrape against the cement floor, and it's all I pay attention to before giving the rest to Cedric. He hears her escaping too and roars, kicking my stomach and managing to toss me off him, my back thudding against the far wall. It cracks beneath my weight.

Cedric and I are minutes apart in immortal age, so he's nearly as strong as I am. But he also knows my tells. A lifetime of friendship rolls into his next punch and my next bite. Of knowing one another's incoming move even before it happens.

He lunges, but I reach for his ankle, yanking him to the ground. He yells out, rolling and forcing me to my back. I reach for his head, intending to yank it off his shoulders.

He blocks every oncoming hit with his own.

On and on it goes. Two vampires battling through the old building, every knock into the wall making it deteriorate more, a testament to the life Cedric once had with my sister.

When he grabs onto me again, the ground shakes.

FIFTY-EIGHT

Harlow

The moment Alec commands me to move, I know what he's about to do, so his attack on Cedric isn't a surprise.

Once making it across the room, I scramble to my feet. Now Alec is on top of Cedric, fist after fist coming down on his face while being equally blocked with Cedric's own hits.

Leave!

Realistically, I know I'm no good to him, especially like this.

The cup catches my eye, and I run towards the broken fireplace.

Six months ago, I would have died before doing what I'm about to, but then again, six months ago I wasn't the same person I am now.

It's with very little thought that I place my lips to the cup at the same time a crash comes from behind me. The two vampires continue to throw one another around the small structure, evenly matched. I only hope that drinking the blood finalizes the change instantly and I can be of some help to Alec.

Darkness cuffs my neck, making me shiver at its abrupt arrival. *Drink*, it demands, and I don't hesitate to tip the cup back, swallowing every last drop of the earthy flavour that's nothing like the sweetness of Alec's blood. *Welcome back,* it whispers.

The blood pours into every corner of my body. Every nerve

vibrates awake. Every sense becomes sharper, more aware. I can hear every curse, hiss, and grunt from the fighting vampires.

My hand lets the cup go, feeling oddly weak while the rest of me has never felt stronger.

My gums throb again, but this time, my incisors lengthen into full fangs. I reach up to touch the pointed ends, knowing later I'll have time to dissect my new body.

For now, I turn back to my mate.

Just the sight of him has an impression snapping inside me. Something that makes me *feel* him—his rage while he battles. The grey connection I spotted after drinking from him strengthens into a brilliant bold colour, a myriad of black and purple.

I once said that, while I was his Bride, witches don't have mates.

Now, I'm a vampire. One of them.

His.

Darkness slithers around my body, a reminder it's still here. My hands flex, heat surging into my palms. My magick never left; I was simply too drained to call upon it, but becoming a vampire has made me strong enough to control it.

The sight of Alec being slammed into a wall has red coating my vision. Fire ignites in one of my palms, a perfect little fireball to destroy the one threatening what's mine.

Beneath my feet, the ground rumbles the same way my Darkness caused the cave-in. The same black tendrils wrap my arms, mingling with my flames and melding together, forming a black flame. Just as hot. Just as deadly.

You're ours for good now, it whispers, but for once, I'm not frightened. I embrace it both as a witch who controls black magick and as a vampire who is a Dark creature.

Both vampires look up from their fight with different expressions. Cedric's mouth slips open, his barely audible, *"Shit!"* heard as though I'm standing beside him. Alec smiles, his gaze hotter than the black flame. He backs up, leaving Cedric a rumpled, bloody mess on the ground, who's trying to regain his footing.

His lip curls. "You're both idiots. You have no idea the mistake you've made, Sinclair. You're the combination of a vampire and a witch—the exact weapon they'll desire. Witches will follow you into Darkness, an army for the vampires. You'll never have a side because you're straddling the line of both. There's nowhere you can hide where they won't search."

"Good thing it's no longer your problem."

I lift my hand, the black flame dancing around my fingers as I move them back and forth, almost thoughtfully. But his death isn't mine, no matter what he's done to me.

"What would you like done? He's your best friend."

My question seems to spark a bit of hope in Cedric, who uses the wall to get partially upright. "Alec...don't do this. You know how much Cora's death broke me. I don't blame you, not really."

The plea rolls off Alec, who gives him a look of disgust mingled with a bit of sorrow, but also encompassed in a lot of indifference. "He *was* my best friend, but he stopped being that the second he thought to take your life."

"No!"

Striding over to Cedric, whose final escape attempt is hindered by Alec, I tip my hand to allow the fire to roll off my palm and onto his body, his scream for help shifting into a howl of death.

His body bursts into flames, a mirage of black and orange, and Alec yanks me away. My tendrils unwrap the flame and link themselves around Cedric, holding him still as the fire bursts rather than burns, the combustion throwing Alec and me backwards. Within a moment, Cedric's body is a pile of ash, and the crumbling home falls victim to silence.

Alec slowly turns towards me, his gaze wandering my face and then my body as he reaches for me. He grazes the spot on my neck Cedric gripped, a flash of fury coming through the bond, but he doesn't linger for long, moving to stroke my cheek, following the line towards my mouth, thumb parting my lips. He pokes the tip of one of my new fangs, amazement brightening his eyes.

"Fuck, Hellion," he breathes. "Look at you. Your eyes—one's still purple and one's black."

A sign of both sides of me.

"You're a vampire. Forever. You know what this means?"

"That your obsession gets to continue until the end of time. Which, according to Cedric, will be any year now."

His expression doesn't falter with my sarcasm. "I was always told that, as a vampire, we lost our ability to love and the closest thing we can feel to that level of longing is obsession. Miss Sinclair, while I've been obsessed with you since the moment we met, obsessions, even for immortals, can be fleeting once satisfied. With you... I'll never be satisfied. There is nothing that'll ever fulfill this need inside me. Obsessions end, but you'll never be my ending. You're my middle, my forever, until eternity reaches a conclusion—*if* there is an end. What I feel for you now is different than when we first met, and if it is possible for an immortal to love, then this might be it, because obsession...obsession is too weak a word. You were the unexpected in my life. My lungs inhale air only so I can take your scent inside me. I blink so each time my eyes open, I'll see you all over. And if my heart could beat, it would beat to the rhythm yours used to. Now, it beats to you. *Only* you. All of you. I don't know what to say, what words to use, what title to give it. Love, obsession, something grander. Not that it matters, because it doesn't change the simple fact that you're a part of me now—the best parts of me— and I'll never let you go."

The feeling of completion upon finishing the change wasn't true completion, because this right here, right now, my heart knitting its final few stitches together is true completion. A conclusion.

"You claimed to not know what words to use, but that was a lot of them. I'm no longer Harlow Sinclair, the witch with the cure.

Are you okay with that?" Is the cure even still a part of me, or did my dying end the curse for good? As an immortal, I'll never have a child, so I'll forever be the last of my line.

"You'll always be my Sinclair."

"I'm still a witch. Still have powers."

"You're a fucking *miracle*. You're perfect." He angles my face up, his fingers sliding into my hair and keeping me trapped. "My feelings aren't dependent on your magick and—" He stops abruptly, loosening his grip on my scalp to bring forward a chunk of hair, allowing me to see what he has.

My normally orange-red hair is mingled with black streaks, like a dye job. The Darkness within me chuckles before slithering back to sleep. It's black like Violet's and Arthur's hair was before their deaths, which was obviously an effect from black magick, based on their early wedding photo where Violet's hair was brown.

"What does this mean?"

"It means I've fully embraced black magick." But not entirely, because I still retain my red. Violet and Arthur still used elemental magick right up until the end and they had no physical signs of it. So many questions that I might never have answers to, though perhaps Morgan knows something.

Morgan. Coven. Shit. If they could barely look at me after seeing what Violet and Arthur did to me, how will they take this? Alec may be my forever, but I don't want to lose the family I've just gained.

"You're a creature of Darkness in every sense of the word. How do you feel about that?"

Comforted, in a way. Fulfilled in another. For so long, my fire was enough, but now my worries over going completely Dark and losing myself seem so silly. Darkness is power, not evil.

"I feel perfect."

"You *are* perfect," he growls, hauling me closer. His body feels impenetrable. His scent is stronger. Everything about him is *more*. "You're all mine, Sinclair."

I feel it, I tell him in his head. *The moment the change happened, I felt your emotions. Felt you. Guess you're my mate too.*

His eyes narrow. *As though I'd allow another outcome.*

"Earlier you mentioned being told vampires don't feel love. If that were true, then what I felt for you this morning would have disappeared, maybe been replaced by something else. But it hasn't. If anything, it's more intense. A festering *need* inside me I can't ignore. I love you, Alec. I don't have a big speech, though. Call it the shitty education of the twenty-first century, but we don't profess our love with sonnets or anything like that. Just three simple words."

Three simple words are all I want from you, Hellion.

I love you.

He growls again before my back is shoved against the wall, the aged stone cracking beneath the force. What would have broken my back hours ago feels like nothing more than me leaning. Such a strange thing, to gain so much strength within minutes.

He yanks me up until I'm suspended in his arms, his hands splayed across my ass. His mouth clashes with mine, his kiss hard and possessive, teeth nicking my bottom lip. His tongue lays his claim as surely as his speech moments ago.

I no longer have to be gentle with you. Even his inner voice holds a sense of wonder to it.

You've been gentle? Each time with him hasn't been hearts and flowers—not that I wanted it to be—but I can't imagine harder.

Introducing to you every aspect of immortality will be my undoing, Hellion. He pulls back from the kiss to rest his forehead on mine. "I'm still trying to convince myself you're real. That all of *this* is real." His finger strokes the side of my face before pausing, his hand flattening on both cheeks as he lifts away, a slight shake making his hair bounce. "Harlow, I felt you die. *I* died too, only returning to life when you did."

"I'm sorry," I whisper. "I had to kill them. I remembered your blood was still in my body, though I wasn't sure if it'd work considering I know next to nothing about the process. I took a gamble that paid off."

"You knew you'd transition." His hold tightens on my face. "You chose it anyway."

"I chose *you*."

His eyes ignite into black molten, but before he reacts on it, he asks, "Who took you? By the time I arrived, the witches who kidnapped you were already dead and gone."

"My parents."

His hand slips from my hair, the vein at his wrist gaining my attention. My gums throb again, this time with the memory of the taste of his blood. Craving strikes me, one driven by newly discovered bloodlust, not mortal curiosity.

"What—"

"Shh." I turn his hand so the meaty part is facing me. "Later."

And then I sink my fangs into his hand, this time *truly* tasting him. Beneath the metal flavour, there's power. A dominance that comes through his blood, demanding I drink, to never stop drinking.

He groans, shifting his hips, making another kind of craving quickly escalate. He mentioned no longer having to be gentle with me, so now I want proof of it.

"This feels fucking fantastic," he groans. "I never imagined..."

He's an old vampire; surely at some point over the centuries he would have drank from another?

I lift my fangs from his skin. "You've never...?"

"From them, yes," he replies, and instantly I despise the unknown vampire who once had Alec's mouth on them, "but I never allowed them to drink from me. Allowing another to feed from you is a vulnerability, and I never trusted anyone enough for that."

His attention falls to his bleeding hand, his unspoken words louder than anything he could say. He lowers his hand to his side, but disappointment doesn't hover for long before he's pulling me close and baring his neck.

Feed from here.

My fangs break the skin where his pulse, if he still had one, would beat.

As his blood flows into me, connecting us in other ways than anything prior, he brings my wrist to his mouth, his bite nothing more than a tickle. Any of that mortal discomfort at having my skin broken into is gone. Now, there's nothing righter.

No one will ever touch you, Harlow. I dare anyone—witch, vampire, or otherwise—to attempt to take you from me again.

If someone tries, I'll burn them alive. I don't like the idea of you being harmed either.

He removes his teeth from my wrist, and I pull away when his hands slide between us. My legs tighten around his waist, and he unzips his pants before tearing mine.

Carina's gonna kill you if you keep ruining her clothes.

I'll buy her a whole fucking mall if it keeps her quiet, as long as I can keep doing this.

He braces at my centre before sliding cleanly in and—*holy fuck.*

He chuckles, and I realize my exclamation wasn't only in my head. *Different than before,* he comments.

"Mhm." *So much more.*

An intense amount more. I feel every little ridge of his cock sliding against my walls. Sex as an immortal feels like what I do after multiple orgasms as a mortal, when I'm hypersensitive and tight, any little movement able to shove me over the edge. As a vampire, I'm already on the edge, despite the increased stamina.

Show me how a vampire fucks, Alec.

My pleasure, Hellion.

FIFTY-NINE

Alec

Still inside her, I run her outside, not wanting her anywhere near what nearly happened tonight. That house was once a place where my sister and Cedric lived, and out of respect for Cora, I'd rather not fuck my mate inside it.

I take her a little ways away, to the edge of the thicket of trees, and stretch her on the ground beneath the moon. Her skin, now paler than this morning, contrasts against the deep green of the grass. She's never looked sexier, her natural beauty coupled with the vampiric quality of perfection, even smudged from her brief meeting with death earlier.

I come down on top of her, linking my arms beneath her thighs to change the angle and stare into her face, unwilling to ever look away.

I felt you die.

She stares back, seeing what I haven't said aloud. The complete and utter fear I thought we'd never have this again.

I thrust into her harder. *I never want to feel that again.*

You won't.

It doesn't make you unkillable. Promise me, Hellion. Promise me you won't do anything stupid again, because next time, there is no coming back. This is your second and final chance at life. Die again, and I'll be selling my soul to the devil to get you back.

She rolls her eyes. *Doubt it works like that.*

It will by the time I'm through with him. I pause, pulling out until only my tip remains in her tight heat. She releases a frustrated growl that's adorable, but nothing like the noise I'll make if I lose her again. "Vow it," I demand. "Promise me you'll never put your-self in danger again. I won't survive losing you."

"I promise, Alec, as long as you do the same."

I promise, unless it means saving you.

She rolls her eyes, but I fuck the attitude from her with my next thrust, pushing her to the brink before her new body's sensitivities take her over. Her hair, the shades of fire and shadows, mixes with the blades of grass when she throws her head back, her noises making birds flutter away.

She comes down quicker than she did as a mortal, her new stamina allowing her to keep going without a break. In a flash, she pushes a knee into my side and flips us both, landing on top with me still buried inside her. Her hair flings to the other side, leaves and debris dirtying it again, but it's her expression that renders me thoughtless.

She reminds me of last night, when she took control, and I realize it won't be a one-time thing—nor do I want it to be. She rotates her hips over me, but her gasp suggests she's surprised herself.

"Fucking Christ, how am I this sensitive?"

I grab her hips, my fingers getting a grip tighter than I ever allowed myself to before tonight. "Part of the perks."

She controls the pace and direction, her eyes fluttering shut. I miss them already. One violet and one black, like her hair. She's a conundrum; something in all my centuries I've never heard of happening. She can't be the first witch to be changed, and once we're home, I'll do everything in my power to track evidence of this happening before. Like her hair, she's two perfect sides of power and immortality.

Her mouth slips open, revealing those little fangs I want to have buried in my body again. Fuck, if I believed her perfect before today, then perfection now has an entirely new definition. She's a natural; vampirism was always intended for her.

Perhaps that's what fate, or whatever brought us together, was thinking. She was always meant to be a vampire alongside me while retaining her witch side.

So caught up in studying my perfect Bride, I at first miss the shadows emerging from her, forming a tangled mess of tendrils, of torn ropes, in the backdrop. One tendril breaks away and wisps over her shoulder, as though petting her. It's fascinatingly beautiful, but chilling too, seeing it touch what's mine. How she's owning it.

Her eyes flash as three tendrils dart towards me, two cuffing my wrists and tying my hands to the ground and away from her body, the other collaring my neck. It bends, lifting me upright, and she readjusts on my lap, grinning when the magick hauls my chest towards hers.

"Sneaky, powerful witch."

"Your witch." The tendrils coil tighter, angling my face towards hers, her possessive claim as strong as those reassuring words were.

Her body trembles before she sinks lower, jamming her knees into the grass to get as close as possible. Darkness tickles her spine while making me powerless, left all to her mercy—a place I once would have despised.

The stems of Darkness clench and tighten and hiss around my body in line with her orgasm, her pussy making the same sensation around my cock. As she comes down with a hissed sigh, the tendrils slither away and back into her, freeing my hands to grip her hips again.

She grins, her hips slowing. "Well. Those certainly added to it. I didn't mean for them to come out; they just did. But once they had, everything else was me."

Amazed, I rub a hand over her side, tangling with her hair. "You're incredible."

She shifts on my lap, her tongue dabbing her bottom lip. "How do I still want more?"

"You're immortal, and with that comes the feeling of never being satisfied."

"How have you survived this long?"

"Easier after a while. The cravings become normal." With her, though, I hope they never go away. That *this* will be our normal, because I'll happily spend eternity buried in her.

She lifts off me and inches down my body, lowering onto her hands and knees as my cock rises in front of her face. She licks her lips and wraps her hand around my length, lazily stroking up and down, and it takes centuries of strength to allow her this control.

"I've been wondering about something." She adds no further explanation before parting her lips and taking me down her throat, no longer worried about mortal limitations such as a gag reflex.

She slides back to the tip before turning her head slightly and dragging her fangs down my shaft in a move that would render a human male extreme pain. Once she has me filling her mouth again, she sinks her teeth into my cock, drinking the body's worth of blood that filled my cock the instant she flashed her pretty little fangs.

You'll destroy me, Hellion.

Does this hurt?

Hurt? This is the furthest thing from pain. This is...paradise. This is...I don't fucking know, because my words aren't exactly working, but remembering she asked me a question that if I don't reply to will make her end this, I say, *Fuck no. This is everything.*

She sucks harder.

Pleasure sweeps me away and, much too soon, she's destroying all my self-control as I thrust a final time into her mouth, my cum joining the blood in her throat.

She keeps sucking until she's swallowed all the blood that made my erection and cleans me of every last drop of cum before lifting her head, her grin adorable and carnal.

I reach for her, yanking her up and over me until I'm kissing the taste of me from her. It's primal, possessive, and I fucking *love it*.

Love her...if such a thing is possible.

With a contented giggle, she slides off me and into my arms, her head on my shoulder. "What a fucking day," she murmurs. "I feel like I lived three lives today."

"I do as well. Including a death. Ready for a life entirely in the nighttime?" I stare at the star-splattered sky, the moon nearly full, and mourn the sun for her. She'll never feel its heat again. Never see daylight again outside of my castle with its sunproof windows. She'll be trading the sun for the moon.

She pulls from my arms to sit up, staring at the twinkling stars. "Strangely...yeah. Since I was homeschooled, I missed out on having a regular life like others my age. In a way, I was always in the dark, so this won't be any different. Except you'll be by my side."

Always, I slip into her head, earning a smile. I reach for her, fingering the ends of her hair and marvelling at the fact she's *here*, even when hours ago, the bond dissipated with her death.

But she's here. Alive. Fuck, more than alive.

"What happened tonight?" I won't go much longer without the details of *how* all this came to be. How did I not pick up on the familiar scents in the shop or at their gravesite? They would have been the same as what I smelled in their bedroom, but I suppose the months passing since their deaths faded their trace enough.

She sighs, shutting her eyes as she talks. "There was a note in the kitchen, which I assumed was from Morgan, asking me to go to her shop. When I got there, the place was unlocked but empty. I wandered into the back room and got ambushed by my parents instead. Woke up in a cave, cuffed." Her attention drops to her scarred wrists—marks she'll carry forever. "Same cave they used when I was a kid."

"How were they alive?"

She recounts everything about Arthur and Violet's plan, the murder of her birth parents, her kidnapping, what changed to them raising her. Everything they told her about her powers, their deception, and the night of their "deaths." Freya mentioned some of this, but she neglected to mention that the fire didn't kill the right people and they were alive.

"I killed innocents," she finishes, her expression somber. "I don't even know who, so I can't apologize to the family, give them something...or something."

Killing humans isn't anything special to vampires. They're on a different level than us; they're prey. Food. For some, entertainment, though I was never so bored. One day, Harlow may see her stress as pointless, but for now, she retains her human moralities.

"It doesn't matter." I sweep her hair away from her face. "I don't mean to sound callous, but it's long over. And you weren't at fault. Arthur and Violet tricked you."

"Still...no wonder Darkness latched onto me so easily."

"It doesn't mean you're evil, Harlow. It means you might lead a grimier path than others, but so have I. So will you again, but now, our paths are aligned. Your magic—both kinds—have embraced you. It'll be okay. You're powerful as all hell."

She glances at the spattering of stars. Ones that'll soon disappear with the coming sun. Morning's a few hours away, and we should seek cover soon, but I also don't have it in me to move quite yet. "Do you think Hecate has officially forsaken me now that I'm a vampire?"

Their deity means nothing to me, but I know it means everything to her. "Your diety doesn't seem like someone who'd be judgemental. You still have your element, so I assume you still have her. Hell, who knows if she's ever turned away from anyone who's gone Dark. Perhaps they turned from her, but she's still waiting for them to find their way back."

She purses her lips. "You might be right. Good insight for a non-believer." Her gaze goes between the trees, towards the crumbled house in the distance, now a resting place for one of the souls who lived there in another life. "I'm sorry for your friend."

"Seems he stopped being my friend a while ago."

Cedric's betrayal twisted the blade in parts of me I didn't know existed. A friend who was once like my brother, who loved my sister, wouldn't have chosen himself over my Bride. Just like if roles were reversed, I'd damn well do anything to protect his mate.

Immortality is long. And so many things—people included—are fleeting. Cedric, like Cora, is now someone from my past.

Harlow's fingers slide down my arm before linking between mine. "Still. He's the only one you had from your time. Even when he was against you, you still thought of him as a friend."

Except her. Harlow isn't fleeting.

"It doesn't matter," I say, my throat filling with an emotion I don't understand. "It's over."

She huffs, shaking her head. "Take the sympathy, ancient bloodsucker."

"Ancient bloodsucker," I repeat, amused with her moniker. "You're a bloodsucker too, in case you've forgotten."

"I won't call you ancient if you *finally* admit how old you are. You're so weird about your age, but if we have forever together, it's only fair I know."

"Make you a deal; we have to find shelter within the next few hours. We can find somewhere close by or begin the trek back to Banff. It's a couple hours away. Your choice, because I don't know how you feel about returning."

She blinks. "Didn't catch a deal in that."

I knock against her shoulder. "Answer the question."

Amusement slides away, replaced by a deep pondering that darkens her purple eye. She nods after a moment. "Yeah, I should let Morgan know I'm alright, and thank her for all she's done."

"Okay. Let's use the journey to test your new abilities. If you beat me back to Banff, I'll tell you my true age. If I beat you, I won't."

Her eyes narrow, calculating her chances of beating me. "Only if you teach me how to run."

"The same way you did as a human. One foot in front of the other."

She scowls. "Smartass. Seriously, though."

"I am serious. It's exactly like you'd run as a mortal, except there's no need to pace your breathing. Your instincts will take over and do the rest."

"Fine." She stands, reaching down to offer a hand.

Once I'm zipped up, I gesture in the direction we'll need to go. "I'll give you a five-minute head start so you can get comfortable in your new body." She doesn't move, needing another urge. "Tick, tock, Hellion, your head start is dwindling. If you want to win..."

With a determined, set expression, she takes off, her speed making her a blur to the untrained eye. But mine? I see every luscious curve of her body, every dip in the path she takes.

I give her ten minutes. As a new vampire, there's no chance she'll beat me. My strength is greater than hers, but her attempt to win will be an enjoyment regardless.

The monster inside paces at the sight of our Bride getting farther away, especially after she was already placed in danger today. But I force myself still, counting down the seconds before following.

Just like the time I chased her after her escape attempt, few urges carry me towards her:

Chase.

Hunt.
Fuck.
And fuck again...
And again.

SIXTY

Harlow

Alec's speed proves I have no shot of beating him all the way to Banff, which means I *still* don't get his age.

Yet. I *will* figure it out.

When we approach the mountains, I pull him to a stop. "Could we find a cave or something instead of using Morgan's basement? It'll be right before sunrise when we arrive, and I won't have time to fully explain everything like they'll want. I'd rather avoid them until necessary."

No doubt Morgan's worried based on Alec's story about what happened after the sun set and he realized I wasn't with her. But she deserves the time to ask what she needs to and not be rushed through that shocking conversation within minutes.

He leads me in another direction, seemingly knowing where he's going, and we reach a large cave in the side of a mountain.

"It goes far back enough that sunlight never reaches inside."

I head to the very back as he recommends, taking a seat on the ground that no longer feels hard. Alec settles beside me, leaning against the cave wall.

"You should rest. Your body went through a lot with the transformation. The first couple days as a vampire are the most difficult."

He pulls me close, his body a perfect fit against mine. "I think I will too. Dying really takes it out of a person."

Maybe, but sleep feels like the furthest thing in my abilities.

"I don't know if I'm able to." I straighten off of him, inching to the side. "But you feel free to. No need to hold me."

Abruptly, he yanks me on top of him, my legs around his thighs like I slept last night in Morgan's basement.

From now on, you'll sleep in my arms.

Possessive. But I'm okay with it.

I have something to be possessive over.

I love you too.

He stares at me, murmuring in a wondrous tone, "How have I gone so long without you?"

"How long exactly would that be?'

He lightly slaps my ass. *Nice try.*

I had to give it an honest effort. What happens tomorrow?

What do you want to happen?

When I first rejoined the coven, it felt right to be home. But now...

You're still a witch. You still belong there.

I'm in between. Vampires won't want me around because I'm the enemy. Witches will be scared of me.

He tightens his arm around my waist, but it doesn't do anything to my despondent mood. "*I* want you, so fuck everyone else."

"They're my coven, Alec; it's not that easy. Even if I was raised away, my magick recognizes them. Sinclairs *made* Highridge, so it's like my legacy. Since I'll never have kids, I'll forever be the remaining Sinclair. Feels wrong to leave."

He stiffens. "Did you want kids?"

I shake my head into his side, answering in his head rather than pushing the words from my tight throat. *Not really, but I can't say where the future would have ended up. Did you want kids in your human life?*

They were expected of me. Wants did not matter. I was heir to my father's throne and would have been arranged to wed a woman, a princess from another kingdom most likely. She would have become my queen and bore my children. At least one son, one spare, and then however many more she wanted.

When Alec speaks of his past, it always strikes me how strange the differences between history and now are. His explanation seems so cold and impersonal, but normal for his time.

It's the life he would have had if my ancestor made different choices. If the vampires who hunted him didn't turn them. If his father didn't give Cora to the coven.

"Do you wish that was the life you had instead of being a vampire?"

Silence stretches between us like an uncomfortable band that's too tight around my sternum. When he finally answers, it seems to be with the weight of all his choices. "The transition freed me. Then, yes, I'd believed I'd miss my old life, but I soon realized being beneath my father's reign was a set of unbreakable shackles. As vampires, Cora and I were free, and while it may have taken a bit to get used to the idea of drinking blood and living forever, I much preferred it. If you're asking if I wished I'd stayed human to take a wife and have a brood of children..." Abruptly, the angle changes as I'm flipped onto my back, Alec coming over me. "Then no. Not the kids, not the wife. They were all part of the role expected of me. When I met you, I officially woke up. Like my immortal life had meaning."

"That's because my blood gave you purpose. Dormer, asshole vampire, and businessman."

He flicks my nose, grinning. "Your sarcasm is half your charm, Miss Sinclair. No, I don't miss the life I might have had. I wouldn't give up my future with you for any version of my past."

He kisses me until I forget what we were talking about. If I were still mortal, I'd be breathless. He kisses me like his mouth holds the answers, and for a moment, I slip into the safety of the unknown. That everything will be fine.

Alec remains behind me as I let myself into Morgan's home, pausing as two bodies lurch upright from their seats, having been woken from a nap. Morgan lunges from the chair in the far corner while Carina lifts her head from the couch's arm and tosses her cell to the side.

"Fuck, Harlow, I've been so worried." Morgan flies across the room towards me, stopping short when my physical changes register, and she falters, arms lowering back to her side.

This is what I was afraid of.

"Goddess...you—you're a—"

"A vampire," I finish, mentally preparing myself to be tossed out of the coven. "And a witch." I make a fireball, then quickly extinguish it by curling my hand around it, the sizzle of flames settling back into my skin.

"Holy shit," Carina murmurs, coming beside her mother, who's shifting between being composed and shocked.

"How is this possible? Your hair..."

"I've embraced black magick too."

"How? This goes against everything the Goddess holds dear."

I flinch as though she slapped me, hearing another statement entirely: *You go against everything the Goddess holds dear.*

Alec's mental touch slithers around my dead heart. *Ignore her.*

The door opens abruptly, another person striding in. A witch, given the way purple eyes scan the four of us. A cloak swirls around her legs, contrasting the skinny jeans, Keds, and hoodie with the slogan *Suck It*, she's wearing.

The stranger stops on me and flicks waist-length red hair over her shoulder. "Harlow Sinclair. *Finally*, I'm meeting the woman of the hour. You inspired the colour today." She lifts a chunk of her hair.

Of course, she's here, Alec mutters, gaining a sharp look from me. He knows the witch when I don't? I understand being raised away from covens limits my connection to all things of my culture, but *him?*

Morgan all but pushes by Alec and me, dipping her head. "Blessed Be, Priestess. Freya. We didn't realize you'd be visiting."

The name sounds familiar, like I've heard it recently, but there's been so much new information jammed into my brain lately, it's difficult to sort through.

"Blessed Be," the witch, Freya, replies primly. "It wasn't in the plans, but we need to chat." All her peace slips away when she twists towards Alec lingering by my shoulder. "Glad you got your head out of your ass, vamp. Like my sweater? Wore it for you."

"As unhelpful as always, witch. If you're offering...I have a few friends who'd love a bite of your power."

She jabs her tongue out before flouncing by us all and into Morgan's living room, making herself at home on the chair Morgan recently vacated. "You're about to eat those words, moron."

"You know her?" I ask.

"She's been around, unfortunately. Noting that, she's the reason the barrier around your house fell and I was able to get to you."

I stare at the witch, my rage bristling until my palms warm. "You *helped* him kidnap me?" Not that it didn't work out in the end, but fuck if it wasn't a journey of hatred and suicidal escape attempts that got us there.

Morgan, like an energetic bee, practically buzzes right by me. "Forgive her, please. She wasn't raised in the coven and doesn't understand the position you hold."

Amusement lines Freya's mouth, and she kicks one leg over the other. "It's cool. I'm well versed in the tragic story of *Harlow*

Sinclair and Her Vampire King—ooh! Goddess, I am *so* trade-marking that. Eventually we'll see you two on the big screen." She waves her hand in the air, spreading them like showing something off. "*The Witch Who Beat the Vampire King*—nah, too basic. *Spells Like Mate*—ha, that's cute. *The Fire Witch and the Asshole Blood-sucker*—that has a nice ring."

Morgan settles into the couch beside Carina. "Remember I mentioned the First Witch? Freya is her."

"She's crazy as fuck," Alec rumbles. "Not quite there. Missing a few incantations, if you know what I mean. You should really see someone about that, witch."

"Suck it, vamp." She kicks her legs out and randomly conjures a movie bucket of popcorn. After popping two kernels into her mouth, she tosses a handful towards Alec, but they fall short. "Keep it up, Your Highness. I'll ensure someone ugly plays you in the movie."

"It's Your Majesty, and you know it."

"I helped you. Be nice. You wouldn't be here without me." She pointedly looks towards me.

"Maybe. None of it changes that 'quirky' isn't apt enough to describe you."

"'Kay, you carry centuries of knowledge on your shoulders and see what it does to your brain." She sticks out her tongue again before gesturing towards me. "Enough chatting. We have business to discuss. Sit. Standing there is so vampire-like of you."

I obey only because I don't know what to make of the witch—the *first* of our kind. An air of superiority floats around her that demands obedience, and regardless of my new abilities, pissing off the original witch isn't something I'd like to do.

I cross the room and sit on the opposite end of the couch beside Carina, who's holding her phone up but taps the red recording button to end it and lowers her phone at her mother's scowl.

"Jasper will never believe it if I don't have proof."

Freya clasps her hands together, making the popcorn bucket disappear along with the ones she threw at Alec. "I'm sure we can all agree, Harlow being both a vampire and a witch is the most interesting thing to happen today, and that you're all wondering the answer to the magick question: how, considering the laws of nature shouldn't allow it. *Well*...I don't have answers. Like, at all."

Weight I didn't realize I was holding crashes to the ground. If anyone on the planet had an answer, she seemed the most likely. Alec notices, or feels, the change in my disposition and hisses at Freya, who only waves him off with an eye roll.

"Down boy. I get you've already pissed on her, but stay calm."

"If you don't know, why come?" he demands, and Morgan makes a face like she's swallowed a lemon.

"Let me talk, and I'll get to it. No idea how I put up with your ass all these weeks. *Anyway*..." She flicks hair over her shoulder, shifting to the edge of the seat. "I have to confer with Hecate and get answers. Until then, I guarantee you'll still be vital to the future. More important than when you had the cure, which, if you haven't figured out, is no longer a thing. You are the only hybrid in the world and will be targeted by both sides *for now*"—a sharp gaze darts to Alec, daring him to comment—"but it won't be like that forever. Witches will be wary of you, vampires won't know how to take you. Your elemental powers remain the Goddess's gift to you, and you will not be overtaken by black magick now that you are a creature of Darkness. Essentially, you're the ideal balance."

"What about this supposed oncoming war?"

Wariness flicks over her expression so quickly I don't know what to make of it. "I can't say much at this time. You were allowed to become a hybrid for reasons, though. It's fate. Everything that's happened was. When the Twilight Grove Coven turned to black magick, this went into motion."

Morgan curses softly, looking away. "That's who...fuck, Jasper will be..." She trails off, mumbling, and Freya speaks overtop her.

"Motion being your family's deaths, your kidnapping, the ongoing memory wipes, meeting Alec. I helped him because fate designed him to take you at *that* moment. Not the next day, not the previous. Everything had to happen for the path pre-laid to be walked at the correct speeds. I am sorry for my role, including *not* helping you. You can hate me, scream at me, attack me, whatever, but know Hecate never abandoned you, even if it felt that way at times. You are an important woman, Harlow Sinclair."

"So you're using her," Alec interjects coldly, wandering closer. "I'll protect her from whatever plans you have."

"We want nothing less from you," she replies. "You two being mates will be important for the future. I won't say why, how, or when, but it'll come to pass."

This is all vague at best and unsettles me. "Arthur and Violet mentioned four witches. The descendants from the four original bloodlines that their coven—Twilight Grove, I assume—will be joining together in some ceremony."

Freya glances towards Carina and Morgan, her lips pinching. "They were telling the truth, but the path I'm seeing laid and the path that coven believes they're following are different. They'll be the same for a while, but will eventually deviate. More couples will come together, but that's all I can say at this time."

"More vampires and witches?" Carina asks, sitting forward.

"Not quite." Freya tips her head. "I'm not allowed to say anything more. Until then, though..." She shifts to me. "You and Alec can't stay."

"Why not?" That's Morgan, and something inside me lights a bit brighter. "The coven respects her connection to Alec. Once they digest the fact she's a hybrid, this is her home."

Carina slips her hand into mine, and like that, I'm welcomed to the coven all over. "My childhood friend was already stolen from me. Don't make her leave again."

Freya purses her lips, glancing at her hands. "I'm sorry. But from here on out, having one-point-five vampires hanging around Banff will disrupt the future. You need to return to your castle."

"Can I visit?" Carina asks, directing her question to Freya.

She glances towards the ceiling, making me wonder what she's looking for, before replying, "In a few months, sure. Not for a while, though. And now, I must go." She stands with a slap of her thighs, tucking her cloak in tighter. "It's been lovely chatting. Nice to meet you, Sinclair. Blessed Be, everyone!" By the doorway, she flicks her finger towards Alec. "Except you, bloodsucker. No blessing for you."

She steps from the room and disappears into thin air.

SIXTY-ONE

Alec

The room is eerily silent after Freya leaves, and it's only after a heavy moment the silence is broken by the High Priestess's daughter.

"Mom, she can't be serious! We just got Harlow back."

Morgan stands, wandering across the room to Freya's seat. She doesn't want to make us leave, but her expression says she will. Honestly, I'm okay with it. I'd much rather have Harlow to myself in our castle, but I was also fine with camping in Banff so Harlow could reconnect with her coven.

"Freya knows best," she murmurs, defeated. "She's following Hecate's orders, which means we must as well. Harlow, you are welcome back anytime. *Anytime.*" Her repeated word, spoken with emphasis, is directed towards me.

Harlow stands, pulling Carina up with her. The two share a look I can't distinguish before she heads my way. "It's probably best, anyway. Settling into the coven after all this time was one thing, but as a newly changed vampire...I wouldn't want anyone to fear me, especially if something triggers my control. Then there's my black magick. I don't want to accidentally corrupt anyone."

Morgan nods, understanding, but her lips are tight. "I suppose this is it then."

Carina pouts and throws her arms around my mate. She whispers something in Harlow's ear, causing a mutual grin between the two women and a head shake from Harlow.

Next, Morgan sweeps her up in her arms. "At least this time I get to say a proper goodbye and know that you may be gone, but you're alive and well." She sighs. "You've probably had enough parents to last a lifetime, but I truly think of you as my own. Always have, always will, which is why if you need *anything*, do not hesitate to reach out." She cups Harlow's face, gazing at her in awe. "No matter what's happened, you'll always be a part of this coven. If you want to come for a Circle, or a holiday celebration, you do that. You were a witch before you were a vampire, and that'll never change. Vampirism suits you."

"Bit ironic," Carina chimes. "The witch once holding the cure to vampirism ended up as one."

That earns a laugh from Harlow. "Maybe it was fate. Morgan, thank you for finding me that night, for bringing me home, for showing me what I've always had...even if I didn't know it."

The two share a final hug before Harlow returns to my side, taking my hand. "Ready if you are."

Harlow heads for the door, but I'm stopped by the High Priestess. She holds out a hand for me to shake. "You're not so bad, vampire. Take care of our Harlow, won't you?"

"Always."

Taking Harlow's hand, we exit the house and walk through the quiet night with the two witches watching from the doorway. We pass the Sinclair house, where Harlow pauses.

I'm sure Morgan would allow you to make it your own. We'll redo the windows to ensure it's safe for us to visit.

She doesn't reply, but a gentle feeling brushes against the bond before she pulls me along and past the other houses, its residents tucked in for the night. We walk through the deserted streets of the main strip, and she points out some of the places Carina showed her the other day, including a restaurant titled BeaverTails, lamenting how she'll miss those in her diet.

We exit Banff hand in hand and run home.

Hours later, we arrive on my territory, the grounds a welcome familiarity.

"Crazy how different everything feels now. I can smell it so much more intensely."

I tug her close, dropping my face into her neck and inhaling her scent. It's mingled with dirt and blood from yesterday.

"Now you know how it was for me. Imagine all the forest's varying scents, and then you dropped into the centre of it. Your blood pounding, your heartbeat racing, your feet disrupting the landscape. You were impossible to *not* find. A beacon amongst nature."

"What did I smell like to you?"

"Bliss," I reply simply, tightening my arm around her body. "From the minute I met you, you smelled different to me. I assumed it was the cure, but none of your ancestors held the same intrigue for me. Somehow, I believe my body recognized you as my Bride."

"And what do I smell like now?"

"Mine."

She smacks my chest. "I'm serious."

"I am too. Our scents are intermingled so others see my claim on you. Then there's the additional scents you layer onto your natural one: shampoo, perfume, and such. You smell even sweeter now as a vampire, but the hunger I feel for you no longer makes me want to rip you apart. I'll destroy you, certainly, but without lasting damage."

She tips her head back, brows furrowing. "You say that like you weren't in control the entire time."

"Age helped. Doesn't mean you didn't smell like a fucking meal every second of the day."

"Huh. Well, damn." Her nose wrinkles. "I'd say sorry, but you were the asshole who kidnapped me."

"Damn right, and I'm not apologizing." My lips trail up the side of her neck and over my bite marks. I tickle the base of her ear, my whisper for her alone, unheard by the creatures around. "You have no fucking idea how much I enjoyed hunting you that night, so I'd like to propose round two. Up the stakes a bit. Train you in your new abilities."

Her eyes flash red, the purple returning slowly. She's intrigued as she twists in my arm. "Do tell."

"Hunt me, Hellion. Give me a two-minute head start to hide somewhere in this forest. I won't make it easy on you. Use your senses, not the bond. Sight and hearing; track me as if I were any other vampire, or even prey."

She grins and nods eagerly, jerking her chin. "Two minutes then. Run fast."

With a final wink, I take off into the trees, running straight for a while, knowing her newfound abilities will allow her to track me. Once a distance away, I change direction.

It's strange being the prey, but for Harlow, I'll be whatever she needs.

SIXTY-TWO

He winks before becoming a blur through the trees, only, unlike every other time I watched him with human eyes, this time I'm able to track his precise path, right down to the last-minute direction change he takes before disappearing deeper into the undergrowth, using the closely packed trees to successfully hide.

Once two minutes have passed, I take off after him, merging into the forest and following his scent. It weaves around trees and doubles back in places, reminding me of how I once ran away from him in this same forest.

Around another tree, and then...he's gone.

I pause, inhaling deeply. His familiar scent is definitely on the wind, but muted. My eyes flick around the dark forest, examining the shadows, seeking signs of the being who'd stick out but finding nothing. Far away, a bird chirps, and elsewhere, squirrels scurry, but no vampire.

I pace backwards a few feet, picking up his scent once more. Stronger now, clinging to the ground. It leads me in the same path around the tree, then it's gone once again.

"Where are you?" I whisper to myself, but it's as much to him as well.

He's close. He's watching. It's a test.

I *feel* him.

I tilt my head back to regard the branches high above my head, barely finishing the movement before my vision is overtaken with complete blackness as a figure drops from a branch and comes down on top of me.

At the last second, I duck to the side, my speed making it possible, causing him to fall messily. He peers up at me, his crimson eyes flashing in the dark and his lips pulling apart in a way that's both sexy and alluring.

"Good job. Now, let's see if you can catch me. Ready or not."

He zips off.

By the time we make it out of the forest, I'm more than excited for a shower. In fact, I never plan on leaving the damn room. Alec leads me towards the castle at a mortal walking pace, which I find interesting, but it allows me to take in everything. He pushes open the large wooden doors with as much effort as a human would opening a closet door.

I enter the castle, this time in a much different manner than him dragging me in as a captive and me running away as an escapee. There is no more being locked in a dungeon. No more claustrophobia—

"Shit, vampires don't get phobias, do they? Do those transfer from human life?"

"Never heard of it happening."

"Yet another bonus of being immortal." After the run home, the chase through the forest, and pretty much everything since chugging the cup Cedric taunted me with, I've loved it.

Being a vampire is like being reborn. Harlow Sinclair—witch, holder of the cure, last living Sinclair—died, and in her place is a witch-vampire hybrid who embraces both kinds of magick. With a mate by my side, who I could never have guessed I wanted.

"You know what's funny?" I ask, trailing Alec to the stairs. "When you once taunted me with keeping me alive forever, I thought I'd rather burn in Hell before ever letting you bite me."

His grin is full of heat, rivalling my fire. "I'm a persuasive man when I want to be."

At the base of the stairs, my attention goes down the hallway, where the ballroom is. His throne, where he lorded over all the vampires he tried to sell me off to. "If you're king, does that make me the queen of vampires?"

"Queen of vampires. Queen of me. Queen of the witches, if your power doesn't stop developing."

"How will the other vampires take you having a witch as your consort?"

He yanks me against his body, his growl echoing around the staircase. "First, you're not only a witch. Second, fuck them. Third, you're my equal, not my consort. Now, let's find a shower so I can show you how I bow to my queen."

is tribute is worthy of a queen.

Later, an hour before the sun is scheduled to rise, I lean on the balcony attached to his bedroom. A feature I hadn't noticed last time. Perhaps if I did, I would have saved the trouble of breaking the window in my room and propelled myself down from here.

Alec lingers beside me, his hands resting on the railing as he monitors his property. He seems calm, but every once in a while his nostrils will flare and his gaze pauses on something in the distance before continuing his watch, apparently deeming whatever he sees as no threat.

Me...I'm too focused on the moon above. It's a bright white, a beacon in the darkness. Exactly like what Alec ended up being for me.

The wind blows, warm and gentle, and wraps around me like black magick does. Like it's Hecate's way of greeting me.

"Do you think She's mad?"

"Who?" Alec looks away from the treeline.

"Hecate. The Goddess. I'm a combination of three things, two of which go against what She believes."

"If that's true, she sucks as a leader. Besides, Freya said she isn't." He pushes off the balcony, trailing his lips over my bare shoulder, only a towel wrapped around my frame from the shower. "Come to bed, Hellion, so I may show you what eternity will be like."

It's tempting but doesn't feel right to abandon the outdoors yet. "Five minutes, then I'll come in."

He drops a kiss to my forehead before entering his room, shutting the door to give me privacy.

The wind blows again, this time gentler. With it, there's the scent of flames, like two old friends meeting one another.

"Is this your sign, Hecate, that you're watching over me? Freya says you are. Is it true?"

Utter and empty silence.

No more wind.

With a defeated sigh, I push off the balcony, twisting to go inside when a voice, silky and soft, comes from a form without a physical shape. Different from Darkness and Alec, with an influence only She has.

Yes, daughter, it is true I have not forsaken you. You've become exactly what you were meant to. You are the hybrid of Light and Dark, of witch and vampire. You are the reason the cure has been extinguished. The reason vampires and witches will one day unite for good. You are the only witch truly capable of wielding the Dark gift in a manner that will not destroy yourself. I am very proud of you, Harlow Sinclair, and very pleased to call you mine. Blessed Be.

And then, all is silent once more.

Blessed Be, Hecate.

I enter the bedroom, finding Alec seated in one of the chairs by the unlit fireplace, a drink in hand. I slide into his lap and take the glass, sipping from it. The strong alcohol doesn't have the same kick it once did.

"Find everything you were looking for out there?"

"I did, yeah."

We fall silent, sharing the drink. With a mindless wave of my hand, a spell ignites in the fireplace, setting the wood on fire and casting a heat neither of us needs around the room. The flames flickering against the stone backing reminds me of how Alec and I came together.

Thank you for kidnapping me. For not killing me. For helping me get my powers back. For apparently fulfilling fate.

Fuck fate, Hellion. No matter what, I would have found you and made you mine. My powerful witch, my Bride...all mine.

I love you, Alec Dormer, asshole bloodsucker.

Forever?

Only if you tell me your true age.

He smirks and *finally* admits it.

Apparently, I like older men.

SIXTH INTERMISSION

Freya

And that's it! For these two idiots, anyway. Whew, are you tired? I'm tired. Fucking exhausted is more like it.

They ended up winning me over. Like I told the vampire, it's been fun tormenting him. Hopefully, the next one is as amusing, because if he's too friendly, it robs me of fun.

If you have questions, I do too. As I said earlier, it seems I wasn't told everything about these two and the upcoming future. I don't like being left out, because how else can I become my best helpful self?

I'm going to talk to Hecate, but while I do, rather than reporting back here, I'm going to show you an outsider's perspective, the same way I did in the beginning. I know, I know, the perspective change might be annoying, but stick with me. It's easier. I'll recap at the end, though, so you end on a high note. (The high note being me talking to you, if you didn't figure that out.)

Anyhoo, here we go.

Freya stands above the same small pond of water she typically uses to communicate with the Goddess. The water immediately ripples, forming the shapeless figure of Hecate.

Daughter, She greets, her melodic voice chiming through Freya's mind.

"You left out important information."

I did, because it was necessary to prevent you from knowing everything at the time. What I told you wasn't a lie; I truly am tired of my witches dying from their ongoing wars with other beings. The vampire race was the most pressing, and with Harlow mated to one of the kings, peace will eventually settle. Alec Dormer will do what he must to keep his new Bride happy by erecting rules that'll protect witches in the end.

"There's obviously more to it. Harlow Sinclair isn't *only* mated to a vampire. She became one! She embraced Darkness in a way I've never seen another witch do. Why would you want that for her? Why are we not eradicating it altogether? I assumed your plan was to counter the actions of the Twilight Grove Coven."

Twilight Grove's errors will be resolved in the future. Freya, you know more than anyone that there is no Light without Dark. No good without evil. It is the entire precipice the Celestials base their existence on.

"The Celestials...so the war is true then?"

The wind blows the Goddess's sigh over Freya. *Unfortunately, and while I have remained out of Heaven's and Hell's ways, keeping Earth and my children safe, I will be unable to for much longer. The war will not happen for a few more years, but I will not overload you with these details quite yet. Harlow becoming a vampire made her a hybrid, one that eventually both races will come to respect. Having her mated to a vampire was never enough. Sides would still be drawn, forcing the couple to choose. I once said to you balance may be needed, and this has come to pass.*

As if Alec would choose anyone but Harlow, but Freya understands the sentiment.

This ensures Harlow appeals to both. As for black magick, it will be important one day. Her vampire side ensures she can control it as a child of the Darkness, so she will never be overtaken.

"What is your role in the war?"

While Hecate and the rulers of Heaven and Hell follow different systems, they do intersect occasionally. Earth was created by Heaven's leader, but Hecate, as his sister, so to speak, was allowed to give life to her own beings: humans with an inclination for the natural world, who gained the ability to influence and control elements in ways regular mortals could never. God and the Goddess do not coincide, each fostering their children in their own ways.

Protecting the witches and all living things.

"And the other couples, will they also fall into Darkness?"

I cannot say. They will be tested by Twilight Grove, though. Once again, you must only guide and not interfere.

Freya recalls the second couple once shown in this same pool. A witch standing beside a wolf, her hand buried in its fur. The wolf shifts into a man and pulls her into his arms. Around them: a pack bonded.

A witch with water magick, currently living amongst a coven filled with air magick and the singular fire witch, now turned hybrid. The witch who was seated in the living room of the High Priestess's home, so unaware of her future about to unfold.

Carina Hargrove.

Me again. Yeah, so back to Highridge Coven I go. This time for Carina, a witch with quite the history behind her, not unlike Harlow.

And the shifter pack who has a long-standing deal with the coven.

And the recently promoted alpha whom Carina enjoys spying on.

Carina and the shifter sitting in a tree—No, that's not right.

*Carina and the shifter running around a tree...*that's a mouthful.

Eh. I'll get it right. Give me time.

Anyhoo, wanna come along?

Do you? Do you wanna come along? If so, be sure to continue the series with Dark Mist (Black Magick #2), a fated mates romance between Carina and a possessive alpha wolf.

C OVEN INDEX

For convenience, here is a breakdown of covens/characters. The list will be expanded throughout the series as characters from each coven, as well as the shifter pack (and other groups to be announced) are featured. These are only the characters relevant to this book. Read on for the hierarchy of witches.

<u>**Covens**</u>

Highridge Coven - Banff, Alberta
Twilight Grove - Northern Ontario
Coven of the Silver Seas - British Columbia
Starfall Coven - Quebec

<u>**Highridge Coven**</u>

Morgan Hargrove - High Priestess - Air magick
Carina Hargrove - Witch, High Priestess' daughter - Water magick
Jasper - Warlock, Carina's cousin - Air magick
Harlow Sinclair - Witch - Fire magick
Emily Sinclair - Witch - Fire magick (deceased)
John Sinclair - Warlock - Fire magick (deceased)

<u>Twilight Grove</u>

Sloane Yarrow - Witch - Earth/Dark magick
Arthur Hartman - Warlock - Earth/Dark magick (deceased)
Violet Hartman - Witch - Earth/Dark magick (deceased)
(More TBA...)

WITCH HIERARCHY

Like the index, as the series expands, so will the hierarchy of creatures to include both Celestials and Otherworldly beings to portray how they are linked together.

HECATE, GODDESS OF MAGICK & WITCHCRAFT

↓

FREYA, THE FIRST WITCH
EARTHLY REPRESENTATIVE OF THE GODDESS.
COMMUNICATES DIRECTLY WITH HIGH PRIESTESSES

↓

HIGH PRIESTESSES

↓

INDIVIDUAL WITCHES/WARLOCKS

Also By M.L. Philpitt

Fractured Ever Afters

A 6-book (& 2 novellas) mafia romance series of interconnected standalones based on fairytales, featuring the Montreal mafia and the New York Famiglia.

The Desire in Deception (Prequel Novella)

The Hunt in Elusion

The Craving in Slumber

The Beauty in Scars

The Freedom in Captivity

The Sound in Silence

The Obscurity in Wishing

The Bonds in Christmas (Epilogue Novella)

The Bratva's Elite

A 4-book mafia series of interconnected standalones featuring the Russian Bratva.

Merciless Queen

Deadly Knight

Defensive Rook

Violent Pawn

Captive Writings

A new adult suspenseful romance series that progressively gets darker with each book

Ruthless Letters

Obsessive Messages

Vicious Texts

Burning Notes

Twisted Holidays

A series of dark romance holiday novellas

Silent Night

Egg Hunt

Fright Night

Be Mine

Midnight Kiss

Lucky Clover

Black Magick

A 5-book paranormal romance series of interconnected standalones featuring witches, vampires, shifters, mortals, and demons.

Dark Flame

Dark Mist

Dark Storm

Standalones

A Vampire for Christmas

Audiobooks

Silent Night

Acknowledgements

Thanks goes to:

- The readers who've been with me from the beginning. The people who gave Cure Bound a shot and gave me the courage to keep publishing, keep getting better. They're the ones I wrote this for. Because Cure Bound wasn't great (and yes, I can say that now) but I still loved the characters, general idea, and the fact it gave me a foothold into the author world. Realizing they deserve better. A story with character depth and better writing encouraged this rewrite turned basically a whole new book.

- My betas: Megan, Colleen, & Lee Jacquot

- My PA: Megan who puts up with my ever changing mind.

- Rebecca Barney from Fairest Reviews Editing Services for the edits

- Lauren from The Eclectic Editor for the thorough proof-reading

- Silviya Andreeva who was a damn saint through the cover design process

ABOUT THE AUTHOR

USA Today Bestselling author M.L. Philpitt writes both dark romance and paranormal romance. When she's not writing made-up realities, she's reading them. She lives in Canada with her four pets and survives life with coffee and an obsession with fictional characters, especially the morally grey kind.

WARNINGS

- Murder
- Recollection of parental death
- Depictions of trauma
- Kidnapping
- Physical violence
- Suicide ideation (brief)
- Blood
- Primal play/chasing
- Captivity
- Explicit sexual content